WORD

Also by Coerte V. W. Felske

The Shallow Man

WORD

COERTE v.w. FELSKE

WARNER BOOKS

A Time Warner Company

Warner Books, Inc., 1271 Avenue of the Americas, New York, NY 10020
Visit our Web site at http://warnerbooks.com

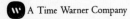 A Time Warner Company

Printed in the United States of America
First Printing: November 1998
10 9 8 7 6 5 4 3 2 I

Library of Congress Cataloging-in-Publication Data
Felske, Coerte V. W.
    Word / Coerte V. W. Felske.
      p. cm.
    ISBN 0-446-52331-3
    I. Title.
PS3556.E47259W67 1998   98-19557
813'.54—dc21   CIP

For
Richard Norman

Acknowledgments

I would like to thank the following individuals for their support during the making of *Word*.

Bill Adams, Tina Andreadis, Helen Breitweiser, Alex Campbell, Vikram Chatwal, Conrad, LuLu, and Stefan de Kwiatkowski, Michael De Luca, Ulf Ekberg, T. S. Eliot, Anneke Felske, Norman Felske, Alan Finkelstein, Yann Gamblin, Simon Green, Laura Handman, Anne Jones, Jack Nicholson, Jeremy Nussbaum, Theodore Owen, Theresa Pantazopoulos, Ann Patty, Chuck Pfeifer, Random House, Dr. and Mrs. Thomas D. Rees, Emma S, J. D. Salinger, Amy Schiffman, Ingrid Seynhaeve, Travels with Men, Michiel van der Wal, Charlie Von Muffling, Ellen von Unwerth, Alan Watts, Neil Young, Nick Wechsler, Michael White, and Sandra Zita.

I give special thanks to my editor Rick Horgan for his patience and Owen Laster for his guidance.

I offer special dedication to dear friends Billy Way and Joe Cole, both of whom were taken away from us far too soon, but their spirits will remain with me forever, in memories that I would consider nothing less than intensely vital and action-packed.

Most of the world's troubles are caused by people's needs to be important.

—*T. S. Eliot*

The "Heart of Gold" song put me in the middle of the road. Travelling there soon became a bore so I headed for the ditch. A rougher ride but I saw more interesting people there.

—*Neil Young, 1977*

WORD

The Age of A

Word is, nobody wants to be sentenced to a life at the edge of somebody else's table. Someone spread that about a year ago. That someone was me.

It was the first day of spring in Los Angeles, and nobody gave a damn. The seasons had their significance back east. But on America's left edge, they were meaningless. It added to the surreal nature of the city. I could always recall what I had done the day before, but I'd be damned if I could tell you what happened the day before that. The days were all the same. And they all blended together with no dividers. L.A. was a uni-day. If you divided yesterday by today, added a day two weeks ago, then three days next month, then sliced all of that in half, what you got was still a day that was warm, with hazy sun and a touch of smog. Just another L.A. day.

But that day in March was a day I'll never forget. That's when it all started.

I was racing west on Sunset Boulevard in the Bavarian Citrus Sled en route to the ocean. Normally, you could characterize my mood as Hollywood-bitter. But on this day I was slightly more perturbed. I needed to get away. So I was going to the place the fam and I always went whenever I felt that way. It was one of my better survival rituals.

I hated L.A., everything about it. Right down to its socks. But I loved Sunset Boulevard. It always gave you a sense of emancipation. It was a de-shackling. The winding turns, the sunshine, the wind blowing in your face. Your life could actually suck. But Sunset had the ability to make all the negativity fizzle away. You could be held at a light next to the finest Rolls and it had nothing on you. 'Cause you were sharing the same asphalt. Sunset was an equalizer. It gave you the sense that anything was possible, which is the myth the entire city was founded on. It is the greatest street in America next to Bleecker or West Broadway.

The Bavarian Citrus Sled was my car. It was a green BMW 2002, a real rattrap. The frame needed resoddering, the muffler was half-gone, and my tires were short on tread. But I can tell you without hesitation, it was my faithful friend. It looked like a wreck and sounded like a lawn mower, but it had a heart like a St. Bernard. It took me where I wanted to go, wherever, whenever.

I called it a Sled because it was so broken down to its bare mechanical essentials, it had nothing more going for it than my childhood Flexible Flyer. It was miraculous that it even turned over consistently. In my estimation it glided along by pure magic.

"I know what you're thinking, Bob," I said.

Bob the Riot was riding shotgun, of course. His presence allowed me to use the High-Occupancy Vehicle lane and get through vicious freeway gridlock. He had blond hair, a doughboy face, and he wore denim overalls. Though his expression never changed, his thoughts did. Bob was my HOV dummy and a contrarian by nature. If I considered an idea to be bold, he would consider it risky. But that was okay. My life needed a second opinion.

Though Bob was short on words he was an integral part of my family. Along with the Sled, my designer NFL football The Duke, and my childhood sleeping bag lodged in the trunk, we were one proud unit. Mildly dysfunctional, but proud.

I took a back-door drive into Bel-Air and docked opposite the tree, not before setting off the car alarm of a parked Benz. My engine was that outspoken. The tree's unpicked fruit had turned from green to yellow since my last visit. I picked as many lemons as my T-shirt could hold. I then placed them with all their little yellow brothers in the Sled's console, and on the front and rear dashboards. The old, dried ones I tossed.

Filling my car with lemons was another one of my survival rituals. It made me feel good. On any given morning, I could open that door and get a fresh lemon scent. It was a happy smell. It made me feel like maybe life wasn't so bad after all—that the day had potential. In addition, the lemon was an appropriate mascot for my Bavarian friend who had seen better days.

I didn't have a stereo so I relied upon my portable cassette player that rode beside Bob. Wearing headphones and listening to grime rock was a dangerous way to drive. But it was effective. I was thirty years old and I figured I could forgo my hearing capabilities. My vision was good enough and my eyes still had enough dart left in them that I could foresee any traffic troubles before they posed problems.

I rejoined the flow of cars on Sunset and sidled beside a Blip on a roaring Harley. He looked at my rig and smiled smugly, convinced I thought his wheels were cherry. Little did he know, I wouldn't be caught dead on his piece of scrap. A Harley was about as original as a tattoo. And those you could get in cereal boxes. So I changed lanes and let him coast alone in all his predictability.

As I drove, my mind drifted. I wanted to think positive thoughts. And I wanted to forget the day. It had been a rough one. It started with an outlaw producer calling me nasty names in an arbitration hearing, my second arbitration hearing in three years.

I also met with Agent Orange. Agent Orange was my movie agent. Or at least he was when the day began. He told me my new work was totally uncommercial. Sure, I'd heard it before. That was the word on me and my product. Unsellable. But I was damn good at producing work that didn't sell. So why ruin a good thing? He told me I should look for new representation. I told him he should look at my tallest finger.

As I drove Sunset I tried to get off the morose track. But it was difficult. The depressing thoughts of my life and times wouldn't let go. I pondered the first three letters of my license plate. They were NFW. It was a plate I'd received randomly from the state. But it was thematically correct for me and my attitude of disbelief about the era we were living in.

No Fuckin' Way.

I considered my era the Age of Astonishment. I'm talking the nineties. If you're hazy on the labeling, let me ask you one question. Aren't you astonished by what's happened so far? Even if you weren't paying attention, you should have noticed that murder pays, justice weeps, viruses rule, your wife's lover is not a man, fashion models are running for office, the boyfriend-back-home is extinct, Mother Nature now has balls, curse words have lost theirs, statistics show you've got as good a chance of marrying your stalker as the romantic mismatch you're forcing down the throat of a church, that money, no matter how ill-gotten, gets the worship manners and cultural achievement used to, that beauty and fame have rewritten the Ten Commandments, that frivolous lawsuits are the country's new flavor-of-the-millennium melanoma, that the very scandal that used to ruin you now makes you a millionaire, that the Tabloid Boys have taken over, creating a lust for sensational news that has body-snatched the populace like a bad propaganda machine with the potency of the worst isms you can recall, Despotism, Nazism, and Fascism included.

Sure, it was a bitter way to see the world. But I was bitter. Bitterness and my profession went hand in hand. After all, I was a screenwriter.

Quotable Agent Orange

Papers fluttered in my backseat as I motored past Brentwood. They were the loose contents of an unbound copy of my latest work. It had a title. But *Wallpaper* was a better one. I had written thirteen spec scripts already and none had been produced. I was murder on trees.

An acid song named "Cynical" came on my phones and I liked it.

As I came down the slope where Sunset meets Pacific Coast Highway, I recalled what Agent Orange had said to me in the parking lot of that fashionable eatery. As he took the keys from the red Vesty to his black Aston Martin, he made an attempt at kindness—the type of kindness that made me refer to him, and all of my previous unscrupulous agents, as a horrific nerve gas that choked, tortured, and paralyzed our soldiers in the Nam; the type of kindness that made me want to be kind in return and rip his fucking throat out.

"Your life is more interesting than your work," he said. "Quit inventing stories. If you want to write, write about your life."

In fairness to him, he did cover the check.

Only later did I realize that Agent Orange was absolutely right. Because in the end, it wasn't what I wrote, or thought, or preached, or pitched. It was the life I led that made the difference. A year later, I'm taking his advice and I'm not going to leave out a single detail.

It's true. Word was my work was uncommercial. I'd never had a script produced. Maybe my writing was elitist. Maybe pretentious. Maybe the concepts were not high and hook-y enough to make them sell. But I knew enough about writing to know it's a sin to bore your audience. What I'm saying is I'm not going to bludgeon your attention span with ridiculous tales about Star Camp. Too many writers out there can do it better. What I am going to do is tell you about my last year and the life I led in Los Angeles at the height of the Age of Astonishment. I am going to put you in the belly of a creative who was trying to get his first big break. I apologize if you get indigestion.

Frisbee No Be

I pulled off PCH and into an Arco AM-PM and filled up the Sled. Sure enough, gas sprinkled on my lounge shoes. The Sled had its share of rust from the brutal eastern winters we'd endured and the flow from nozzle to tank always involved some leakage.

I slipped into the station's minimart and bought some diet cola. It was my afternoon drink. I'm not going to name the brand because I'm sick of giving those overstuffed cats free advertising. I'd done enough work for free already. What's crucial is that my drink had caffeine. I was a caffeine addict. It was always coffee in the morning—astonishing quantities—and diet cola in the afternoon. By the time evening fell, I'd had so much caffeine I was wondering where the enemy was.

As I saw my favorite beach in the distance, I began to simmer down. La Piedra was past Malibu right off the highway, as all beaches were. It was where I went when I wanted to get away from my smog-belt community in Follywood. It was where I went when I was down.

I guided the Sled down the serpentinely gravel drive and parked. The lot literally was situated on a cliff overlooking the ocean. There were only two vehicles there with surfboard racks on top. And I recognized them both. That was a good sign. No tourists. I didn't want to have to fake a smile for someone's kid.

I checked out the waves and the swell was pretty small. Still, I could see a brace of surfers crowding each other out for the choicest morsels.

I hiked down the dusty trail that bisected the break in the cliff. The sea mist in the air moistened my skin and I could feel the ocean's ions performing their calming magic.

In this town, writers do all sorts of things to keep up the morale. Some do vitamins, some work out, some teach, some do drugs, lots booze, some chase hi-glam ladies, others chase lo-glam ladies, and very few, but some, read. I sought the dusty brown sands of La Piedra. Music, running my five miles, making my daily drive-bys, and gathering lemons were soothing. But Piedra kept me sane.

Someone asked me to play Frisbee and I said no. I'd rather do the hula hoop and let my hips gyrate than look like a Mo and toss around that little saucer. Aren't you suspect of people who are good at Frisbee? The ones who can throw it backhanded, forehanded, reverse, inverted, and catch it on their fingertips. They think they're so cool but they're really Mos. You and I know it. Then they turn their dogs into jerks too. Teaching them to catch it in their teeth. If you want to look like a Mo-ron, fine. But why do it to your dog? He's probably cool on his own. He doesn't need you to mess with his program. I hated Frisbees.

POST-IT: Wordsmithing
Writers spend a lot of time alone. You have so many downtime hours, studying, pondering, ideating, and analyzing, that eventually your mind locks onto every subject imaginable. You contemplate your scarred kneecap, your receding hairline, the relative cleanliness of each article of clothing you're wearing. Thoughts are your blood. Words are your weapons. Thoughts can also be your downfall. Paranoia drops in from the outer banks and says howdy too. Your imagination is a finely tuned instrument. You can take any given set of circumstances and credibly concoct a hundred stories to match them. So you play games with language, with words. Like

a child with blocks. Inventing neologisms. It can be dangerous. But always invigorating. Without the capacity to express myself, I am no one. And nothing.

I watched Shred and some unrecognizable wet suits vie for waves. But I knew no one was going to outdo him if he wanted a piece of the ripple. Shred was amazing. He truly beat the hell out of the ocean. Hot. You wouldn't know it if you saw him. He looked awkward on land. During his growth years, his ribs had formed to the contour of the deck of his board. He walked funny, he couldn't catch a ball. But on water, he was master. He had a slender frame but thick, high, broad shoulders from all the paddling.

Shred had everything the prototypical L.A. surfer had—the long, sun-bleached hair, the no-shoes, the one article of clothing, and the offbeat language. He was tan as a brownie, a lover of all that was natural, and had the is-there-a-pulse? mellow disposition. But he did not employ the word *dude* and I liked him more for it. Though he and I never hung out, he was a very pleasant person, harmless and good-natured. Not only did I like him, I envied him. He wasn't on any Wannabeast track like me. He was just happy to follow the sun, get up early for waves, check the weather and the swell, in essence, to be down with Mother Nature.

When Shred looked to the shore and saw me, he gave me that Hawaiian hand greeting with thumb and pinky wagging. Then he took off on a midget wave and stood up in half-assed posture, bored with a swell that was far beneath his level of proficiency. After the finger-food thrill, he went back to his belly and paddled in. Once onshore, he wedged his board beneath his arm and advanced. He unzipped his spring suit top and squatted beside me.

"Not too exciting out there, huh?"

"It's all mush," he said with a Malibu droplet desperately clinging to his chin.

"Those storms must have kicked it up some."

"It was huge. Twelve foot last weekend. Major juice."

"Really?"

Then Shred's usual mellow countenance slashed serious all of a sudden.

Eddy No More

"Hear about Eddy?"

"Your friend?"

He nodded. "He lost it."

"Surfing?"

He nodded again.

"Where?"

"Up at Mavericks."

"I'm sorry to hear that, man."

"Yeah . . . Funeral was Wednesday. Bunch of us paddled to the horizon and dumped his ashes."

I had nothing to say to that. We sat there and let the silence bring us back together.

"I've heard Mavericks is huge on a big day."

He didn't say anything for a moment. Finally, he offered something I'll never forget. "It's like . . ." He paused, shaking his head. ". . . *word.*"

I didn't know exactly what it meant. But I loved hearing it. I'd heard the term *word* in the Homeboy ranks, meaning *seriously, man,* or *honestly, I swear,* or *word-up,* that kind of thing. But never like this. So I asked him.

"It's something you can't describe, man," he explained. "Words don't tell it. It's just . . . *word.*"

I was a language freak and whenever I heard something that crackled with brilliance, which I thought this did, I placed it in my memory banks. For the future. This one made my day. It may give you an indication as to how great my days were. But still, *word* was a great word. It was the greatest thing I'd heard all year. It was even better than "solosexual," my latest prize.

Solosexual was my cyberlife term for a futuristic American hero, who, as the separation of the sexes continues to flourish, becomes a self-sufficient, self-satisfying salon-chair ghoul who holds the TV remote in one hand, offs his you know what in the other, and talks to his remaining pals on speakerphone, all the while getting a vicarious thrill from television imagery or computer communication.

But *word* was a better word.

Shred looked at me and then turned away again when he saw my mind was grinding away at something.

"How big does Mavericks get?"

"Twenty-five feet. That's what Eddy lost it on."

"Fuck."

"Yeah. If it's ten here it's twenty there. Monster."

He then settled into a blank stare. I could have sworn he was reconstructing Eddy's final descent in his mind. Living it a little.

"Someone got it on video too."

"Did you see it?"

"No. I don't want to."

"Why not?"

He looked at me. It might have been considered an insensitive or at least bizarre question. But knowing Shred, I had my reasons. Then I got an answer.

"Don't want to get spooked," he said, proving me right.

See, it had nothing to do with the macabre aspect of a death video. It was the intangible, maybe superstitious factor. He didn't want to psych himself out of the big waters there.

"You've never done Mavericks?"

"Not on a big day."

Then there was more silence. Eventually, Shred asked me how writing was going. I asked him not to. He just looked at me and gave me the Hollywood Big Three, and love had nothing to do with it.

"Tough business, man."

It was the one cliché uttered by almost anybody you discussed the film industry with. If you knew nothing about it, you knew that much. It was the one phrase that made people fearful of getting involved in it. It was also the one phrase that had me irrefutably sold on wanting to succeed in it. I wanted the toughest challenge in the toughest business. It offered that.

You see, I was what you call "Ivy League dim." Though I'd attended accredited private secondary schools in New York City and showed enough aptitude to get accepted to and graduate from an institution of higher learning like Brown University, I was also just dumb enough to think I could buck all the odds and actually make it in the film industry.

I guess uttering the Big Three was a showstopper. I was tortured and quiet. He was mellow and quiet. We just sat there silently and drank in some more sunlight and mist.

"Be cool, man," Shred said eventually.

"I be, you be."

We nudged fists and then he sashayed off with his awkward gait. He paused once to tilt an ear and outed the last surviving sea drops.

Screenwriter Schizo

I enjoyed a lengthy stare-down with the big blue beyond and then decided it was time to go. I found a nice jagged pebble and stuffed it in my shoe. Then I hiked back up the ravine. For some reason I didn't even snarl at the Frisbee that whizzed overhead.

As I glided south on PCH, I thought about my professional predicament. *I'm a Hollywood screenwriter . . . And so am I.* That was the best way to describe the difficulty of the profession. Faulkner had faced it. Fitzgerald had faced it. So had Hammett and Chandler and Mailer. And now Heyward Hoon. What it was, was forced schizophrenia.

Screenwriters, if they've had any real-life experience in the business, usually suffer from a personality split. On one hand, they're forced to conform to the industry requirement that America is the Land of the Happy Ending, that the work they live and breathe, their art, must end up in the Rose Garden, that good triumphs over evil, that Jack ends up marrying Jill. On the other side, the *lives* screenwriters lead, the shit they have to deal with, the unctuous people they must face and get sweet with, make them a most pessimistic, bitter, and brooding lot.

Hence, me.

In essence, your real life sucks. So there you are trying to uplift the spirits of the world while your blood is boiling and you're disliking a good portion of humanity. So even if you're lucky enough to get a picture made, chances are you'll still want to rip open your producer's rib cage and grab a few things.

I then thought about Shred again and how uncomplicated his life was—how he just enjoyed the simple pleasures. And that he was *able* to enjoy them. I was having trouble smiling while eating a Chipwich. And I loved them. The only competitive thing Shred involved himself with was that big green wall. He had all that simplicity and I was envious.

I daydreamed about what it would be like to let all the pressures to accomplish which had mounted up over the years ooze out of my body. If I could just open up the gates and let all those lifelong goals flow right on out, I'd probably be a better person. I'd definitely be happier. After all, I could go back home.

But returning to New York would prove my family right. And me wrong. I still considered that worse than failure. Good old family angst is never anything you can turn your back on. There's nothing more empowering than a brace of East Coast, white-haired, **boldfacing** WASPs rooting on your demise.

Right then, I realized I wasn't dead. Right then, I realized I wasn't going back to New York any more than I was going to eat a chickpea pita sandwich in a Cabriolet convertible.

The drive back to my neighborhood of West Hollywood was an easy one. Though it may not seem like it, I felt much better. La Piedra never failed me in that regard.

There's one thing I forgot to tell you. Though I had this dark stream looping through my veins, I never let anyone know it. That would have been professional suicide. As soon as you showed weakness in this town, you were finished. You'd be eaten like a roadkill carcass. If your company was folding, you were better off taking out a full-page ad in the *Hollywood Reporter* claiming you had a banner fucking year. L.A. was many things. But it was not a town in which to wear your heart on your sleeve. You'd find a jagged blade in it before the blood had cooled.

In the end, I didn't talk a lot. Nor was I outspoken or judgmental. Which means I didn't ruffle any feathers. It also means I didn't employ my personality, and I was known back east to have a pretty effective one. I played it down. Way down.

I dressed my mind down. I dressed my family background down. I dressed my education down. In essence, I dressed my ass down. I let the Star Campers think that I wasn't more communicative because I didn't really have anything going on. And I didn't. Yet. But the difference between me and a Muffin Head is, I was ready.

I was not a threat and I didn't let anyone feel I had the potential to be a threat. And in L.A., being a person who was not a threat made you as popular as you might imagine. It came off as charming.

In L.A., Heyward Hoon was charming. That's how well the town knew me. Which was fine, just fine.

Strugs at the Olive

The Olive was my neighborhood haunt. I always paid a visit there to start off the evening. It was right down Fairfax, so it was a short slide in the Sled. I'd park around the corner to avoid the omnipresent valet crew, usually a six-pack of south-of-the-borders with little mustaches and little vests, and pop in to see what was going on.

"I know—you're a friend of the Valets. You went to school together," the chief Vesty cracked.

Sure, it was my line he was using on me. It made me smile. So I coughed up a buck for him. But when he said he was going to frame it, I took it back. Our private little contest would continue. Love that. I'll take a wholesome grudge whenever I can.

My thoughts on valet parking were this. Not only did I not want to give up the jack—usually a five-spot because they'd expect and get the $1.50 in tip—but I didn't want anyone messing with the Sled. It was my good friend, remember? As I slipped through the Olive's dungeon-style doors, the head Vesty gave me an icy glare. And guess how much I cared.

The place had a nice dark, dank feel to it. The prominent features were the horseshoe-shaped bar, the paintings of famous geniuses few people could recognize, and the oddly presented food. French fries came in the shape of a box. I liked the Olive because it had a pleasant New York feel to it, and for good reason. The owners were from New York, as were most proprietors of the hip places in Hell-A. The interior was smoky, low-lit, and had a reputation for spontaneous cameos.

"Hey there," a voice chirped up.

I looked to the center booth beneath Einstein and Gandhi and saw it was Bridget seated there, flanked by a couple of Strugs. Bridget was from Arizona. She was brunette and pretty, well-constructed, and had a face charged with cosmetics. The girl had quite a reputation too. Oddly, it wasn't what she had done that gave her this kind of curious word. It was what she hadn't done. Bridget was the Last American Virgin. Word was she had never given it up. And she let you know it. It was an odd set of bragging rights but she made it very clear that no one had ever snapped her radish.

Her unblemished status made me skeptical, as did most novel ideas. For one thing, she had Beverly Hills Bumpers, meaning her chest had been manufactured in one of Rodeo Drive's formidable labs. It made me wonder how a girl who'd never had sex could get into the mutilation thing. She was nice though, despite her odd claim to fame.

"Why don't you sit down?" she offered warmly. She loved male attention and liked to bathe herself in more whenever she could.

My moment's apprehension began to look like rudeness so I did put it down. And as soon as one of the Strugs heard I was from New York, he initiated one of those New York–Los Angeles comparison dialogues which I truly detested. Comparing the two cities was Star Camp's version of discussing the weather because talk of the climes wasn't an issue. The weather never changed. But opinions did and he wanted mine. When I didn't offer up my views, I was forced to hear his. They came out slowly to a disturbing degree, but what was more annoying was he really thought he was saying something clever, something no one had ever heard. It was all that studied acting technique that gave him the confidence to master half of the art of conversation.

Strugs are struggling actors. They have the jeans, the white V-neck T-shirt, the black distressed-leather coat, the disheveled gamy hair, the unshaved cheeks, the generic handsome look you've seen in a couple soda commercials, and the last but most important piece of Strug garb, the ubiquitous go-down-on-you goatee. You may think I'm being harsh on actors here, but really, how can you take anyone seriously who is using all his might and life experience to scream out at the top of his lungs, *"Look at me!"* The vanity quotient is too goddamn high. Everybody needs a little applause in their life. I was no different. But this was identity starvation on a stick, no wrappers.

These two were L.A. dogs as well. Real barkers. Among the best. They looked good, were attractively dim, and spoke good *Girlie,* which was an essential tool for landing La-La's ladies. They had all the key monosyllabic phrases down like "wow," "cool," "huh," "s'up," "sure," "hey," "whoa," "right," "yeah," "ooh," "gee," "slick," "hmmm," "cool," etc. The phrases would make them come off as politely indifferent, and we know how the chikitas respond to that. A few of those gems thrown in properly in a conversation could get a guy every bit closer to some memorable wildtime. These two spoke it fluently.

Though the Strugs had the Girlie verbiage down, they still didn't know the best one-syllable term to date: *word.* But they would. Two years from now. Once I gave it to them to regurgitate. Sure, I was cocky at times. But mostly when it came to words and language. I felt confidence was the least of what you had to possess in your chosen craft. After all, I had to prop up my self-esteem on something.

I'd seen the Strugs around before and they had a pretty good handle on all the ladies in town. They night-notched on a nightly basis and tonight was no different. Night-notching involves a bedpost, a Swiss Army knife, and a desire to bullshit your ass off until a partner lays it down. And once she does, she gets her own carved notch that, as the championship athletes mime after winning a title, *no one will ever be able to take away* from her. As if anybody would want to. Or care.

I knew the Strugs were doing their respective technique finest to outwit and outmaneuver each other for that prized piece of Bridget. They wanted that radish. It was a real Ping-Pong match as they battled with their *wows* and their *cools* and all that macho slop in an attempt to talk her out of her panties. But they had their work cut out for them. The girl was not going to go yard without something. Like a trip around the globe, some large sparkles, or a serious Cupid shot in the ass. At the risk of sounding unoriginal, I'm not even going to mention a speaking role in a flick.

Still mired in the comparison dialogue, I got up after the Strugs' explanation of how the Los Angeles Dodgers had kept the blue and white colors of their Brooklyn forebears. I was in no mood for more conversational horse pill sedatives so I saluted them all. As I moseyed up to the bar, Bridget gave me a good-bye smile and the Strugs gave me *see-ya*s in stereo. I contemplated a "Go get 'em, tiger" but refrained. I asked X-Boy if he'd seen Joe the owner, but he said he wasn't in yet. Then I took off after having found out the Olive's version of what L.A.'s twilight hour had to offer.

Absolutely nothing.

Swinging at the Monkey Bar

I got in the Sled, slashed a U-y, and cruised down Beverly. I found a nice parking slot on the Boulevard and asked the Sled to wait for me. She would.

I sidestepped a snow-white stretch docked in front of the restaurant and slipped beneath the awning. The car obviously belonged to Starman. I didn't wait to find out but the reputation of the Monkey Bar was such that it was a good bet.

Less anonymous than the Olive, the Monkey Bar was the town's celebrity-friendly restaurant. It was the Elaine's of L.A. It was where Starman and Stargal mingled with the rest of the world. The owner was a New Yorker, of course, and had put together a damn good slammin' place. It even had TVs angling down from the ceiling so you could catch any essential ring, hoop, and pigskin contests.

I strode in and was met by some smiles and some handshakes. I ordered up a brew and eyed the long line of Mom-I-Got-the-Part girls perched on the stools. They were wearing their best "please don't rape me, honest" clothes, their painted claws digging into the bartop. Each had one eye on the dining room and one eye on the door, hoping for Starman to enter, to maybe get seen and invited over by Starman's P&B, pimp and bodyguard, or parachute in to his table later and play faux reluctant to overtures for a nice stardust ball.

I greeted a couple whose faces were familiar from ancient hot tub wars and then peeked into the dining room. There was the normal cluster of Woodies—moguls and Noguls, Strugs, Wams, random 8x10s, and girlie-whirlies. Girlie-whirlies are girls who are not serious. And therefore, they can't be taken seriously. In that way, they're like the male Blips. The town was sudsing over with them.

I also eyed the empty coveted booth with towered napkins pointed high waiting to be mashed by Starman and his thick-fingered and thuggy entourage. The town's requisite Model Dinner was there too. Not so long ago, L.A. had been told that models were hip, so by now there was an appreciation for the species and you could find some Model Dinner somewhere in town on any given night. That was the thing about L.A. It had to be told what was cool. In art. In literature. In fashion. And in girls. And then they'd make three movies about it.

"Yum," Kelly the Bullet said after I kissed her hello. The other Bullets—Mindy, Suzy, and Heidi—were there too with their lit-up faces.

"Girls, girls, girls" went my group greeting.

"How are you, Heyward?" Kelly the Bullet asked with an already amused sparkle in her eye.

"Miserably wonderful."

"So nothing's changed."

"Only calendar days."

And Kelly the Bullet giggled and looked at the others. Kelly got the biggest kick out of me. She'd display me like a windup angst toy and make me serve a dour dose for everyone's amusement. But the other Bullets didn't find my gloom and doom as enthralling as she did. Of all the Bullets Kelly was my closest pal.

"Heyward, this is Jack," Heidi the Bullet said.

I looked at him and he nodded at me. We shook hands. I didn't know what to expect. So I beckoned the waiter for a round of beverages. I saw the Bullets already had their party punch but I asked anyway.

"Would you guys like another?"

With that the four finished off their half-gone drinks and held up their glasses for a refill like little alcoholic orphans at mealtime.

"Red," Kelly said.

"Red, please," Heidi dittoed.

"Me too," Suzy added.

"Me three," said Mindy.

Their choice of beverage was Red, anything red, meaning cranberry juice–based. Baybreezes, Seabreezes, Cosmopolitans, and Cape Codders did it for them. They tasted great and it got them fucked up fast. I ordered another round of Red for them, a beer for Jack, and a double Stoli on cubes for me.

The Bullets

I first met Kelly the Bullet one summer day at an outdoor block party hosted by a few collegiate guys. My initial glimpse of her was more like a flash than a direct, eyes-on sighting. I just remembered a striking blond mane, lip gloss galore, miniskirt hiked high, platform shoes, and the whole package was traveling through the crowd at the speed of light. What was more impressive was she had three more striking Bullet pals in tow, all with electric hair, exaggerated ruby mouths, browned legs supported by heels and left naked by mini-minis, and the Toys "R" Us mentality. Each held on to the other's hand so as not to get separated, while putting on urgent expressions as if they were pressed to get somewhere fast. Which was a lie.

I saw them whip past me again moments later and if I'd had a plastic lobster bib on, it would have slapped me in the face. The way these chippies carved through the thick throng with no interruption, preoccupation, or need for a pit stop reminded me of hot, speeding bullets. And from then on, every time I went out with them I felt like I had been shot out of a barrel.

The reality was that they weren't going anywhere. The Bullets had only one gear. *Through.* They just shot through places and stopped only if they absolutely had to. They would convene or regroup in the bathroom and have a conference to share party data: what cute guys there were, what creeps had shown up, gossip games of who'd done who, and most important, where they should go next.

Together the Bullets were like a roaring party engine stuck in that one gear and they would zoom all over the flats and hills of Hollywood in search of a good time. They were striking. They were fast. They were two tons of fun. They were anywhere from 5'2" to 5'7" but not fashion-gal height. They were L.A. hot. They were the best of the L.A. party girls.

The Bullets were good representations of what L.A. had to offer with respect to attractive women. L.A. girls were pretty. I would not say beautiful in the classic sense, with the occasional exception. The Bullets were L.A.'s pretty girls. They were the pretty offspring of pretty people. I have my own home-baked explanation for this phenomenon.

If you consider Hell-A the dream dumping ground of the world, then it should be no surprise that over time, time defined by the beginning of the film industry, there have been droves of people who have gone west to become a movie star, mogul, or writer, God help the last group. They have enough ego saved up from their respective little towns all across America, egos massaged by good God-fearing people who told them that they were pretty, handsome, funny, or talented enough to make it in Star Camp and become the next Starman or Stargal. The praises repeated in their youths would eventually take root in their brain and it would eventually drive them to make the Move. The Move was the same move the California gold rush people made in the 1840s. Only instead of gold, the prize was celluloid fame.

Now, of those seemingly pretty and talented people, some made it. But the overwhelming majority did not. Still, many would not return to their hometowns. Maybe they couldn't face family and friends after failing. Maybe they were black sheep who'd hated their past lives. Maybe they wanted to be in a place where there were no expectations to meet and no one to report to. Maybe they got a taste of the good weather and the sun baked them in place. Or maybe they just found a new life, or even a life they would never let their loved ones ever know about. Sure, L.A. had broken the hearts, backs, and souls of many an American, and not in good old American ways.

In the end, what you had was a huge pool of pretty and talented also-rans who settled in Southern California. And they passed on pretty and talented also-ran genes to their offspring. Some of these offspring were Muffin Heads. The handsome ones were 8x10s. The pretty ones were the Bullets. And when they came of age, they would try their sexiest at the fame thing and another tiny percentage would make it and most wouldn't but they'd regenerate and the L.A. cycle of pretty also-rans would continue.

Noguls and Moguls

"Jack and I went to high school together," Kelly the Bullet offered. The revelation was a pleasant surprise.

"In San Diego?" I asked. He nodded. "Is that where you live now?"

Then he told me how he worked for a real estate company down there, that the area wasn't that exciting but it was pretty peaceful. I thought of a passive life in San Diego for a few seconds and they were nice thoughts.

"I don't know how you live up here," he added.

I just nodded.

Jack was a nice guy, an average guy. That was refreshing. I told him I was familiar with the San Diego area because my family used to vacation in La Jolla.

"Nice town," he remarked.

I looked over and saw the Bullets were competing to see who'd be the first to tie a knot in the stem of a maraschino cherry with their tongue. Their eyes darted to and from each other, as their mouths were busy at work. Then all of a sudden Heidi, the brunette, drew the winning knot from her mouth and screamed.

"Done!" she exclaimed. Then commanded them to "Chug!"

With that the other three Bullets grabbed their Red and sucked them down in one haul. It was a previously agreed-upon punishment.

Then Kelly turned to me and asked me if I was going to Disneyland on Saturday with them and I said no.

"Thought I'd ask anyway." Then she sighed. "Heyward, you're so weird."

"Thank you."

"But wonderfully so."

Though she was teasing me, that's how many L.A. people thought of me. *Weird.* It was either that or *cool.* Or, in rare cases, *great.* L.A. natives used words sparingly so most people fit into those categories. If they didn't like you, you were weird. If they liked you, you were cool. If they really liked you, you were great.

I thought briefly about Mickey Mouse and how nice it would be to go to the park to find him, dodge and weave a little, then grab him by his fat black ears, pull him to the ground, and give him a few choice rib shots.

Just then I saw two Thickies advancing, really suffocating the aisle, their tree stump necks spreading the lapels of their leisure jackets wide. Drinks on tabletops shook when they passed. I knew who they were. They were Starman's heavies. And I knew which Starman. It was Starman Steroids. And his Thickies were casing the joint to see if there was anyone who might pose a problem for him.

Starman Steroids was one of your typical ethnic action-adventure heroes who looked six and a half feet tall on-screen, but in reality, was a foot shorter, and worked out incessantly and juiced up big on anabolic steroids to come as close as possible to the maniacal characters he played on-screen. This Starman was so juiced up and paranoid he had to have bodyguards comb the place and search out any undesirables. If the coast was clear, then he'd enter the joint. This ritual had all the subtlety of a prizefight and was witnessed by nobody—nobody in Sacramento anyway. Starman Steroids' entourage and clinger-ons were at the mercy of his runaway ego, whims, and mood fluctuations—which were, in turn, at the mercy of his anabolic intake. In essence, it was a gathering held hostage by 'Roids.

The Age of A.

Can you imagine Cary Grant, Gary Cooper, or Clark Gable, or any other Golden Ager who had made you dream about being in this business as a kid, pulling this kind of stunt? NFW.

As I continued to swap suburban tales with Jack, a guy with a huge head and Duracell People features approached the table and I felt a sharp pain in my side. He had the industry uniform on, the black Armani blazer over black turtleneck, and gave Kelly the Bullet the big, zealous, enthusiastic, warm, friendly kiss of a professional bullshitter. Though I'd never met him, I knew exactly what he was. And my stomach started to bubble a special brew.

Kelly said it to him. "This is Heyward." He then shook my hand. "And Jack," she added. Then he shook Jack's hand. I swear this guy's nut was so big he was a headhunter's dream in any forest.

Jack smiled with genuine warmth and told him it was nice to meet him. That made me sigh. Jack didn't know what he was up against. I didn't have the heart to tell him this guy wasn't worth the energy it takes to be a nice person. He was ego on a parade float.

After the introductions, he still didn't say his name. As if we should know it already. So I made sure he knew I didn't know who the hell he was.

"What's your name?"

"What?"

"Your name. What do people call you?"

"Easy there, trigger. What do people call me? Depends on who you're talking about."

And he laughed smugly and tried to get the Bullets to laugh along with him like he was such a sensation and so well known he could be called lots of different names by lots of different people. That he was that popular. My feeling was "Get outta town."

The Bullets just smiled. I considered it very kind of them. The Bullets were always good-natured—too good in this case.

"Say, anybody got a cigarette?" he asked, looking at the girls. Heidi gave him one, offered him a chair, and he sat down, to my dismay. Kelly the Bullet looked at me and shrugged. She sensed my sentiments on that development.

Though he hadn't given us a name, I had one for him. He was a Nogul. The Noguls were like the movie moguls only without the power. They dressed like moguls, they talked like moguls, they had the designer specs and short-groomed beards like the moguls. The difference is they had no authority or juice to get any movie project off the ground. About the only thing the Noguls could green-light was a VCR.

But the way they shoveled it, you'd think they had a string of hits along with a shelf full of Oscars. To be a Nogul, all you needed was the black-on-black uni, a decent knowledge of *Daily Variety,* and the clankers to boast you just had lunch with Jack. And not Jack from San Diego.

Star Camp has only a handful of producers with green-light capabilities. They're known quantities. The rest have to talk up their clout. The Noguls were Beasts on the lowest rung.

This Nogul I was sure was king of the water cooler crowd at some temp job somewhere. He was already chatting up the Bullets. When they started talking shop, I dropped out. But the shop talk beat up the girls too. They were more interested in other things. Like life at the moment. They made a mass exodus to the bathroom for a conference. That left us all alone in the booth with only parcels of uncertainty about each other. A writer, a real estate salesman, and a Nogul. The Nogul, conditioned to schmooze on a dime, fired a couple quick character profile queries at Jack to see where he stood. When he got wind of the San Diego thing, somehow, some way, the conversation died. Another galactic surprise.

"You live in L.A.?" he asked me.

"Yeah."

"What do you do?"

"I'm a rock sculptor."

"Really," Jack intervened, looking surprised. "I thought you were a writer."

"That too."

The Nogul snickered somewhat, fully aware I'd taken him lightly enough to bullshit and toy with him. That's what these guys were always concerned about. How they were being perceived in the eyes of others. My glib behavior implied he had no movie muscle. It made him take on a stern look.

"Movies?" he asked in a serious tone.

"Yeah."

"God, everyone I meet is a writer." That was a partial comeback, implying I was just another cliché. And now he would try to confirm it. "What have you done?"

"Specs mostly. Couple contracts."

"WGA contracts?"

I nodded. The question asked whether or not I was a professional WGA member or just a Scabby, who would take a few grand from low-ballers and call it a contract. Another indirect barb.

"Any titles I might know?"

"Yeah. I did *Sanka Man,*" I said earnestly, convinced he knew of the project.

"*Sanka Man?*"

"It's a story of a decaf superhero who just can't seem to get to the crime on time. He's just too tired. And in the second culmination of the second act someone slips him a cup of regular coffee and he figures it out just in time to save the world."

The Nogul looked at me scornfully, fully embracing the extent to which I was fucking with him. Once he knew he couldn't compete with my snap he tried at some *where you from?*s and *where'd you go to school?*s. That's when I decided to return to my shell and let his ego brush itself off and climb back onto the swing. My modus operandi was to play it down, remember? I would make him think the flurry I dealt him wasn't intentional. Meaning maybe it never happened. His ego was dying to process it that way anyway.

When he told me he'd attended Stanford, I said SUNY Binghamton. It gave him more confidence, I could tell.

"Who's your agent?"

"I handle my own stuff."

He just nodded condescendingly, blew out a lungful of smoke, and let my response stand out there all by itself. It was a gesture intended to dash me off. He was telling me that he knew if I didn't have an agent, my work must not be good enough to get an agent.

More important than the verbal barbs, he'd decided I couldn't help him and that's all he really wanted to know. I didn't want to hear about his imaginary résumé, so I didn't even bother asking.

But Jack did and then we got an earful. And all I could think of were the sounds of metal scraping on concrete, the sounds my snow shovel made when I helped Paddy the doorman shovel the icy walk outside my family's New York apartment after a snowstorm.

Since his head was steadied again with a gloat injection, he warmed a bit and did the one thing that proved he was every bit the Nogul I'd suspected. He handed me his card and asked me to send him a script. In Star Camp, it was the same thing as saying "Nice to meet you." He knew there was no point in burning bridges with a writer no matter how snippy or unaccomplished he seemed, because, you never know, he may be drafting the next *Dumb and Dumber* at home. And the Nogul wouldn't want to miss out on his first vehicle. I swore I wouldn't even give him a pastel Charmin sequence.

We watched the Nogul look sharply away and it made us do the same. He was looking at Starman Steroids, who was settling into his booth across the room. Then he said it perfectly, right in character.

"Excuse me a second," he said bluntly.

"Absolutely," I said, though I meant "gladly."

I'd seen this hundreds of times before. A Nogul posturing, wanting to make us believe that he was on such the mighty inside track that Starman's entrance would affect his behavior enough for him to get up from the table and go pay a visit. I knew he didn't know Starman any better than he knew his second cousins.

I watched it go down for kicks.

The no-name Nogul waved at Starman, who smiled faintly in return with a glazed, who-is-dis-fuggin-guy? look. Then Starman's paranoia got the best of him and he put it to one of his Thickies, who shrugged. This Nogul had potential. He could make it up a few rungs of the Woody hierarchy on chutzpah alone. Which was the only way anyhow.

The Bullets returned from the powder room with no powder but fresh red grease, the kind that would lay messy tracks on a guy's face if given the chance. Their expressions were predictably urgent as well.

"There's a party up on Bellagio," the Bullet announced. That meant nothing to Jack. It meant Bel-Air to me. "Let's go," she added.

"What about dinner?" I asked.

"Shine dinner!" Suzy the Bullet blurted, and Heidi the Bullet high-fived her. And so did Kelly.

We got up and motored down the aisle. As we did, one of Starman's Thickies bear-trapped Kelly the Bullet in a conversation. Starman spotted me and offered that synthetic smile and said, "Hey, Shakespeare. How ya doin'?"

"Not bad, Starman," I said.

And I continued on my way. I didn't know all Starmen, but I knew Starman Steroids. And it's not that he liked me. He liked the girls I knew and that I knew a lot of them. You see, for some of the players in town, Hollywood was not about fame or money or power. Crudely put, it was about pussy. It was the other things that got you the pussy. Starman Steroids was one of them.

On the way out, we almost ran down a few frustrated Mom-I-Got-the-Part gals who were loitering around, not wanting to shell out for another drink, waiting for that table invite that didn't seem to be coming. And it wouldn't. Unless Starman didn't infiltrate the Model Dinner or run into any other hi-heeled, hi-glammers. It was a tough road for the Mom-I-Got-the-Parters. No one likes being a last resort.

No More Glam Rock

The Bullets suggested I join them in Mindy's Cabriolet. I didn't like the convertible aspect with my hair getting blown around, in addition to the blaring eighties glam rock that some radio station let slip on their turntable and was now brutalizing our ears. Right then I wanted to be in the Sled cruising alone, biting on some grunge, and sniffing lemons. I didn't like glam rock. It had no edge. It was written by light-footed Englishmen with faggy cuts, parachute clothing, and no cause. Those glamour boys nearly destroyed the rep Zep and company had established during the British Invasion in the sixties. With songs like "Girls on Film" how can you argue this point? The only cause they were fighting for was bisexuality.

"What are you talking about?" Mindy asked. "Adam Ant has a great new CD."

"Spare time, Mindy. Spare time."

"It's coming back, Heyward," the Bullet added.

"Only because the world is bored," I contended.

"You're so weird."

I continued my vociferous protest of the retro sounds and Suzy finally stepped up to play deejay and put on some solid acid. It was a song called "Shit Towne," and I liked it.

The Bullets began looking at each other and mouthing the words like they were the band. It was obviously one of their theme songs when they were raging. It made me stop brooding about the cotton candy causeless melodies of the glam era. In the end, Adam Ant and his comeback could eat my belt.

"Say, Heyward," Heidi the Bullet asked, "who do you think has the best *fuck you* in music?"

It was a typical subject for Bullet debate and I was not knocked off-stride. "*Fuck you* or just the word *fuck* in it?"

"Fuck."

"In rock? Or grunge?"

"Either."

"Pearl Jam's 'Some stupid fuck!' is pretty good."

"Yeah, I like that," Suzy contended.

"Then there's the Dead President's 'Fuck you kitty, you're gonna spend the night . . .'"

"Right . . ." And she didn't sound satisfied.

"The Nixons' 'You ignorant fuck' isn't bad."

"Yes! That was my favorite!" Kelly shouted.

"But I must say, Bullet, the best fuck I know is by Soundgarden from their first album. 'I know what to do/I'm gonna fuck, fuck, fuck, fuck you/Fuck you!'"

"That's right. How could we forget that? That's so killer. I knew you'd know."

"Hey, *Writer Is Rock Star*," I said. I was referring to one of my mock titles depicting a sci-fi world where writers ruled. We were obviously thousands of years away from that kind of development.

I looked over at Jack, who was in back with me but free from my thought process, and lucky for him. He just hung on to the door handle and listened.

"Whose party is this?" I had to ask.

"Some music biz guy," Kelly the Bullet shot back effortlessly.

"No, he's a musician," Mindy the Bullet said.

"What kind?" Suzy the Bullet asked.

"The rich kind," I snapped back.

"Charlie something," Heidi added.

"Charlie and the Afterbirths?" I asked.

"Heyward!"

"Yuck!"

I told them I was just kidding.

"I'm so over these names," Mindy the Bullet said anyway.

"What's the address?" Suzy the Bullet asked.

"Just look for the cars," Kelly the Bullet said.

In case it was unclear, Kelly was the mastermind of the group. And she was echoing the formula for crashing a party in L.A. Just look for the cars. Party crashing was an almost accepted and expected phenomenon. Especially if you were bringing along four thrusters like the Bullets. You'd have a hard time getting turned away.

In New York, you'd never go to a party if you weren't invited, unless you were drunk or you wanted to spy on your girlfriend. But that was in the jealous twenties when it mattered how many guys your girlfriend had had wildtime with before you, and who she'd been flirting with when you weren't around. Later in life, it doesn't matter. And in the Age of A, it's an absurd consideration. As long as you've boned more than she has, you're okay. If you haven't, don't worry. She probably won't end up your bride anyway.

Lord of the Launching Pad

No town ripped the American Dream a new rim as severely as Bel-Air. It had a real stench of success. Too much success. You could smell it as soon as you passed through those black wrought-iron gates. It was big on privacy too. Most of the homes were shrouded in greenery. But once you gained entry, they often unfolded before you like quaint palaces. It was always interesting to crash in Bel-Air. You were almost guaranteed an exercise in have and have-not psychology. In essence you were dramatically reminded you were a have-not.

As we climbed up Bellagio, the headlights illuminated my favorite lemon tree and I saluted it. Pickings were a strong yellow and looked good. Soon enough we saw a row of cars on both sides of the street, nearly choking off the middle. And these weren't ordinary cars. Each had its own net worth alone. A Vesty with a ratty, dome rug tried to take our car and we heckled him. Then we slid into a spot vacated by an impatient Porsche with a peroxided couple in midargument. We hopped out and heard music. The loud kind.

We then strode up to another iron gate where there was a flock of people all trying to bark their way in. The Bullets did the hold-hands thing and we slithered past the restless crowd, getting some annoyed looks along the way. I looked at the four of them and their cranberry-red mustaches. It made me smile.

Kelly the Bullet found herself opposite a hefty man wearing a tux and holding a list, his head wrapped in electronic gear. There was another sidekick Thickie too who seemed to be the Go-To Guy, meaning he had more juice than Hefty. He had the ubiquitous goatee and there was a good chance he was a Strug in his free time. I'd seen him in this capacity before. I tried to get a glance of recognition from him but his face didn't budge.

"What's the name?" Hefty said in a voice that could have cracked a Brazil nut.

"Kerry. Kelly Kerry."

"We know Charlie," Suzy forced. And it was not a good move.

"Wrong party," he snapped. "He lives up the street."

With that he was done with us and beckoned the next bash smashers in line.

I knew what had happened. The long line of parked cars was for both parties and we'd chosen the wrong fete. I leaned over to the guy next to me.

"Whose party is this?"

"Sydney Swinburn's."

"Ah-hah," I said. But I really meant "Ouch." Because I'd just gotten hit on the head with the envy mallet.

You bet I had heard of Sydney Swinburn. He was one of the town's true Lords of the Launching Pad. A guy with some real bang. He was everything a Nogul wanted to be. The real thing. So I stepped up and layered it on thick.

"I'm a friend of Mr. Swinburn's."

"Name?"

I told him.

Hefty scanned his clipboard and searched. As he did, the Go-To Guy did exactly what I was hoping he would. He looked the Bullets up and down, a real X-ray once-over. He saw them nude by now and I'm sure it was a good time. Even if his imagination was dim. One thing about L.A. girls. They've got the curves. They may not be their own from their original genetic map, but they're there. When Hefty raised his gaze at me he was shaking his head with a face that said negatory. That's when I saw the Go-To Guy raise a walkie-talkie and speak into it. He mouthed my name and added in a low tone, "He's plus four."

"Let's go," Kelly the Bullet said in a huff.

"Hold on," I told her.

With that the Go-To Guy tapped Hefty on the shoulder and gave him a short nod, the short nod of a party autocrat. It was a power move.

It translated to let this group in. I let the four slide ahead. When Jack
tried to follow, he received a log of a forearm in his chest.

"Sorry, guy," the bruiser said. It's funny how just a nice guy from out
of town gives off that reject-me odor.

"He's with us," I said.

The Go-To Guy nodded and Hefty's arm dropped.

The Bullet Tour

Before I knew it the group was advancing on a driveway that snaked up
and up and up. Our ascent took a few minutes. We were coming upon
one mother of a Bel-Air estate. It was groomed everywhere. People in as-
sorted codes of dress passed by us, doing their best to explore the
grounds and find hidden places to party and make a mess or do whatever reckless partyers do.

The doors to this modern castle were hand-carved and high enough
to comfortably greet a guy with stilts and a top hat. And stepping into
the house was stepping into a certain way of life. A different one. There
was no hunger here, no struggle, no stress. Day-to-day bills were not a
problem and never would be. I wondered if I'd left my Southern California Edison past-duesy on a table, would it have gotten paid? That's
how removed this place was from reality. I did a quick frisk for any out-
standing bills but realized they were all stuffed under the seat of the
Sled.

One look at the guests and I could tell they were making out big by
having made it inside. Few were worthy of the hospitality, the surroundings, and the ambience of the place, including me. The place was
mobbed. Anyone who was anyone in town was there, from moguls to
Strugs to Noguls to Wams to Starman and Stargal. I expected to see
Abraham Lincoln there too.

The ceilings were vaulted and palatial, the rooms impeccably deco-
rated. As impressed as I was with the place, the Bullets were less affected.
They stepped on the clutch and put the party machine in the only gear
they knew. They grabbed my hand and I held on tightly to avoid it being

ripped out of my socket. Jack tried to keep up, but the me-firsters ate him whole.

In no time I got a view of bedrooms with canopy beds, playrooms, game rooms, screening rooms, a pantry that could have fed a small nation, secret stairs, bars off of bars, a pool the size of an ocean, and a tennis court that could have been bigger if it wanted to be.

I was panting when the Bullet tour took a break inside a third-floor bathroom surrounded by art, a lot of marble, gold fixtures, and a minichandelier overhead. This bathroom was worth more than my entire apartment complex. I turned away as Suzy the Bullet moved for a quick squirt. Her skirt was so short there was nothing to hike up.

"What do you guys think?"

"It's raging."

"What's this guy's name again?"

"Sydney Swinburn," I said.

"What does he do?"

"Whatever he wants," I added.

"Guess he wanted to throw a party."

"Or someone did."

"He's probably not even here."

The reality is, next to Eisner and Ovitz, Sydney Swinburn was the guy in the movie industry. *Premier* magazine had him ranked number three in movie muscle. He was CEO of Novastar Studios, the second most successful studio in Hollywood over the last ten years. They'd put out a dozen blockbusters and won a Best Picture Oscar for a film entitled *The Gods of Gunfire*. You bet I knew who Swinburn was. He had big-time whites, meaning motion picture credits. Personally, I knew very little about the man. I'd heard he was married and rather private. It was very clear, however, his party sure as hell wasn't.

When everyone was ready, I opened the bathroom door, which was wide enough for all of us to come out at once. When we did, there were spectators witnessing our exit thinking the usual dark and perverted thoughts, but there was one set of eyes beaming at us that caught my attention. They belonged to a guy in his late forties, medium height, perched against the railing of the stairwell. He had a nicely groomed

Woody beard, horn-rims, and a gray suit. Though his gaze was piercing it wasn't offensive. He seemed to be smiling, as if he liked the thought of my being in there with the Bullets. One on four. Good ratio. We nodded hellos with smiles and then passed him in a whoosh. A mental flash told me this might be the party's host. I'd seen a picture of Sydney Swinburn and I recalled some similar glasses. I remembered his face as being rather nondescript. So I wasn't sure. But we were on to new thoughts and new territory two floors down already.

Gerbilized

As soon as we were in the main living room where the music was pulsating, I saw a little swirl of confusion. There were girlie-whirlies, a whole pack of them, on their hands and knees scanning the ground. Someone had obviously lost a contact lens. I hung around just long enough for the Bullets to shoot off. That was okay. I needed to slow it down.

"What are they looking for?" I asked one of the crawlers.

"Lisa-Anne lost her stone."

"What stone?"

"Her five-carat diamond."

I looked at the group of diamond hunters and saw one girl in particular who had a face full of water.

"It was her mother's. And her mother just died."

"Shit," I said with genuine remorse.

"It popped out of the setting."

"Really."

I don't know why but I was always good at this sort of thing. Back in Long Island in the summertime we used to shoot BB guns at trees. And I was always able to find the fallen BBs in the grass. It saved BB money.

What I did was maneuver around the perimeter of the group. Mind you there were revelers everywhere dancing, pushing, laughing. It made a find difficult. In addition, the stone was worth about fifty grand. For some people, pocketing it would be easy and involve no guilts. I moved quickly. For different reasons.

Sure enough, beneath a chair that had a drunken human water balloon floundering on it, I saw a quick flash of glitter. I bent down and picked up the stone. Then I tapped Lisa-Anne on the shoulder and held it up. She cried even more at the sight of it and wrapped her arms around me. Before I knew it, all the girls were surrounding me, planting kisses on my cheek and neck like a swarm of little gerbils. It was kind of a sisterhood they shared in jewelry—lost jewelry. It made them bond immediately and, together, love me like the white knight. As I was being gerbilized, I looked in the distance and saw that same man from upstairs eyeing me. While listening to some hotty, he offered me another weak smile. I smiled back.

More important, finding the diamond was a nice moment for Lisa-Anne. She didn't say much to me. She was too overcome with emotion. What she did say was, "I'll never forget you."

I'm sure that was partially true. I also knew I wouldn't forget her. I thought of all the things I could buy with that 50G. I was doing without in L.A. and a few essentials would come in handy. Basically, most everything I owned had a flat tire. My eyeglasses had no left earpiece, my cowboy boots needed resoling, my molars were like rock boulders that sliced my tongue whenever it rolled over them, my printer needed ink, my PC needed a new hard drive, not to mention all the little things the Sled could use. Like a wash for starters. I didn't let the thought last and I wasn't serious about it. The good, bright life that returned to the girl's eyes was well worth it, the sap that I am.

8x10s

Just then I looked over and saw that same guy who gave me the polite smiles chatting up the hotty. Only now, a striking 8x10 had joined them. 8x10s are the just-another-pretty-face group. All look, little content, and few goals. Except for what's in arm's reach. Like a bag of chips, the TV remote, or a set of fine nightclub fishnets. And this snapshot saw a momentary lapse in security on the hotty and recognized his chance to move in. And his dim, monosyllabic phrases were just enough to carve into the guy's rap and box him out. With nothing else to say, the guy asked the hotty if he could get her something to drink. The 8x10 finished it off with "I'll have what she's having." After putting in their orders, they resumed the yak-yak.

"I'll be right back," the guy said in a runner-up's tone.

And all I could think was "rookie move." One axiom I'd learned in the art of aggressive womanizing is to never employ an 8x10 masher as your Storage Man. Storage Man is the overly dependable guy you store a hotty with while you tend to other business. You use bespectacled, clammy-handed Blips as your Storage Men. Why? They're not a threat. They're nothing. They're blips on a radar screen. They dutifully converse with her and watch her until you return from your mission. I had used guys like this a million times. And they were always Blippy and foolish and the hotty always came to that realization very fast. The moment he opened his mouth, she didn't know what he was talking about. Why? Because she didn't want to. Why? Because he's not a quick, flash-fuck 8x10 or someone who can further her career. Most female Woodies are agenda chicks and they do think that way. How did I know? They rarely hit on me.

Sure enough, when the poor guy came back to his storage closet, his hotty was no longer hanging there. She was grinding away on the dance floor with the smiley, vacant 8x10, his hands already tugging away at her hems.

I loved watching human behavior. And particularly, in pursuit of behavior. So predictable. But so entertaining. Which wasn't to say I was above scrutiny. I had my own patterns of behavior that easily tagged and categorized me. In fact I'd categorized myself. I was a Blippy Scribe. That was one thing about Wannabeasts. We all imbibed in a little bit of hypocrisy. It may sound self-serving but it was really true. Why? Because this town, and more specifically this business, did not run on pleasant deeds done pleasantly, or nice gestures performed nicely. In order to play, you had to wear the right gear. If you want to play pro football, you don't step on the turf with shorts and a T-shirt. You wear a helmet and pads, not to mention a firm athletic supporter for the real creeps. More on them later.

The reality is, however, I wasn't well-equipped. I hadn't grown up in this environment nor had I been exposed to it. As a result, I depended upon my powers of analysis, judgment, and awareness. I called it my Blade. I was pretty good at cutting away the fat, seeing people as they really were. And it was crucial for me. And my survival in L.A. It was my only defense. Sometimes I was harsh, sometimes I was wrong, but I figured it was better to be overly acute and protectionary than naive and an underestimator. That would only result in the Big Hurt, which would occur faster and more furiously.

In any case, I had done my good deed for the evening and I figured it was time to do something for myself—like go to the bar.

"Stoli cubes," I said soon after.

"Scotch," some other barfly chimed. Then eyed me. "Ron Cashman," he said with an all-too-enthusiastic hand extended. After all, I was a New Yorker and hadn't yet shed that general skepticism of people with a gift for splashy greetings.

"Heyward."

"Quite a bash, huh?"

I nodded absently.

"You know Sydney Swinburn?"

I mumbled something noncommittal.

"Quite a guy. I wrote two pictures for him."

And that was just about the worst thing I could have heard. Maybe he was a nice guy. Maybe not. But experience had told me to get my liquid silver and move. Only the bartender was too damn slow.

"You a writer too?" he followed up with.

"Why do you ask?"

"You have that look."

"What look?" I said, somewhat put off.

"That pale, underfed artist thing and out here those types are usually movie writers." He belched out at the jibe too and I smelled his gamy, foie gras breath. Brutal.

My response was to reach for the drink coming to me. I pivoted away.

Maybe it was rude, in fact I'm pretty sure of it. But have you ever seen a couple of screenwriters together? It becomes a seminar in ugly war stories of the Business that no one wants to hear. It's a downer. I liken it to the soldiers who participated in and witnessed the goriest in Korea or the Nam and are reluctant to talk about it. They don't want reminders. It's too goddam painful. On a lighter scale, that's the way it is with most movie writers. You'd just rather talk sports, women, or—even better— talk to someone else.

But if you came upon a writer with some whites, it's even worse. He doesn't want you to move on. For all the crap, bullshit, and demoralizing dues he's paid to get where he is, he'll make sure to take out a little revenge on your hide. He'll gloat and brag and twist the knife in your ribs. He can't wait for you to ask him what he's written so that he can let you know he's not a suffering bastard anymore. He'll gleefully watch your expression deflate, your face lose all its glow. And you'll silently slip out of the party and drive home and hate L.A. all over again. There's nothing like the ego of a successful Hollywood player. They're worse than tennis players. Or boxers. Or professional wrestlers.

"Where you going?" he asked.

"Outside."

Sure, he wanted me to stick around so he could rub my face in his glittering feces.

"Tell me about . . . ," he started with.

"NFW," I finished with.

The Walking Nightclub

The throng was so thick I knew I had little chance of finding the Bullets unless I anchored at the bar and they made a pit stop for some Red. But that gloating writer was keeping me away. So I crept at my own pace through the kitchen, out the back door, past the fountains and gardens, and I decided to just kick back for a while on the changeover bench of the tennis court. There were sky-high trees hovering over it, no doubt photosynthesizing away, working overtime to fight off the smoggy Hollywood easterlies, trying to give the place some good air. I sat there for a while, took in a deep wedge of it, chewed on cubes, and pondered what a lucky sonofabitch Sydney Swinburn was.

Way beyond the gardens in the back of the property, I glimpsed a modest cottage, modest compared to the rest of the oversized place. I decided to take a little walk back there, but the yard was so deep it became a big one.

Upon closer look, the cottage was more like the little Trianon palaces at Versailles. A lot of estates in Beverly Hills and Bel-Air had guest cottages but this was the nicest I had ever seen. It had its own pool and Jacuzzi, of course. And its own gross national product statistic, I'm sure. It was dark inside and I wasn't sure if there was anybody in it. I advanced silently until something in my peripheral line made me turn sharply around. I could have sworn I saw someone spying on me from the corner of the cottage. I listened and heard nothing but the pool heater.

As I drifted back toward the mansion I saw a curious figure making movements on the baseline of the tennis court. She was dancing, performing very graceful ballet pirouettes. Hands floating high, legs hearing some far-off Mahler symphony. Every time she spun, her silver minidress would come up and what was beneath was worth looking at. She had underwear on, yes. But the underwear was trying to hide the flesh. And losing. It was a battle it would never win. Not with this body.

Suddenly, the young woman saw me standing there and gasped in fright. It was a frail gasp, not what I expected from someone so tall and physically superior.

"You scared me."

"Sorry," I said.

Then she laughed.

"I'm just doing a few exercises."

"You do them well."

She smiled shyly.

"I'll leave you alone." And I started to go.

"Don't have to," she said in a voice labored from limbs still pumping.

"You don't mind if I watch?"

"No. Not at all."

So I sat down, sipped my silver, and sighed.

"Are you a friend of Sydney's?" she asked.

"No."

It made her half smile and I don't know why. Then she made some elaborate movements which included some twists and spins. And I watched.

Forget anything I already said. This girl was a walking nightclub. Wherever she went people would circle around, gather, loiter, check their coats, sit down beside her, turn on music, smoke, order drinks, watch, and wish a lot. There was no need for a party. She was it. On a sidewalk, in a garden, or on a boat, there would be a scene developing around her. If she entered a room couples would inevitably argue, separate, and divorce. She was all that and a mile more. Genetically, she was off the charts.

When she was done with her spins, I clapped.

She took in the applause with a smile, looked away, and let her knees knock a bit. She was either way shy or trying to be. But her face couldn't cover a rush of enthusiasm.

"Do you want to see me do a flying split?"

"Only if you want to make my night."

She flew across the court and the legs parted and jutted out wide. It was a gorgeous move and let's not forget the sensual aspects. She landed perfectly.

I put down my glass and clapped again. She was laughing.

"How am I doing?"

I told her she was doing great and I meant it. Anyone would. Her movements were all but anesthesia against any of life's troubles in the Age of A.

Then she walked closer and I slid over on the bench but she did not sit down. She put a hand on the net cord and dragged her index finger along it. I decided she really was a shy girl, painfully so.

"What's your name?"

"Teal."

I was going to say it was a nice one but didn't. "Funny time to do your exercises, huh?"

"The best time. No one bothers me."

"Other than wayward partygoers like me."

"Right," she agreed with a smile. "They're too involved with their own . . ." And she bent over and made fingers touch toes instead of finishing her comment.

"Agendas?" I supplied.

"Yes. Agendas . . . than to worry about me," she added.

"What can I tell ya," I quipped. "It's tough being a girl."

And she thought about it. "It's tough being a *good* girl," she sent right back. And a killer smile came with it. And I laughed. This girl had all that *and* some wit. And of course she made me feel pretty average male, meaning I was forced to wonder what it would be like to go toe-to-toe with her.

I kept my eyes on her. When she looked at me again we both held each other's gaze for a long second and it was wonderful how neither of us worried about the mutual stare or what it might have meant. She trusted me enough to keep her eyes on me not fearing I would take it the wrong way. She was a beautiful girl with long strawberry-blond hair and that murderous body. I'm sure there had been many times when her stares had falsely excited the hopes of many men.

This was different. I think we had an interior vision of each other. Like we both knew exactly where each other was coming from. The vision I had of her was telling me that she was somewhat melancholic. Maybe even lonely. I knew the symptoms all too well. Maybe she saw them in me too.

Then something odd happened. She put her hand back through her hair, scuffed a toe, and seemed to flash on something disturbing. Then, without saying anything, not a word, she just took off. And she didn't walk. She ran. I sensed she was on the verge of tears but maybe it was my imagination. Either that, or the low-light conditions were making a fool out of me.

I stayed on the bench for a while and finished off my silver. One thing I wondered was how Teal knew Sydney Swinburn. And how well. No one was around to give me any answers. But at least I was curious about something. In that town my curiosity wasn't always aroused. Even-tually, I walked back to the party, but my mind was on leaving it.

The Real Rookie

The marble stairs I climbed up to reenter the house dwarfed me. I drifted across the wide patio toward the sky-high French doors.

"Nice night," someone said. It came from my left in the darkness of the patio.

"Yeah," I said. And I slowed a bit not knowing what to make of the overture. Then the face the voice belonged to appeared in the light and slowly advanced my way. I could see it was that same guy—the one who'd seen me emerge from the bathroom with the Bullets, then recover that diamond, the one who had lost a hotty to a snapshot.

"Hey there," I said amiably, acknowledging our silent run-ins earlier.

"Have we met before?" he asked with a look that seemed to be gen-uinely puzzled.

"I don't think so." Then I smiled.

"What's funny?"

"Rookie move." And I said it nicely even though it was kind of rude. But I was kind of bored.

He tilted his head. "Excuse me?"

And I explained it off to him. Normally, I would have refrained from critiquing a total stranger. But there was something open and unthreat-ening about him. I told him he had achieved a solid Breakthrough with that hotty. There was no reason to have put her in storage. And not with an 8x10. He laughed. When he finished making a mild excuse for his behavior as all men do when poor performance is pointed up in their womanizing, the air went dead between us. Then he said this: "I'm Syd-ney Swinburn."

I immediately froze. My premonition earlier had been correct. I laughed from nervousness.

"I'm sorry. It's obvious who the real rookie here is."

He laughed at that. "Quite all right," he said. And the awkward quality of the exchange died away.

He spoke somewhat swiftly, in short, quick bursts. I could tell he had a very active mind. Love that. It always gave me a charge when I found it. He looked at me with an expectant gaze and extended his hand. It prompted me to introduce myself. So I did.

"Heyward," he repeated, then tilted his head to take in my name's music. "That's a different name."

"An old southern name."

"It's in a Tennessee Williams play."

And not many people knew that.

"Precisely."

"I saw you recover that girl's diamond."

"Yeah, well."

"Nice gesture."

Then we both stood there and let the silence do whatever it does to people when they've exhausted all meaningless chitchatty topics of conversation.

"What do you do?"

"I'm a writer." Then I laughed punishingly and looked off. And I don't know why. But it was the first time I felt really embarrassed about saying it. Maybe because he was so much a part of the business and I so much was not.

"What kind of writer?"

"Is there any other kind?"

"Out here, I suppose you're right," he said with a smile.

That's when I wanted to get the fuck out of there. I didn't want to have to confess to a career that boasted no whites. And no agent. Not to someone his size.

"You have anything you're working on?"

The question caught me off guard. The way he said it almost indicated he was seriously inquiring about my work.

"Just finished a new spec."

"Has it been around?"

"Uh, no. No one's seen it."

"No one ever has," he said with a sardonic smile, and I knew what he meant. Writers always tell movie executives they're getting first look even though the piece may have been distributed to fans at a Dodgers home opener. The hope is they'll get someone to read it within two weeks. Instead of never.

"In this case it happens to be true. Very true."

He then looked at me and pulled out a wallet. He handed me a card.

"Send it to my office. I'll read it overnight and get back to you."

It made me smile. I was speechless. But more so, skeptical. No one reads the work of an unheralded writer overnight. No one with any bang reads the work of an unheralded writer at all. Still, I had to thank him. After all, he was Sydney Swinburn. So I did. Rarely does a Blippy Scribe ever get the chance to be bullshitted to by a man of his stature.

"Great party," I added.

And he just nodded absently. It was a couple of words I'm sure he heard thousands of times. He'd probably hear it another thousand times before the night was over.

As I stepped back inside, I couldn't help thinking what a strange meeting it was. But it lifted my spirits and that didn't happen too often. I fended off a few drunken marauders and invitations to dance from sloppy girls playing a losing game of hard-to-get. Then I planted myself on the large staircase that overlooked the main room of the party. I looked for anything meteoric. I found it but it was more cometlike. And it had a slow trailer named Jack. I ran down and caught up to it and asked it what it wanted to do.

Two of the Bullets said "I'm over this!" and two said "Let's get out of here!" and Jack did the San Diego thing. He shrugged.

I said, "Agreed."

The Mighty Hippo

On the ride home the Bullets tried to kidnap me and take me to the Viper Room, the place on the Strip that had been slamming ever since Starboy had gone down there. Nothing buzzes a place more these days than a Star Murder, Star Overdose, or Star Death. You know the era. But I declined. I wanted to cave. After all, I had to be at work at nine. So they dropped me off on Beverly where I left the Sled, and then they speeded back up to the Sunset Strip.

My apartment house was your usual L.A. prefabricated number, typical of the Hollywood flats. It straddled a corner at Fairfax and Melrose in the heart of the smog belt. In fact, my apartment was wedged beneath a huge movie advertisement billboard which never ceased to depress me. It was a modest one-bedroom, with some nice Swiss chalet beam work. That's what you got in L.A. Random architectural choices, stuff erected without planning or forethought and piled right next to each other. *Zoning* and *taste* were terms from other cultures.

I got in bed and thought about a few things. Like the standard of living at that house on Bellagio. And the odd meeting with its owner. The word on Sydney Swinburn was that he was incredibly intelligent, ruthless in business, and possessed an acute commercial sense. We obviously didn't have a lot in common. Other than that, I knew nothing about him. I was impressed with how accessible he was, however. I guess if you're that powerful, sometimes you don't have to be a Mo anymore. Maybe he was beyond it. Or maybe he was full of shit. I didn't know for sure.

Then I started to tally up the lies. It was a night ripe with them. We'd covered a lot of ground and the Beasts were out in full force. I often tallied up the lies after an evening in Hollywood. Because that's what everyone did when they came to L.A. They came here to tell lies. Most tried their nastiest to back up the lies with truths. It's what was called a career. Few succeeded. But if someone has just arrived in town with a burning desire to alter his status as one of the planet's Blips, he'd quickly find himself telling lies. Little ones *and* big ones. Why? It's too easy. No one has a track on a newcomer. It's a modern prospector's dream.

Tallying up the lies was kind of fun. It also kept me sharp. And untrusting. And preserved my Blade. It was a dark way to look at life. But it was a dark town, definitely. Sometimes I overshot the truth with my own neuroses, paranoia, and other mental mechanisms for self-defense. But it helped quash the naiveté that tried to seep into my brain. Sometimes I made a list too. But tonight I wasn't in the mood. I got bored after the sixth falsehood. I took a note instead.

POST-IT: It's true I reduce life to the bare bones. It's a writer's gift. Or curse. To see the world in such minimalist terms. But whenever I see the bullshit of life piling up, I out it. For my own good. When you look from a distance, you see the patterns that evolve. I see the patterns, process them, reduce them, and label them. 8x10s, Strugs, Stowaways, Noguls, Wams, Star Campers, and Blippy Scribes like me. I consider my analyses to be informal anthropological surveys. I like to reveal the harsh, raw reality of a situation. Nor am I immune to scrutiny. I'm the Mighty Hippo. I am in the barest bone form a hypocrite. I hate the plastic trappings of fame. But I need recognition. I despise silly, hollow Star Camp chatter but I schmooze with the best of them. I out the Age of A offenders but I am part of the weave. I have my reasons, my drive. When I ponder whether my actions meet up with my philosophies, I know there are inconsistencies. But sometimes you do things that aren't really in your nature. L.A. extends you this way. It encourages momentary lapses of rationale. For some the lapses last longer. It is my goal and duty to keep that behavior to a minimum. I am a finger-pointing offender. I am the Mighty Hippo. But I am aware of it. I'm confident that awareness will keep me in check.

One more thing. I couldn't help thinking about the fragile Teal, the ethereal danseuse, and what her little riddle was. She was perfect subject matter. She was a perfect Project. In fact, she was so refreshing she made me think of Eleanor.

Eleanor was my girlfriend even though she wasn't. I wasn't involved with women in those days, but if I had been *she* would have been the girl. Eleanor was from the high-hedge district in Newport, Rhode Island. She was a product of old money and lofty social stature. Which I didn't give a shit about. And neither did she—for the most part. Still, there was an element of style and class she'd never lose. She was the coveted New York wondergirl. She was a fashion editrix for a national hi-glam magazine but she really could do anything. She was beautiful, educated, very smart, and most important, cool.

But if there was any hope of us getting together romantically, I needed to be established. I needed to produce. Not because she was into money—she wasn't. She would prefer, however, to avoid any major struggle.

I reread the last postcard she'd written me. She'd been in Florence, Italy, at the time. I'd only read it seventy-five times. So I hadn't squeezed all the good feeling out of it yet.

And then I drifted away. It had been a long day and I wanted it to end.

The Folgers Farewell

When I woke up that morning, there was someone lying next to me and she still had her motorcycle helmet on. The Road Bitch was lying peacefully enough but a thick film of breath condensation had formed on the visor. And I noticed her lips were purple. It looked like she was suffocating. Or already had. I quickly flipped up her visor so she could breathe. An awful waft of booze busted out of the helmet. I couldn't tell what it was, but her purple vampire lips—and it wasn't lipstick—led me to believe that she had been sucking down some house merlot. And that was not a good sign. Baby Garbo was not supposed to drink.

Baby Garbo had motored over on her bike late-late that night, after I was already asleep. I knew her. I knew her well. And liked her very much. And she liked me. She was a Stowaway from the previous year when I was active. I didn't get involved with her anymore. I didn't get involved with anyone anymore. That's probably why she dropped by. Not to do me. But to avoid doing someone else. She felt safe with me. I had given her a key and told her she could stay over anytime.

Women are necessary. But they're secondary. Maybe even tertiary. That was my sentiment in those days and, for the most part, I stuck to it. Sure, I would get involved with the occasional Stowaway, to stave off the horny crunch, but I hadn't recently. And didn't plan on it. I was inactive.

I was beyond that ego satisfaction which derived from a conquest mentality. Certainly, if I saw a piece of mind-boggling glamour stroll past, I would conjure up the usual number of heavy male thoughts, perverse sexual atrocities included. But I stayed away. I'd had enough sweet thing in my younger years. Now I was a cheerleader for the rest. If you wanted that piece of Strange, meaning a strange girlie-whirlie from the odd rim of life, I rooted you on. Go get it, tiger! was my rallying cry.

What was a Stowaway? She was the type of girl who you'd phone up late at night and have her come over and play rape games with until the wee hours. Then she would magically slip out of your apartment in the early morning, not hearing from you again until the next rendezvous. If she got sluggish and showed signs of wanting to sleep in, a Stowaway no-no, you would tiptoe over to the venetians, open them silently, let the slashes of sun slice the bed and tickle her eyelids. Then you'd pump her with coffee and ask her tons of questions about her day until she realized she had a lot of errands to run. And she better get to them. Then she'd buzz off wired on your brand. All you had to do was see her to the door. Then you'd wait until you knew she hadn't forgotten something, then draw all your blinds, make a dark bear den, and rerack until springtime. Or noon, whichever came first. I called it the Folgers Farewell. Coffee is fucking great. So many uses.

Sometimes, of course, she'd stay for a day and maybe wash your clothes or cook you lunch and then take you down again in the afternoon. By and large she was not a girl you went out with in public. She was *stowed away*. And so were you. You were both satisfying the loneliness thing, a large part of L.A. single life, as well as the creeping biological urges. There was a lot of that independent, secretive body mashing among the Wannabeasts of L.A. What's equally amusing is that if you ended up at her place, the next morning you found your mitt clutching a hot mug of a Colombian brew just as fast. Or faster.

The reality is everybody was so independent, on such a course, no one really wanted to commit because they were already linked up with someone far more important: their career. When you want to be a star, a relationship takes backseat. And when a relationship takes backseat, well, it's on pretty shaky ground. Stowaways were necessary, though. They usually exhibited good character and were, in general, good sports. I liked Stowaways.

That's not to say all Stowaways were happy with their status. Some, of course, wanted more out of a relationship. Unfortunately, they had chosen a difficult town for old-fashioned love. Star Camp was a selfish place in many ways. The way I saw it, conditional love ruled. At least for the Wannabeasts. I felt if you came out there for true love, and were having difficulties, hopefully one day you'd realize there were better places to find it.

Anyway, I wasn't getting involved anymore. In fact, I hadn't gotten laid in a year. I would never have even confessed to that fact in my mid-twenties. But I didn't care anymore. I really didn't. I'd forgotten as many rolls in the rack as I could remember. Even the good ones.

That's not to say I didn't interact with the opposite sex. On the contrary, I may have been as popular as ever. Most of my phone calls were with women. But in romantic terms, I was no longer considered a threat. The ladies of Los Angeles did not have to worry about me. It even led to speculation that I was seeking pastures of a different color. But many things were incomprehensible to people in Los Angeles. *The rest of the world* being one.

If the truth be known, the Beach Boys had it all wrong about the girls of California. "I wish they all could be . . ." is the most melodious piece of propaganda, false propaganda, meaning *bullshit*, I have ever heard. I wished *none* could be California girls. The more they wanted to giggle, the more I wanted to sneer. The more they wanted to catch rays and look tan, the more I wanted to stay inside and get pasty. The more they wanted to flash their bright whites, the more I wanted to flash my coffee-stained choppers. The more they wanted to show off those Beverly Hills Bumpers, the more I wanted to stick a pin in and watch them pop.

Sure, you could have fun playing around with them. But I wasn't playing around anymore. I wasn't in any frame of mind to settle for something I didn't want. That is not to say there weren't some great, interesting girls in Los Angeles. But that is to say they usually came from somewhere else, and they were usually married. That is also to say that if my movie career had been slamming, I probably would have loved all the girls of the world, Californians included.

Wam Bam, Nothing Happened

I looked at Baby Garbo from head to toe. She looked pretty uncomfortable in her heavy leather and boots. But since she was passed out it didn't matter. To me anyway. There's no doubt she was sexy. She had those great left coast curves, a Mom-I-Got-the-Part body, with your usual amount of surgical enhancements in all areas that gave her a sense of pride about herself. She sported some Italian blood too and had thick wavy brown hair and a great chewing-gum smile.

Baby Garbo was a Wam. Wams are the waitress-actress-model group. They were Wannabeasts, the girlie versions of the Strugs. Baby Garbo worked tables at a Sunset Plaza bistro called Le Petit Four, always had a few television commercials running, and modeled lingerie. All Wams wanted more than the thirty seconds of airtime their commerical work yielded. Their goal was very simple. Wams wanted a feature. Just like the Strugs. As you might imagine, Wams were a pretty insecure group for all that wishing upon a star they had to do. Maybe, like, the writers.

I smelled the fresh brew in the kitchen. My Braun coffeemaker had a timer feature and its percolating slurps in the morning made for sweet music. It meant I was going to get a damn good jolt. And soon. I checked the clock on my PC and it was eight-thirty. I had to be at work at nine. I poured myself a bowl of java and sipped it like cereal milk. Then I showered quickly and stepped into the bedroom.

"How's my little depth charge?" I asked. And my affectionate lick was not hyperbole. Baby Garbo was explosive. She didn't have a good personality. She had *too much.* She had twenty-one personalities and I liked twenty of them. And they took her in many directions. This was a girl who, when jealous over a classmate's tooth retainer, wrapped a paper clip around her fangs and wore it to school. This was a girl who made a pet of a tree frog and called it Tree Frog Fred.

"Fine, fine, okay, fine," she rattled off.

"Want some coffee or something?"

"Void."

"Tell me, Baby Garbo." And I said it like a *Father Knows Best* stand-in. "Were you out drinky-drink last night?"

"Nope."

"Then why are your lips purple?"

"Are they?"

And she rubbed them. Then laughed. "Oh, I had a Popsicle."

"A Popsicle?"

"Yeah, grape," and she laughed some more.

I just cast heavy, skeptical eyes on her and stepped out of the bedroom. Baby Garbo's transmission sported four gears, those of denial, avoidance, avoidance, and denial.

"Where are you going?" she asked, sounding left out.

"To get the mail."

"Wait for me!"

And I did. We did it together. We wrapped ourselves in his and her towels and went downstairs. That was one bonus about California. You could go outside with a towel and not freeze. That and the fact that there was no such thing as Fashion Week.

Getting the mail wasn't usually a good time. I had four enemies. Pacific Bell, Southern California Edison, the water company, and the Van Wagoner Ambulance Service from the night I dialed 911 with massive palpitations from an anxiety attack; all due to the galloping rot of the Age of A on my soul. And let's not forget the No Script Contract in sight. I'm sure you understand. With the exception of those four, all other letters I carried into my apartment with the warmth of a southern gentleman.

This day's mail was different. I got a letter, the personal kind. From the person in my life who mattered most.

I was intently reading it when Baby Garbo purred up next to me in her towel looking all sleepy-sexy. Yes, for some girls it goes together. I don't know how guys ever let them get out of bed when they're this type. But I was you know what anyway.

"Who's the letter from?" she asked pointedly.

I didn't answer. To be honest, I didn't hear her. I was too immersed.

"Eleanor?" she added in a curious way.

I nodded.

Baby Garbo didn't say anything. Baby Garbo didn't like Eleanor. But Baby Garbo didn't like anyone who took attention off her. She stayed silent. And I didn't say anything more. I didn't want to initiate a conversation with her. It would end up in a lecture. From me. About other things.

As I dried off with my towel, Baby Garbo tugged at me and made me sit down.

"Oh no you don't."

"Yes."

"No."

"How long has it been?"

"Dunno."

"Be right back."

"No, Baby Garbo. I'm feeling good," I whined. And I was. Hot blood was flowing through my veins. After all, Eleanor had just written me and the caf-jolt was making me realize it in all its Technicolor splendor.

But Baby Garbo came right back as promised. With Q-tips, hydrogen peroxide, and some nail clippers. She loved doing this stuff. If she got a splinter she couldn't wait to go home to play with it. Scabs too. And new zits were heaven.

"I don't have time."

"Hush. And tilt your head."

Baby Garbo mothered me. She considered me a throwback, a real Neanderthal. Like a big overgrown shrub. And I needed pruning. So she did my ears, my nails, my toenails. Baby Garbo was a Stowaway, the maternal kind. I loved Baby Garbo.

And when she was finished jabbing a cotton swab into my ear, I heard her whisper it.

"Heyward?"

"What?"

"Do you think I'm a good actress?"

"Top-shelf."

She smiled faintly, curled into the couch, and didn't say anything more. Wams. The only thing they needed for breakfast was a little reassurance. It could serve as lunch and dinner too.

Drinky-Drink

As I drove south on Fairfax en route to my job at Loser Inc. in Culver City, I put a few thoughts to Baby Garbo. I was disturbed by her appearance in my bed. Not the fact that she was there. The fact that she'd gone drinky-drink the night before. *Drinky-drink* was her term and a cute one at that. With those pretty eyes she'd just look at you and go "I'm going to go to the ladies' room. Can you get me another drinky-drink? For the road?" And she'd flash that bright smile with a mischievous look. Very sexy. And of course you'd get her one more. What man wouldn't? And all of them did. And that was her problem.

We had had numerous scenes, spectacles, and public outbursts. All due to her slamming the hard stuff. Alcohol was a drug to her. When she drank, her mind became a moralistic jungle gym. Anything went. And in a town full of enablers who all wanted in to her private spaces? Forget it.

It made me replay that confrontation we'd once had. And my mind went right to the meat of the discourse as your memory always provides it. I gave it to her. I gave it to her hard.

"I'm going to tell you, Baby Garbo. You don't have a chance in hell of making it. Unless you clean it up. You're anesthetizing your failure with the Hollywood one-two. Booze and drugs. I've seen those with talent that roars. *Not* hampered by this shit. They still can't make it. Every time the Oscar show is beamed to the world, or a hit movie opens up the valves of sensation of the world's youth, droves of people are inspired to make this lifelong craft. And they all pour out here to wedge themselves into the fray. And hardly anyone gets through. As a Wam, you start with a one in one hundred thousand shot of making it. But consumption puts you in the one in a million group. It's hard enough if you're clean and in control."

Normally, I'm not such a righteous, boring, pedantic, and proselytizing nightmare of a guy. I'm a live-and-let-live type as long as it's not my life. The reality is I knew she was never going to make it. But I at least wanted her to have a fighting chance. Baby Garbo was an original. But she had no discipline. And you can't fly on talent alone. She could impress a dinner table, but a group of moguls who are investing millions in her delivering?
NFW.

Grand Master Filer

Of course I had my own statistical struggle. At present, I had a bullshit job with bullshit people awaiting me. Real rock dwellers. *Where the hell did they come from anyway?* I wondered. The only fun I had was the drive there and back during which I would emerge from the A.M. grog with a little Radio Stern until he would do something stupid like put his mother on. When my mind finally awoke I would let it take over and float through a few subjects which could amuse me. That was how I spent most of my time in L.A. With myself.

I pulled into the lot of Loser Industries Inc. at ten after the hour. That wasn't really the name but it may as well have been. I was bummed I had missed the Danish cart. It was one of the day's highlights. That and lunch break made work a real hootenanny.

The company I worked for had some real estate scam going down. Apparently, they were using federally funded housing projects for tax shelters and doing it with an illegal spin. They were under current federal investigation. I didn't know the specifics. And I didn't care. You see, I was the Grand Master Filer, meaning I was the Go-To Guy when it came to filing. Believe me the thought of paying $75,000 for an Ivy diploma and using it to insert little index tabs into Pendaflex files had uppercut me more than once. I was better educated than my bosses. But I never let anyone know it.

It started as a three-day assignment and turned into a reasonably permanent thing. I made about $350 a week and cleared just over three bills after Sam's bite. My agency told me to stick with the assignment because the temp biz was slow. So I did. And hated every minute of it. The only perk was the fact that I could sneak a few phone calls to New York at lunchtime. But even that had its element of danger. There was some in-house Mo named Russ who pretended to be some kind of security figure. He goofed off all day except for some phony moment when he'd try to bust someone for something just to show he was earning his pay. Let's face it, they were all Mos at that job. So I did my work silently with no interaction with the Mos.

If I wasn't sneaking a phone call, I went to Tito's Tacos for lunch. The tacos were greasy but good. I think it always reminded me of that grim quote I saw every morning in the bathroom stall of my fraternity at Brown. "If God hadn't meant for man to eat pussy, he wouldn't have made it look like a taco." It was a nasty quote but memorable. Whether or not it made Tito's tacos taste better I couldn't be sure. I knew it didn't hurt.

For me the job was just a paycheck. I'm not going to bore you any more with it. Sure, I gave them my time. What I didn't do was give them my mind. I thought up script stories and dialogue and took notes while I shuffled all the cardboard.

After the day's work, I pinballed through freeway traffic at high speed and got off on Pico Boulevard. I sidled up to the security gate at Novastar Studios.

"Your name?"

I told him. "I'm dropping off a script for Sydney Swinburn," I added. And I felt pretty damn good about saying it. I loved that feeling—that I was entering the Novastar lot for a reason. It meant that I was part of the business. However slightly.

The guard pecked at his computer, confirmed my claim, then handed me a pass. Then my car followed the blue line to Swinburn's building. I ran down the hall and slowed three yards before Sydney's office door. I stepped in and found out he wasn't there. But his secretary was. I wanted to see him in person but he was out at a meeting. That was a disappointment.

It was a great office, however. So great I took my time handing over my work. I slowly flapped over the envelope, slowly licked it, slowly asked for a pen, slowly wrote down Sydney's name and address, then slowly added "By Hand." When the secretary asked if I wanted a diet cola, I took my time to decide. When she went to the fridge, I just studied the walls covered with the posters from Swinburn's movies. It was an impressive wall. Not a bomb on it.

"We met at the party, Sydney and me," I announced proudly.

"That's nice," the secretary said absently without lifting her head.

I drove home sucking on my diet cola, in a decent frame of mind. And a new Novastar Studios pen.

At a stoplight a Mexican guy tried to sell me a bag of oranges and I said no. I hated oranges. Besides, I was the lemon type. It's like the difference between being a Rangers and an Islanders fan. You're either one or the other. Never both.

That night, I avoided all phone-ins and resisted the temptations of joining people for another silly L.A. Nerf-ball social affair. I stayed in. Of course, I wondered what Sydney Swinburn was thinking about my project. That included what his reader thought of it, since Sydney would be relying on his coverage. These guys never read anything themselves. Movie projects were always cut down to something Woody-witty like Killer Warts meets Breaker Morant.

I didn't have much hope. I was sure Sydney would find it as unsellable as anyone else. But maybe he'd flip through and see the quality of the writing. I knew I was that good anyway. He would know I wasn't a Muffin Head.

Maybe he was full of shit. Maybe he wasn't even going to read the coverage. That was usually the case in Jollywood. Maybe he wasn't going to call at all. I was used to that. That was the main play in town. Never call back. After all, someone might be in.

At Loser Inc. the following day I tried to suppress my excitement for the studio chief's response. But that kind of wait, meaning a report on your art, was always nerve-racking. It was like waiting to see if your ticket had won the lottery. You always felt you had a chance. *Maybe, just maybe,* the thinking went.

Maybe he wasn't going to call at all was another thought. But he said he would. I don't know why I believed him.

The Call

At lunchtime, I retreated to the back room and dialed into my machine. Kelly the Bullet wanted to go out and get good and Red. I owed money at Kinko's for all my wallpaper. Fux Young Boys was having a cocktail party in the Hills. Travels with Men was off to Rome. The Pumpster was going to a screening at Bob Evans's house. A bunch of hot tub crashers were heading up to Hef's. And Baby Garbo wanted to have dinner. She said she hadn't been eating well. Then I heard this from the secretary:

"Sydney Swinburn is calling you. It is 10:30 A.M. The number is 310-779-9022."

A surge of adrenaline shot through my insides. I dialed up the super-M. And got reception. Then her. Then I waited for him. I smacked my chest to make my heart shut up.

"Hello, Heyward?"

"Hi there."

"Listen. I read your script. I've got to tell you. You are a great writer. I have a meeting now, but I'd like to talk to you more about it. Would you like to have dinner tonight?"

"Sure thing."

And I thought about it. Why not bring Baby Garbo? A beauty jolt is always refreshing. Besides, it may make me look better, which may make the business go even better.

"Would you mind if I bring a lady friend?"

"Not at all."

I looked over my shoulder and saw that in-house dick named Russ standing there. He was slashing a finger across his throat indicating I should get off the phone now.

"Say Morton's at nine?"

"Great."

"See you then."

I hung up the phone and looked at Russ. If the studio chief had told me my work sucked I probably would have strung Russ up against the wall and gripped his stones until he went sea blue in the face. But since I was happy, elated even, I just made a yo-yo of him.

"Something wrong with your Adam's apple?" I asked.

"No personal calls on the job."

"That was business."

"Yeah? Whose?"

"Mine." And then I started to redial. "But this is personal." And I added a wink. "Baby Garbo? Dinner's on. I'll be by you at 8:45."

Russ was so miffed he had no lips. But so what? It was a job that I didn't care if I lost. Besides, I was the company's only superhero, Super-filer, and everyone knew it.

Yo Garbo!

The episode was the type I was not used to. Not in Gollywood. A studio head had actually stuck to his word. Unfuckingbelievable.

For the first time in a long time I was actually excited about going out. Sure, I put on some nice clothes. I wore my remaining pressed shirt and wore a linen jacket over that. Then I did a quick blast of the eau de toilette someone had left in my medicine chest. I didn't forget to put the pebble in my shoe either.

I picked up Baby Garbo on time. I wanted to be on time for Sydney. She lived in a West Woody apartment complex—you know, the style thought up in the early sixties over coffee and built a few weeks later. Real color-by-numbers architorture. It was horseshoe-shaped with a pool in the middle. Brutal.

Baby Garbo lived on the second tier like me. And down the stairs she came, wearing turn-of-the-century hooker clothing which, these days, probably cost a fortune. It was all frill and ruffles and lace and sexy. Baby Garbo loved to dress up like a ho. From any era. She had the wildest selection of dresses, hats, furry stuff, and boots for every occasion.

With her personality it was overkill. With her body it just wasn't fair. I mean what were all the other girls going to do to compete? The fact is few could. This girl, left to the male eye, had the best package in Hollywood.

Baby Garbo also had a signature tat in her panty line which was the sister tat of another. Her former lover, yes, a girlie-whirlie named Boots, had the same one. And had showed it already on the big screen. Some sleazoid got to her. And it irked Baby Garbo to no end that her former mate's tat had made it into theaters first. There'd been a race. And Baby G lost.

"Hi, baby. How do I look?" she asked, spinning around.

"Better than me."

"Really?" Her facial glow upped a notch.

See? *Reassurance.* "Really." I peeled off a few more compliments as we drove. Then I proceeded to give her the word on Sydney.

"Impressive" was her only remark.

As we rode west down Santa Monica Boulevard, she played with a couple lemons. Passing through Boys Town I went against the grain and gave her a very hetero kiss. So the soft ice creamers could see where I stood. Not to overcompensate because I was one hinge away from busting out of the closet. Rather, to show all of them I was happy as hell to have the ability to be turned on by a being as exquisite as Baby Garbo.

Big Monday at Morton's

Around the corner from Morton's, I found my favorite back alley spot and parked. When Baby Garbo wasn't looking, I drew out an old parking ticket from the console and slapped it under my wiper just in case.

The lazy meter maids would see it and consider it one less ticket to give out.

Morton's was the industry's favorite joint. They had the most prestigious Oscar party every year as well as Big Monday. Big Monday was the restaurant's well-known Monday evening dinner lineup, which featured all the supermoguls breaking bread with Starman, trying to grease him with a little goodwill.

We were ushered to a table against the far wall beneath a real Francis Bacon. It showed a contorted figure lying on its side angst-ridden and twisted, his soul just oozing out. Obviously, it was a screenwriter.

Sydney was there already, seated at the table by himself, sipping on some mineral water. There was a bottle of red wine too. When he caught sight of us he stood up and beamed a bit.

"Hi there, Heyward."

We shook. "Sydney, meet Baby Garbo."

And it made him smile. "Pleasure, Baby Garbo."

She was all smiles and we sat down. I let Baby Garbo slide ahead of me so she could sit between us.

"Is that your real name?"

"No, it's his name. But I like it better than mine."

"Do you like wine?" he asked.

"No, I'll have soda water," Baby Garbo said. But I nodded out of politeness. Sydney poured. He did it shakily however. I sensed he was nervous.

"So how long have you been out here?" he asked her.

"Five years now."

"You enjoying it?"

"Yeah, well, it's L.A."

"Were you with Heyward at my party?"

"No, she wasn't."

"Yeah, why didn't you invite me to that party?"

"I crashed it," I confessed.

"Where was I?" she asked herself. "At another party," she finished with, and laughed. So did Sydney. And he eyed me. I just nodded with a smile. "No, I was rehearsing some sides," she corrected herself.

"For what?" Sydney asked.

"A commercial," she said with an unsatisfied sneer. But I was glad she did. Because it got Sydney to talk to her about acting. In no time, they covered movies, her favorites, his, and she inquired about his movies too. As she spoke, he had trouble looking at her. I could tell he liked her. Baby Garbo was a beauty after all.

"Sydney, this one's an original," I followed up with.

"Really."

"This is what actresses are trying to be."

"The real thing?"

"The realest," I said.

And Baby Garbo glowed a little from the praise.

"Tell Sydney about creatures and robots," I said to her.

She looked at me for assurance. She obviously wasn't ripped at all. Or she would have just plowed headfirst into her zaniness.

"Well, the world is made up of just that. Creatures. And Robots."

"What's a Creature?" he asked.

"A Creature is someone of this place and dimension and not at the same time. It's a whole set of movements, gestures, and ways of being. That are specific to a person. Things you say, things you do. It's kind of animal-like. Like, I'm a monkey."

"Is Heyward a Creature?"

"Definitely. He's a cross between a water buffalo and an ape."

I just smiled and nodded to Sydney. Sydney started grinning as well, somewhat charmed.

"I'm serious," Baby Garbo stressed. "He's a Creature because he can write about the Robots."

"What are Robots, then? Cliché people?" Sydney asked.

"Kind of. Robots, well, Robots try to be Creatures. Like this room is filled with Robots who think they're Creatures when really they're malfunctioning Robots. They're all overdoing it, they're all performing. It doesn't come naturally."

"Welcome to Hollywood."

"Exakkalactly," she said.

"So what then would you call me?" Sydney asked.

"Can't tell. I just met you."

"But what do you think so far?"

"You're a rich Robot." And Baby Garbo burst out at that.

Sydney smiled somewhat but looked off and away nervously. And I thought, Shit.

"Just kidding," she said.

"See, Sydney? Playin' with fire."

He didn't say anything. I don't think he expected it. He wasn't used to getting teased. Either that, or Baby Garbo's gorgeous face clocked on him, intimidated him. Finally, he looked at me. It was the moment I had been waiting for. I took a deep breath. I felt I was looking out the hatch about to leap into the clouds on my first sky dive. I was so nervous trying to anticipate what he was going to say, my insides were dropping right out of me.

"So, Heyward, I've got to tell you, you're a very good writer. The script is professionally written. It has a good beginning, is well-paced throughout, with enough action and a central romance. There are plenty of twists and turns though sometimes they get a little complex. But the suspense is nicely held. The trouble is it's not quite commercial enough."

I must say I was a bit disappointed. I remained silent a moment. I didn't want to sound bitter or argumentative.

"Have you read his script?"

"No," Baby Garbo said.

"It's the kind of movie I would like to see. But it's not the kind of movie I would make."

"What kind of movie would you like to make?" Baby Garbo put to him.

"For me this business is just that. A business. That which will sell to a wide audience."

"That's understandable," I added.

"A lot of money is at stake," she added with a nod.

There was a moment of silence, and Sydney again fidgeted with the base of his glass. I guessed he was probably uncomfortable. Maybe Baby Garbo was just too beautiful. It's amazing how beauty can cripple even the toughest negotiators and stoics. If they're vulnerable to it. It can be like kryptonite that way. Maybe I shouldn't have brought her, I thought.

"But I gave your script to a friend. Ruth Yizerman. It is the kind of picture she makes. She's going to call you about it."

I thanked him. And assimilated his comments. "What do you think I need to do?" I asked.

"You need the right story. One that has wider appeal. You have all the skills. You write like people talk. You just need an architecture that is commercial. If you want to break into those leagues. The studio A and B lists. Of course you can write pictures that have more narrow appeal and hope that some independent will pick them up. But there aren't that many made each year. You have to widen your accessibility. You have to have vision."

"To see where the market is?" I interjected.

"To see where the market *will be*. Don't write sci-fi, or farm movies, or comic book stuff because that's what's hot now. You want what is hot two years from now. It's hard to predict. Gear your efforts toward what players will pay dearly for. What no one else has. You have to be two steps ahead."

Then he took a sip of water. It was inspiring to hear this kind of critique from such a pro. At this moment, I looked up and was startled. Starman All-American was smiling down on us. He immediately thanked Sydney for the party on Saturday. This Starman was big. He had that Gary Cooper appeal. Word was he had just recently gotten divorced. But his career was on a roll. Sydney immediately introduced us. Starman sat down for a few minutes and talked shop with Sydney.

"He's a nice man," Baby Garbo said of Sydney. "Is he a good friend?"

"We just met really, but . . ."

"He likes you. I can tell."

"Think so?"

She nodded and we clanked glasses.

"Heyward is a great writer," I heard Sydney say to Starman.

Starman nodded with his famous big-screen smile but the comment meant more to me than I let appear. In reality, I was floored. No one had ever given me validation in such lofty circles.

If that wasn't enough, Sydney started to pitch my script story to Star-man. We had a discussion and Starman said he liked it. So did Baby Garbo. Then someone tapped Starman on the shoulder to say hello. Eventually, he drifted off to his table, but only after bidding us farewell and calling me by my first name. He wished me luck on my project too. I was impressed.

The waiter came by and we ordered up. After giving our selections, I saw Baby Garbo lay a curious eye on Sydney.

"Have you always been in the movie business?" she asked.

And I was truly interested in how he'd respond. We had never talked personally before and I knew nothing about Sydney and his life.

Sydney recounted his march to Hollywood. He grew up in Brook-lyn and as a young teen was a nighttime janitor in the local movie house. Then he went to college and was a business major. He got mar-ried after college and moved to Hollywood in the sixties and started in the mail room at William Morris. Then he was promoted to junior agent. Then agent. From there he got a job at 20th Century-Fox as a development executive and was made head of production in 1979. They had a tremendous run of hits. His record was amazing. In 1985 he was offered the top job at Novastar and has been riding high ever since.

"Are you still married?" Baby Garbo asked.

"I'm going through a divorce."

"That's tough."

"Yeah, well. We've been together for fifteen years. We actually met in college."

"Where'd you go to school?" I asked.

"In Providence, Rhode Island."

That was interesting to me.

"Really? Where?"

"Uh, Brown University."

At that moment, I decided not to lie. "Really? So did I."

"That's funny," he said.

Then we discussed the campus life when he was there compared to when I had gone nineteen years later. He hadn't returned in a long time and didn't know any of the names of my professors.

"Any kids?" Baby Garbo asked.

"No. Thank God. That's who it's toughest on."

"Why not?"

"Well, my wife couldn't have kids. And we were going to adopt but we started having problems. So we decided not to."

Then a woman glided toward the table. Her movements created a stir at every table she passed like ripples on a pond. Her strawberry locks bounced off her shoulders and her figure sliced through the air, carving it in half. Her demeanor of sexy confidence didn't hurt. Sydney stood up. And so did I. It was the least I could do. For that mysterious girl.

"You made it," Sydney said to her. And for some reason my whole body started heating up, my pores prickling with a new rush of hot blood. After all, it was her. The Walking Nightclub.

"Teal, meet Heyward."

"We met," she said.

"You did?" Sydney asked. He seemed surprised.

"Yes, at the party," I said with a smile. She returned it and it didn't fade.

And Sydney looked at me and then at her. The moment almost seemed uncomfortable and I didn't know why. "And this is, can I really say it?" He looked at me. I nodded. ". . . Baby Garbo."

And they both gave off smiles. And their smiles were like Connors and Borg hitting forehands. They were supremely talented in areas other women only dream about and delicious smiles came easy to them. The two of them looked so good we were making enemies nearby. They made married men want to be single. They made married women want to be them. We sat down, retired the open spectacle, and kept divorce rates down.

"How did it go?" Sydney asked.

"All right, I guess," Teal answered in a pressured way. She then explained how she had just come from a movie audition. "The director is kind of a jerk."

To be honest I wasn't listening to her. I just watched. Her lips, her neck, her eyebrows. I watched how all the features worked together in harmony to give off such a beautiful gift. The gift that was her. It surged out of her person. Baby Garbo was a sensual beauty. But Teal was a better version, if that was possible. When she looked my way I had trouble holding my gaze. And soon was forced to divert my eyes to Bacon's tortured and oozing soul hanging over us. I considered it less pleasing to the eye. But safer.

"So you two became friends after we spoke," she said to me.

"I told you Heyward is a writer."

"I'm enjoying your script," she said. "I'm halfway through."

"I hope you don't mind, Heyward. I let Teal read anything I find interesting."

"That's fine," I said.

"I like it so far," she continued. "You know women."

"What?" I asked.

"You write women characters well. You understand them."

And that embarrassed me.

"He should," Baby Garbo said. "All his friends are women."

My eyes darted around. For some reason I didn't like that burst of attention. I wanted to give the spotlight to someone else. It was Sydney's presence there. It's amazing how different types at a table give a different taste to the broth. Had it just been Teal and Baby Garbo at the table I probably would have cracked-wise at Teal's compliment. But add a dash of Sydney Swinburn and it clammed me right up. I guess I didn't want to come off as cocky, or a know-it-all, or so advantaged with the opposite sex that his darker sentiments like envy and such could be kindled. So advantaged that I didn't need help. I didn't want to come off like a star. Because it was all too clear to me I wasn't one. Play it down, was my feeling.

A couple more moguls passed by the table to help me out. Sydney again introduced me. Finally, some guy in the uniform slid past and Sydney gave him the real brush.

"That guy's so full of it," he added.

"I call them Noguls." I told them why. They laughed.

"That's very funny," Teal said.

And Baby Garbo got up and went to the bathroom. Teal gave her the once-over as she did.

Me Magazine

"Great girl," Sydney said after she was out of earshot.

And I knew he felt that way. He had been spying on her movements throughout dinner.

"What's the word on her?" Teal asked. I was surprised by her directness. While dancing those pirouettes on the tennis court she seemed much more ethereal, more light and elusive, than someone who would be involved in phrases like getting *the word* on someone.

"How do you mean?" I asked faux-innocently. I didn't want to chop Baby Garbo up into sound bites. I wanted to come off less affected and less calculated.

"Is she your girlfriend?"

"No," I said.

"You don't sound so sure of your answer," Sydney said.

"Well, she's a close friend. Let's say that."

"Great girl," Sydney repeated.

When dinner came, more of Star Camp's power set paid their respects to Mr. Swinburn. And he continued to introduce me and praise me to people I had always read about but never met. The respect factor I felt was instantaneous. That was clear. A seat at Sydney Swinburn's table was a window on the grass roots of the industry where shit really did happen. I had the distinct feeling I was in an entirely different world. And I was.

When Teal asked Sydney how we'd met, Sydney recounted how I had emerged from an upstairs bathroom with the flock of party comets, then found some poor girl's stone. He didn't include the rookie move part of the story, naturally.

"How big was it?" she asked.

"Five carats."

"Better than WGA minimums," Sydney joked.

"Don't remind me," I said with a smile.

Baby Garbo returned and Sydney patted the space beside him indicating she should sit by him. Teal slid down right next to me. As she did, her skirt rolled up from the friction and it revealed that her black stockings were not full waist-high hose, but thigh-highs. An inch of tan flesh between stocking band and skirt hem peeked out. Sexy. One more slide and her skirt hiked up higher and her thigh touched mine and pressured it. Sexier. It's amazing how the slightest touch can send ripples of sensuality through your body. This gal flicked on all of my fuses.

She smiled at me and we touched glasses. Then she sipped and placed the glass back down. But it was the look in her eyes that impressed me. It betrayed a mind grinding away. There was a strong point of view there and it had a lot to say. The scenery, the crowd, the ambience of the place had nothing on her. It all remained mute and in relief. What was important was in her head. She was in control. And I was about to find out.

"I'm kind of puzzled," I initiated.

"How so?"

"When I first met you I thought you were a shy, reserved type."

"And now?"

"Now you seem . . ." I hesitated. I was choosing my words carefully.

"Less innocent?"

"Like you have more of an edge."

"Edge. Such a funny nineties word. Tell me. Does it come from the term *cutting edge?*"

I didn't answer. And she didn't say anything more. She didn't have to. Instead of responding to my query she turned it into her own question, which in effect nullified my comment and let her go. It was right out of my own bag of verbal weasel maneuvers. Instead, she took on a curious expression. It was an attempt to look blank but there was nothing blank about it. It was erupting with some kind of life deep within, like it was hiding something. It didn't surprise me. The town was fueled on these types. But I wasn't ready to turn this one into a type. She had a different way about her. Something original, something different. Maybe.

Baby Garbo and Sydney were by now in deep discussion about the movie business. Which I considered a good sign. Baby Garbo could use a push and maybe Sydney could give it to her.

Further discussion with Teal yielded a quick impressionistic background portrait. She came from a big family in Wyoming. Three sisters, two brothers. She'd attended the University of California at Berkeley and had helped put herself through school by working in a hospital. After school she went to Kenya and helped with the Flying Doctors, a group that flew from trouble flash point to flash point to give medical aid to destitute African villages. But after a year there, all the famine and sickness got to her. She returned to New York and revived a passion for ballet and studied theater there. Eventually, she moved to Los Angeles to do the acting thing.

When she was done with her background flash, she came right at me. "Do you want to be famous, Heyward?"

She asked it almost nonchalantly, as if she was asking me where I was born.

The question caught me off guard, of course. Wouldn't it you? I had no preparation for it. In less than five minutes, she was hitting me where I lived. What was scarier was I sensed she probably only needed thirty seconds.

"No more than the next man," I countered eventually.

"The next man, or the next Hollywood man?"

"Define your demographics. Good point, Teal. I want spoils for toils, yes."

"And rightly you should."

For some reason this person sparked my bizarre sense of humor. I said it with a smile. "In fact, I'd like to be feted."

"Fetid or feted?"

I laughed at that. She was good.

"Feted. Lavishly. With all the attention on me. With all my lawyers and agents and business cheerleaders semicircling me. In fact, I'm going to be on the cover of *Me Magazine* next month. And every month after."

She laughed at that. And goaded me further. "Just simple Q&A?"

"Q&A, my viewpoints on life, love, taxidermy, golf, everything. Isn't golf the silliest game?"

We were both laughing now. I loved it.

"Not as silly as snooker," she added.

And we both burst out. It took a while to get back to more dialogue. Our sides were splitting.

"What's so funny?" Sydney asked.

"Tell me, tell me, tell me," Garbo added.

We just shook and cracked up even harder.

"Yeah, but back to me," I said faux-arrogantly. And it primed more cackling laughter. "So, cover of *Me Magazine*, maybe a press conference or two, and my little sound bites will be sent all over the world and everyone will want to hear more. Then I'll color my hair and do it all over again."

"Do you color your hair?"

"I used to. But my colorist moved away."

"That's sad."

"But I got a new liposculpturist. He's such an artist."

She loved that. So did Baby Garbo. And I don't know why. It was just free-association nonsense about societal weirdness.

"He really knows how to handle a roll," I said.

"A roll?" Sydney asked.

"Of fat!!" Teal and I said in hysterical unison.

"I'm sure Michelangelo would be proud," Teal forced out through her laughter.

I had one more narcissistic push. "Where are the wind machines? I need more wind." And I rubbed my nipples for emphasis.

"What does that mean?" Sydney asked. He was either trying to join in the conversation or slow us down. I wasn't sure.

"It's a reference to having fans blowing around you at all times, the kind they use in fashion photo shoots, so your hair gets gusted around heroically. It gives you the constant windswept look. It's the ultimate in vanity," I explained. "Silly me."

And the whole group was laughing now, Sydney included. It was stupid restaurant booth banter but nonetheless entertaining. We calmed eventually and Baby Garbo and Teal got into a discussion about acting, where they studied, Meisner vs. Strasberg, etc. Sydney and I discussed recent pictures we'd liked.

We left Morton's after a few spoons of key lime pie. Sydney told me to call him the next day. I felt pretty damn good as we stepped outside. I considered the dinner a success. The best I'd had in my two years in L.A.

In the end, I was glad I had invited Baby Garbo. She helped ease the tensions of Sydney and me first getting to know each other. She also added to my stature. It's amazing what a little show of pulchritude can do for business. I could tell Sydney was impressed with her. Even though he had a gem in Teal.

Baby Garbo had a good time too. She said so. I drove her home afterward.

When I got home I plopped right in bed. I was exhausted. I considered it the biggest meeting of my life to date.

Before drifting off, I thought about Teal. This gal got me. It's amazing how quickly a connection can be ignited. And we had one. She seemed to know exactly who I was. It was the second time in as many meetings. She had shown different colors the first time. Shy, mildly spiritual, detached colors. She exhibited a sharpness, an endearing cynicism the second time. In both cases she was mysterious. And wildly sensual. And while exhibiting such different character hues, we still ended up at that place of common understanding. Both times we connected. It was more than mildly frightening.

Of course I wondered what her relationship was with Sydney still. Were they romantically involved? I sensed the answer was no the way he was taking a shine to Baby Garbo. But you never know. Especially in Hell-A.

Certainly, I could have asked her directly. After all, she hit me with the fame thing. And I turned it into satire. To take the attention off myself, of course. Weasel maneuvers, remember? I sensed the answer to the Teal-Sydney issue would say a lot about her. And him. It was as loaded a question as she'd hit me with. But in the end, I felt it could only hurt. I didn't need to know. It might just make her uncomfortable and turn her against me. If she knew Sydney as well as she did, she probably had some degree of influence with him. And I needed allies, not enemies. So I put my Blade back in my sheath and let it go.

If the truth be known, Teal reminded me of Eleanor. Eleanor may have been more literary and possessed a better vocab but I thought Teal was a tad quicker and wittier. And less cosmopolitan conscious. As cool as she was, Eleanor never would have seriously entertained leaving the big city and going to Africa to help out have-not villagers. She could write about them with compassion, but to get physically involved was another story.

Then I found something wrong about comparing the two of them. For some reason it didn't seem right. They were two great ladies. Basta.

I watched the ceiling for a while and decided against counting up the night's lies. It had been a nice evening and I didn't need to end it on a bitter note. Maybe because I didn't feel bitter. Just maybe.

The Little Riddle

A bunch of L.A. uni-days passed and you know what that means happened. Nothing. Flip, flip, flip went the daily calendar pages. I tapped out some more leaves, gave the Sled a lemon change, and clocked a couple good five-milers. I also introduced a new Project file into my "Gold," my computer data base. The entry came under the name "Teal." It was my most exciting science project to date.

Though I thought I had made a solid connection with Sydney Swinburn, I wasn't going to hound him. If anything, I was determined to do the opposite. Moguls are like beautiful women. Never chase them. Let them chase you. But if they don't pursue you on face value, meaning on your character alone, make sure you possess something they want. And let them come after you. And that's exactly what I did.

No less than a day later, the call came. His call. He had finished a meeting in Santa Monica. He wanted to have lunch. He sounded a little off-kilter, his voice charged with immediacy.

"Any preference?" he asked.

"Uh . . ."

Here it was. My big moment. I was asked to come up with an idea. My first idea for him. The idea machine all writers are supposed to be. But I had a block. The supermogul meets the Blippy Scribe block. Then the Gods of Good Ideas spared me. A morsel of ingenuity crept into my skull.

Contrast was the theme. I asked him when he'd last been down to the beach. He said three years. I didn't say I figured as much. But I thought it. I suggested meeting at a little burger hut north of the Santa Monica pier. He said that was fine. But he asked me to get there as soon as possible. He needed to tell me something. I said I would get there as fast as the Sled would permit.

Which wasn't that fast. I couldn't ask the Sled to do more than sixty-five and even that was a little much. As I drove, I replayed my brief conversation with Sydney. It made me wonder about the urgency in his voice.

When I found an open slot on PCH with cars whizzing past, I trotted over to the hut and saw Sydney sitting at one of the plastic tables. His face brightened when he saw me. I asked him what he wanted and he said he wasn't really hungry. He was fidgety, even anxious. I asked him what was up. He urged me to order up first so I did.

I ordered a big-ass cheeseburger and gigantic diet cola. It was the afternoon and I needed a caf-jolt. The cutesy Burger Girl asked me if I wanted that burger on pita and I asked her if she was out of her mind. I contemplated asking if she could wipe the burger down with mayonnaise and lard to show her what I thought about all that left coast health-consciousness crap she had been brainwashed with. But I didn't. I saved my O_2 for the studio chief.

I then sat on the same side of the table as Sydney. He looked at me oddly when I did.

"Don't like the sun," I explained.

Then he took a sip of water. And we sat there a minute. Sydney remained silent and looked out at the ocean. I wondered what he was thinking. I wondered what the ocean meant to him, if anything. I continued to eat. His face grew taut and his eyes narrowed. He was either agitated or confused. I couldn't tell. I wasn't master of his facial expressions yet.

The 55-Degree Rule

"Is there something on your mind, Sydney?"

He hesitated and then some air shot out of his mouth. "I don't know."

"What's up?"

"I just felt like talking, I guess."

"Talking?"

"Yeah. To someone. I've been thinking about a lot of things."

As I munched I listened. And I wasn't surprised by what I heard. You see, screenwriters, if they're any good at all, are students of human behavior. Oftentimes they can sense what is going on in someone's head. After all, each person on the planet is a little riddle. And every screenwriter, *and it is his duty,* wants to solve it. Usually, the better the screenwriter, the better the analyst.

Actually, that's total bullshit. The better the screenwriter, the better he is at getting his script bought. Basta.

"Like?"

"Like, my life for once. Funny. I've never put it that way."

"What way?"

"I've never said *my life* to anyone."

I guessed that was a compliment to me.

Then he just looked at me and I broke down the seriousness of his confession with a big chomp of my burger and ketchup just oozed out all over the plate and hit my knee too. I did it for him. To make him feel comfortable with opening up to me. He knew the dangers and pitfalls of letting loose personal thoughts in Hell-A. He could get distracted in my slobby ways. It worked.

"How do you mean, your life?"

"Well, here I am," he started. He paused and pondered. "Look, I started with nothing. A dollar and a dream. Not even. Twenty-five cents and a dream. I came out here to do something different. And I've had a great ride. And now I have, shall we say, a lot of advantages. I have an advantaged life."

"Well, *you* made it happen."

"There is a feeling of gratification I have about it. I'm not saying that."

At that moment, I made a major decision. It was time to use my Blade. I'd been holding off in all our conversations previously. But playing it down would only get me so far. Meaning right where I was now. With a power guy. Alone. Now I needed to show a point of view. To let him know that I wasn't going to be a pushover. That I wasn't going to be one of those ass-kissing studio Vanilla Boys who'd crawl under the conference table and suck a superior's member at a moment's notice. I was going to treat Sydney like a peer—tell him what I really felt and take no shit. It was the only way to get respect.

"What are you saying?" I challenged him with, to let him know his message wasn't coming through yet.

"I'm not . . ." and he stopped. "I guess sometimes I feel like I'm going through the motions. I don't know what for. What for, all this? You know?"

"Tell you what. I'll trade you my West Hollywood chalet for your house."

He laughed at that, though I'm sure he didn't know what the chalet reference meant.

"But what am I doing it all for?"

"For your own sense of accomplishment. If you didn't do it, what would you do? How could you wake up in the morning?"

"I suppose. But today, I was sitting in a meeting and I found myself not listening. *Me. Not listening.* We're talking a forty-million-dollar picture. And where was I?"

"Dunno. Where were you?"

"I guess I felt I haven't been having any fun at all. Every day's the same. It doesn't inspire me. I just want to have some fun for once."

"You sound like a song I know." His face flashed cool for a moment.

He was being serious and I was cracking-wise. "Just kidding," I added. "You know what, Sydney? Let's have some fun."

He just looked at me. He didn't yield a smile though I sensed he wanted to. And after we said our good-byes and I let all my burger wrappings slide off my tray and into a trash receptacle, I gave him another chance.

As he was pulling out, I ran across the parking lot and waved him down. He stopped and motored down the driver's side window. I shuffled up to his purring Jag, leaned in, and gave him a risky blast.

"There's one thing I want to impart to you. It's something I do and maybe you'll discover its merits as well. The next time you're entertaining a young lady, and you invite her to your home, you must try something. If it's summertime, raise the air-conditioning temperature in your bedroom to hi-cool. Or in winter, make sure the heat is way down. In either case, you want the temperature in that chamber no more than fifty-five degrees. Why? When she maneuvers her head into your lap to give you a zippy and then employs that up-and-down motion, the sensation is marvelous. Each time she comes up you'll feel the coolness of the room all over your exposed shaft. It has the effect of making her mouth feel like a hot cave. It adds sensation to an already delightful act."

I looked at him and he was broken wide. That means I got the smile I was looking for.

"I'll keep that in mind," he said.

When Sydney and I parted company I told him I'd phone in with a plan of attack. And I would.

My Gold

I didn't consider our meeting business. I didn't consider it pleasure. It was more of a calling-out. And it was Sydney, not me, who was doing the calling out. And I heard what he said.

I sensed Sydney Swinburn was a lonely guy. I also sensed he was in need of friends. Friends he could trust with his personal thoughts.

Without fearing any reprisal. Friends who would not give him the answers he wanted to hear. Friends who had balls. But more important, friends who were connected in ways he was not. I had something he wanted. It wasn't my smile, my sarcastic jokes, or the first-look he got on my script. It was the absurd quantity of women I knew.

I'm sure Sydney was absolutely serious when he claimed to be disillusioned with his present life. There was a hole in it the size of a moon crater. And he wanted to fill it. He wanted deliverance from his boring routine. And he had taken this occasion to drive the point home. Men like Sydney don't mince messages. They like fast results. It's part of their character—it's part of their job.

The brutal fact was all the king's horses and all the king's men couldn't yield Sydney Swinburn a hot little hen. I had no idea what skills he had to offer in this area. He'd just bailed out of a marriage and maybe he didn't know either. But Sydney's successes had yielded him respect, headlines, and big box office tallies. But no one to share them with. Sydney wanted to take a little walk on the wild side. And he chose me to bring him there.

Perhaps you're wondering how I knew so many women. The answer is far more logical than you'd expect. It certainly wasn't because I had been trying to wedge myself between every set of legs I could find. That my libido was so explosive that I needed to do the plunge at a moment's notice. And that I had a little black book as fat as *Bartlett's Quotations* to reflect it all. I had that book but it wasn't for conquest-oriented purposes. Just the opposite. I loved being inactive. The act of sexual intercourse was a mere by-product of what my true motives were with the opposite sex.

Very simply, I wanted to probe their puzzle. I wanted to figure them out. Each and every one of them. I wanted to get into their soul and take a good long look. For my writing purposes, of course. I felt the key to all good writing for a man was understanding a woman. Woman is the key. Woman is life. Woman is the key.

I felt I had spent enough time in the locker rooms to understand men. They're pretty obvious, uncomplicated creatures with the occasional exception. Men are Johnny One-Notes. They want the 4 Ps and little more. They want some power, some press, some pesos, and some pussy. And maybe tickets to the Knicks. And delineating their character is not difficult. Their psychology is based on which of the 4 Ps they aren't getting. The less, the more bitter. The more, the more abusive.

But I truly felt if you had your finger on the pulse of Woman, if you could master her psychology, you were in a prime position, ahead of the rest of the robotic, clammy-handed keyboard mashers. That your tools of expression were intensely keen and you could properly record on any given subject, the art of human interaction, and achieve in manuscript form, the real bouquet of life.

The problem with sex was, more often than not, once you penetrated a woman, you ruined everything. You ruined the honesty you once had. Sure, you'd achieve a heightened intimacy. But the subjects you could discuss freely were drastically reduced. Because now you were *doing it.* That gain in carnal knowledge would bring on a loss of opening up. Woman would avoid certain topics because of that. Just as you would. You'd get the surface stuff but not the deeper depths. You'd get the gossip but not the gold. I wanted the gold.

In a relationship, women are wary about how you're going to feel about them if they divulge. They're conditioned from early on to be silent, to keep their legs pressed together or crossed, to close down. They don't want to expose themselves. Their real fear is to be judged. Women hate being judged. Don't you? As maturity hits, they open their legs but still shut down their private thoughts. The real private ones, the ones that surge forth from the soul, the ones that are essential for a writer. To stay close friends with women is to stay in their private circle—where the thoughts they fear to tell a loved one ooze out. To stay close friends with them is to stay close to their soul. And that's where the gold is. That's where I wanted to be.

Over time, many years in fact, and covering a few countries and cities, I met a lot of gals who had given me the gold. Sometimes their private parts came with it. But less often than you'd think. I had quite a list to draw from. Though I wasn't active, I had an active roster. I knew tons of girls in L.A., as I did in New York. I had made it my business. They were my science projects. I studied their psychologies, habits, fears, passions, favorite spits of dialogue, astrological data, musings, wanderings, their likes, their dislikes, and their capacities for unpredictability. I wanted to know everything about them. I wanted to know how they felt at any moment. Whenever I witnessed something behaviorally interesting, I inputted the data into the file.

Part of the process was, of course, figuring out their weaknesses. Weakness is the key to deep character. Understanding the fragile aspects of any human being is crucial. A person's puzzle was not complete until I owned their weakness. My database included entries on socialites, valedictorians, preppettes, gold diggers, stockbrokers, lawyers, prostitutes, waitresses, next-door neighbors, actresses, you name it. My life story could be told with the girls I came in contact with.

And Sydney Swinburn, supermogul and head of Novastar Studios, had come to me to give him a chunk of that Gold. I wasn't sure if he knew I knew where he was coming from when he gave me his little seaside spiel. I guessed he did. It was one of those tacit understandings between savvy people. Nothing needed to be discussed or spelled out. Clearly, fun did not mean going to a Lakers game together, playing pool, teasing Scientologists, or even attending a screening. Fun meant ladies. And for me, ladies were only one printout away.

One last thing. Implicit in those tacit understandings between savvy people is usually a pastel shade of business being transacted. If I was going to give Sydney Swinburn a piece of my Gold, then, of course, it was understood he'd do the same for me. And you know what he had that I didn't. Take a track record in the business, a nice wedge of respect, and the capacity to green-light multiple pictures, for starters. And I wanted some or all of the above . . .

In life, you sometimes don't know what the hell you're doing. *Most* of the time. Add a wedge of fear to that. Being lost and afraid go together. They're married. I was at a point close to that. It's what made me sign on with Sydney. But let me address one issue. Knowing I was going to call on my Gold in this way, I immediately set up some stiff parameters. The Darwinian kind. Only the fittest would I call. I would only call on ladies who were tough enough to get involved with a movie studio chief.

I would not invite a woman who I thought would be in peril of losing anything that could be lost. They were going to be carefully selected, sifted through my strainer. If a girl was too vulnerable, she wouldn't make the cut. The ones who remained would want to remain and be happy doing so. Unless I sensed they were servicing some self-destructive drive. Then I would let them go and let someone else take them down the alpine slide. I didn't want to mess up anybody's life. I was going to do my part and keep it clean.

The New Breed: The Wannabeasts

I went to bed that night with some specific thoughts about Sydney, me, and my Gold. Even though I had quite a roster of ladies to draw from, it never stopped me from seeking out more. More puzzles, more mysteries, more Projects, more gold. It was a cache I wanted to build up even further. It helped me alleviate the boredom of L.A. life, it staved off the cabin fever I would get writing, and it helped enrich it. Though I was writing wallpaper, I'd be damned to tell you if it wasn't rich wallpaper.

A football coach once said, "Winning is better than sex." I'll modify that. Success is better than sex. I was determined. I was a dog with a bone and blinders. But I had my work cut out for me. After all, I was up against a vicious breed. The Wannabeasts. They were the fame-seeking hounds. They wanted their names in whites in the credits and in **boldface** in the columns.

It was a new breed, a generation within a generation. It wasn't a breed entirely peculiar to the film industry. Any modern industry that offered fame and glory had its share of the Beasts. But given its reputation for overnight worldwide recognition, the movie business was the ultimate Wannabeast profession. That made L.A. the Wannabeast capital of the world. The town was full of them.

When I first arrived, I thought I could survive on good hard work alone. That way of thinking was less than naive. In Hollywood you had to turn yourself into an animal and growl like a garbage truck, with a snout that could peel back and show vicious points to go along with the don't-fuck-with-me attitude. Unfortunately, I had grown up soft. I had never had a callus. My only blisters had come from tennis rackets. To survive in Star Camp, I had to deny my past and strip away all that cocktail party conditioning and useless WASPery I'd been teething on all those years. I had to reinvent myself.

The life-sustaining fluid of a Wannabeast is one part blood, one part dreamer, one part family angst, and seven parts identity starvation. The angst/ID starvation quotient varied with socioeconomic background. From my perspective, the greater the social advantage, the higher the family angst variable. There's less to prove to the world and more to the parents. Likewise, the lower the economic advantage, the higher the identity starvation variable. There's less to live up to and more to prove to the world. My blood was weighted more in family angst. But it made me no less the Beast.

However they got there, Wannabeasts breathed envy and coughed deception in the attempt to grasp their chunk of notoriety. They were the young Machiavellians. They were the tragic-heroes of the nineties. Why tragic? Because they usually had to dabble with darkness to make things happen. Like I said before, they were all Mighty Hippos, meaning they had to swallow some hypocrisy. And if I wanted to beat them, I had to join them. I considered linking up with Sydney Swinburn and sharing my Gold with him, joining them.

No doubt I had my work cut out for me. Others didn't have it so nice growing up. Others didn't have the comfortable pad on Park Avenue. Others didn't have the Ivy League pelt. Others didn't have the social standing. That all means others had a head start. They had dibs on motivation, on incentive. If they were lucky, they had a real chip. They were more have-notted than me and it translated to added drive for them. I was playing catch-up.

We were the Wannabeasts and we danced the Boulevard growling away with daggers poised at each other's throats trying to stave each other off and make our way out of the pack. It remained to be seen who would and who would not.

Heyward Holiday

I shot out of bed the next morning like a jack-in-the-box. It was only seven and I was an hour ahead of my coffee timer. So I used manual override and made a hot pot. I was feeling happy. Or at least less than miserable. I even dipped into the freezer and drew from my special stash of flavored coffee. I know it's pretty lame to enjoy flavored coffee. It's for Mos. You and I know it. And I wouldn't admit to it in front of a crowd. But it was a Christmas gift from Kelly the Bullet, who was in tune with my caf addiction. And I used it only for special occasions. And it was a special day. After all, it was the first day of the rest of my life.

As the chocolate-amaretto aroma crawled up my sniffer, I reviewed the previous day. I knew I had made a solid contact in Hollywood. My first move was to call in sick at Loser Inc. I was taking a Heyward Holiday and they were going to just have to get along without their Master Filer. I wondered what they'd say. But not for too long. After all, what could they say? They couldn't fire me. I hadn't been hired. It was one of the perks of being a temp. Companies generally like to hold on to competent temps. They usually get stuck with idiots and have to send them home by noon. That wasn't the case with me. I was dispensably indispensable. That means I had job security.

I booted up my Gold files and took a good look. I had thousands of entries. Each entry was its own profile. For each profile I logged in a treasure chest full of short, snappy sound bites that instantaneously delineated deep character. Ever since college I had been doing profiles. I remember that Fran, who worked at Baskin-Robbins in Providence, was my first Project. I didn't wonder what she was doing now. She wasn't that riveting. Or smart. Or sexy. I did men at first too, but it got repetitive. Though the women could stack up the big clichés too, they usually had some particular quirk that captivated me and merited a few bytes of space on my hard drive.

As I scanned my files, I compiled a list of potential candidates. From that list I would phone around to see who was in town, who was single or linked up, and, if they were linked, whether it mattered.

Think Duh

It was about eleven-thirty that night when I picked up the phone. It was Sydney. He said he was having difficulty sleeping. I believed him. He said he had a lot on his mind, but he wanted to ask me something very specific.

"Well, it's kind of silly. And maybe I shouldn't say anything."

"Go ahead," I said.

"Well, jees, it sounds so stupid."

"Sydney, fire away," I said sternly, using my Blade.

"Well, sometimes I don't know what to talk about."

"Where? With who?"

"Girlie, uh, whirlies."

I knew what he meant. And I knew what to tell him.

"Just whack seventy-five points off," I said.

"Off what?"

"Off your I.Q."

"Seventy-five points?"

"Right off the top. Don't think smart. Don't think witty. Think duh."

Sydney laughed at that. "Think duh?"

"Yeah. Dumb up."

"How do you mean?"

"Well, often brains, acumen, and intelligence are attractive. And let's face it. Sexy. But they also can be intimidating. And a turnoff. They can make you inaccessible."

"Really?"

"It all depends on the configuration."

"What configuration?"

"Of the person you're interacting with. I stay away from sweepers but, in general, intelligence is an easier sell back east. Or in the more cosmopolitan urban centers. But out here, in this milieu, our milieu, especially with the opposite sex, intelligence can work in the reverse. Dumbing up lets someone intellectually less fortunate in."

"What would you say is appealing out here?"

"Simply put, fun & stuff."

"Fun and stuff?"

"It comes with an ampersand. Haven't you ever heard one of these girlies talk about fun & stuff?"

"Not really."

"They don't want to recite the day's news, or discuss the failing environmental movement, or compete with you cerebrally. They just want to hear you say something funny. Once you've got 'em laughing and having a good time, you're on your way."

"To what?"

"Whatever you want. A friendship, a dinner invitation, sex."

"How do you go about it?"

"Relax."

"Relax . . . ?"

"Don't feel compelled to be an entertainment center. If there's an awkward moment, eventually her own nervousness will take over. Because everyone wants to take situations out of the high pressure and put them into the low pressure. If you're feeling the stiff vibe, chances are she is too. Maybe more so. Because you are a power figure. You have all that advantage. She will feel compelled to act. She may have the goods, the great body, and the silver-dollar smile, but you've got the keys."

"Keys to what?"

"Her future."

"Huh."

"And she knows it." It needed qualifying. "Even if she doesn't want a career in entertainment, she can still feel the force of a power guy in control. All you have to do is sit back, relax, and think duh when spoken to. Then wait for her to open up. To smile. To laugh. Laughter is the most disarming emotion. It knocks her, and you, right out of the uncomfortable and into the familiar."

"Give me an example."

"If your lady friend talks about where she grew up, let her discuss her family. If she's comfortable with that, then it gives her an easy path of discussion. But if family chatter makes her stiffen, ease the conversation out of it. Don't go there. But if all goes well, follow up her account of family life with your own version. But add a humorous spin. Make it sound self-deprecating, like how silly you were as a kid. When you can laugh at yourself, it's a very appealing quality. How many times have you seen downright grotesques landing a lady of stature. Why? *'Because he makes me laugh.'* If I've heard it once, I've heard it a million times."

"So have I."

"It loosens a woman up. And it takes some, but not all, of the intimidation out of your presence. Because you don't want to give it *all* away. Ever. Never."

"It's so basic."

"Human interaction is. You don't need to shove your brilliance down her throat. Your reputation has given you that. Consider your brain like a car with five speeds and shift the gears accordingly. Keep it in a low accessible gear, running smoothly, offending no one, and rev it if necessary. That's the key to the art of aggressive womanizing in Hell-A."

"In general terms."

"The most general. Obviously, it's not going to work for that hot, sexy, but serious and career-minded studio sharpie. Or the well-bred, educated New Yorker. Their turn-on is a different thing."

"Like what?"

"Are you playing dumb, Sydney?"

"No. It helps to hear it from you. You put it very well and it's refreshing."

"Sharpies are interested in stature, power, money. Savage sex is not the priority. Still, they pick and choose their spots to be vulnerable. Like weekends."

"Girls dumb up too?"

"Those sharpies who have given up a social life for a shot at a movie career need a release too. After maintaining their shaky hold on their job for yet another week, they can get real stupid. With the 8x10s, the Strugs, some Valley Blip, as well as Starman."

As soon as I finished saying it, I thought of Teal—how she'd clearly dumbed up on me in our first encounter. She'd camouflaged her education and acted five yards shy of a Mom-I-Got-the-Part dancer. It was the image she had chosen for me. To make herself accessible. To let me in. To show me she wasn't a threat. Maybe.

"I know the type. They work for me."

"Precisely."

"But how do you do it?"

"Just sit back, take a lazy hold on your body, and shorten your thoughts. To bite-size. Make your moves slowly, like pouring wine or lighting her cig. And don't do everything. Let her do some work. Let her talk, and pretend you don't know what she's talking about. Make her explain things. Give your face a glaze too. Pretend there's a Nerf ball between your ears. But don't get carried away. You don't want to come off like a retard. Smile a lot and use Girlie-speak."

"Those one-syllable words?"

"Wow, cool, yeah, yo, hip, slick, great. *Exactly.* You'll find *wow* has so many uses."

"Frightening."

"Frightening, yes, Sydney. But that's the charm of this place."

"Think duh, huh?"

"Think duh." And that needed qualifying too. "For now. Later I'll teach you the Naughty Law."

After a moment I heard it. "Wow . . . ," he said airily.

And I smiled. "Perfect."

We hung up soon after.

FBI: The Kissing Bandit

Tennis jocks are familiar with the First Ball In scenario at the commencement of a tennis match. It's a cumbersome term and it's appropriately shortened to FBI. When your game is a bit rusty it always helps to invoke the FBI privilege, which allows you as many serves as necessary to get the first ball in play. You can have as many tries as needed with no fear of a double fault. It relaxes you. It's a nice way to begin a match.

This is precisely how I viewed Sydney's first dalliance with the opposite sex. At my arranging. I was determined to give him FBI. I wanted him to get on base his first time up. It would be good for his self-esteem and confidence, which would allow us to progress more precipitously. I didn't consider myself any kind of Svengali type, but I thought some simple tampering could help us both get where we wanted to be, faster. If pressed, I'd say my duties were that of a coach's, in the area of Romantics.

I had a gal in mind. She had to be perfect for the job and she was. Dana was from Utah and all Mormon. And like all good Mormons she was not going to go yard without a trip to the altar. But Dana did like to have a good time. And she was really open and nice and a Breakthrough wouldn't be difficult.

I did a fingerdance on my computer and pulled up my Gold. She was in the Miscellaneous directory. Normally, I grouped by country. My files included Irish girls, German girls, Swedish girls, Africans; every nation where there were girls was represented as well as every state in the United States except Idaho. And that's a sore point, let me tell you. I remember chasing down a ski bunny once whom I hadn't met but who I'd heard was from Boise. Unfortunately, I was very stoned at the time and I don't smoke pot. But that day I did and as I chased her down an intermediate trail, I caught an edge, and did a double blowout release of the skis which resulted in a face plant in the snow. Stupid Mo, for sure. And I never got my potato.

Girls in the Miscellaneous directory had some special or unusual characteristic that preempted their nationality. Hookers, religious fanatics, and women with handicaps were common Miscellaneous entries. In Dana's case, being a Mormon set her apart. Hell yes, a girl who didn't readily give it up in the Age of A, I considered special.

I read my notes on Dana. I scratched down her number and remembered her favorite piece of dialogue. She'd say *It's all about this,* or *It's all about that,* or *It's not about this* or *that,* as a way of expressing things. It was her own little construction which she used to lean her personality on. A detail like that could prove invaluable to a guy like Sydney.

In the Art of the Breakthrough, it was a simple device. Use the humor, language, and artillery of a desired party and throw it back at them. It's totally endearing. Aren't you secretly flattered when someone adopts a phrase, habit, or quirk of yours? It's a compliment. And if planted correctly it can be humorous. Which is a desired effect. Sydney could repeat Dana's phraseologies either to sweetly mimic her or to show he'd adopted her language. In both cases, it comes off as charming.

Dana was a nice girl. Though she wouldn't go deep, she would throw back a few margaritas and get affectionately sloppy. In fact, if she really put on a buzz, she might play pathological make-out games, meaning she would French-kiss you all night, but the next day she would treat you like nothing ever happened. And she would not be faithful. I called her The Kissing Bandit.

I figured Dana was a girl who was going to enjoy sex once she got her chance. Her passionate personality was the giveaway. But since she hadn't done the deed yet, she was intensely frustrated. So she found her naughty excitement in dumping her newest conquest and landing a new guy to kiss and fondle. The former's bewilderment would give her a charge and serve as some form of emotional compensation. *The Kissing Bandit.*

An asterisk at the bottom of *Dana-Ut.doc* told me it had been alleged that Dana had given a blow job to some Strug, but I didn't believe it. Once she had succumbed to that activity, more episodes would surely follow, and there'd be an outbreak of braggadocio because men can't shut up. And the word would get out. That hadn't happened. Besides, she wasn't impressed with Hollywood. She was a student at UCLA, she hung out with Blips, and she just liked to have clean fun.

I called her up and found her home. Even better, she was excited at the prospect of having dinner with me and my friend, though she didn't know who he was.

The Art of the Breakthrough

When I dialed up Sydney to give him the word on her, I was sure to tell him her passion for "it's all about . . ."

"Is she a model?" he asked immediately.

"She's a Could-Be. In a small city."

I then told him to be polite, a nice guy, not to force things. The general stuff. And then I mentioned to him the Art of the Breakthrough and its tenets.

"A breakthrough is your goal. Without it you don't have a chance. Women are skeptical. They don't let just anyone into their private space. You have to break through. And the tougher the girl, the tougher it is to do it."

"Is Dana tough?"

"No. But she is a hotty. She gets offers all the time. And she's a nice girl."

Then I told Sydney the philosophy for the nice girl. I explained he should employ her language, agree with her points of view, unless he could turn it into something more overtly sensitive than what she had postulated. In essence, harmony and honey.

"For example, order the drink she's ordered as if you're trying it the first time. Search for points of commonality. And think duh if it helps."

"Does that work on all girls?"

"Not a chance. The formula for the Breakthrough changes with each personality. You would never utilize the nice-girl formula with a Dysfuncionado, Bianco Trasher, or abrasive type. Those gals need resistance, rudeness, and rock and roll. Give them honey and harmony and they'll eat you for lunch. They need to know you're going to put on a gremlin mask and bevel them from behind if they touch the remote, just so they can touch the remote anyway and have the threat realized."

I had to pause for a moment. "Did I really say that?"

"I think so."

"Anyway, that's further down the road, Sydney. First things first. With nice, straightforward girls, looking for and accentuating the harmony is the call."

"Should I tell her about my business?"

"Only if she asks. She may be fed up with the industry. Feed her what she wants."

I found myself oddly amused at his rapt interest in what I had to say. No one gave me this much airtime, not even family. I got less respect from Noguls. Overall, I wasn't sure how much Sydney Swinburn actually knew about women. How much or how little. He was tight-lipped. Sometimes I felt like I was a mob consigliere who did all the talking as the capo listened. And made up his mind. One thing I did know is that Sydney may well have been a shy Casanova for all I knew. But if he was, he was definitely rusty.

By the way, I was always taking notes. Whenever something struck a certain chord in my mind I jotted it down. It remained in my head for three days or so. If I didn't get it down on paper it usually flew free only to be recaptured by dumb luck or if some similar circumstance occurred that brought it to mind. I jotted potential titles, snippets of dialogue, movie ideas, self-help notations, and forgotten memories unearthed through some sort of image association or holographic delivery. It's crucial for a writer, even the unsuccessful kind. Like me.

"So where's dinner?" Sydney asked.

"I told Dana the Atrium but I'm going to change it."

"To where?"

"The track."

"What track?"

"Malibu Grand Prix."

"You're kidding."

"No. She'll love it."

"But she's expecting dinner."

"That's my reasoning. We're going to take her unexpectedly."

"Why?"

"It's a turn-on."

"What is?"

"The unexpected. Wouldn't you get a rush if someone told you you were going to dinner and then they abducted you to some glorified go-cart track?"

He stuttered.

"Well, if you're configured correctly, the little kid in you should be screaming."

"Huh?"

"It will free her up, take her away from herself. Everybody loves a little adventure. It will free you up too. It lets you interact in a place that's not staid and boring where you are forced to depend upon earth-shattering witticisms and brilliant chatter. How did you meet your wife?"

"Tobogganing in Sun Valley."

"Precisely. It takes you both out of your comfort zones and you become more like teammates. Together you try to get through the set of unknown obstacles. The chaos of the situation will force you to talk about all sorts of things and you'll forget it's even a date. It lubricates a Breakthrough. Got me?"

I sensed he was smiling but I wasn't sure.

"Okay," he said finally. "Who are you going to bring?"

"A Bullet. Maybe Kelly. Maybe Mindy."

"I like them. Good."

I then imparted to Sydney the secret to double-dating. It's not in the spontaneity of the date itself. It happens hours before. It's in the socio-chemical mix. It's like an exercise in casting. You have to cast correctly, to get the right interaction, to get the right performances, to get the right results. Combinants rule. If you get the chemistry mix right, everything flows correctly.

You don't want girls who are mutually antagonistic, like a Paglian neo-feminist with pyro leanings and a Melrose kitten in a No-Not-There dress. You don't want roommates or best friends because they can bury themselves in each other. You don't want physical contrasts like "one pretty, one not." You alleviate the jealousy factor wherever possible. Because jealousy is kryptonite for a double date. Everyone buckles at the knees when one girl greens up on another.

You also don't want one guy to be inferior to the other. The girls will team up on him. Or they'll both go for the more interesting guy. Again you end up with a big dinner tab and nothing else. The parts must be balanced. Sydney brought power and fame to the table. I brought looks and personality. And we both brought brains. Enough said.

For reasons above, Kelly the Bullet was the right choice. After all, I wanted First Ball In and no surprises. Kelly was a team player. There's nothing as Breakthrough-effective as one girl's whispers of endorsement in another girl's ears. And a pretty girl's whispers? Forget about it. That was the best feature of a Bullet choice. It would be three against one. Star Camp always liked those odds.

On Track

Like most of the natives in Hell-A, I tended to dump on the San Fernando Valley. Why? The Valley was draped in that thick blanket of amber-gray. Everything had that hue. The houses, the sidewalks, the streets, even the people. You only went into the Valley if you had to. It's kind of like how New Yorkers think of New Jersey. *Only if you have to.*

That's where the nearest Malibu Grand Prix was located. So Sydney picked me up in his Jag, then we picked Dana up, and then all of us picked up the Bullet. But the Bullet demanded to ride the motorcycle a friend had left in her garage. And she wanted me to go with her. So I strapped on a helmet and obliged her, against the angels of my better nature. I didn't like the concept of two wheels and a motor. I didn't have screen whites yet and the thought of skidding out on such a worthless piece of machinery made me feel equally moronic. But I did it for Sydney.

Though Sydney and Dana thought the bike idea was a completely spontaneous development, it had been nothing of the sort. I'd asked the Bullet to press for it during our phone chat earlier. I wanted Sydney to ride alone with Dana. I was forcing them to communicate immediately. All the social jitters of interaction would be relieved by the time they arrived at the track. When they did arrive I noticed they were both in fine, spirited moods.

We paid our entrance fees and hopped in the minicars. The attendant strapped us in harnesses that crossed at the chest. The cars had roll bars for extra safety.

We were four in a line revving it up. Sydney and Dana took turns alternately roaring their engines. Good communication established already, I thought. It was nice to see. If they could do it in a go-cart they could do it in a tighter space. The Bullet was her typical shriek and shout. Excited about another day in another amusement park. Dana was somewhat shy.

If the truth be known, it was Sydney whose world I was trying to alter. There's no way he had ever been to a track like this. That was the point. Dana was sufficiently in touch with her child within. But I sensed Sydney had layers of bullshit that needed to be peeled away before he could start having a good time. The track at Malibu Grand Prix was a start.

The Bullet took off predictably fast. I tried to catch up with her and incite a mild crack-up. On the other side of the track's figure eight, I saw Dana laughing hysterically as she drove without talent. Sydney looked somewhat awkward strapped in his seat, but he had a huge grin on his face.

We took three rides apiece. I clocked a 4:54 on my second run. The Bullet's best was about ten seconds above that. Sydney had a 5:02 and Dana's best was 5:35. She didn't go for a third because she swerved mightily and crashed over the tires. She hit her knee and at that point I knew Sydney was in great shape. Dana had been successfully taken out of her element. Her zone of comfort had been bludgeoned to the point of crashing a go-cart. She was asking for someone to take her, meaning kiss her. It was an easy read. Mormons really are cute.

"It's all about crashing into the tires . . . ," she quipped with a self-deprecating laugh.

Seduction Sonata

With the group peaking with joy and good feeling, we decided to hit the road. I suggested Sydney follow the Bullet and me on bike. Then I told

the Bullet to take Laurel Canyon Boulevard. We climbed the winding ascent of Laurel and made a right on Mulholland Drive. After some vicious turns, we pulled over at the lookout point. It offered a full
sweeping view of the Valley on one side and Follywood on the other.

If the Valley had been a woman she would have asked to be pho-
tographed from this angle. It was her best profile. And the darkness aced
the smog, leaving her contours to the imagination. All the depressing little stories of all the also-rans who never made it on the other side of the
hill receded into invisible relief. At night the Valley was like a sensual,
masked beauty, a wide and deep wipe of lights. Darkness was the Valley's best friend.

We stood there and gazed out. And when we did I gave some
thoughts to Kelly the Bullet. Some warm thoughts. I looked at her body
and an urge tried to grip me at the waist. We never slept together when
I was active. We did seventh-grade stuff, meaning seventh grade in the
seventies not the nineties. You get a few more bases nowadays.

Kelly had a tremendous shape. She wasn't statuesque but she wasn't a
Spinner either. She was 5'7" and a fun version. Everything was done to
scale. She had nice measurements, great skin, and tight feminine sym-
metry.

I had a secret crush on her, I must confess. If there was any girl I
wanted in Hell-A it was the Bullet. When we started first hanging I was
wild about her. But for some reason I didn't want to press it. Then we
went too far in the friend direction. And then Eleanor came into my life.
So it never went beyond the crush stage. But our feelings for each other
never waned.

Oddly, the Bullet was inactive too. She'd had a bad breakup with a guy
she had set her hopes on marrying. You know, real doggy-dog stuff on
his part. Kelly was a straight shooter and an old-fashioned rarity. If she
was in love with you there was no one else in the room. She had no star
bug, no desire for fame or Follywood. She just wanted to find a mate she
loved and mate with him. Kelly the Bullet was a graceful, beautiful swan.
I loved her for it.

Maybe that was what was so wonderful. We were these two beings attracted to each other who just couldn't get it together. It was an exciting

union in that way. We were constantly on the verge of saying good-bye to each other. And neither of us wanted to let that happen. When Sydney and Dana piled out of the Jag, the urge to do push-ups on the Bullet left me like a disobedient dog. Quickly and without warning.

It was nice to see Sydney not depending on me to be the social generator. The two of them were smiling and interacting and were caught up in their own conversation.

"It's all about hating your sister because she's your sister," I heard her remark to him.

I'm sure they had followed several conversations to their conclusions, probably shared some similar views, and if Sydney had any female sense at all he'd agree with mostly everything she said anyway. It looked like he was in good shape.

"Should we get a bite?" the Bullet asked. Everyone looked at everyone else, and oddly enough, no one seemed to be hungry. No one wanted to go to a restaurant. Another good sign.

That's when I nodded to Sydney. "Why don't we go for a drink?"

We both waited for the girls to say where. But they didn't. Sydney looked at me for support since our script needed some improvisation. I hadn't foreseen the supermogul factor. That the girls were hesitant to call the shots in the face of a power guy. Or risk naming a place that would invoke class judgment. It was better to shut up and they did.

So I did the tugging. "Where do you like to go, Dana?" She shrugged shyly. "Bullet?"

"Wherever."

At that moment I gave Sydney the clapboard wink and he swallowed his cue, stepped on his marker, and responded in turn.

"Why don't we go back to my house? We can have a drink and listen to some music."

The girls looked at each other and nodded.

"That sounds cool. What do you like?" Dana asked.

"Aw, Benny Goodman, Artie Shaw," Sydney piped in out of the blue.

The girls looked at him funny. But I laughed. Then so did Sydney. It was the first of its kind. At least in my presence. Sydney had cracked a joke. Not a great one, but one indicating a metamorphosis could be under way.

I could tell by the way Sydney watched me and listened to what I said, he was trying to get to the bottom of what it might take to have charisma or at least a popular personality. He sensed I had the goods. I sensed I was a science project for him. He was beginning to incorporate my language, expressions, and warmed-over sound bites. I'm sure he had seen my gregarious, Mr. Popular type many times before, in school and after. He wasn't the most handsome or electric guy and I'm sure he figured he could get back at all those popular jerks that got the pretty girls in high school by becoming an atomic success. Sculpted personal skills which did not come naturally to him were secondary. Anyway, he could work on them later.

Now was later, though. Now he wanted to dip into my world. He knew it was the causeway to a more rounded and fulfilling life. And sex.

Going back to Sydney's was the right idea. It was met with no further questions or suggestions. Except one modification. I said it to the Bullet.

"Mind taking Dana on the bike?"

The Bullet just smiled. Very cool chick. She knew what was going down and got it.

"As long as you get me some Red when we get there."

"Done, baby, done."

"I'm going with Sydney," I announced.

"Hey, Dana," the Bullet blurted. "You're on the bike. With me."

She was hesitant as I knew she would be. When she wavered, I nudged her a little with something I remembered from the Dana.doc file. She hated Mormon barbs.

"Oh, that's right. She's a Mormon. No bikes, no booze, no balls. No fun."

The taunt was enough to spark her little reserve of rebellion. Her next move was a hop.

I slipped into Sydney's Jag and extended a closed fist. Our knuckles met. Our evening was sounding like a symphony. So far.

"I really like her," he added.

I didn't respond to that and I had my reasons.

In case the notion is foggy, putting that Mormon on the bike was the last movement of the seduction sonata. It was going to yield dividends in three ways. First, Dana was going to bond with the Bullet, but not so much that she would find escape or refuge in her, allowing her to get all girlie-whirlie and lose her nerve. The Bullet knew not to let that happen.

Second, the Bullet would pump her with good word on Sydney.

Third, Dana would get one more surge of adrenaline in her system while straddling a big piece of mean machinery. By the time we arrived in Bel-Air, I figured it was a pretty good bet the Mormon would be tugging down her undies that had climbed up her crotch on the ride and would have some specific taboo-type ideas about what could be done next. Of course I knew the charge would manifest itself not through an expression by her lower half, but it would all come up through her smacker. The Kissing Bandit.

And sure enough it did.

Of course Dana was impressed with Sydney's digs. There was nothing not to like. Envy? Yes. Hate? Even more. But like? Nothing. What we did was have a little champagne party on the outdoor patio overlooking a backyard that rivaled a Vermont farm. Bubbly, bubbly, bubbly went the spirits and, before long, we had jack-o'-lantern grins, four across.

Then Sydney piped, "It's all about living well." I smiled at him and winked. After some more toasts, some more Star Camp chatter, because sometimes you can't avoid it, and some laughs about Dana's shitty driving, I offered up the inevitable.

"I want to show you something," I said directly to the Bullet.

That left Sydney alone with Dana. A drunk Dana. An excited Dana. After she went to the bathroom and returned, a freshly lip-glossed Dana. Clearly, it was time for the Bullet and me to explore the rest of the house, the part they call the door.

Cough went the Bullet's bike and we were three and out. I figured the only thing that could fuck up Sydney at this point was something wildly improbable like Dana going flatline from a coronary, and, even in that case, he could lip-smack her when she passed out. Bad weather wouldn't hurt because it would give him a chance to take shelter, hold her close, and kiss her often. If a natural disaster hit, he'd hold her so close he'd probably get laid. After all, even a Mormon would consider an earthquake extenuating circumstances.

The Bullet dropped me off at home and we pecked each other.

"Too bad we're not in love, huh?" she asked me, and it was a surprise.

"Yeah," I said. "But then we might not get along as well."

She smiled through my sarcasm.

The Stable

Men can bond in many ways. Through sports. At work. In school. But there is no better way than achieving some good wildtime with ladies together in the same evening. A shared financial windfall with a guy can certainly cement a friendship. But it pales next to the act of hunting and gathering together. If you're the right kind of guy. And Sydney Swinburn was that kind. Ladies meant a lot to him. I could tell. Just how much, I didn't know.

When Sydney called me the next day, it sounded like he'd just won Wimbledon. They kissed, he petted, he felt, he got felt, and he was assured of another date. And soon. I certainly understood his excited quality. You don't need to consummate to have a great time. A simple kiss can fill you with the greatest emotional highs. I'm sure that's what Sydney was feeling. He was dancing on clouds.

You know what I thought. *FBI.*

Until he added this. "But, but, I really like her."

"Well, reconsider." I felt comfortable enough with Sydney to be so deliberate and opinionated.

"Why?"

"I told you. She's The Kissing Bandit. She plays pathological make-out games. She's on to the next one already."

"We're going out again tonight."

"Okay," I said. And dropped it.

"Hold on," Sydney said, and he switched over to another line.

I thought we were done. But when Sydney returned, he asked me another question that caught me off guard.

"What about you, Heyward?"

"What do you mean?"

"Why don't you get involved with women anymore?"

It was an odd moment for me. I didn't know what to say at first. Meaning I didn't know if I should answer truthfully, or at all. But I found myself stripped of any analytical-forethought mechanisms. I was alone, with only the truth. And it came out.

"In general, Sydney. I'm not interested. Not now anyway."

"Why not?"

"I'd rather watch *Letterman*. Or read my *New York* magazine. Or spruce up my New York accent with some Radio Stern. Or buy the hell out of a new caffeine product that's just come on the market."

"What does all that mean?"

I didn't say I wanted my Blade sharp and ready to slice. And anything that had a dulling effect, I avoided, girlie-whirlies included. It would sound weird. And make him suspect. But that was my real answer. Forethought mechanisms had returned. All the better.

But I wanted to tell him. I wanted to blast it right at him. *Sydney, no one wants to be sentenced to life at somebody else's table. Otherwise you're just a hanger-on. A Blip. With no credits and no identity. I want the reservation in my name. I want my own table and I want to fill it with whomever I fancy.*

"I guess career is too important," I mustered up. "Women take time."

"You don't have time?"

And I wasn't sure if I liked the sound of it.

"Not for a relationship. I've had some unions that have sapped me of my productivity. Forty years old is only ten years away, Sydney. I've always planned to have my house in order by then. That's my plan. I have no other. That's why women take backseat status."

There was a long pause. I was ready for something, something from him to me. Something positive. After all, I was giving him something of myself, a UPS package from my soul. But it wasn't coming back. Nothing was coming. Just the silence. So I followed it up.

"Besides, I think when you fuck around with too many people, you end up fucking yourself."

And it was something I truly believed. It was a void filler, but I was unaware of the special effect it would have on Sydney.

After another few beats, he responded. Defensively.

"I was married a long time, Heyward. Before that, I had two girl-friends, only one with whom I slept, and that was only twice. And I wake up, divorced, at age forty-nine, and it's a different world out there. And I hadn't even experienced the old one."

I didn't say anything. Nothing needed to be said. And I thought it was overreactive of me to expect Sydney to offer up something to me. Like a pledge. He'd been wrapped in years of monogamy, some of them painful, wondering what it was like on the other side of the fence. He wasn't thinking about my fight for whites and my get-my-shit-together timetable. I figured he'd ponder what I said later, and some of the message would get through.

"Let's talk later," I said eventually.

When we hung up it was midmorning already. I decided it was time for some drive-bys. I looked at my watch. I had fifteen minutes to catch the morning special at Swinger's, the grunge breakfast joint on Beverly. It was like a fifties retro diner and filled with the type of people I liked to waste time with. I'd often go there, take notes on My Newest, and chew it with any Projects who showed up. Some people can't write with all that chaos. Dishes clanking, orders being shouted, let's not forget the social whirl. But I loved it. I had no problem digging into my stories. My characters could talk to me and to each other even as my eyes followed those omelettes going from kitchen window to table, transported by a busy Wam.

I made it to Swinger's swiftly, found a parking slot with some time left on the meter, and perched at the counter. The Wam came up to me with a pencil and a pad.

"Recommend anything?" I asked to make her feel useful.

She suggested the tofu quesadilla and I said no. Or *not on your life*. I wanted the special.

"How do you like your eggs?"

"Scrambled soft with wheat toast."

I scanned the *L.A. Times,* ate quickly, and seeing nothing, no Projects, or no one interesting, I moved out of there.

Like my morning, that afternoon had a different feel. I had an added agenda. It was frozen yogurt with a mission. It was gym workout with a mission. It was an afternoon cappuccino with a mission. I wasn't searching necessarily for Sydney because for him I wanted a Known Quantity, meaning a girl with no surprises. And any new find might be full of them. For Sydney I needed candidates I knew well and could depend on. The new acquaintances I would eventually get to know and once the consistency in their personalities was established, or lack thereof, only then would I involve them.

And at that moment I made a decision.

I decided I was going to provide Sydney with more than he had bargained for. Even though it was him who was calling for it. Not that he had called for it per se, but the way he moved, the way he talked, the way he looked at me, I could tell it was what he desired. He wanted to know what it was like to be one of the planet's smooth operators. He wanted to know what it was like to have ladies on any given night. And he wanted to experience the self-esteem jolt he thought it would give him. As I was doing without credits and the spoils that accompany a successful Hollywood writer, Sydney had never felt the sensation of being a bon-vivant playboy. He'd experienced everything else but. I decided to help him get there.

There was going to be a stable. And a rotation. That's what my mission became. A full nest of honeys and a capacity to rotate girls in and out of Sydney Swinburn's life. That was the secret to making this honcho happy. He needed numbers. He needed variety. He needed a Stable.

The Sled slid down Santa Monica Boulevard into Beverly Hills and I made a left on Canon. I motored into the Public Parking garage and ran out pretty fast. I wanted to stay under the two-hour free parking limit so I wouldn't have to pay. I made good use of my time.

I slipped into the Canon Arcade and checked out the anthropology at Caffe Roma but it was still too early for all the brats who never work but sip away their lives in European-style cafés. I then slipped into

Giuseppe Franco with a huff and a puff. Giuseppe Franco was another one of my daily drive-bys. It was a beauty salon and there was always a nice quantity of L.A.'s finer kittens.

Let me point out here that I was pretty good at finding the girlies if they were around. And Giuseppe's on a weekday morning was a damn good bet. The prime feature was it was a spontaneous stage. You would run into those types you had never seen before, the ones who never went out. The ones locked in their houses and their lives. The unavailable ones. Giuseppe's salon made them available. And if not available, at least accessible and maybe approachable. In the end, everyone was approachable in Hell-A. The "bigger-better-deal" was on everyone's mind. Or they wouldn't have been there in the first place. That was the charming nature of the town.

Reverse Roots

Josie the cashier greeted me as I slipped inside. I knew Josie pretty well. After all I wasn't just a loiterer. I did some business there too. The music was blasting and all the eyes were on the door and me as I stepped in. It was that kind of place. Everyone looked to see what the new intruder looked like, in essence, whether he was a celeb or not. The place broke the sound barrier on vanity.

"Do you have an appointment?" Josie asked. "I didn't think so."

Josie asked me if I wanted some flavored seltzer water and I said no.

"I just came in to say hi." That meant I came in to check out the anthro and Josie knew it. It made her smile appreciatively. Then Bettina flew past me and gave my head a good look.

"Need a touch-up?"

"I hadn't thought about it."

"I have a batch mixed up already."

"My batch?"

"Yup. My eleven o'clock didn't show."

"Well . . ."

Before I knew it, I was taking off my shirt and putting on the black smock.

Bettina did me. She did me well. That included bringing me to the upstairs parlor where it was more private. I couldn't stand the thought of having all those foil wrappers on my head, let alone a public display in the downstairs section. It had traffic marching through it like a stadium portal. It made me feel like a lab rat. Besides, I didn't like the vast implications that I colored my hair. By all accounts it was a reflection of my character. Guys who colored their hair I found moronic and would generally stay away from. But I had to live with me. I did half a head instead of a full. It was cheaper, took less time, and was psychologically less compromising.

I played it down, remember? And part of that was to stamp out all traces of my WASPiness. You see, I was a blond, a real towhead through my teens, and a dirtier version of that later on. So I had Bettina keep my golden roots away. She dyed my hair dark brown. Billions of dollars are spent all over the world by people desperate to have a hair color that came naturally to me. But I did not want to look like the just-showered country club tennis pro. There were enough obstacles out there in the field. I dressed it down. I wanted no tan and no blond. I wanted underfed, sickly, pasty, and limp dark brown. I was giving those industry bastards nothing to hate.

I plopped into my reserved chair, the chair I always sat in. Bettina chatted up a storm. Told me what she'd been hearing. It was always torrid gossip. She said her chair was better than a gin and tonic. The gals came in and gushed.

There were only two chairs up there but when I looked over in the mirror, I saw someone sitting beside me. She was attractive and it made me uncomfortable. Naturally because I knew she was the type I could run into out and about. She was what all the L.A. dogs wanted, Strugs and 8x10s and such, and eventually she'd turn up. I didn't like anyone seeing me this way. I was comforted when her beautician appeared. It took the attention off me.

And I listened as they conversed. And what I heard surprised me. She wasn't a seasoned vet of the Hollywood Hills at all. She was a tourist from Indiana with thoughts of making the Move. She confessed to being a walk-on, meaning she just entered the shop, unaware of its reputation. And her name was Puddy.

She was a real field mouse too, so impressionable, so trusting, so sweet and together, with the kind of moral fiber that made her perfect pickings for the dark mayors of the town who, if given the chance, would eventually take all that innocence and churn it up in their meat grinders and spit out an exploited, tainted, used and abused version of her over the course of a long weekend. It made me sick to think about it. The Field Mice Tourists. Each goaded on by the hopes and hypes of a better life on America's left edge. If I'd seen one I'd seen a thousand. It made me want to buy her a return ticket to Terre Haute that afternoon.

That was the beauty of the Giuseppe Franco salon, however. It had a draw that couldn't be replicated in any hip bar, high-profile restaurant, or girlie-whirlie dance club. It appealed to all women. No matter how big a hermit you were, if you were in L.A. you still wanted to look good. Some women were totally bored too—so much that a hair appointment was their only excitement. Of course others were just dying to get away from their mattress status with daddies so old they couldn't even remember whether they had done them or not and so they would just have to do them again. The salon was a welcomed retreat for them too.

I left Giuseppi's feeling shiny and shampooed with some new Reverse Roots. *Sassy* is how the Soft Boysies put it. And that was irksome. How could anyone describe anything as sassy other than someone who just gives you too much lip? I also left with Puddy's number at the world-famous Sunset Motel on the Strip. She claimed to be free that night. So was her roommate. See, we chatted during the drying. Nice pickings at Giuseppe Franco's.

Didn't Wanda

I neglected to say before, I also ran into Wanda. She was pretty in an L.A. way. But running into Wanda was never a good time, if only because of the negative-vibe factor. She was never nice to me. When I slid up to the counter to pay for my reverse roots, she was there buying hair products. And true to her spirit and angst, she gave me that "Hey there, Mr. North of the Equator" greeting.

It was an odd phenomenon, my relationship with Wanda. Wanda had been a Stowaway for a few months. We had a pretty nice time. We cooked in a lot. She made a great stir-fry. We did the Blockbuster Video thing. We did lots together. But there was one thing I would not do with her. I would not kiss her coochie.

I wasn't known for that kind of abstinence. I was known for high-velocity penetration, absurd turns of the flesh, licking everywhere, and when I went down I was La Machine. If I do say so myself. But somehow, for some reason, I could not go low on Wanda. Maybe it was an intimacy issue. Maybe it was our lack of chemistry. Or maybe I was having a Paglian episode, seeing Woman as one big vagina with teeth and being repelled by the thought of returning to the slime from whence I came at birth. Her name was suitably perfect for our predicament. Because I didn't really wanda. And her name for me was equally appropriate, Mr. North of the Equator, as I would not go south on her. I was aware that to tell someone you will not ingest her most personal fluids is a real knee-in-the-stomach insult. Complexes result and not all of them justified. So, whenever she saw me, she saw me as a guy who had insulted her tremendously. To her I was as popular as the lights-out midnight mosquito.

Right then I had a surge of an idea.

"What are you up to, Wanda?"

"You know, SOS."

"Look, I don't think we've been hitting it off so well lately. I know it's my fault. A bunch of friends are getting ready for dinner tonight. Why don't you come?"

After some fakes at other engagements, she was on board for the night. Wanda was a good sport.

I checked my watch and made quick speed back to the parking garage. I had two minutes to go. I hopped in the Sled and hauled ass to the gate and handed the booth attendant my ticket. I sighed in relief when the gate opened. I hated giving the city of Beverly Hills any more money than they deserved. And I didn't think they deserved any at all.

In the end, I decided against Wanda. I thought the invitation would ultimately result in a disaster. After I had positioned her in a booth next to Sydney, pumped her with all sorts of good word and propaganda on him, then positioned myself on the side of the table that was so far away I could get a head cold, she'd realize I was dishing her to him. Given our previous history, I knew this wasn't the right way to go. How would you feel if a guy wouldn't go low on you and then he offered you to someone else?

I dialed up Wanda and asked her to join me for coffee some other time instead.

Model Repulsion

Sydney and I talked that night. At six. Right after Dana had called him to cancel on that evening's date.

"You were right."

"Yeah. But you never know, Sydney."

"Hey, there are other girls around. Right?"

"Only two hemispheres full."

And I had already spent the last hour on my Gold files. I was scanning them in search of the next candidate for Bel-Air's newest Romeo. I was looking for someone more experienced, where the payoff would be a little more than a few wet, moonlight smooches. I would consider that progress.

I tapped a few more keys as I felt I was onto something. Sydney heard the taps.

"Are you writing now?"

"No . . ."

Sydney wanted to have dinner. I think he wanted to discuss things some more. We went to Indochine, just the two of us. I met another parade of Hollywood power brokers as well as Starman Lead Guitar. Midway through the meal Sydney hit me with this.

"What about the models?"

"What do you mean?"

"Don't you know any?"

"Sure, I know some." That was true.

"I mean, what do you think about that?"

"I think it's a bad idea."

"Why?"

"Because, first of all, L.A. is not a good model town."

"Why not?"

"The models in L.A. are the second tier. You've got to go to New York or Paris for the big game."

"Big game?"

"Second, they're difficult."

"How so?"

"The beauty contamination aspects. Makes them attention junkies."

"More than the Wams?"

"Yes. Besides that, it's all over for them."

"How do you mean?"

"They've peaked."

"Peaked how so?"

"They hit their prime and it's all downhill from here on in."

"Think so?"

"I'm not a betting man. But I'd bet a limb on that."

"Beautiful women will always be appreciated."

"But this frenzy won't last. They had their bang. And the human being, the normal human being, the ones who don't have those China doll looks, are fed up with them."

"I don't think so."

"Let me explain. In the sixties the world asked models to look good and shut up. In the seventies they learned how to look good, smile please, and swing with us. They learned how to look good and do drugs with us in the eighties."

"And in the nineties?"

"They've been asked to look good, stand up, and speak. And the world found out what the models had to say. Nothing. The majority anyway. So by century's end, they're going to ask them to look good, sit down, and shut up."

"Is that the word?"

"It's my word."

"How do you know all this?"

"Just the nervous system of an artist responding to his environment as his sensibilities move onward in time."

He thought about it and didn't call my bluff. If he had, I still wouldn't have come off my position.

"Who do you think they'll be replaced by?"

"How do you mean?"

"Well, if this phenomenon dies flat, who will take their place?"

I thought about it.

"In terms of women?"

"If the models are out, who's in?"

Bianco Trash

"The Millennium Girl."

"Who's she? That's a great title, by the way."

I knew that already. I had come up with it a year before. It was in my title file and it was the subject of a future script.

He asked me again. "Who's the Millennium Girl?"

"She's a woman uniquely qualified to handle life in America at century's end." I paused and thought a moment more. "Let me qualify that. You want to know who's in right now?"

"Yeah."

I hesitated briefly before I gave it to him. "Bianco Trash," I said flatly.

"Who?"

"Bianco Trash is where it's at."

"You mean white trash?"

"Yes."

"Why?"

"They have everything the mannequins don't. A full and colorful past. Rich interiors. They're multifaceted."

"So?"

"It's given them a point of view. They have something to say. It makes them more interesting. POVs always do."

"Everyone's talking models, though. They're so striking."

"To hell with the models," I shot back. "I'll take Bianco Trash any day. You have some wildtime with a model ten times then what? You're waiting for the waiter to bring more bread. You have nothing to talk about. Their tanks are empty. The only things they know are what they've been told in the van. And that they don't remember. So all you end up with is the wildtime and when that wears off, the fact that they can't say anything makes you resent them faster. But they'll get lathered in attention by any newcomer. That's even more maddening. That someone can gain that kind of attention and you know it's propped up by nothing more than the fact that some crawler wants to slam her. Grim.

"Now, Bianco Trashers, you know, gals who've had difficult childhoods, or some kinds of trauma, or they've worked all their lives, or they've been in life-threatening situations—there's nothing better. They have all that delicious psychological baggage. Real Dysfuncionados. They're the best."

"Is it the fact that they're white trash, as you say, or dysfunctional, that makes them so great?"

"Good question. It's the combination of both. Obviously, not all Bianco Trashers are dysfunctional. And it's not the only group susceptible to dysfunction either. There's dysfunction at all levels of society and in all socioeconomic groups. We're all damaged in some ways. But the dysfunction translates to different behavioral patterns in the different groups. Dysfunctional Bianco Trashers are behaviorally the most colorful. Because, usually, they've lived a more colorful life. It makes them singularly fascinating. To me it's like going to an amusement park. On a daily basis. It's unpredictable. Exciting. You don't know what's going to happen. Every day is a new day. It's the action you pay for. That's the girl for me."

"Really . . ." He had never heard this before.

And to be honest, neither had I. I'd become Gym Boy. And the locker room chatter was just flowing freely from me. But I knew what I was doing. I needed to show structure, to show knowledge, to show precision and timing, to show absolute authority on the issues of aggressive womanizing in the nineties. And that's why I came up with monikers like Bianco Trash as well as the colorful Gym Boy coinings. I needed to show I knew the ropes, that groups were classified and their behavior and habits had been studied in depth and detail. Which they had. For my writing purposes. But why did I flaunt my knowledge? I needed Sydney to fully understand the extent of my abilities and, therefore, my worth. To him.

There was an extended silence from Sydney. "But these models are so . . . glamorous," he said finally. *Damn*, I thought. He'd gone back to the generic beauties thing.

"You say look at all that glamour of the models? I say look at all that interiority, color, and personality of the Bianco Trash."

"Don't tell me there aren't any dysfunctional models out there."

I roared. It was funny. I'd met a few, that was for sure.

"Sure there are. Many models *are* Bianco Trashers. But with the beauty often comes some form of contamination. And it's not their fault. They've been treated differently all their lives. Their daily life experience is very different from yours and mine. It makes them different. It makes them contaminated. Normal Bianco Trash doesn't have that contamination."

"Maybe it's because you're a writer. You want to soak up the bizarre quirks."

"Maybe," I said, and leaned back in my chair. I was really stuffed. "But just name one of those models, even one of the famous ones, who hasn't had one boyfriend or husband after another. They can never find love. Know why? Because they choose guys who are wrong for them. Guys who want them for their beauty. Guys who've had a roster of beauties to their name since childhood."

I was babbling now. Gym Boy was running amok. The meal had made me tired and I was experiencing food coma. I ordered a double espresso.

"Where was I? Oh yeah. The problem with these guys is that, if they get off so completely on a girl's beauty once, they'll seek the same experience again with another stunner. These beauty junkies can't ever get enough. It's a drug. I'm rambling. Sorry."

"No. It's interesting."

"Talking girlies always is," I said. Sydney smiled at that.

The reality is I was dissing the shit out of the models not only because I partially believed it but because I was orchestrating a situation that would yield a big payoff.

The waiter came back with the espresso and I downed it. It helped me regain clarity.

"They're the keepers, the Bianco Trash," I asserted.

"Are you Bianco Trash?"

"Half. My mother's side."

"Is Eleanor Bianco Trash?"

"Not at all," I responded. "Is Teal?"

He looked serious suddenly. The question had caught him off guard. He said "No" and slowly sipped his water. "When you say keepers you mean the ones to marry?"

"No. They're the ones you keep in your stable. The diversions in between. It's like going out with a depth charge. How can you argue with that? And the sex? Forget about it. They're overrun with complexes. Daddy, Mommy, incestuous, mild and major abuse. It makes them wildly naughty. Before you know it you're getting a blow job on a barstool in broad daylight while the bartender is timidly asking you if you'd like another round. For my money, pound for pound, it's the Bianco Trash."

More locker room banter. Gym Boy was on a caffeine roll now. But I would keep it coming. Until I got the response I was waiting for.

"Tell me about the Naughty Law."

I smiled. He had trapped the term. I had made it up on the spot and forgotten about it. But it didn't make it any less true. I thought about how I was going to introduce the concept, and decided to bring up an anecdote from my past.

When I was young, I loved doing mischievous things. But my favorite pastime of all was to ring on doorbells and run. It would make me laugh until my sides needed restructuring. And I explained to Sydney that I used to tell women about that.

"What would you say?" he asked.

"I told them, *Deep down inside me there's a little boy who likes to ring door-bells and run.*"

"What would they say?"

"Nothing. They would just smile. It showed them I was fun, playful, and a little bit naughty."

"So?"

"Ladies are dying to be appealed to in a naughty way. Not all, but a major proportion. They've all been societally conditioned to close down, to show coy and shy and refined. It's not 'proper' for them to be the naughty, passion instigators. So they're waiting for the chance. If you take the lead, oftentimes they're right there with you. With skates on." I looked at him. "See? Even you're smiling right now."

And that made Sydney laugh. "And the Bianco Trash pick up on it sooner, right?"

"You bet they do. Either that, or they initiate it in the first place."

And then I got the response I was waiting for. "Where do you find them?"

"Sydney, are you shitting me? It's America. We're known for baseball, apple pie, and poor white trash."

"So what do we do about it?"

"I have a plan."

"A plan?"

Sydney was pretty shocked at my dissertation on modern cultural trends, I think. Specifically the science of model repulsion. Maybe it was a little over the top. In fact I'm sure of it. And maybe he'd hit an accurate chord when he asked me if it was the writer in me that was responding to this other group of hot Dysfuncionados.

We didn't say much more that night. Starman Action Adventure Director came up to the table and whined about uncontrollable Starman Grunge. It was interesting to get the real dish on the moviemaking life. It had never been presented to me in such an uncut form.

Sydney dropped me off at home. And I thought about a few things. My mind was very active. It had been sparked in some way. My synapses were firing again. Like they used to in New York. I attributed it to my new relationship. I had made a friend and it had an inspiring effect on me.

The Plan

A few things happened over the next few days. One day my hair looked so good I sprayed it in place periodically throughout the day. It kept its nice shape and fall and you know how important it is to look good in the Age of A. It's everything. Sure, L.A. was giving me a lot of kidney punches on a daily basis—its people, its language, its customs—they were all beating me down, trying to dull my Blade. So I would succumb on occasion to moronic acts like vanity concerns. I wasn't worried yet. Only if it started happening regularly would I dial 911.

I had a few Mocha Chillers at Humphrey Yogurt and I ran a few laps around Fairfax High School track. I also changed lemons in the Sled and dusted off Bob the Riot. In essence, I didn't do anything. So no one had anything on me in town.

Oh, I almost forgot. I had a meeting with Sydney's friend Ruth Yizerman. We'd met in her office in the Valley at which time she told me she passed on my script. That was disappointing. But she suggested I take a quick read of an old pulp detective novel that they were going to resurrect and make into a film. She said using my script as a sample, I'd be right for the job. Hot shit, was my feeling. But that's all there is to say about it. A potential writing assignment. Hell-A life was looking up. The details I won't bore you with. They're too fucking boring.

What I did was a quick read of the book and then wrote a one-pager demonstrating how I would approach the script. I dropped it by Ruth's office and hoped for the best.

That night I tried to stomach a movie with Kelly the Bullet but as soon as the opening whites rolled, I saw that some Mo I disliked had written the screenplay and everything in my stomach curdled.

On Thursday night, I went to work. I had a plan in mind. I booted up and searched for two of the meanest Bianco Trashers I could find. It didn't last long. Tiffany and Tammy were their names. With names so similar, there could be some confusion. But we'd get beyond it. We were bright guys. Tammy's entry came from my Manhattan Beach file. I didn't know if she still lived there or not. A call confirmed she did and her spontaneous ramblings told me she was as crazy as ever. That was Tammy. I'd known her for three years. She liked to have fun in bulk.

Tiffany was a Valley girl with a body built for war. I didn't know her as well but she seemed perfect for what I had in mind. I knew the two would get on well. Both their fathers were in the army. And like all army kids, they'd moved around a lot when they were young. Besides, neither of them was an attention junkie. They could share a spotlight. All the better for the sociochemical mix.

When Sydney told me to spare no expense in setting up some fun, I got real serious about the next adventure. Even the Pentagon would have been proud of my plan. I rang up Sydney and asked him if he would trust me with his weekend. He said he had a black-tie benefit to attend. But he would cancel if I told him he should. I did. After a flurry of snoopy questions, he asked if there was anything preparatory the weekend required of or from him.

I told him there wasn't. I told him I would pay my own way. He insisted against it. I insisted further. He respected that. For the rest of the reservations, he gave me his Amex number.

I think he liked the idea of the surprise. Who doesn't like a surprise party?

When the day of departure rolled around I had my work cut out for me. It would have been easier had Tiffany not canceled. Out the window went all that army background chemistry. I phoned aggressively. It was difficult to get someone on board that fast, even though I was using some strong desperate charm. One pretty girl would be fine logistically. She could assist in corralling another contender. But it looked bad. It looked like I couldn't deliver.

Remember: in Hell-A, you have to produce. If not for yourself, at least the moguls. Especially the super ones. They're used to getting things done, and done the right way. They win.

We were a limping threesome in need of a fourth.

The Unknown

Of course there were many girls in my Gold, but not all were suited for this trip. It was a very specific niche I was battling for. There was not a wide margin for error, meaning not just anyone would do. You'll understand why. I promise.

Even though L.A. was laid-back-bordering-upon-flatline-brain-dead by nature, by Friday, even the aimless Muffin Heads had trouble dropping plans and getting spontaneous. Not good, was my thought.

That was when I thought of the right girl at the right time. *Crunch* time.

"Hello, Sunset Motel?" the raspy voice chimed.

"Is Puddy there?"

The woman left the line. And plugged me in elsewhere. And someone picked up. I asked to speak to Puddy again.

"This is Puddy."

I told her who it was. And there was silence. "We met at Giuseppe's. The other day."

"Oh right." Then she giggled.

"What are you laughing at?"

"You were the one getting your roots done black, right?"

"Uh, what did I tell you when we spoke?"

"You told me it was our secret."

"That's right."

"Don't worry. It is."

"Are you sure?"

"Of course."

"Where's your roommate?"

"She's not here. She met some guy."

I liked hearing that. "Movie guy?"

"I think a writer."

"Is she Polish?"

"What?"

I didn't tell her the infamous joke. But it meant her girlfriend was already playing the town wrong. She was fucking her way to the middle.

"Nothing."

She laughed again. "In that chair you looked pretty funny."

"Well, I am funny. A real cutup."

"I've never heard of a blond going black." She followed it up with more guffaws. I took it. "Sorry. I'm in a funny mood," she added.

With that, my mind held up the winning bingo card. Puddy was happy, carefree, and in that funny mood. Funny moods are the best moods. If a girlie-whirlie's in a funny mood it's a good sign. All reason and rationale go out the window. She's controlled by something otherworldly. Girls on funny moods are as good as girls on barbiturates. Or so I'd heard. They just might do anything.

"Well, you came to the right place."

"Really, why?"

"I want to take you on a voyage."

She left a void of no response, meaning she allowed me to surge forth and make my pitch. I told her a little bit about Sydney. And Tammy. She told me she needed to know where we were going. I wouldn't tell her. She said she wasn't going to come unless I did. So I did. And the girl laughed and uttered two gems.

"I'm in."

"Great. We'll pick you up in an hour."

I knew that meant two but I wanted her ready.

"Wait. Can I bring my bird?"

"Uh, sure."

I didn't bother to ask what her bird was, if it in fact was a bird, or a stuffed animal or a toy. I chalked it up to the good old Bianco Trash behaviorial rainbow. The fact that I had nailed her at the eleventh hour was all that mattered.

"Are you sure I'm going to recognize you without all those foils on your head?"

I hung up soon after. But hell. I liked this girl. She was giving me shit already and I always liked a girl who had enough verve to do that.

Let me make another point. And it's an important one. The trip worried me. It's true I didn't know Puddy well. She was a U.Q., an Unknown Quantity. The results weren't in on her yet. I'll explain. Dinner in a local eaterie with a U.Q. is fine. If there's a problem, if personalities clash and the get-together unravels, dinner is soon over. Everyone goes home. But to venture off into the unknown with an Unknown is incredibly risky. Especially when the stakes are high. Supermogul stakes.

Ours was a long trip. An Unknown could turn out to be wonderful, but also a disaster. She could ruin everything. But we were under a severe time constraint. Baby Garbo was out of town shooting a commercial. I didn't want to invite Kelly the Bullet because being one of the guys constantly was wearing on her. She knew we weren't going to get it on and she knew she wouldn't go for Sydney.

That's how an Unknown became our Fill-In. And it was a gamble.

Bianco Trash Holiday

The Sled brought me up to Sydney's house where the limousine was awaiting. It was an ugly limo. It was long and black and the guy perched at the wheel seemed scornful of Sydney's overwhelming Bel-Air digs. Either that or me. Whichever, he had certainly preserved his finest bitter face. He puffed away and let me hang there, waiting for him to quash it out. He was letting me know I had nothing on him. He took my garment bags without a smile.

"Which airline?"

"American," I said, since I was still the only one who knew the travel details.

Sydney emerged from those big front doors wearing some inappropriate clothes that were punishingly safari-like. The driver smiled at Sydney and right there I knew he was just another Hell-A whore. Be nice to Mr. Huge and shit on the guy with the noisy muffler because the only difference between him and you is dumb luck. Guess he forgot the 100 I.Q. points. And a few evolutionary steps. I called him Monkey Man from then on. Fuck him, was another thought.

"What's the next destination?" Monkey Man asked Sydney. Not only was he a prick, he spoke Brooklynese, a dialect that makes rudeness soar.

"Heyward. Where are the girlie-whirlies?" Sydney asked me in turn.

"They're next."

"Where we goin'?" Monkey Man repeated.

I wanted to give it to him turn by turn and drive his mind wild. But I didn't want to be a Mo in front of Sydney. "Genesee, a block south of Sunset."

Sydney looked over at me. "Do I need a bathing suit?"

"Nope. Skis."

"What?" And he burst with an excited smile. This guy must have been deprived as a child, I thought. He loved this surprise stuff.

We climbed into the limo. I let him ride with eyes forward, while I sat opposite. As soon as our asses hit the leather, Sydney popped it.

"So where are we going?"

With that, I drew out one of four airline tickets, the one with Sydney's name on it, and handed it to him. He scanned it.

"Memphis, Tennessee?"

"Graceland."

"Graceland?"

"We're taking a Bianco Trash Holiday."

He laughed at the absurdity of it and that was a positive sign. It was the sign I wanted from him. And all of them. Like the Malibu Grand Prix, it was intended to bust them out of their normal lives and thought patterns, and, if we were lucky, into our beds. At least, Sydney's.

"Are you some kind of Elvis freak?"

I told him I wasn't. I couldn't give a damn about Elvis. He may have been a pioneer of the rock and roll beat, but I liked what the others had done with it. The Beatles, Floyd, the Stones, U2. Elvis's shtick was too corny, too Gracelandy. Besides, he didn't write any of his own stuff. How could he be the King of Rock and Roll if he never wrote any? To me he was a Strug with an 8x10 face and a decent voice.

One Bad Mood Away

As we zoomed down Sunset into Smogwood, I asked Monkey Man to pull into Tower Records. He agreed only because he had to. I dashed in and grabbed some trashy, hair spray rock. Like Boston, Foreigner, Journey—you know, the Sweet and Low stuff. I also snagged an Elvis tape in case one of the girls called for it. I could already hear the high-pitched "How could you go to Graceland and not listen to any Elvis?" shattering my drums.

When I got back in the limo, Sydney had a question for me I'd anticipated.

"So what's the word on Tiffany?"

"Tiffany couldn't make it."

"No?"

"I got a Fill-In. Her name is Puddy."

"Is Puddy for me?"

"She's for whoever she wants to get close to. Can't force these things. But since I'm inactive you're her only shot. So yes, I'd say she is for you. In essence, they're both for you. We'll have to see how it plays out."

He nodded silently. "But what if it helps for you to get involved?"

"Cross that bridge when we get to it. But don't worry: I know how to be an assist man."

"So what's the word on the Fill-In?"

"Actually, she's more than a Fill-In. She's an Unknown."

Sydney paused a moment to process the terminology. It wasn't difficult and he soon awaited my follow-up.

"I met her the other day. But the fact that she just upped and came on short notice is a good sign. She's from Indiana and has a playful disposition. But I could sense a few cracks there."

"Which is good, right?" He smiled as he said it, poking fun at me and my appreciation for fractured types.

"Last I knew."

"Where did you meet?"

"Out and about. King's Road Cafe I think." Sure it was a lie. And you know why.

"And what's the word on Tammy?"

"Tammy I know better. Major abuse. Her old man was a real scumbag. He did it all. Whacked her around, did the nasty. An old boyfriend used to cage her too. She had some years of low-budget, quack therapy and it helped. She's completely unpredictable. But in a good way. She'd do anything for you."

As I continued to give Sydney the word on her, I watched his face initiate a glow. He was warming nicely to the profile.

"Where's she from?"

"Galveston, Texas. But she lives in Manhattan Beach. Which is also good."

"Why?"

"If you hit it off and get involved, but don't want to see her every night—*and you shouldn't*—it will work out nicely. She lives out of town. This way she can become part of the stable."

Sydney laughed. "You mean I'm going to have a stable?"

"And the rotation that comes with it."

He let the passing sights of the passing road outside snag his eyes, making them flick and return like a typewriter. But he was grinning from ear to ear like a kid you tell not to touch you.

Of course I was talking out of my ass. But I wanted Sydney to have high hopes.

"Why shouldn't I?" It was a question he had on delay, blockaded from his dreamy state, but I knew what he was asking. I was waiting for it.

"Settle down?" I completed for him. "Because you're just starting out again. See what's around." Then I held up a V sign. "V is not for victory. It's for variety. It's the ultimate spice. For a while anyway."

"I don't think I'm capable of having a stable."

I felt it was now time to give him another axiom in the art of seduction. The ultimate axiom. One Bad Mood Away.

"Any woman, Sydney, is *one bad mood away* from being in your bed."

"What? One bad mood?" he asked with a confused expression.

"When things aren't going right for a woman, whether in her life, her marriage, or her relationship, she hits a point of vulnerability. And she feels lacking in some way. She may feel the need for a quick fix. And oftentimes, if the right set of circumstances comes up, and the right things are said, in the right way, it's all over. Then . . ."

"She's yours," Sydney finished off.

"Precisely. And when she's confused like that, there's always a guy to push her over the edge. Marauders smell the blood of a wounded bird and dig right in. Mercilessly. With sensitivity, or sweetness, kind gestures, out-of-town offers, gifts, or just a patient ear. Her weakened quality is the lure."

"But it's true of men too," Sydney interjected. "When they're bummed out they seek out other women."

"They may want some substitution satisfaction. But they usually won't get it. It's just the opposite. A guy is *one good mood away* from being in a woman's bed. If a guy is having a problem, it's written all over his face. He gives off that bad energy, and a woman can feel it. No one likes being around bad energy. It's a repellent. But if he's happy and feeling good, his energy is positive and he's attractive. To you. To me. To the opposite sex. And the opposite sex will avail themselves of him. And a guy, being a guy, if he's that kind of guy, whether he's in a relationship, marriage, or not, will oblige her."

"It's easier for a woman to get it, that's for sure."

"What I'm saying to you is, no woman is out of reach. Ever. It may not happen tonight. Or tomorrow. But down the road. Patience is key. Don't forget. A woman is run by the moon. Not by your commands or a slap on the wrist or a marriage license or a clasp of the hands or an engagement ring or four ones and a thumb to the jaw. It's the moon, baby. Go ahead, try and compete with the moon. How small do you feel now?"

He looked at me a moment. "No wonder men have such a fragile sense," he said. And it was the most naked comment I'd ever heard him make. It was aimed at himself. Obviously, he found all this romance stuff a bit daunting. I didn't let on and I didn't give in to it. I pressed on.

"If you meet a girl at one bar, but get lost on the way and find your way to another crowded restaurant, and then go to a different dance hall later that night but wind up at someone's after-party at a house? That girl sitting at the end of the couch watching you come in, no matter how married, how involved, or how celibate she may claim to be, is also— one bad mood away from being with you. It's true of any woman, no matter where, at whatever time, in whatever place or station in their life. Look how many women end up with their bodyguards. Princess Stephanie, Patty Hearst. Why? They were right there when they became vulnerable. One bad mood away."

Sydney looked off and away. "I sat in on a casting for one of our new pictures. Some models were there."

I looked at him squarely. Again.

Fuck the models! I didn't say it but I thought it. Here I was racing around to get this mo-fo some unforgettable Dysfuncionado wildtime and here he was once again expressing a desire for that overexposed, low-probability, meteoric maintenance group. Silence blanketed the rear of the limo. That left the sounds of Monkey Man making the grumpy movements of a bitter have-not up front.

So Far

Monkey Man may have been a Mo-ron but he knew where to go. He turned off the Strip into the parking lot of the Sunset Motel. He'd been there before. The motel was legendary. Freshly arrived musicians, Strugs, and those contemplating the Move holed up there. Along with the nightly mates they scrounged up on the Boulevard. Lodging there made newly Woodies feel a part of it. Fast. It had the glow of the Strip and the taste of sleaze all around it.

Puddy was waiting there with her new golden strands being tugged by a light breeze. She had her entire suitcase. And the little bags that always accompany the big one. Like baby turtles following their mother. To come with us she had to move out of her room. I got out and kissed her on the cheek, then helped her with her bags and Monkey Man let me. Mo.

In her other hand, Puddy was holding something aloft with a cover on it. She looked springtime cheery in her white miniskirt and baby-blue baby T. It pronounced her chest and no one was confused. I bypassed Monkey Man and introduced her to Sydney. But Sydney introduced her to Monkey Man. I didn't apologize. Then we were off.

"So what's under the wrap?" I asked.

With that, she lifted the cover.

"It's my bird." And it was. It was more multicolored than a beach towel.

"What kind?"

"It's a love bird."

I accessed my mems on that breed. "Shouldn't it have a mate?"

"It has one."

"Where is it?"

"Right here. *Me*. Right, Francesco?"

Puddy had a love bird named Francesco. From Sydney's faint smile I could tell he considered that interesting. I considered it a check mark. Puddy was wonderfully wacky.

"But when I move here, I'm going to be gone a lot. On auditions and stuff. So I'm going to get it a mate."

"Another bird?"

"No, a cat." And she was on the verge of giggles when she said it.

"A cat?"

"Yup."

I looked at Sydney. I let him take it. "Excuse me, but you know cats make food out of birds," he stated politely.

"Yeah, but I want a cat. And I'll hang Francesco real high."

"Bad idea," I said. "You're aiming for a house pet version of *Wild Kingdom*."

"Well, I don't want him to be alone all day. Maybe I'll get him another love bird."

I decided to tease her. Her big playful grin told me she could take it.

"But then what will you do?"

"What do you mean?"

"Francesco will love the new mate. And not you."

She thought about that one. "That's when I'll get the cat!" she said demonically.

We all found humor in that. Puddy was good news. So far.

Saved by the Floyd

On the ride out to Manhattan Beach, Puddy gave us a seminar on the Midwest. She claimed to be tired of it. And the way she described it anyone would be. She had only been in town a few days and she was already sold on the Move.

We pulled off the San Diego Freeway and moved through the Manhattan Beach business district. Nature has a tough time surviving in Hell-A, was my thought. Even the beach towns choked off the greenery.

We glided up to a small bungalow on a small scrap of crabgrass. I stepped out and looked for Tammy. She soon emerged in something her parents would not have approved of. She was wearing a peach full-length slip-dress and a pair of see-through platform gels, almost as see-through as her slip, but the shoes' sparkles got in the way.

"So hot," she said, smiling.

I didn't tell her she looked great. She knew already. When we slipped back into the car, Sydney did a short squirm in his seat. He eyed both girlie-whirlies and then looked at me. He angled his head out the window to hide his smile. We got back in motion and I barked an order to Monkey Man because he'd been so unaccommodating to me all day.

"Can you pull over here?"

He looked in the rearview at Sydney, who nodded. *Mo.*

"What are you doing?" Puddy asked.

"Party favors," I answered with.

That was only half-true. I wanted the three of them to have a forced early moment together. To see if some synergistic give-and-take would be unleashed.

Moments later, I returned with a bag.

"What did you get?" Tammy asked. I let her hold the bag and look in. "Rods?"

"What good's a road trip without Rods?" I quipped.

"He's got Pop-Tarts, Doritos, and snack cakes too," she added.

"Not just snack cakes. Twinkies."

"Why did you buy all the junk?" Puddy asked.

"We're on holiday."

With that I mashed open the bag and cracked a Rod. I didn't have the heart to tell the others the trashy food was thematically correct for our upcoming voyage. But I thought it, digested it happily, and that's what counts. Let's not forget the phallic slant either. *Writers.* They're always looking in the oddest places for their little morsels of irony and symbolism. It gives them a perverse little charge. And they'll take one whenever they can. After all, they're usually despondent from not working, so why not soak up some good feeling when it comes? I was no different.

As I munched, Tammy cracked one too. So did Puddy. And Sydney was compelled to do the same. So there we were munching away on the long pretzel sticks wondering what might happen next on our little odyssey.

"What kind of name is that?" It was Tammy asking the question. To Puddy.

"Nickname," she shot back in a tone that cut further queries off. She didn't want to explain and that was it. At that moment, it seemed like we were in store for some friction. But I interjected and told Tammy a few things about Puddy's background. Then they discussed music and Puddy claimed to like grunge, while Tammy was a seventies rock and roll fan. They found commonality with Pink Floyd. What woman doesn't like the Floyd? I quickly slipped some in the limo deck. All was peaceful.

I must say I felt pretty damn good about the trip. The fact that I was getting away from L.A. made it all the better. Maybe I would come back and appreciate it more. I didn't bet on it.

Lady's Choice

All I can say is the Cristal champagne began flowing on the way to the airport and we were besieged by giggles and uncontrollable kindergarten behavior. We needed coloring books. And a Crayola 24-pack. Sydney couldn't believe his eyes. But when you get two spontaneous, original, unique, funny lunatics together, you've got enough raw power to light up Shea Stadium. Highlights included kisses for both of us by both girls, which gave no clues as to who was leaning toward whom in the flesh raffle. I considered us still back at romantic ground zero. Make that romantic par. We had progressed past ground zero.

The reason I popped the champagne in the limo was to induce a little *in vino veritas* probe. I wanted to know the early returns on which girl was interested in Sydney. If either. What I saw was Tammy sending a few questions his way. And him giving answers back she seemed to appreciate. She even smiled.

Puddy, however, was so busy alternately righting her miniskirt and blinding us with her bright yellow panties, in addition to playing footsy with me, that she had very little attention left for Sydney. As a result of my findings, I made sure the first-class flight attendant seated Tammy next to Sydney and Puddy next to me.

It all could change of course. We know girlie-whirlies. At any given time, they're you-know-how-many-moods-away from dumping present company and showing interest elsewhere. In any case, we were off to a good start, the potential heightened by Tammy nesting her tired, bubbled-up head on Sydney's shoulder. The booze in the car had made for the big sleep on the plane and I was sawing logs right along with the girlies. Sydney, however, stayed awake. He scanned company memos.

POST-IT: The plane ride overall was fine except for my usual desire to sucker-punch the Mos who clapped after the landing. I hate that, I really do. It's so rah-rah. I hate rah-rah. I hated the idea of all the fake spirit you're supposed to show for the team, or the school, or the town. It made you feel part of a mass of dependent, needy, parasitic, nonindividuated, Simon-says, sheeplike rejects.

The rest of the journey was pretty standard.

I administered Advil to the girls when they awoke. It was dark out and we wanted to get to our lodging. We retrieved our luggage quickly and took our rental car to the Blueswater Motel. We had a choice between Memphis's version of a four-star hotel, a middle-ranged number, and your sawdust, low-life motel. We went for the sawdust. It was my decision and I know you understand why.

The front desk clerk, Ansel, had a southern drawl that twanged around the block. Old Ansel was a dirty son of a bitch too. After telling us about the region's nightlife, he warned the girls about the mechanical bull.

"Watch out for that auto-bull down in Genny. You're likely to come back with a bald monkey."

The girls loved it. They even asked Ansel to join us. That's how off and beyond these two were.

We ordered three rooms between us. Sydney checked in as Sydney Swinburn. The girls checked in as themselves. And I checked in as Boy George. Sydney and I each took a single and the girls shared a double. It wasn't that they loved each other so much. I think they were scared of being alone in a fleabag motel.

After showering and giving stick to my underarms, I knocked on Sydney's door. I felt we needed a preliminary chat.

"How are we doing?" he asked as he was putting on a button-down.

"Fine."

"Should I wear this or a T-shirt?"

"T-shirt."

"Really?"

"It's up to you. But that's what I think."

I felt Sydney needed to be stripped down to ordinary, accessible dimensions. And I told him so. He opted for the T-shirt.

"Puddy's into you," Sydney then asserted.

"You think?"

"Totally."

"I wasn't so sure. I felt it at first but then I felt a frost come over her.

But that could be her way. Tell me about Tammy. You making progress?"

"I don't know. We talked a lot."

"It looked pretty animated."

"We talked about everything. Her growing up in Fairbanks, Alaska. Her old boyfriend. What she likes in a guy."

"Perfect," I said resolutely. "What does she like? Or what does she say she likes?"

"There is a difference, isn't there?" It made him think about it and then replay the ear music she'd gaven him to see if this new filter altered his impressions.

Finally, he said with a sigh, "Sincerity. She's tired of playboys. Wants to settle down."

"That's standard. The quasi-virginal stuff. She wants you to respect her. She's learned the importance of it. What are her interests?"

He looked straight through my question and locked on me straighter. "But I don't think she's . . . into me."

I couldn't tell if he was serious or he just wanted to probe my brain and get my read, or if he was begging for a belt of confidence. Probably all three. When it comes to women they can split and divide your thoughts like no one else. Insecurity is always waiting on deck for its chance at bat.

"She's probably intimidated. I mean it's a girl like that's dream to land a guy like you. You kiddin' me?"

"Yeah . . ." It came out extra hollow.

"No 'yeah,'" I mimicked. "Yeah!" I exclaimed it. "And maybe she doesn't know it yet. But by the end of this trip, she will."

"I thought she might be into you."

"Me? I didn't even talk to her."

"But she was looking at you a lot."

"'Cause she knows me. I'm familiar. Puts her in her comfort zone."

"I'm serious, I think she likes you."

"All right, if a switch takes place, and I'm not saying it will, but if it does, hey, it's Lady's Choice."

"What do you mean?"

"I mean in the end, it's their decision, not yours."

"How come?"

"They're going to get involved with whoever they want. For whatever reason. Looks, money, astrological propaganda, or some perceived connection. You can't force a mismatch. You can't force a guy down a girl's throat any more than a girl can be forced down yours. Even less so. 'Cause you might take the wildtime anyway. Lady's Choice, Sydney."

"So?" he asked.

"So we go with the flow."

He made it for about ten more seconds and he had another question for me. He really was nervous.

"What about protection?"

"What about it?"

"Do you use condoms?"

"No."

"You don't?"

"Nope. Rubber gloves."

"What?"

"I use rubber gloves. You know, the kind with five fingers."

"Bull."

"No bull."

"Why?"

"A condom works once. A rubber glove you can use five times."

"You're kidding." He paused. I was poker-faced.

"You're right, Sydney. I'm kidding."

And we both broke it, him harder than me. And that's what I wanted to do. Get him laughing. To get rid of his jitters.

Tennessee Cat Scratch

We found the dive bar Ansel suggested and pulled in. It was between our motel and Memphis. The dirt driveway was packed with redneck vehicles and clinging paraphernalia. Confederate flags, decals, and stickers. Our rental car took a slot and was dwarfed by monster trucks with wheels as big as merry-go-rounds. We slipped in. I sensed our entrance would be noticed. The girls looked pretty fresh. And the cultural clash was immediately obvious.

The bar was called Ronny's or Bobby's or something like that. The matches wouldn't tell me. They were generic and advertised a massage service on one side and low-priced lawyers on the other, which, in the Age of A, was a suitable pairing. I was grazing elbows with Tammy at the bar. She was telling me about being a contestant in the Hawaiian Tropic beauty pageant. We were talking in a shit-kickin', chicken-lickin', finger-snappin' kind of way. The joint seemed to bring it out in us.

"Did you win?"

"Hell no. I came in second. But I shoulda."

Coulda been a model, coulda been Ms. Hawaiian Tropic. There's always a hierarchy of couldas and shouldas, was my thought. With writers too. If I didn't achieve a breakthrough soon I was gonna be the Coulda Been Scribe.

"Who won?"

"Some girl from Alabama," she scoffed. "But I had a good time," she added.

Meanwhile, Sydney was making good time with Puddy. I ordered another round of beers and some buffalo wings and cheese fries. Beside me at the bar was a southern Thickie with his straw-haired barroom sweetie. She looked like a real veteran of this bar, of all bars. And this town. And all towns. She would bark orders and jokes at everyone in earshot, with a deep voice that had been cracked long ago from too many cigarettes. Her smoker's voice and cackle could have sent dogs whimpering. She had that unpredictability in her gaze too, the one all alcoholics do, only more so. I won't leave out the South's-Gonna-Do-It-Again brands and the nasty scar above her brow. I figured scars were the adhesives holding up her overworked skeleton.

Her friend, the Alabama Thickie, had a set of guns on him that could have collared a mammoth. He had a big-ass Robert E. Lee tat on his shoulder. If we were in search of some astonishing Bianco Trash, which we were, we had just found big game. The bar was off-the-charts redneck.

Sydney, on his way to the bathroom, slapped my shoulder and redirected my attention back to our own girlies. In comparison to the rest of the gals, they seemed like reluctant debutantes. Or so I thought. I watched Puddy slam down a shot of something gold. That's when everything started to change a little. I looked into her eyes and she smiled back. It was as if I was looking at another person. Or someone close. But not her. I hoped that wasn't the case.

"So you were in the Hawaiian Tropic pageant?" I heard Puddy ask Tammy. And she didn't say it so sweetly.

"Yeah . . ."

"Didn't you feel weird?"

"How do you mean?"

"Well, I mean kind of stupid? All those jerks slobbering all over you. And . . ."

"Not at all. I think it was a great opportunity."

"Opportunity for what?" Puddy spat back derisively.

This was an odd development. I didn't see it coming. I thought everything was copacetic between the two. Prior to this, they'd treated each other with politeness. And they had even spent some time in the motel room together. The booze must have given the underlying tension a shove. Puddy was now abrupt, deliberate, and devoid of the shyness she'd displayed in the daylight hours.

Tammy sensed Puddy's judgmental slant but ignored it. For the time being. She answered offhandedly.

"Well, I got a lot of work from it."

"What kind of work?" Puddy threw back with a snicker. Then looked at us. "Hide-a-Bed maintenance?" And she laughed too.

"Yeah, whatever."

I decided to intervene. "Tammy does commercials. Lots."

"Besides, the pageant paid well," she followed up with.

Puddy bobbed and nodded condescendingly. Her boozy refills had obviously hit her system and reactivated all the slurp we'd consumed on the plane. She was still buzzed. I hoped she wasn't what I feared, the type whose personality changed along with it. But I had that uneasy feeling. She was Indiana field mouse sweet on one side. But on the other, who knew? She was an Unknown. I was relieved to see her drift quietly over to the music box and flip through the catalog. But I knew this much. She left Tammy with that "you whore" feeling.

"Are you okay?" I asked gently.

She was silent but resembled a dam ready to break. She couldn't hold off. "How do you know that girl?"

"I don't, really," I said.

"Nice find," she said sarcastically. And it took something for Tammy to use sarcasm. It wasn't in her nature.

"Didn't you make friends in the room?"

"There wasn't time. I took a shower. And she drank."

"Drank what?"

"That bottle she snagged off the plane."

I said something forgettable, just to downplay the significance of what I was being told. I wanted to keep things on an even keel. It was my responsibility.

I sensed something foul in the air. It wasn't a smell or a disturbance. It was something intangible. A feeling of dark energy bordering on ill-will. I decided our best move was to get the hell out of there. But before I could assemble everyone, shit happened.

It began like this: An unidentified country song burst through the speakers from the juke. Puddy rejoined us with a little dance step. But when she looked over at me I could see the look in her face had changed. Her expression showed an unpredictability, even danger. The alcohol was registering in the way her eye slashed severely. Her movements were now blunt and careless. She slapped the bartop twice.

"Bartender, let's have a couple Cuervos for me and my pal, Miss Hawaiian Tropic."

"No," Tammy interjected. "I don't like liqueurs."

Puddy laughed. "It's not liqueur. It's tequila," she said with more attitude.

"I don't like tequila."

"Yes you do."

"No I don't."

"Come on, precious. Loosen up."

"I am loose."

"You're not loose. You're a trained seal."

"What the hell is that supposed to mean?"

"Arf! Arf!"

"Fuck off," Tammy snapped.

"Ooh. Ms. Hawaiian Tropic just said a bad word."

And the local bar folk started to get interested.

"Easy, you guys," I said.

"Who do you think you are?" Tammy continued with.

"Me. And not a jewel less," Puddy countered.

"Yeah, well you and your prime-time pussy can take it and shove it."

"Bitch!"

And Puddy's arm motion knocked a beer mug off the bartop, sending the suds down the shirt of the Thickie's woman.

"Hey! Knock it off, you two!" she cracked.

They looked over. The husky redneck gal was glaring at them.

But Puddy was already in provoke-and-fight mode. She wasn't going to take nothin' from nobody.

"Who asked you?"

"No one's gotta ask me nothin'. I say what I want when I want and that's all there is to it. Got it, honey chile?"

"Honey chile? You guys hear that? Chile. You damn ass-backwards southern bitch and three-quarters."

"What did you say, sister?"

"I said don't move over here."

"I don't think you heard me. I go wherever I damn well please. And no scrawny Yankee bitch is going to say otherwise. Got it?"

"Don't be calling her names," Tammy interjected.

That was an interesting twist. In times of trouble, Tammy was standing tall for a gal who had insulted her massively minutes before. It was an odd show of sisterhood.

"Oh, is that a chirp I heard from the airheaded dumb bitch with the blimpy tits?"

Then it came down like lightning. Puddy gave the redneck woman a backhand the likes of which I'd never seen. The woman reeled against the bar. Then surged at her, grabbing Puddy by the throat. Tammy then lunged at them, grabbed the woman to pull her off. And a full-fledged catfight was in session with all the southern fixings.

I lunged forward to break it up but the Alabama Thickie and his buddy squared opposite Sydney and me, the way hockey players neutralize each other off during a brawl.

The redneck woman was tough and certainly our girls were no match for her on their own. This woman could last a few rounds with any tough guy. She was a real sweetie.

Puddy got the Redneck Sweetie's grip off her neck but the Sweetie got hold of Puddy's collar, tearing it all the way down to Puddy's chest. Her breasts just poured out. By this time Tammy had the Sweetie in a headlock and had pulled her to the ground. Again Sydney and I just looked at each other, incredulous.

What was most shocking was that no one tried to, or dared to, break up the fight. The spectacle created a boxing-arena-style frenzy. The patrons of Bobby's Bar were eating it up. I made another move to break up the two but the Thickie shoved me back. I didn't like being touched, but the numbers against us told me I shouldn't crack-wise.

We watched tensely. To remove herself from the lock, the Redneck Sweetie got serious. She started grabbing. Grabbing at anything she could get a grip on. That involved thrusting a hand up Tammy's mini-mini and I swear to God, holding her like a six-pack, meaning she stuck her thumb and her index finger in the only available holes and yanked until Tammy screamed in agony. That pissed Puddy off. Like a team of sisters who hate each other, but hate outsiders even more, they made the Redneck Sweetie pay.

Puddy gave her a buck to the head and blood flowed freely from her nostrils. Then came the hair pulling. Puddy had a hunk of the Sweetie's fried locks, and when her hair gave, Puddy had a fistful of it. It started to get more ugly and finally the cheering men had had enough. So they grabbed hold of their roughette while Sydney and I separated our girls from them.

All would have been jake but suddenly I saw Sydney shoot forward with a grimace. As he hit the floor face-first, I saw what had caused it.

A jealous, Yankee-hating, territorial, southern-fried, country-ass, fat fuck, in an International Harvester cap, standing over him like the conquering caveman. And from the looks of him looking at me, he wasn't done.

"Come on, poster boy," he growled.

I charged him and gave him a stick that knocked him backward an inch. But no more. He looked up and gave me a fist to the nose that felt like a burro kick. But what really pissed me off was that he followed up by spitting in my face. I don't know if the following events happened or not because they linger on in my mind like some far-off dream. But I think a manifestation of some less than subtle frustration had been requested of me. Let's not forget that I always had some kind of brewing reserve of angst. The angst of the unaccomplished. It boiled over.

A two-fisted bolo punch whacked said fat fuck into a stunned, stagnant, stupid stand. He moved neither forward nor back. He was standing there bobbing like a buoy. That's when I drove a fist right through him. It was intended to connect somewhere around his face but it hit his chin and this tub went down like a pop machine.

I didn't feel the arms of my mates pulling me out and into the car. I do remember a towel wrapping Sydney's bleeding head. He looked at me and I looked at him. We were in the backseat together. Puddy was driving. Tammy was seated right beside her sweetly holding her hand. Though I was in pain, that vision was a comfort.

Sydney combed my face expecting a comment. I didn't have one.

"How about them Dysfuncionados," he whispered instead. It made me laugh. Sure, it was sarcastic. I thought of the dissertation I'd given him on the dysfunctional breeds: their rich interiors; their colorful behavior. And here we were bleeding profusely from our first date. It was the funniest thing I ever heard Sydney say.

I laughed harder. Until he joined me. Until the girls asked what was up. When we had no answer but laughter, the girls started to laugh too. We were one hell of a sight. Four bleeding and bruised itinerants only four hours into our white trash holiday. Laughing to old Boston riffs in a rental car. And the gas gauge still read almost full.

"Let's go back to the motel," I suggested.

"Let's make one stop first," Puddy countered with.

"What for?"

She didn't answer, which was okay. My attitude had changed about her during that cat fight and it fell somewhere between shock and respect. I saw all those tough, hard, trashy years come out in her flash of animalism. She was no Field Mouse Tourist. If she was going to make the Move, it was Hell-A that would have to do some bracing. Not her. I liked her for that.

When she emerged from the spirits shop, she had three bottles and they all had the same black label. Jack. The finest over-the-counter Tennessee whiskey.

"I asked for some shine but he said they were all out," she added. No one protested.

After a long silence, and the bumps of the road hurting my frame, I broke all the quiet with:

"I feel like shit."

"I do too" came a second opinion.

"I'm wasted" was a third.

"I hurt all over," a fourth.

"Fuck." It was the last thing we heard. And it didn't matter who said it.

Walls No More

We had a radio and four plastic cups. And that was all we needed. We knocked on their door.

"It's open," Tammy said.

"Like my head," Sydney cracked as we stepped in.

Puddy was lying on her bed when we slipped through their door. We heard the shower turn off and some bad plumbing noises.

"Do we want to move?" Sydney asked.

"To where?" Puddy chimed.

"Another hotel. A better one."

"Why? I love this place," she said.

"Yeah, who wants to move? I can barely walk," I muttered as I limped over to Puddy's bed and sat down lightly. I was favoring everything, which means I had no control. It hurt big when I settled down on my ass.

Tammy emerged from the bathroom in a cloud of mist and a towel wrapped around her which covered the serious stuff. But barely. Her body was bursting out of it.

She chuckled slightly when she said, "Motel towels are always so small."

Though Sydney and I didn't miss the flesh sighting, it didn't have the same raw power it would have had we not been involved in such an absurd melee an hour before. The nervous tension that comes with members of the opposite sex meeting and wondering all the psychological uncertainties of *will he like me?, will she like me?, can I get close to her?, what does she look like naked?, how enthusiastically does she make love?, does she like oral sex?, does she like giving it?*, etc. . . . It flies out the window when you've shared a scene as colorful and delicious as a catfight followed by an all-out brawl. There was no tension in the room. If you wanted tension you would have had to pay big coin for it. The ice had not only been broken but melted and sent off in a mist to make the air just a little more moist.

And this holiday condition—no walls, no barriers, no tension—was exactly what I'd hoped for. It was what we needed. A quiet existential moment in the motel with everyone in the same space saying nothing but with a collective consciousness that could have conquered the rest of the county. We were a team. We were brothers and sisters. We were lovers. We were anything we wanted to be.

At that moment, I knew it was all over. For them. And for us. Our trip was a success waiting to begin. The bowling pins were standing straight. All we had to do was send the ball down the lane. At this hour, only retards need not apply. We were going to close in on the negative spaces. We were going to take them down. Hard.

The Layup

When the girls apologized to each other and hugged, Sydney leaned in to me. "This is genius."

"That brawl was genius," I added. "I didn't plan on that."

"Did we get our Breakthrough?"

And that made us both laugh.

It was like every cliché old movie you've seen that shows a man and woman getting together. One actor, usually the male lead, gets hurt while performing heroic deeds, and the woman must care for him. She cleans the wound, bandages him, caresses him, feeds him. It's meant to be erotic. Then she kisses him into a dissolve into the next day, which in those days meant they have wildtime. As a screenwriter I knew it was an easy play. And you would try not to use it. Too easy. Overdone. A crutch. All the four of us had to do was administer a little first aid to each other and we'd all be on easy street.

The first move was not a pass or a sexual advance. It involved cracking one of those amber soldiers. I poured while Sydney held the cups.

"Now, it's a layup," I whispered to him.

"How do you mean?"

"It's all over."

"Think so?"

"Sure."

"What should we do?"

"They're bruised and battered. Let's just play doctor. In addition we have three quarts of whiskey. *Layup*."

Sydney went on an ice run and came back with a bucket and four towels. He filled each towel with ice. Each of us had a different body part that had been injured and needed to be targeted with cool. Sydney had a huge bump on the back of his head. Puddy had a cut on her hand. But Tammy was hurt the most. She'd had her privates mauled by the beer-hold the Redneck Sweetie had on her. And my nose was swollen. Comparatively, I felt my injuries were pretty unmacho.

POST-IT: The word *grim*. It's the most contagious word I know. I added it to my vocabulary at Brown. It has so many uses. As a kid you said gross, and later, disgusting, bogus, and repulsive. But grim says it all. Everywhere I go, usage of it is immediately imitated. It describes any unpleasant or ugly situation succinctly and without need for follow-up. I love the word. One of my favorites.

Remember how in high school you did stuff together as kids and you just fell into your crushes and went from there? Romances occurred naturally and were born out of nature and natural activity. Not some contrived meeting or date in which you both gave conversational curricula vitae in between Caesar salads and another warmed-over life-inventory roll call between your entree and dessert. And then you were poised to decide whether you wanted to make out, grope, or have sex. Or not. Going to Graceland was like going to the Malibu Grand Prix. Or back to high school. It was just on a grander scale.

We all lay down on the big bed and commiserated silently. Puddy held ice to my nose. Sydney lay back on his ice pack. And everyone wanted to administer ice to Tammy and her privates.

After a few minutes of calm after the mighty storm, Puddy shot up from the bed and made an announcement.

"Fuck it!"

"Say what?" I said.

She moved over to the little table and poured herself another shot. Immediately, she slammed it home and lit up. "Redneck bitch," she scoffed.

I beckoned her to pour me one and she did.

"Come on, Sydney," I urged. Then I snapped on the shitty bedside radio. "Searchin' for a Rainbow" by the Marshall Tucker Band was playing and I loved hearing it.

Before long, we were all singing along, doing shots, multiple shots, for no other reason than our bodies were making the right movements necessary for debauched boozing, and there wasn't anything else to do. We certainly didn't want to go out again. It would have been okay for Sydney and me but these two Dysfuncionados fueled on booze were too unpredictable. Whatever we were going to do had to be within arm's reach. And that wasn't a letdown. After all, anything we wanted was. Anything *Sydney* wanted, that is.

After everyone was sufficiently sloshed, we traded first-fuck stories. All of us except Puddy. She didn't like the game. She said hers wasn't very interesting, not that ours were. Mine involved inserting myself in some girl and then not moving. I didn't know you had to pump to hump. I thought it just happened. That magically you would get this surge of erotic feeling and then blast off from the mere fact that you were inside. Sure, I was a moron. If there was ever anyone I never wanted to see again, it was that girl. I was sure she had told the whole world what a lousy fuck I was. And I had been.

It reminded Tammy of a joke. "Why do so many women fake orgasms?" We weren't sure. "Because they think men care." It was a bad joke, so bad we were rolling on the floor, crying with laughter.

That's when it happened. Sydney made a power move and all it involved was lying on his side and facing Tammy. From there, he caressed her leg. I almost forgot to tell you. Tammy never got dressed. She was still wrapped in that little motel towel. So sexy. So accessible. A brainstorm wasn't needed to tell me to fake the Packer Power Sweep left and head back to my room.

"Where are you going?" Puddy asked.

"To change my shirt." It had gotten wet from the melted ice in the towel.

My move was premised on knowing Puddy would eventually feel uncomfortable staying there. Not even eventually. She upped, slammed another shot, grabbed the last bottle of J.D., and opened the door for me. No one behind us objected, asked for the time, or gave us any message to hook up later. We left in a puff of silence.

Word on Tammy

The next morning I woke up with a whiplash snap. And adrenaline shot through me. I wasn't sure why. I looked around. It was a room unfamiliar to me. Puddy was in the other twin bed. Her ass was hanging out of the covers so I knew she was fully naked. Certain things came back but a vicious Jack head sting overrode them. It made it unfun to piece it together. But my adrenaline surge had nothing to do with me. I was anxious to hear what had happened to Sydney.

I sat up on the edge of the bed. Then I saw a shadow walk across the window and stay there. Someone was looking in. I opened the door the width of the latch. Sydney was there grinning like a schoolboy in June. His smile was contagious. I cracked one wide.

"Let's get some coffee," I said.

And we took off in the car and landed in a grits diner. I ordered the omelette special.

"So give me the word on Tammy."

"Oh, man, you can't believe it," he said with a waterfall of glee pouring forth. "We started having this conversation. I mean, really weird. She's telling me about her move from Alaska and her dad who beat her up and all that stuff, which was fine. You know, real Bianco Trash. The good stuff."

Don't think I didn't consider it a victory that Sydney, the power guy, Mr. Greenlight, had incorporated my language into his own. What he wasn't aware of was how that Trash moniker now made me cringe. Or why.

"But then she went into this talk about, you're not going to believe it. I asked her, 'So what do you want to do with your life?' She said she wanted to buy a farm out in Idaho or Montana."

" 'A farm?' I asked."

" 'Yeah, you know, with horses,' she responded."

" 'Like a ranch?' "

" 'Oh, I'd love a ranch. Yeah. In fact, I've been looking already.' "

" 'You have the money?' "

" 'Some. But after my egg sale, I'll have enough for the full down payment.' "

" 'Your egg sale?' "

" 'Yeah.' "

" 'What's that?' "

" 'I'm selling my eggs.' "

" 'Your eggs?' "

" 'Yes.' "

" 'What eggs do you have?' "

" '*My* eggs.' "

" 'Like from the ovaries?' "

" 'No, my pet chicken's eggs. Of course my eggs.' "

" 'I see.' Then I told her I didn't think it was such a good idea. To sell her eggs."

"What did she say to that?"

"Well, she tried to rationalize it. Like she would never see the children. That it wouldn't come from her womb."

"And what did you say?"

"I said, 'Yeah, but what about the fact that there would be someone out there with your genes, your genetic map, someone with your color hair and eyes, personality, and cleft chin? Wouldn't that make you feel weird?' "

"Good," I mouthed with the tone of a coach's approval.

"Guess what happened next?"

"She cried."

"How did you know?" And he had a look of surprise.

So I told him.

It wasn't all magic. It's very simple psychology. When confronted with the dark stuff they've been suppressing for years, the Dysfuncionados lose it, break down, and cry. Like most people. But here's the difference. Since emotional turmoil has oftentimes been coupled with random acts of kindness in their past, they naturally seek support. Like some token warmth. I'm talking being broken down and sexually maneuvered. In many cases, it's all they know. It's where they get their jolts of self-esteem. In times of turmoil, Dysfuncionados get wildly sexual. And expect to. The more turmoil, the more the turn-on. It's dysfunctional for sure, but if it's all you know, it's all you know.

"Are you telling me you got laid?"

He broke the big grin. "It was great," he blasted. "She's so sexy. I mean everything. We did almost everything."

He then stopped and looked straight at me. Almost like his mind had slammed on the brakes. He extended a paw.

"I want to thank you. It was one of the best, if not the best, nights of my life."

"Cheers," and we touched coffee cups. I smiled. For him. It wasn't for me, I knew that. My night had made for a different kind of memory. The kind you like to forget.

And not surprisingly, he turned the question on me. "So what happened with Puddy?" he asked.

In answer to his question I responded somewhat flatly, somewhat reservedly, and somewhat deceptively. In essence, I bullshitted my ass off and it took one word to do it.

"Nothing."

"What?" and he was incredulous.

"Nothing happened." His mouth was still on a lower floor. "We just went to sleep."

"You're kidding me."

"You know me, Sydney. I'm not active."

That was true. I wasn't active. But like I said before, it really behooves you to know your subject when it comes to women like Tammy and Puddy. The No Surprises Law is important. Because what unfolded on that strange, brawl-filled and J.D.-drenched night in Tennessee, I definitely hadn't been prepared for.

Untold Tales

The previous night, when we'd slipped out to leave Sydney and Tammy be, Puddy had followed me to my room. She planted at the little desk, forearmed away the Bible atop, mashed open the last bottle of Jack, and took a big slam. As soon as she finished guzzling, she started telling me about her life, knowledge I should have had prior to her joining us, but there hadn't been time. And had I known what she was about to tell me, I would have never taken her to Elvis country.

It all started when she stumbled over to the bed I was lying on. She was drunk as hell, and the Breakthroughs we had experienced in the salon and in the bar were enough for her to be stripped of any fears of me, and so she planted a wide 90-proof smooch on my kisser. The brand of fluid that came with it was only slightly diluted by her saliva and tasted like half a shot on its own.

She lay next to me and grabbed me in the area of my basket and I pushed away her hand.

"Are you okay?"

"Yeah . . ."

"Don't you like girls?"

"I like girls fine."

"Come on, really. What's your deal?"

Of course I told her what I told everyone.

"What the hell is that supposed to mean?" she asked.

"That means my switches are turned off."

"Oh yeah?"

"Yeah."

"Bullshit."

I took a swig of our amber friend and said nothing.

"Every guy I know who is *not active* as you say, it means they're soft. Or close to it."

Soft. I loved hearing it. It was a great word for the term *homosexual.* And what was surprising was it came from her, which means it must have come from her home state of Indiana. But the term seemed too advanced and jaded to come from there. On further reflection, I realized gals like Puddy are privy to all sorts of road color, weird run-ins, and personal odysseys in general, that normal citizens just never experience. You can't really categorize a Dysfuncionado by the normal qualities of their region or state. Their dysfunctional character makes them much more a student of the world, and, usually, the darker side of it. I wondered no longer how Puddy had a term like *soft* in her arsenal. I quickly put it in mine.

"Maybe I'm soft. Or close to it."

She yanked at my zipper and I pushed her away again. She sat up and lit up. A long gap of nothing happened. Then she turned away for another noiseless gap. The outdoor light that was streaming through the window found a home on the thin stream of water that was breaking new ground on her shadowed face. It was a beautiful stream. So free. It let me know what was happening to her. And it was my turn to ask.

"Are you okay?"

She nodded and wiped her face.

"What's the matter?"

She shook.

"Tell me. What's the matter?"

She said nothing. I leaned forward and touched her shoulder. The mere touch made the dam break. She erupted in a kind of sobbing that turned into convulsive heaves. I held her close, but the heaves kept coming. I felt very sorry for her. And I felt even sorrier when she told me her stepfather had murdered her mother the year before and had gotten away with the murder completely. It was an awful tale especially since this stepdaddy had stormed into Puddy's room one night and introduced her to his brand of darkness.

I asked her what happened. And now I wished I hadn't.

"He was beating the hell out of Mama, like usual," she sobbed. "And I heard her cry and yell and scream. Like usual. Only this time I couldn't take it anymore."

"What did you do?"

"I yelled at him. Told him he was a drunk. And a mean sonofabitch. I said other things too. That he was a little man. In every way. A very little man. A coward. For beating on her that way."

Then there was a pause that I couldn't let linger.

"What did he do?"

She heaved. And sobbed. Then her chest quieted.

"He stopped."

"Beating her?"

She nodded. And then broke down again.

"Is that all he did?" I sensed it wasn't. Then a fist of dread hit me in the chest.

"No," she let go quietly.

"What did he do?"

"He came into my room. I was in bed. With the lights out. When he found me he slapped me. In the face. And he ripped open the covers. I was just lying there. In a nightgown. He tore away the nightgown. And started touching me."

"Did you fight him?"

"No."

"Why not?"

"I just wanted him to stop beating Mama. I didn't care what he did . . . ," she cried. "To me," she added.

"Stop," I said. I'd had enough. I didn't like what was happening. To me.

"No, I want to tell you," she shot back. "I've never told anyone."

She collected, then gave me a difficult burst with all the harmony of a mouth trembling and a voice cracking in two.

"He ripped off my nightgown. Then . . . I had never done it before."

It became clear why Puddy hadn't offered up her tale of The First Time with the group earlier.

"Then he turned me over. You know, the way drunk men do. And continued to do it. Then he went away. And I went to sleep." She paused and I wasn't sure why. "He came back a couple hours later. My eyes were barely open and . . ." She cracked into sobs. I held both her hands. Tight.

"Don't."

". . . he grabbed me by the back of the neck and made me . . ." She couldn't finish it. And that was okay with me. "And he told me he was going to beat up Mama every night unless I did what he wanted."

There was just a hallway's worth of silence. No other sounds enveloped us.

"Why didn't you leave?" I said eventually.

"I couldn't leave her. I knew he would hurt her if I did. And I wanted to finish school. Mama wanted me to graduate."

Twin tears made it down my face on that last line. More than two went down hers.

"How old were you when he did this?"

"Fifteen."

"When did you leave?"

"When I graduated."

So he did this to you for two years?

I asked only in my mind. Somehow she heard it anyway. Because her face was a wash of water when she looked to me. And then her eyes drifted absently down my torso. When she spotted the lump in my pants, her eyes gripped shortly, then raised again to mine. We just looked at each other.

"I'm sorry," she said.

"Don't be."

"I needed to tell someone. It's been so long. I've held it in. I just wanted someone else to know. What some men do."

I kissed her on the forehead. Then I got up from the bed.

"Where are you going?" she asked.

I closed the bathroom door behind me. I stood there in the darkness and let my mind process her horror. I thought about the millions of stories just like Puddy's, now and over time, that never get told, that never get resolved, that never get a trial for justice, that never give the victim the benefit of the doubt, that never allow the victim a right to a free and happy life—that ruin them forever.

I settled on the toilet cover. And wiped my face. And cursed myself. For being part of the same creed as her stepdaddy. And all those grim motherfuckers from those untold tales.

I wondered why our biology was set up in such a way that I could get aroused from hearing a story that served as someone's life-altering pain. It didn't seem right. I'd experienced the sensation before in certain movie scenes. Was it a dysfunction singular to me? Was it the male in me? Or was it the animal? I wondered if I was the only one. I didn't think so.

We're all animals, I decided. And, sometimes, it manifests itself in ugly forms. That's all there is to it.

My little bathroom séance was over.

Eventually, I traipsed back into the bedroom. As I lay down, Puddy coiled beside me and wrapped an arm across my chest. I kissed her on the cheek. Her eyes had dried up, her breathing was normal again, and a look of peace, satisfaction, and contentment had come over her. I held on to her warmly, gently, and didn't let go.

Then I saw her eyes die. She fell asleep in my arms. I watched her have puppy dreams with all the shudders and jerks. She talked a bit too. I was sure she had her own nightly stage. With a library of horrifying home movies housed in her head, who wouldn't? I caressed her as she slept and I stayed up long after she'd switched positions.

I never told Sydney Swinburn what Puddy had told me. There are just some things you should never divulge. That was Puddy's private horror. And releasing it to others could only hurt her.

That night with Puddy in that grim little hotel on our grim little holiday in Tennessee was one of the strangest I had ever experienced. It was also the night I swore off Bianco Trash. And Dysfuncionados. Forever. The terms went with it.

After several refills, Sydney and I returned to the motel. The girls eventually woke and did what girls usually do after a night of drinking, fighting, and frolicking. They showered. We reconvened for a late break-fast and then made a strong move. We took the next flight back to Star Camp.

The reality is, nobody gave a damn about staying. We were sore from the brawl and hung over from the J.D. After all, we hadn't flown there to visit that tacky tourist shrine to Elvis anyway. With all due respect to the King, whose name I respected but whose music I never liked, nobody gave a good goddam about Graceland. We never even saw it. Or gave it another thought. We partied and fought in Tennessee and that was enough. And that's how our holiday came to an end. If the South was going to do it again, they were going to do it on somebody else's time. Not ours.

A Pebble for Your Thoughts

As soon as I slipped inside my door, I was manning the phone. I had re-ceived so many calls I was impressed. I also noticed that several delicate objects were resting on the floor. The remote, my pens, and, in the kitchen, a broken glass. This meant there had been a mild quake. Or aftershock.

The phone never seems to ring when you're sitting around looking at the cheap art on your walls, contemplating your pamphlet of a life and what went wrong and whether you should be doing something else. But when you're out there, making things happen—anything—like fighting and fornicating down south, the world has a way of missing you. And calls in.

The most exciting call came from a revered agent at the revered International Creative Management agency, one of the most powerful talent trusts in the business and, therefore, the world. Marty was his name and he wanted to meet me. I'd been recommended to him by Ruth Yizerman, and he asked me to drop by midweek. An immediate sit-down between a creditless scenariste and a power agent was a real rarity.

The evenings prior to my meeting, I arranged some nice tables for Sydney and me and he snared two more dates out of them. Again, the invitees were carefully selected from my Gold files. One was a black girl named Chenille. Chenille worked the bar at an offbeat restaurant downtown. The other girl was a Wam named Patti though I nicknamed her Boldface. She was pretty but her features were just too pronounced. Her eyebrows were too bushy, her eyes bulged, she had a short forehead, and a chin that jutted out like a pier. But she had a world-class keister and Sydney found her sexy.

Even as I played attentive at the dinners, my mind was elsewhere. On that superagent meeting to be specific. On the day of my meeting, I got up early, made a pot of flavored, and primed my mind with some Radio Stern. No matter what you think about him, to listen to his banter is a quick clinic in wit and repartee. I wore a pastel shirt to show sensitivity, and a black blazer over that to demonstrate I was not a pushover. Dark clothes make you appear more assertive. I wore my favorite pants, the ones that made me feel bony. I loved feeling bony. I loved the thought of being thin. The trousers were magically cut to make me feel svelte, in good shape, and ready to take some money from someone.

I didn't forget my pebble either. Whenever I had meetings I placed a pebble in my shoe. When I walked, the little stone would irritate and annoy me. It was a way of keeping my Blade sharp and my angst intact.

I'm not going to bore you with a description of the cloud I was floating on during the ride over, or the fact that I didn't even hear the Sled's muffler music. I'm not going to mention the satisfaction I got from seeing those smiling faces at ICM belonging to people who didn't know who I was. But since I was in the building looking sufficiently underfed, pasty, and angst-ridden to be a genius, they treated me like I might be the newest Tolstoy. I'm just not going to bore you.

Other than to tell you Marty was very cool, so cool, he was *kewell*. He told me he wanted to represent me. He advised me to write a spec. I pitched him a few stories, he selected the most commercial and told me to go nuts. And to call him whenever I wanted advice, story help, or to bounce any ideas off him. *Kewell.*

A Clink and a Sip

I was so ecstatic I zoomed over to Sydney's place. Docking the Sled in front of his house created a formidable contrast, not to mention humor. On a purely metallic level, minus sentimental attachments, my car was worth less than his front door knob. And all the other knobs too.

"Nice doorknob," I said to Armando, his valet, as I slipped inside.

"You like that?"

I nodded. Because I did. The finer things in life I appreciated and was accustomed to somewhat. They still resided peacefully in my backstory, heritage propaganda included.

Sydney was in his study, seated at his desk. He had been in meetings all day. He was in a lighter afternoon mood and it seemed as if he was reflecting on his life that evening. He just smiled when I stepped in. It was a friendship smile and showed our bond had taken on another notch of firmness. Clearly, our holiday was a smash. I was happy for that.

"I'd like to thank you for setting me up with Marty Abrams."

"How did it go?"

And I told him.

"Good" was all he said. Then he stood up and asked me to follow him. We stepped out of his study, went down the hall, through the living room, giving greetings to Monet's *Lilies in the Field* along the way. We were a minute into our walk when we finally reached the French doors that opened out to the patio. We sashayed across the patio and down the back steps. Sydney remained curiously silent and some form of excitement began to brew inside me. I wasn't sure why.

We continued past the pool. But there was a sight there that caused my pace to slow and my pulse to increase. Had I not been with Sydney, I would have stopped. I waved to her, though, and her "hello" in return caught Sydney's attention.

"Heyward, you remember Teal . . ."

My heart was doing a little jig when I answered him. Teal was lying stomach-flat on a chaise lounge and looking as fine as a tight spiral. Her body came with her too and I did my damnedest not to look at it and blow a gasket. No top was strapping her back and her ass was facing up with some butt floss placed between her halves just for kicks, doing its best to provide some mock protection of an ass that Rodin would have been happy to work from. In clay or bronze. A sketch even, and he wasn't known for them.

Shit, was the cleanest of my feelings.

"Hello, Teal," I said, desperately trying to keep my voice even and unwavering.

"Hi, Heyward," she offered nonchalantly. "Sydney, you're blocking my sun."

"Sorry." And it was true, his shadow was slashing across her back.

It gave birth to an awkward moment. We all stood there a moment saying nothing. But I knew Teal was clocking me. It made me more uncomfortable. Enough to ask her a question.

"What are you reading?" I forced out.

"My Wodehouse," she said matter-of-factly, like it was as normal as brushing her teeth. "Ever read Wodehouse?"

I told her I hadn't.

Sydney looked my way and then hers and said, "I'm going to show Heyward something."

I reacted to that with a polite smile and she added a slight twitch wink at me. I think it was a torn wink. She was torn between giving me a full clapper and not one at all. That was when I was certain Sydney had some power over her, romantic or otherwise. I wondered how extensive it was.

We continued our march past the little tennis court that was a bastard cousin compared to the rest of the yard. We came upon that house in back, the maid's quarters. Sydney went inside and I stepped in after. It was impeccably furnished with a sunken living room and tasteful orgy-style couches that went on and on. The pillows were so deep, quick-stop love affairs could be conducted between the cracks.

Sydney spread wide the fridge and drew out two Cokes. He handed me one and cracked his and sipped.

"This is the guesthouse," he uttered, and a carbonation burp eased out of his mouth.

"You don't say?"

"Friends from out of town stay here."

"Or husbands who need a retreat?"

"That too," he said, grinning. "Come on outside."

We settled into the upholstered chairs next to the Jacuzzi. This house had its own pool too. For an impoverished writer the house was a dream. For a millionaire it was comfortable. For Sydney Swinburn it was just a place to stuff guests.

"Mind if I ask you a personal question?"

"I think we're at that point," I said, and a respectful smile came too.

"What do you pay for that apartment of yours?"

"Six-fifty a month."

"For that, what do you get?"

"It's a one-bedroom with a walk-in kitchen, dining and living room together, and a bitch of a landlady."

"I'll offer you a deal. You pay my accountant six-fifty a month and I'll give you the guesthouse. What do you say to that?"

I didn't answer him at first. Not because I didn't have an answer. You bet your ass I did. Before he'd asked me. But in times like those, when presented with a stroke of generosity, I've always felt embarrassed. In addition, I didn't want to pounce quickly so that it would smack of desperation—even though I already knew where I was going to reposition the wall-size TV. Blame it on all the WASPy politeness propaganda drummed into me from my Prince Charles haircut days.

But after two artificial moments passed, I had an answer that I delivered slowly, assuredly, and not desperately.

"Can I switch from Coke to a beer?" I said with a different sort of smile.

"Of course."

And he moved back into the kitchen. I said after him, "It's the first deal I've had in Hollywood in a long time."

"May it be the first of many," I heard. "Is champagne okay?"

I said it was and the appropriate pop was heard not only around the backyard. Around the fucking world.

"Yes!" I said to myself no fewer than sixty-five times in the next ten minutes. It was better than a game-winner from half-court at the buzzer. That charge was fleeting. The buzzing thoughts of career advancement were not.

Sydney emerged from the sliding glass doors of the guesthouse with two frothing flutes of gold from an embarrassingly superior vintage. Following a predictable toast and a clink and a sip, there was some silence. He took in the view of his house and yard like I'm sure he'd done thousands of times and by now was reasonably, if not totally, immune to its grandeur.

I took in the same vista and confess my interior was very festive. I just landed a kick-ass pad on the best street in Bel-Air. And I was a mere stone's throw away from one of the town's living icons. Not to mention a shared valet named Armando. Scenarios now started debuting in my head. I flashed on the various ways I might be perceived. As someone close to Sydney Swinburn. As someone who had his ear on a daily basis. What I got was bigger than a studio appointment job. It was worthy of a *Variety* front-page liner. It was a position that would make any Wannabeast stand aghast in a puddle. After all, I was thisclose to a green-light guy. I had just pole-vaulted over the Beasts and had taken a giant leap for mankind. Mankind meaning me.

"It has an outdoor shower too," Sydney added as an afterthought. "I think everything works. But I'll tell Armando to give it an inspection. From now on you'll deal with him and we will never discuss the arrangement again."

"Thanks, Sydney. Large thanks."

He let out a long sigh.

"Chenille," he said. "Wow" followed it.

"Are you going to see her tonight?"

"Saturday night. Tonight, I'm seeing Patti. And The Kissing Bandit tomorrow night." He looked at me for a reaction. "She called me," he qualified when I had none.

"Always a good sign," I said.

"I still like kissing her."

We both laughed at that. I lightly tapped his flute with mine. I watched bubbles release from the bottom of the glass the way they always do, but this time with new appreciation. It was something I usually didn't focus on. But, suddenly, I had a new perspective. When the worries of life are shelved momentarily, it frees you to take in other things you wouldn't take the time to notice. I was happy that the bees were making honey and the trees had leaves. I was beginning to see life from a new angle. Instead of looking up the mountain, I was on a tram climbing it.

Then came my toast. "To your stable."

"The stable," Sydney said with a triumphant smile.

The Pact

I finished my bubbly and looked up the yard. The fresh visual jarred my senses to think of other things. But my thoughts didn't even leave the yard. They had been affected by something more immediate. As far away as poolside. But not my pool. *Hers.*

"What's Teal's story?" I asked nonchalantly.

With that, Sydney looked sharply at me. Then away. He took a slow sip. "What do you mean?" he said bluntly.

The handed-back question puzzled me. I clarified mine by employing our language.

"What's the word on her?"

"Teal?"

Sydney seemed frozen for a moment as if not knowing where to begin. I figured he must have been thinking other things like making movies. After all, he had a thousand and one daily headaches to conjure up if he was in the mood to wrestle with them.

But I was wrong.

"She's like a daughter to me," he said. And his voice had changed. It was now low, even, and stern. "Her parents died when she was five. I met her at the Playboy Mansion at one of those Sunday night screenings. She was kind of . . ."

And he took his time with it. A long time. Eerily so. Maybe. Maybe not.

". . . disillusioned with life . . ."

"Where's she from?"

"She's from Wyoming, actually."

"And she's an actress?"

"She's doing the—what do you call it?"

And he couldn't come up with it. I knew he meant "the Wam thing."

"She goes on castings," he said instead. "Although she's not very aggressive."

Then he stopped and looked into the middle distance. He picked up that my level of interest in her was above casual.

"You like her, don't you?" he said finally. And he looked away.

"I think she's cool."

He just nodded. Then he finished off his glass. And poured another for the both of us.

"I'm okay," I said, referring to my empty glass.

"No you're not," he said with a funny smile, and maybe it wasn't even a smile at all. Then a certain weight could be seen in his gaze as he delivered this. "Teal is very special to me, Heyward. She lives here sometimes. And in one of my other houses. Teal is to me what Eleanor is to you."

He looked at me and I nodded. But he wasn't done. Add to that the fact that his face tightened and he clamped on his back molars, making his jaw powerfully define itself. He forced a cough to get rid of the emotion that was creeping up his torso.

"I think we should make a pact," he said.

"A pact?"

"I think we should choose one girl, and one girl only, that the other cannot under any circumstances approach. And I am saying this because it seems like there are two ladies that are very important, if not, indeed, sacred, to us both. No matter what, neither can make overtures to the girl each of us has chosen. Agreed?"

"Hey, you know me. I'm not active anyway."

"Whether you are or whether you're not."

In the moments I took to think it over I couldn't help feeling that it was a strange overture as well as a strange arrangement. There was a sudden gust of wind that flapped my trousers at the ankles.

"Agreed," I said.

Then what happened next took the strange out of the exchange and added the frightening.

"Heyward. I'm going to tell you straight." And he looked at me with a glare that could have bent metal. "Don't cross me. Ever. Not on this. Or any other pact we make. I know two ways of playing ball. Hard. And harder. Violations of my agreements result in grave consequences, gravely felt. I'm a bottom-line guy. If you fuck with her, you're fucking with me. And if you fuck her, you're fucking me. In that context, you can consider it a homosexual act. That girl is my soulmate. And my soul is something you don't want to fuck with."

As I met his steely gaze I felt like I had been locked in the refrigerator. A full chill came over my body. And I found my forehead, palms, nuts, and neck going clammy, even though I attempted to appear like I was sipping a piña colada poolside under a Palm Springs desert sun. The indifferent pose was to make Sydney think I was unaffected, that my thoughts for this girl weren't even close to carnal in nature.

"And it's the closest I'll ever come to sounding spiritual," he said, and a faint smile was not making its way out.

In that one short, chilling burst, I knew how this guy had become a success in the business. It was that quality that had sent many flaky directors and producers away thinking they better have their shit together when they deal with him. Because your average con, in the con man's capital, was not nearly good enough. The average con got snuffed in this town. This guy, Sydney Swinburn, was uniquely qualified to scratch, sniff, and do the snuffing.

His face didn't let up for a minute and it would have been nice to see it happen. I felt like I had just taken the SATs. I felt like all the sense of democracy, mutual respect, and my quiet ego-infused consideration that we were equals, and even that I'd held the upper hand somewhat with respect to our womanizing, where I was the Go-To Guy for advice in all matters carnal—all went out the fucking window. With one short blast he put me in the back row of kindergarten class and made me write *"I will not chew gum"* a hundred times. He shifted the balance of power forcefully in his favor.

I started thinking how lucky I was to be in his presence. Any ego satisfaction I had accumulated over the recent fortnight for coaching this power guy in areas of romance meant nothing. Zeroids. At that point, I was nothing more than an impressed admirer. I was nothing more than a fan. I was nothing more than a dime-a-dozen screenwriter with no whites and no batting average. I was all need and no offering.

"Do you choose Eleanor?" he asked finally.

"Yes I do."

And we tapped flutes one last time.

"It's a pact," he said.

Eventually, his vised-up face gave way and a smile came over it.

"So let's have some fun."

"Fun it is," I said.

Then came another comment that wasn't unsettling but it was surprising just the same. And I wasn't sure he was serious because he followed it up with a laugh.

"What about the models?"

But when his goofy chuckle died in his chest, he was still looking at me. It was the third stab at the request. The dreaded M word. And after the previous assault, who was I to deny him anything, let alone a request for models?

"Okay, okay," I said. "As you know this isn't the greatest town for them."

"Right."

"But there is a girl in town from New York. An aspiring-actress type. She's from Massachusetts. I haven't seen her in a while. But I can bring her to dinner."

"When?"

"You tell me."

"I have Patti tonight."

"You have Dana tomorrow night."

"How about Thursday night?"

"The only problem is, with these ones, their dance card gets pretty full, pretty fast. Like, as soon as they set foot on the LAX tarmac. The town is starved for the real beauties. So I would hold off on what you already have and go for something fresh right now. Before the vultures circle and swarm."

He thought about that. "How about tonight?"

The Designated Don't Girl

Sydney then told me he had to see the dailies of one of his flicks over at Novastar. I told him I was going to my apartment to inform my landlady I was moving out, though I didn't tell him how smugly I would do it.

"Do you mind if I move the wall-size TV?"

"The place is yours to do as you wish," Sydney said.

And then he strode back up the expansive green lawn just like any other guy worth fifty million would. *Calmly.*

I sat there for a moment. I was punch-drunk. Something had hit me and I was dazed. I relived the conversation in my mind and my palms erupted in a clammy wash again. I was sure they would no matter how many times I mulled over our guesthouse chat. Then I turned around and looked at my new digs. I poured another flute and downed it. Though my ecstatic feeling had been stymied, I still couldn't help thinking shit was looking up.

I walked an arc that bordered upon a semicircle back to the main house. Not because I wanted to avoid the spitting lawn sprinklers or to test my quads. The last thing I wanted to do was engage in a conversation with Teal. I didn't even want to see her. And that was saying something. I didn't want to see her beautiful shape, her playful mouth, the wit that came out of it, her flowing locks the color of a fruit I loved, or her white-white smile.

"Sydney, you're blocking my sun."

Or the mystery that surged forth from a place deep within. Which was the most tantalizing thing. Women and their private puzzles, remember? Her gold was hers to keep as far as I was concerned. She was no sweet Project of mine. She was a walking nightclub but it was a club I wouldn't bring my business to. Last call had already come and gone. For me, this girl named Teal, who had made my heart hopscotch back and forth in my rib cage, no longer existed.

Then, as if life had no respect for the laws of abstention I had just laid down, I heard this. "Heyward?" It was almost like cheesy irony it was so blatant.

Sure, the voice was familiar and intensely feminine. And smart. And just as dangerous. So I pretended not to hear it and continued my way up to the main house.

"Heyward. I think you hear me."

I looked over reluctantly and saw her standing there with the sun splashing all over her strawberry locks. If she had had a book she would have been a dead ringer for Renoir's *La Lectrice*. And then it appeared in her hand from behind her back.

I mumbled something to show I was human.

"I hear you're moving into the guesthouse."

I nodded and added a half-smile that was as fake as banana candy.

"Need some help moving in?"

"No, thank you. I don't have much stuff."

My nerves were on the rattle. I feared Sydney was watching through the window only minutes after he had just laid down the law, and here I was already chatting with his Designated Don't Girl.

"You look nervous."

No shit, Red, was my thought. "I have a lot on my mind" was my actual response.

"You remind me of my father."

"Really."

"Yes. He was a fireman."

"You don't say?" I asked nervously. And then remembered her father was dead. It made me wish I hadn't sounded so glib.

"I do say. My brother is a fireman too."

She hung there looking at me in a way that was not necessarily provocative but her attractive quality was still surging through. And she was making it surge through. Her charms were mere marionettes of her desires. And beyond. But what were her desires?

"Don't be afraid," she said.

It was worth a "What do you mean?"

"Oh, I don't know." Another pause. "Look. I'm Sydney's best friend. You'll be seeing a lot of me. We're family here, Heyward. Okay?"

"Okay," I said. Then I waved toodles to her and continued on my way.

Modelitis

I turned over the Sled and coughed out of the place. My drive back to West Hollywood was a damn good one. The best I'd ever had. It was the last time I would return there as a resident. I had traded up. Hugely. And beyond. And if the Sled could talk she would have had proud words.

"Now we have our own lemon trees," I told Bob quietly.

Bob the Riot was silently ecstatic. We were one family on the up and everyone knew it. Dysfunctional, but on the up. My good.

Soon after, Armando cruised by with a loading van and two Thickies. Even moving out was going to be easy, I thought. I looked skyward and thanked Someone. With all the help it took an hour. I kissed the east wall and left the flat forever. I didn't even pick up the new mail. I was going to play hide-and-seek with all the past-duesies. And I was going to do the hiding. And then I was gone. It wasn't a wholly sad parting.

At Sydney's I stored some possessions in the garage since some of them were not appropriate for my new residence. I still had collegiate-type leftover items indicative of another mind-set. The loser kind.

As soon as I prepared my new digs, and had all the plugs in place, I booted up my Gold files. I scanned the Massachusetts directory. I was looking for Vanessa Lewis. Her biographical data read like this:

Top model. From Worcester, Mass. Sexier than drop-dead gorgeous. Odd features. Street smarts, not real smarts. But proud sense of self. Medium-Hi Maintenance due to beauty contamination and submodest background. Mostly male friends. Belle of the ball needs. Compliments other women only if they're not beautiful. Multiple girlie tables a no-no. Brunette. Favorite sayings: clichés "kinda-sorta," "never a dull moment," "don't go there," "I'm tellin' ya." Ego derived from near-supermodel status. Favorite gesture: snaps fingers out of nervousness. Wicked temper, severe PMS riots, known for offensive Mace maneuvers. Boyfriends: dark, control freaks. Affairs: handsome Strugs, male models, 8x10s, and womanizing producers with name. BG: father's a steelworker. Raised her. Mother died of C at early age. Affianced to drug dealer in New York. Cocaine abuse. Rehab. Very spontaneous. Big head on slender body. Anal sex a plus. Fellatio-selective. Favorites: *The Twilight Zone.* Cap'n Crunch. Go Ahead, Try and Fuck Me clothing. *Are You My Mother?* book. Lived in all model cities.

I'd heard Vanessa was staying at the Peninsula Hotel, the place where all successful out-of-town models stay. So I rang her and asked her to join us for dinner. She asked where. I told her. She asked what kind of food they served. I told her. She asked who Sydney was. I gave her the word on him. She asked what the temperature was going to be like. I told her that too. She said she didn't want to stay out late. I said that was okay. She had a late casting but she would try be there shortly thereafter.

Like my Gold notes had indicated, she was medium to high maintenance.

Zona was on Robertson. It was another one of L.A.'s identity-
support places. The place was usually thronging with the average quantity of Woodies and Beasts. In essence, it was just another four walls
with new decorations to house the entertainment vermin of Star Camp.
Not a bad place. It probably had six months left before the insects
moved on to new crumbs.

When we entered I saw the Jolly Jumping Lying and Cheating Bastard at the bar. We were seated very soon. I was happy for that.

You know the type. The kind of guy you first meet in a new place
when you don't know anyone. And he comes off like one of the town's
Go-To Guys. And he meets you and within two minutes he knows you
have more to offer. So he clings to you to use you as his ticket. But you
soon find what a jolly, jumping, lying, and cheating bastard he is when
you get the word. So you move on.

His assessment of my worth had been accurate. The weak wave he
sent over to Sydney and me at that prominent table told me as much.

Next, I gave Sydney the word on Vanessa. I told him she was from
Massachusetts, that she was better looking in her photos than real life
but that in real life she was sexier than her photos. She had that quasi-
bizarre look that was in fashion. Her eyes were racoony and she had a
body like Olive Oyl. Photographers had chosen her and made a bronze
star out of her. She wasn't educated but had street smarts that she considered were real smarts. Her face and stature made her believe it too. I
told him her father worked in a steel mill outside Boston and her mother
died of leukemia at an early age. I didn't tell him about her past
boyfriends. Sydney would invariably do the comparative thing, which
can be crippling.

"She doesn't sound very sexy."

"The high-maintenance aspects drive you to get beyond them. And
have grudge sex with her. And once you do, she's wild. Take my word."

I told Sydney he had a shot at her but to take his time. With mod-
elettinis, patience is the supreme virtue because, in the end, it's their
choice. It's always Lady's Choice, but that credo is supersized with the

model group. They'll tell you when the door is open. It's closed until they do. They made the world an unfair place. Too many guys want in, so they have their pick. Possessing a weighty notch up doesn't help. All suitors, to be even considered, have to have a notch up. Even if it's in the area of coolness or lack of hygiene.

What Sydney had going for him was pretty standard. She wanted to be a star. Modeling had teased her into believing she could be. She was needy of praise and attention. She wanted into the movie business so she could glam it up for the rest of her life. She didn't want the cameras to stop snapping. Just the reason for them being snapped.

"How should I act?"

"Just lay down some nice-guy track."

"Think I can . . . take her down?"

I liked hearing his choice of words. It bespoke a confidence he'd never before displayed. It's amazing what a good roll in the hay can do for a man's psyche.

"Eventually, but not tonight, and not next week. Maybe next month. But you never know. That's my full answer. You make the call."

"Really . . ." His face showed predictable disappointment.

"In the meantime you're looking good at a high-profile place, and other potential stablemates will see you with another beauty. Let's not forget the linkage aspects."

"Linkage?"

"When you're out with someone at a table, people think you're fucking anyway. It's the Age of A."

We were seated at a turbo table at the aforementioned restaurant, sipping on a nice Pinot Grigio. We saluted some faux-weighty Woodmen while we waited for Vanessa. Faux-weighties are one-picture wonders. Somehow, someway, they got a picture made but they're years away from repeating. If they ever will.

"What's her last name?"

"Lewis," I said. "But she doesn't use it."

Sooner than later, Vanessa strode in with heavy post-appointment makeup. Her entrance caused a mild shuffle and a pause in conversation. Hell-A is a look-see town, don't forget. She looked damn good, the only way models can. It's that little bit extra they possess on the genetic scope. It separates them from just foxy, sexy, pretty. The X factor. She had that glamorous now-look that I was not a fan of. Thin, underfed, and sleep-deprived.

"Vanessa," I said with a smile. I was standing, as was Sydney. "Meet Sydney Swinburn."

She looked at him and smiled with a nod. Then right back at me. Her energy was scattered.

"That valet guy was so rude. I was over in Century . . ." She drew a blank so I filled it in.

"City."

"Right . . ." And she pulled out a cigarette and leaned in. I found matches and lit it for her. She continued right in stride.

". . . get my car out of a garage, drive here, and the valet guy outside tells me there's no more room. No more room! 'Make room, Buddy. I have a reservation.' And why do you think he did it?"

"Why?" I asked. And for once, a little sorrow for the Vesties crept in.

"I wonder," she trailed off sarcastically. "He was so rude."

She still hadn't sat down, since she was enjoying standing tall and being watched by the watchful room.

"Vanessa, Vanessa," I muttered.

"I know. Never a dull moment."

"Have a seat," Sydney said politely.

"So, Sydney Swinman," she blurted.

"Swinburn's the name," I corrected her.

"That's okay. A lot of people get it wrong," Sydney said.

I knew that wasn't true. It had been running around the press, the papers, the posters, and the credit rolls for too long.

"So you're a director?"

"I used to be a producer," Sydney said. I liked the modesty tack he'd chosen.

She looked at him like his answer was a disappointment. Then she angled away and snapped her fingers. As if the question and the extroverted approach demonstrated a certain intelligence. It gave the illusion of a quick mind microprocessing rapidly. Which is what she wanted. I decided to quiet my skepticism and watch the games play out.

The waiter glided up with a bow tie wrapping his throat and Vanessa ordered.

"A Kir Royale," she said without looking at him.

"So where are you from?" Sydney asked gently.

"We're going to play that game?" She said it and once she saw his frozen look, she laughed to take off the edge.

"What?"

"Where am I from? Hasn't your friend told you?"

"No," I said. And I looked at Sydney, who was definitely taken aback, though he gave off a bemused smile to cover his drain of poise. "I didn't tell him anything about you. You're on your own."

And she said it in monotone like it bored the hell out of her.

"I was born in Worcester and I lived there for four and a half years until we moved to Detroit for another six years and then back to Johnson Falls, Mass, where I lived until I was seventeen."

I was listening in amazement. She was dumping on Sydney and his polite, nice-guy approach, an approach I had instructed him to employ. I could tell he was enduring a self-confidence meltdown and I didn't want him to speak further. I wanted a quick side bar with him to tell him to close down fully. But it was too late.

Game over, was another thought.

"What are you doing in L.A.?" Sydney followed up with.

Vanessa gave the question no respect. She ignored it and switched the subject to what she wanted to talk about, doing it with a question of her own. The self-absorbed kind.

"Who's that looking over here?"

"Where?" I said as we scanned the tables.

"That girl over there. The Pamela Lee wannabe?"

I smiled at that. It was her only offering that coincided with my sensibilities.

"She keeps looking over here."

I said it with pride. "I think she's looking at Sydney."

She then looked Sydney up and down, taking my comment seriously. She just smiled as if to say *yeah, right*.

"A girl like that needs more than you in this town," I said to her.

"I think she's into girls," she countered.

Vanessa was seated in such a way she was showing Sydney little more than a sharp shoulder blade. It was pretty clear she wanted nothing to do with him. It was also cruel the way she was letting it be known. Openly.

"Vanessa," I said as if underscoring the authorship of her quote.

Then she got up from the table and moved off without saying anything. As soon as she did, Sydney didn't hold back. "What a bitch."

"Yeah."

"You knew she was a bitch?"

"She wasn't always this contaminated."

"Christ," he said.

"Well, she's attractive, don't you think?"

His answer was silence, which was a reluctant yes.

"I also know she wants to be an actress. So I figured she'd play it smart."

"If she's thinking I'm going to help her, she's out of her mind."

"I don't get it."

"Let's take off."

"Wait a second."

Then I told Sydney this was only phase one.

"What's phase two?"

"It's different for different girls. But for a pain-in-the-ass high-maintenance model who thinks the world is her own runway ramp, well, see the seat belt in your lap, Sydney? Fasten it."

My Life Story

He smiled faintly. I could see his mind being filled with juices of excitement, pondering my method. He sensed we were the underdog team in the midst of a comeback. We were. It wouldn't end up with super-pussy for the supermogul but it would end up with something just as, if not more important: ego preservation.

Vanessa was at the bar smoking a cigarette and nonchalantly chatting with an 8x10 who obviously couldn't afford dinner. He was looking to see if he could infiltrate a table, number-crunch, or pick off anything at the bar. Like Vanessa. When conversation with the 8x10 tired, and was not reinforced by some silent starfuck energy that would have kept her there longer—for the simple reason that the snapshot was not a star—she squashed out her cig and made a slinky trail back over to our table, a path that took anyone else four seconds but she made it in eight. She had slowed her movements down to a *look at me and my fine ass* crawl.

She sat down and the waiter returned to take our order.

"I've already eaten," Vanessa declared without any prompting.

So I put in an order. So did Sydney.

"So what was the meeting you had?" I asked her.

"I met with a director."

"Which one?" Sydney asked.

"Bernie Meyer."

"Never heard of him," I said. More significantly, Sydney shrugged.

"What's the project?" Sydney asked.

"Well, he wants to do . . ." Then she looked right at me. "Say, you're a writer, right?"

I nodded.

"He wants to do a movie about me."

I loved hearing it. "About what?"

"My life story. And I can't write. I mean I can but I don't have the time. Maybe you could do it."

"I'm flattered," I said with my own brand of sarcasm. But of course she didn't get it. But Sydney did and he smiled faintly.

"What's the main tension of your story?" I asked.

"How do you mean?"

Sydney jumped in. "He means what would compel someone to do your story? Why should your story be told?"

And unbelievably so, Vanessa just ignored him again. She looked back at me. "What do you think?"

"Excuse me, Vanessa," Sydney said. "I just asked you a question."

"Sssssh. Don't be so needy," she said, and flashed a faux-cutesy smile at him. When she looked back at me her smile was gone.

"Well, you don't have to if you don't want. I know lots of writers," she contended.

I let her comment drop. She sighed and looked around the room.

"This place is so boring." And out came another Cleopatra sigh. She would avoid me now for a while because I chipped a chip from her ego by not biting at her script proposal. Finally, at the end of her sigh, as if forced, she asked Sydney a question. After all, he was the only other choice.

"So what do you do now?"

"I work for a studio."

"Is there anyone in this town with a beard who doesn't?" she shot back. "You must all go to the same groomer. Do you all know each other?"

"The ones who really work, do. It is a small circle."

"Come on. Everyone works for a studio or is some sort of *producer* out here. I meet twenty every day. As for me, I don't want to produce. I want to direct. Next year I'm going to NYU Film School. I'm going to direct my own stuff. The crap they're putting out these days. I mean, those comic book movies? Were you involved with those?"

"I did a couple, yes."

"Why?"

"They made three hundred million dollars."

"Is that what it's all about?" And she looked at me. "See? That's why I'm going to direct my own stuff."

And at that point I had had enough.

"Wait a second, Vanessa, you're going to direct?"

"Yes."

"Excuse me, but what are you going to direct?"

"A movie," she claimed. Then added a *"Duh,"* to platform my stupidity.

That's when I let go. Not of her. Rather, any hesitation I had to rip her skin off.

"But, Vanessa. *You are retarded.*"

"What?"

"You are retarded. You have a nice now-face. You have a nice now-body. You have no other now-talent. To sit here and tell my friend this shit, make judgments about his pictures, and judgments about his character without knowing him, also shows your moronic quality. Here's a guy who pulls a lot of weight in this industry. A guy who could actually help you. He deserves your respect. If you could ever get off yourself and dive into the other realm of consciousness which we all call the real world, you might find there are some other ideas out there. A face does not make art. A face does not make shitty art. People do. Minds do. You are not going to direct pictures. You are not going to have your life story made. Your life story is about a guy on the make who is using it as a subject of conversation which might catch your interest. Your life story project is about a guy putting both his middle and index fingers in your pussy and getting some wildtime after an okay dinner somewhere. Or let me give you an equation you can understand. A producer who says he wants to do your life story equals he wants to fuck you. There is no Vanessa Lewis biography story. No model's story is that great."

I paused, then looked over at Sydney as if appealing to him.

"A girl gets worldwide attention for having a marketable face and all of a sudden she thinks she's Anne Fuckin' Frank. You don't know anything about movies. You don't know anything about people. You don't know anything about life. You are a model. Basta. And you are retarded."

She wasn't at the table when I finished. I remember her leaving at the end of the third quarter when the game was already over. But I had wanted to say that piece for a long time to some prima donna model somewhere.

But before she left, I did hear her say, "Fuck you, Heyward. You're an asshole."

And I was. Sure as hell. But I just couldn't take the model-maniacal point of view anymore. I was afflicted with a condition called model repulsion and it was high time I got that load off my chest. Especially since she was so ruthless. Especially since it was taking advantage of my friend. Especially since it was typically modelesque and it had been happening all over the world for years. The thought of those Cleopatra girls truly repulsed me. And beyond.

Obviously, Vanessa didn't make it to dessert. After my last line, all that was left of her was a dead napkin on the table.

"Sorry, Sydney."

He smiled weakly. I could tell this altercation had sunk his ship. I think he thought his chances had been pretty good. He had just come off two successful liaisons. I'm sure he felt on top of his game prior to meeting Vanessa. But models have always been great neutralizers. No one can count on getting new model justice. It's a bad bet. The odds are better in Vegas. I'm sure in that block of twenty-five minutes his mind raced to the things that would rock his psyche, and had rocked his psyche, hitting those little pockets of insecurity he felt were at the root of the problem. The things that prevented a Breakthrough. He had an insecurity flare-up.

I sat there quite silently with silent plans to do nothing. And I didn't move. I'm sure Sydney had thought I was going to salvage the night for him. He had that much confidence in me. But I hadn't delivered. I started to have an insecurity flare-up myself. We didn't say anything and I was watching the distance grow between us at the table. He was across the room from me, separated by the now-giant centerpiece of flowers. I needed a few telephone books to sit up high enough to see. I was feeling that small. I still said nothing.

"Waiter? Can you bring over a bottle of Cristal?" Sydney asked. Then he looked at me.

"I want to acknowledge the way you handled that situation. And the way you handled that situation in the bar in Tennessee. I never thanked you. I am thanking you now. I rarely come across people who stick up for me in genuine terms. They're usually trying to see me slip. If they do, they're doing it for obvious reasons. Thank you, Heyward."

"You're welcome." I said it simply because there was nothing else to say. His words were heartfelt and had been delivered formally. Shocking was another way of putting it.

The champagne came and so did the pop. We both had half a glass and took off.

Not So Fast

Another word was never said about that aborted dinner. And I know why. You don't remind powerful Go-To Guys of their Waterloos. You can remind them of their shortcomings but never their Waterloos. That goes for the rest of the world too.

That night we glided silently back to Bel-Air in Sydney's Jag. We didn't play pool and we didn't take a swim. Sydney went to bed. And so did I. I was rather proud of myself and what I had done. I'll tell you why.

Of course I knew other girlie-whirlies. My Gold files took a half hour to print out. I had 2,237 profiles. Of course I knew other models. I had 212 profiles. But I did not want a pushover for whom Sydney would pay the check and get some quick wildtime. I didn't want him to get too confident. I didn't want him feeling he could do it on his own.

The fact is, Vanessa Lewis had been chosen purposely and purposefully. I knew she was going to come in there feeling like the star of the home team with the fans cheering and fawning and that she'd throw out that model-maniacal catechism which was sure to rip Sydney Swinburn a new rimmer. I knew she was going to give Sydney a slap and a half. That she was going to take his stones in her palm and crush them until they turned into white dust. I also knew I'd lose my friendship with her. I didn't care. A friendship with her was a one-way street anyway. I'd casted correctly. She was the right gal for the job.

Sydney needed to learn that lesson. He needed to know that failure with the girlie-whirlies of the world was only one dinner check away. He needed to be humbled. Simply put, he needed to know my worth.

I told you I was a young Machiavellian. I believed my Blade was as sharp as old Niccolo's. In fairness to him, look how much more I had to work with. Niccolo had all of history. But I had Hollywood. All of history was played out every day on every one of its corners. All the darkness, all the light, all the generosity, all the calculation. Hollywood was surging with intensified life the likes of which Niccolo had never seen. Of that I was sure.

Certainly, I knew some ravishing fashion gals who enjoyed love affairs with tequila and blow-caine, who were nymphomaniacal and easy and would yield body parts on night one, and the rest on night two. I also knew Sydney was vulnerable. If he got the A-I treatment from a smoker, he might not recover. He may want to hang his hat there awhile. Maybe forever. Then where would I be? And my payback? I would have buried my usefulness in a shallow grave and thrown away the shovel. Not so fast, was my credo.

Oh, I almost forgot. There was one thing Sydney never asked about again: the models.

As I lay back in my new digs and stared at the gourmet wallpaper and the moldings and all the expensive little architectural wonders, I didn't think any negatives. Unfortunately, I was so damn excited I couldn't drift off. So I did the proper insomniac thing. I put on a pair of shorts.

I ran fast up the dark yard all the way to the main driveway. There I opened the trunk to the Sled and pulled out The Duke. It was my football, the kind the pros use. It had been with me since I was ten. It had been in the hands of all my childhood friends. It survived all those touch games in Central Park. And all those creeps who wanted to steal it. I handed it to Mark Bavaro in 1986. And he signed it. So did Simms and L.T. Sure, it was family.

I grabbed it and ran back down to the guesthouse. The spotlights on the property guided me like buoys to a lost ship. What I did next, I had a blast doing. I threw the football around my new yard. I threw it in every direction. I threw it left, I threw it right. I threw spirals, I threw ducks. I threw it with my right hand and I threw lefty too. I punted once or twice. I threw it as far as I could. And as far as I could was not far enough. I never hit a wall, a tree, or any kind of fence or boundary. That's how much turf surrounded me. I threw and threw. Until my arm hurt. Really hurt. When I woke up the next day, my arm was sore. But it was the nicest dose of pain I had had in my entire life.

The Fit

A right-cross to the ego was not the only result I was seeking by un-leashing a bitch-model like Vanessa Lewis on Sydney. I wanted him to come to me. So I waited.

I was sitting by the pool sipping some freshly squeezed when he came at me. He was on his way to the office. I was not.

"How you doing, Heyward?"

"Great."

"You all moved in?"

I nodded. Sydney was fidgety. He had something on his mind. I was hoping he would.

"Heyward. I'm going to ask you something you may consider stupid. Perhaps it is."

"Go ahead."

"I want your opinion." He sighed. "What do you think about my look?"

"Your look?"

"Yeah. How I look?"

I was not going to answer him directly. It would make him feel like I had been pondering the subject at length already.

"Physically?"

"Yeah."

"I think you look fine."

"Fine?" he asked somewhat weakly.

"Well, hey, I mean if you're, I don't know, *bored*, it never hurts to change. We all could use a change. What would you like to do?"

"I don't know. I don't know anything about that shit."

I thought about it. In front of him. It made him think it was hitting me fresh. When, in fact, I had thought about it before. But I was wait-ing for him to come to me. After his self-esteem took a mule kick. Like the one the Species Model had given him.

"Let me think about it," I said. "I may have some ideas."

We parted company, which means he took off. I just sat there and took a shark bite of sunlight and got real content with the way things were going. I was going to give Sydney what he needed to progress. I was going to give him what he needed to enhance his chances. I was going to give him a makeover. At his prompting. Almost.

The approach I selected for him was one I had adopted myself. But in the reverse. I'd heard about it in New York actually. Look British, act Yiddish. Sydney already had the Yiddish down. He was tested tough in business affairs and negotiations. Now he just needed the British. He needed a boost in matters of taste. He needed to know how to dress, how to look, and how to carry himself.

I was qualified for the job. I considered myself overbred by a long line of social climbers back east. By the time my generation had arrived we were right up there on society's mantel, anglophiling away, licking up to social etiquette. We were on all the right lists and received all the right invitations to all the right parties. That was my breeding.

But I was lacking in other areas. I needed more savvy in business affairs, more career-minded thoughts, and a confrontational toughness once I got there. In essence, I needed more Yid. My character was unequipped for what the movie business required. I was aware of it. I had my Machiavellian Blade, a certain aptitude for analysis, and a gift for social X-ray, but when it came to business and thinking commercially, I was a blind child. I had to study it, learn it, and adopt it. And Sydney was a pro. I knew he could help me.

Here comes the interesting part. The key to happiness for each of us was in what the other had. He wanted what I had and I wanted what he had. On paper, we were a perfect symbiotic fit.

The Makeover

I mapped out a five-stop itinerary for us. We were going to hit Fred Segal on Melrose, Banana Republic and Tiffany on Rodeo, Giuseppe Franco on Canon, a consultation with Sydney's plastic surgeon pal, and then on to Polo. With a surprise stop along the way.

We zoomed down Melrose first and hit Fred Segal. There, I grabbed a rainbow selection of T-shirts and different styles of jeans. I was looking for a more relaxed, youthful, warmer Sydney Swinburn. To take the "i" out of *stiff* and put it in *accessible.*

Then we hit Banana Republic and got some loose-fitting denim shirts, some braces, and khakis. Sydney was covered with all the foreign wool and silky stuff, the Armani, the Boss, the custom English shirts, Agnes B. and Comme des Garçons. Yawn, yawn, was my feeling. Follywood had been kissing the ass of European clothiers for years. That was the easy part.

Of course, Sydney had plenty of fancy shoes—Gucci, Crisci, and Magli, to name a few. So I got him some understated Kenneth Cole's. And a pair of kick-ass construction boots with steel toes. For the weekends, of course. To kick the shit out of the competition. When I was done with him, there wouldn't be any.

The most enlightening exchange occurred as we left the army-navy store. Sydney was eyeballing his new steel toes.

"These are weird."

"No, they're not."

"This isn't me."

"It's going to be you."

"Oh yeah?" he said, and stopped short.

"Don't be so committed to your personality. Or what you think is you."

"Why?"

" 'Cause it may not be that great. In certain areas."

"That's quite an insult."

"It is? Well, that's what you need."

"Says who?"

"Says me. The person you asked to advise you on this. Would it make you feel any better to know that the qualities you possess—the ones that make you such a big deal in this town—are the ones I have none of?"

He pondered it. "I know what you're doing."

"Oh yeah? What?"

"You're turning me into a WASP."

"That's right."

"Why?" Then he anticipated my response and he was right on the money. " 'Cause that's what I need."

"Listen, Sydney. I need to toughen up. Get hard. Aggressive. And ruthless. And commercial. You need to soften. Refine. Whether you know it or not. We both have what each other needs. I know how to hold a fork. You know how to stick it in."

"You need some Jew in you."

"More Jew."

"I thought you were a WASP," he said with a face showing shock. "You're Jewish?"

"Half. I need whole. And in this town another half on top of that. My old man was a Jew."

Secretly, I loved saying this, for reasons to be discussed later. But what I will say now is what I was telling Sydney was only half-true. I wasn't half-Jewish. I wasn't Jewish at all. In reality, I was total WASP. But Sydney didn't need to know that. Neither did anyone in Follywood. I played it down, remember? Way down. This is not to say WASP was "up." I just didn't want to show different. And ram straight into the territorial leanings of Hollywood. I wanted to show I was part of the same herd, with the same spotted coat, running gingerly along, waiting for my big break.

Sydney started strolling again with an amused smile and a certain lightness. He looked down at his steelies again. I think he liked them a wee bit more.

"Are we done?"

"No. Come on," I said, quickening the pace.

"What's the rush?"

"We have an appointment."

"We do?"

"*You* do."

Foils, Hoops, and Loops

It was a four o'clock slot at Giuseppe Franco with Bettina—upstairs, of course. And as soon as we stepped into the salon Sydney balked.

"What are we doing here?"

At that moment Bettina met us with a cheerful welcome.

"Sydney, meet Bettina. She's your colorist."

"Colorist?"

And that's exactly what we did. We took his mud-brown locks and lightened them a few shades and added some blond. After the grumbling, the complaints, the foils, and the paranoia associated with all the pampering from salon softies and the like, Sydney had a new look. It was warmer, sexier, and overall, a total improvement. The results were clear. Sydney Swinburn was looking less like the hard-ass Jewish studio chief and more like a WASP. He was looking less like himself and more like me. The real blond me. Of course I already looked less like me and more like him. It's what you needed in Lollywood: Dress British, act Yiddish. That was the formula. Mine anyway.

"If anybody sees me here, forget it," he griped. "It's all over town."

"Next time your colorist will make a house call."

"House call?"

"The way the rest of the town does it. Your colleagues included."

"Colorist," he muttered.

He was skeptical and he continued to complain. About everything. Except the results. We had turned his locks from dark brown to a nice chestnut color with blondish streaks.

"It goes nicely with the yellow-brown in his eyes," Bettina added.

That gave me another idea. Across the courtyard was an optical shop. Sydney didn't need sunglasses. He had twenty-four pair. It was the eyes themselves. They were brown with a touch of green and yellow. I figured we could liven up the green. I yanked off his horn-rims and had him fitted for a pair of tinted contacts. His eyes watered heavily and went red. But the results were again strong. It gave him the sweetest hazel-colored eyes.

"What do you think, Sydney?"

He rode the mirror a beat.

"I like them," he said with a smile that showed genuine excitement.

"We're done now, right?"

I shook.

Our last stop on the tour had some shine to it. Silver shine. Again Sydney had no idea why I brought him to Tiffany's. It had nothing to do with purchasing a gift or paying homage to our Huckleberry Friend.

"What are we doing here?"

"You'll see."

"Who are we buying for? A girl?"

I shook my head. And the Tiffany saleswoman strode up, a Valley girl with a carnation, and threw her newly acquired snobbism at us.

"What are you seeking?"

"An earring."

"Just one?"

"Yes."

Sydney looked at me in a puzzled way.

"For the gentleman," I added.

"An earring? I'm not wearing an earring."

"Silver," I said to the saleswoman.

"But I have meetings. Corporate meetings."

"You can always take it off."

"Why do I need an earring?"

"It's a nice touch."

"Touch? I'm not gay. I'm not a black athlete. And I'm not a rock star. I'm a Jew. And I run a company."

"Let's have a look at the small hoops," I suggested.

"Hoops?" Sydney questioned nervously.

"Hush, Sydney." She showed me one. "No. Smaller."

"That's the smallest hoop we have."

"What about the loops?"

She nodded.

"Loops? Are you out of your mind?" Sydney piped.

"Not at all."

"Hoops, loops, I'm not wearing a goddam earring."

"Yes, you are. And you're going to like it."

By now the lady was smiling and she showed us a small silver loop.

"What do you think?" I asked her.

"I think it will look great on you," she delivered to Sydney.

Sydney spent the next seconds shutting up.

"I don't care what anyone says. It makes you look younger, more hip . . ." I reinforced.

"I remember when everyone went with ponytails a few years ago. They looked stupid."

"An earring is different."

"How so?"

"It's not a fad. It's here to stay. And you know what, deep down it'll give you a boost."

"How?"

"You'll have that pirate feeling," she chimed in with. And it was a comment as precious as the shinies in her display case.

"Like you're menacing, threatening, and powerful. Like you don't take any shit. And you close the deal. Confidence is the sexiest quality you can have."

"A G-4 doesn't hurt," the saleswoman added.

"You hush," I said, mock indignant.

"How does wearing that make me seem confident?"

"Like you don't care what people think. You're comfortable enough with yourself to wear it. For starters."

Then I whispered it to him. "Models love confidence."

He had no more defense. His Platinum Card blinded us.

"Wait," I said. "Don't be so hasty."

"You want something?"

"No. Aren't you forgetting someone else?"

"Heyward, step aside. This I know how to do. I'd like three gold bracelets. No stones."

"Tennis bracelets?" she asked.

"Yes. Right?" I nodded in agreement.

And then I added, "And three little silver anklet chains."

Sydney looked up at me surprised. Again.

"For the ones you haven't met yet. It's more a testament of friendship. And it leads to much more. Usually."

"We gotta be done now." His face just hung there, hoping.

The Big Suck

Our last stop was my favorite tattoo shop on Sunset. Not because I liked tattoos. I didn't.

"I'm not getting a tattoo."

"No tattoo."

"Promise?"

"Promise."

We slipped inside and the Green Man stepped up and asked us what we wanted. I called him that because his body was so mapped with tats it was hard to find skin tone.

"A piercing."

"Okay."

Sydney looked nervous. "Wait. Why don't I get a clip-on?"

"A clip-on will get you laughed at. Like you're a pussy."

"Is this the only way?" he asked the Green Man.

"Only way I know, sunshine," the Green Man said.

"Okay. My left ear, right?"

"Wrong," I said.

"My right? We had a script once and this guy says any earring worn in the right means you're a homosexual."

"That's not true."

"Yes it is. Left is right. Right is gay."

"That may have been true but years ago. When was your picture made?" He went silent on that. "The left could mean anything."

"Hey, but I'm not gay."

"It gives you that androgynous appeal. And in the modern era, androgyny works. Girlies love weirdos. Not that you are. You are so grounded and successful and wealthy that it will just add to your mystique. You need an image, Sydney."

"I have an image. One to uphold."

"You're a primary color."

"Meaning?"

And I said it like it was old news. Like telling a pitcher not to hang the curve.

"No mystery, and therefore no allure beyond the norm."

It was the last time he rolled his eyes that day. He took the piercing like a champ too. Except the part where he fainted. I drove the rest of the way.

"What did that guy ask you?" Sydney queried referring to the Green man.

"He asked me why I didn't want a tattoo."

"What did you say?"

"I said, 'Why should I? I have a personality.' "

"Did you say it before or after we paid the bill?"

"After, of course."

Sydney nodded. "So we're done, right?"

"We have one more errand."

"Jees."

"Your plastic surgeon friend?"

Immediately, Sydney looked sharply at me. He got eerily quiet.

"I already had that done."

"What done?"

"Does it look bad?"

"What?"

"Shit, you're making me so fucking insecure."

"What are you talking about?"

"People tell me he did a shitty job. What do you think?"

"On what? Who?"

"My nose, asshole!"

"Oh, I didn't even know about that," I affirmed. "But come to think of it, I did see that old snap of you. Your nose is larger in the photo."

"Yeah, I know."

"No, what I want you to do and, hear this—*I'll do it with you*—a little lipo."

"Liposuction?"

"For the gut."

"You're crazy."

"I need it too. Look . . ." I lifted my shirt and showed him my roll. "And I run."

"I'm not doing liposuction."

"Liposuction, Sydney."

"I'm not doing it."

"There's fat you can't get rid of no matter what your diet is."

"Forget it. There's no way in hell. I'm not doing it."

He said that a few more times before we got out of the car. I only said one more thing.

"Thin to win."

He shut up after that. We stepped into the office and had a consultation with his friend Terrence, the plastic surgeon. The surgeon made several jokes about Sydney's nose Sydney didn't find funny. Mainly that he had gone to the wrong specialist. We made our lipo appointment for the next morning.

The next afternoon was painful. The Big Suck was not a gentle process. But it did give each of us a flat stomach.

The makeover was a success. In the end, Sydney looked pretty damned stylish—a hundred percent better, in fact. And people told him so. It also gave me a sense of gratification.

As we stood outside the clinic in Beverly Hills, the uni-day heat beating down on us, I looked at Sydney and he looked at me. And what he said was quite funny.

"Well, what do we do now?"

A wink was my answer.

The New Drageur

For the rest of the spring, summer, and into the fall, I arranged tables: dinner, lunch, breakfast, and the snack type. And Sydney met the girlie-whirlies in my Gold. The results were as I'd anticipated. Success. And beyond. After one month, he had made out with four, did everything-but with three, received fellatio from another, and slept fully with four, and the women involved in the acts of intercourse performed all of the above. Naturally. Sydney, with his new locks, jewelry, clothes, and shoes, was glowing like the desert sun. He was a happy and spirited man.

We truly played out the tale of *The Sorcerer's Apprentice*, only I was the sorcerer and Sydney was my apprentice. I taught him everything I knew in the Art of Drageurism. A drageur is by definition a netter, a fisherman who works the high seas in a boat, dragging those huge nets to catch fish in mass quantity. But we're talking the French slang version here and I will tell you it has nothing to do with fish.

I taught Sydney the Art of the Breakthrough, I taught him the power of Comparative Beauties, I taught him about One Bad Mood Away, Lady's Choice, Storage Men, Think Duh, and Never Divulge the Whole Truth. I taught him about the Stable and the Rotation Theory. I taught him about Romantic Chess, the Laws of Attraction and Repulsion, and Honey and Harmony. I taught him about Dysfuncionados, Modelitis, Wams, Bullets, girlie-whirlies, and Mom-I-Got-the-Parters. I taught him about the Proper Combinants for a successful double date.

I taught him to stuff his guest room drawers with the latest La Perla lingerie, and stock bathrooms with foreign feminine products and lotions: Embryolisse, the M.A.C. line, and all stuffs Phyto included. I taught him about Never Slam the Boyfriend, the Law of Reconnaissance, and of course, the Naughty Law. I taught him about the 55-Degree Rule and the Mole Game. Everything I knew—gift ideas, the perfect dialogue, gestures, body language, psychological ruses, and locales for maximum results—I imparted to him.

And he learned fast. The results were coming in. He was becoming one smooth, well-oiled drageur. I was happy to see the positive transformation in him.

On a professional note, Sydney taught me a few things too. He stressed the high cost of moviemaking, that a picture has one weekend to flaunt its stuff. And that the weekend's box office tally during those first few days makes or breaks you. It underscored the need to choose my subject matter wisely. *One weekend.* That's all you got.

He taught me the need for stars to ensure the picture opening strongly. The message was to avoid throwing yourself in a vacuum by scripting characters who may be weird and fascinating but totally unplayable by the short list of names needed to ensure that first weekend. He taught me to write parts for stars. Parts where studio executives could say *Ah, that's*

Starman Demento, or *Starman Whitebred Hero,* or *Stargal Afro-American,* or *Stargal StripmeIhavegoodtits.* Sydney taught me the commercial ropes.

I was in the ideation stage for the spec Marty had advised me to write. I couldn't dedicate full-time to it yet. I had an idea and two characters but I needed more meat. I had some research to do as well. I landed two writing jobs with clients of my new agent. The first was a rock video. The other was a half-hour script for a sexy thriller short destined for cable. I titled it *Raincheck.* It depicted a guy who calls on his former high school love, now an oppressed Beverly Hills starwife, and redeems his "raincheck" for one dose of intercourse they promised each other in the future. The pay wasn't bad but it wasn't feature work. The big question still consumed me. When would I break out?

One October afternoon, I arrived back at the guesthouse only to find a nice gift wrapped with red and white ribbon. When I opened it, I had that shoulda-known feeling. It was a mobile phone, something I swore I would never buy. But it was a gift. No one had bought me a gift in a long time. Though I didn't use it, I was touched just the same.

Muffin Heads

There was a uni-day during this stretch that was different from the rest, however. It was a summer day's holdout in the early fall. September I think, the best month in any town. The sky was cloudless, the smog quotient was low, and the city was baked in sunshine. Even the 7-Elevens felt good about themselves. An exceptional day. Only I was having a lowly version of it.

Sydney was attending the film festival in Deauville. It was grating on me. Not that Sydney was a participant in the overseas event. The fact that I was not. The fact that I was treading water with my career. I felt like I was one of those characters in the Waiting Place in Dr. Seuss's *Oh, the Places You'll Go!* Damned forever.

The ruthless truth is I wanted a picture in a festival. Or somewhere. It made me green. It was a nasty Wannabeastly flare-up. I guess my mood was a natural correction to all the overweening optimism I'd been feeling lately. Anyway, I did what I always did when I experienced such a dip.

On the drive up PCH, I noticed my gas gauge was flirting below empty. I slid into my favorite Arco AM-PM. I took my slot, paid inside, inserted nozzle, and filled up my baby. Of course some gas trickled on my dogs.

"Bummer, dude."

I heard it behind me. I didn't have to turn around to know what I was up against. Of course it was a Muffin Head. In the classic tradition. They were everywhere in L.A. Muffin Heads from all over America came to L.A. where they could be with their own dim kind. If you knew anyone in school who was a little spacy, a little stoned, a little out there, wore sandals too long into the fall, had a Lava Lamp, or talked about surfing too much in a town where there were no waves, he probably ended up in L.A. By the time you got to them, L.A. had done a zigzag on their heads so that they were two watts short of a sixty-watt light-bulb and wore slick sunglasses du jour that made them feel like they tested high on insubordination but really they couldn't even hold up a mocha java bar. Muffin Heads.

I came up with the term one afternoon when a Stowaway came over and baked blueberry muffins. I watched them cook through the oven window. They were held in little cups and the high heat turned them brown. When they popped out of the pan they were done. That's what I felt about the L.A. natives. They all started in little cribs and the sun cooked and browned them, and made them mellow and complacent. Once they popped out of their adolescence they were nicely baked Muffin Heads.

Now I give you my rule. A Californian is a terrible thing to waste.

This Head was filling up at the next pump and was still nosily eyeing my soiled dogs and waiting for a response. So I took his cue and did the right thing. I ignored him. It was either that or rip his face off.

You see, it wasn't the fact that he was a Head. You ran into them every day. What irked me was what he called me. I hated hearing that word. If the truth be known, I hated hearing all those L.A. words. Like *bitchin'* and *gnarly* and *to the max* and the cutesy-stupid license plates with cheery messages like JONESIN or 4-PLAY or HI THERE. Every time I saw one, I wanted to ram right into it. But *dude* was the worst. Anyone who called me *dude* I wanted to strangle. And tell them I wanted nothing to do with their foggy, loser world. I wanted to whap and slap the cheeks of all the Muffin-Headed verbal cripples who drove around in cars with no roofs, who possessed the intellectual charge of a penlight, to wake them up and ask them to try the English language for a change. Of course, had my career been a little more eventful, I would have chalked them all up to local color.

Like I said, I was having a Greenie flare-up.

Tahitian Taboo

I hadn't visited Piedra in a while. And I made myself get real useless once I got there. I swam in the ocean, skipped a few stones, and scraped tar off my big toe. I brought a book too. I read from Alan Watts's *The Wisdom of Insecurity*. Like the natives, I wasn't reading much in the city that never reads and I thought it was high time I got back to turning a few pages. It felt good to exercise my eyes again.

The beach was pretty deserted except for a family with toddlers, a stray mustard mutt, and a young lady far in the distance. But the heat waves coming off the sand made for a hazy, impressionistic wipe. Besides, I was too immersed in Watts's contentions that impermanence and insecurity are an inescapable part of life, that we must embrace them and worship the reality of the present. I thought about how I had a spirituality drought going, and these words were good nutrients for my neglected soul. All Wannabeastliness and Mighty Hippo needs took a backseat for a few hours and it was a nice feeling.

Though those career-based tensions took the afternoon off, my nervous system was still given a full workout. It all began with the surfside stroll. The sun assault had made me restless. As I walked I noticed the deep stamps my flat feet were making in the sand. I wondered the difference between my molds and those of an ape. I rounded it off to an evolutionary toss-up, even though the ape's feet probably had more arch.

I sniffed some seaweed, kicked a few shark eggs, and looked to the horizon for a pack of seals, but none had chosen Piedra's cove to frolic in. Then I saw her. It started with a hand waving at me. She was lying on a towel and from the distance, her color was all flesh. Clothing had no part in the vision. Breasts, perfect beautiful breasts, were sunny-side up, pointed high, snobbily looking off and away from the ocean, dashing it off as nothing. It was that Taboo Girl. Looking more than taboo.

Fuck.

I waved back politely and hoped it would be enough. But she sat up. And waved me over. Then stretched an aqua tube top over a torso boasting a chest like one of Gauguin's Tahitian treats. I felt better about approaching her clothed. So I did. One step at a time. I looked around to see if there was anyone in sight. There wasn't.

When I moved within twenty yards, I saw she had a tiny black excuse for suit bottoms that rose up weakly above her hips. I was happy for that. That she had at least something on. Not that her charms would be wasted on me. Just the opposite.

"Hello, Heyward."

"Teal." I remained standing. "Gorgeous one, huh?"

"Sure is," she said, and gripped a tall Evian bottle at the same time.

"Been here a while?"

"We've been here a couple hours."

"Who's we?" I said, my heart starting to drum.

"Just me and my Wodehouse," she said, smiling. And I saw the book spread on the towel.

She then asked me if I wanted some 4 and I said no. And then nothing more. I wasn't going to be the conversation generator. Not that day. And not with her. I let the silence between us be her worry.

"You've done some job with our friend."

"Sydney?"

"You're quite a, shall we say, coach."

"I told him 'thin to win.' That was it really."

"And the colorist and the clothes. He's a different man."

"There you have it. The formula."

"The formula for what?"

And we both laughed. It was one of those laughs that indicated we both knew what she was implying, even though I wasn't exactly sure. I was playing along. But one thing was for sure. With that simple exchange, all the angst and bitterness I'd been feeling had disappeared.

"Why don't you sit down?"

"Well . . ."

"Come on," she said. I found a nice dent in the sand and plopped into it. She smiled and followed up with "Don't you feel it?"

It was an odd question, which means nothing more than there was something unpredictable behind it. "What?"

"Where? is a better question. And I'll answer it. Deep down."

She looked at me. I had a better idea now. But I wasn't going to give in to anything. Perhaps she was just fishing, was my thought.

"Don't play concept-challenged with me."

"So you know?"

"About your little pact? Of course I know." And she cracked the victorious I'm-privy grin. "That's why we feel the way we feel. It's kind of exciting, don't you think? The fact that we're sworn off to each other." Her smile lasted a few seconds, then died. "Just be careful."

"How do you mean?"

"He's tough. I've seen him in action. He can be pretty severe."

"I'm not surprised."

"And vengeful."

"What are you saying? That maybe this isn't such a good idea?"

"Of course it's not," she said. Then her head angled to the sea. "That's what makes it special."

I smiled weakly, then rose up from the sand and gave my sandy legs a brush. Then I started my march back to my book.

"Heyward, don't be silly. We can still be friends. Can't we?" I pivoted around and found myself saying nothing. "We can still have a conversation, right?" I left that alone. "So let's." Then her tone changed. "Besides, there's nothing to worry about. We're in the same camp anyway."

"Camp? What do you mean?" I advanced back a few steps.

"You know what I mean."

"I don't think I do."

"We're neutral."

"Neutral?"

"Our personalities. They neutralize each other. Don't you find we reach a stalemate?"

"Perhaps," I said airily. It was a stall technique. Because I really wasn't sure. Besides, I knew full well she'd define her feelings further and then I could decide. It's what I liked about Teal. She took me to places others didn't. Places I was unfamiliar with. Whether her points were valid or not. They were hers. And different. It's the kind of movie I enjoyed. The type whose ending you can't predict. Until you get there. She was sharp, this Taboo Girl.

"Like we get a buzz from each other's company at first but then we come to an impasse. The tension dies off. Don't you agree?"

After all that, I didn't say anything. Mainly because I disagreed. But I wasn't going to tell her that I felt we had a fierce connection. That she accessed me. And I accessed her. And that I felt the tension therein. There was enough there to get big muscles if you lifted reps of it. But if she was being true to her impulses, I didn't want to alter her mind-set. She looked at me still waiting for an answer. And since she did, only at that moment did I feel compelled to respond. Any further hesitation would seem like I disagreed anyway.

"I suppose . . ."

"I *suppose.* Wiggle words. Next you'll be saying 'Not to my knowledge' and 'I don't recall.' Very evasive."

"Did you attend law school too?"

"Not quite. Think about it, though. We're on the same team, Heyward."

"I don't know enough about you to make such a claim."

"Sure you do. You know me." She uncapped the tall Evian bottle and took a swig. "And I know you."

She offered the bottle to me. I drank too. I wiped my mouth and recapped it.

"You think you know me?" I asked with a dash of challenge to it.

"Of course. You're easy. And not because you are. I see you in myself. You're just a more developed version."

"How so?"

"You actually execute. I just sit around and ponder it."

Now I knew where she was going. So I decided to slow this whole thing down. I waited. So as to show perfect composure. To demonstrate her probe couldn't affect my system, a system whose innocence I would still uphold. She was trying to flirt with my dark side. To make me confess. And I would have none of it.

"It?" I offered finally.

"*It* is the Big Gray Monster."

I laughed at that.

"You know what I'm talking about."

"Maybe. Define your color scheme."

"Gray? It's neither black nor white, but has elements of both. It's the color of life."

"And my behavior?"

"Ditto," she said, and it had been a long time since I'd heard someone use that phrase. "You'll be honestly regretful and naturally sorry about having done certain things. Because deep down you're a good person. But some things get in the way."

"Like?"

"Life."

"You think I'll do anything to make it?"

She said nothing. But kept a confident twinkle in her eye.

"You're an interesting girl."

She laughed at that. "Spew, spew, spew. I bet that kind of comment goes down well at the club bar. Do you follow it up with a reach for cashews too?"

I smiled. "Are you being hostile? I can't tell."

"Just your average beach bitch on a beautiful day."

"I don't know if I'm ready for this kind of conversation. It's only noon."

But she wouldn't leave it alone.

"I know it's tough to wrestle with, someone who's calling you on your double-sided nature. You don't know whether to deny or come clean."

"There are people I wouldn't take it from. That's for sure."

"I'm flattered."

My half-smile turned into words. "Tell me about my two sides."

"Your desire for fame. And your knowledge of the absurdity of it. You can laugh at it, roll it up in a funny ball, and throw it, yet, at the end of the day, you still want that cover of *Me Magazine*."

"Whatever there's a notoriety index, I'll be there," I said.

"Don't hide behind overkill," she sent right back.

"You think I'm a hypocrite?"

"We're all hypocrites," she said flatly. "It's a part of life."

"Is that the cousin comment to 'We're all prostitutes'?"

"If the shoe fits."

We looked at each other a moment.

"Look, I just write wallpaper."

We both laughed. I did because our conversation was consistently ebbing back to a certain seriousness for no apparent reason. I didn't know why the fuck Teal was laughing. It was part of her charm.

"We all contradict ourselves. On a daily basis," she continued.

"Like, 'Sit down, Heyward, I want to talk to you, but be careful, you might get fucked for doing it'?"

She liked that. I saw it in her smile. It was obvious she possessed a similar gray tone to her character and she enjoyed being caught. She wanted to be caught. In fact, she'd made me catch her.

"Precisely," she said finally.

"I've called myself the Mighty Hippo," I confided.

"You are quite the buzzword guy."

"I try."

"Duality is just about the most interesting behavioral trait human beings possess. It's what separates us from the rest of the animal kingdom," she said, and put on a big pair of buggy ovals. I complimented her on them.

"So I am close," she prodded.

"If you claim to know that much, you should know the answer. My guess is you're just poking around. You are good at it. And it is amusing."

"Fuck off. I know what you're doing."

"What?"

"You're studying me."

I burst out loud in laughter, the kind that erupts from deep down when you've been busted. Her Blade was a nice one.

"Right? You're letting me go off on you, quizzing me on you, taking all my barbs and insults, sucking me in, to see what I'll say. Not because you want to know what I know of you. But to reveal myself. You're putting me on the slab and making me a science project. And you're studying my habits."

I casually looked at her from a left angle in a concerned, clinical, scrutinizing way, then from the right. As if giving her a real lab doctor's inspection. "Maybe."

"Do all your maybes come in a set?" she cracked. "That's okay. I've been studied before."

"I'm sure. You have rich interiors. And you have control of them. That's a rarity."

"Thank you."

"Is Teal your real name?"

"It's my middle name. My real name is Amber. But I changed it."

"Why?"

"Because Amber is a stripper name."

"And Teal?"

"Teal takes her clothes off when she wants to. Not because she has to."

"Good answer. I didn't think you were a Saturday Night Girl."

"What's that?"

"A girl who lets anything happen. Providing it's Saturday night."

"Meaning she makes one unscrupulous move a week?"

"Exactly."

"And what are you? Saturday Night Guy?"

"No, I'm Monday Night Guy."

"Who is . . . ?"

"He's the guy you don't want to go out with on the weekend. You save him for early in the week."

"I think you're selling yourself short."

I could only laugh. "Who do you think I am, then?"

"I think you're Friday Night Guy dressed in Monday Night clothing."

"Meaning?"

"You want at least two unscrupulous nights a week."

"Very good," I said with a breaking grin.

"So is Monday Night Girl the most unwanted girl?"

"No. Not to Monday Night Guy. He loves her. He marries her."

"But he still dreams of Saturday Night Girl."

"He is male, yes. It's the same with Saturday Night Guy. He won't be seen with Monday Night Girl until Monday night."

"So Monday Night Girl is the preferred-least girl?"

"Well"—I thought about it for a second—"Tuesday Night Girl is only slightly better. But they're still respectable."

"You mean there's someone lower?"

"Yes."

And hearing that made her excited. It was all over her face. It was scary. It was the way I got when told something fresh. "Tell me. Immediately," she pleaded.

"I can't."

"What?"

"It's too crude."

"Try me, O Dark Lord," she quipped sarcastically.

"Sunday Afternoon Girl. She gets the least respect."

"Really? Why? It sounds religious."

"It's hardly that. Sunday Afternoon Girl comes over during a football game. And then performs fellatio on you at halftime, only to take off soon after."

"Why?"

"Because you want to see the second half."

It broke her in half. She was slapping the sand with her palm. She laughed for minutes on end. I sifted sand between my toes.

"So guess what I am?" she asked playfully.

"You're Friday Night Girl."

"Nope."

I loved it. She was turning my own silly language against me.

"I'm Thursday Night Girl."

My face showed puzzle. I didn't know where she was going with this. I was stumped. "Explain."

"Well, I only go out Thursday night and I'm hard as hell to get, and I play even harder to get, but if you say the right things at the right time, in the right way, provided I like the way you look and the way you move, then you've got me, and you'll get me for three days. Because, remember. I've left the weekend open."

Though a bit wordy, it was brilliant. "Just three days?"

"Three days."

"With no chance for a renewal?"

"Depends how the weekend went."

I smiled. And so did she.

Smart Moods

When a woman is highly intelligent, there's nothing better. But it's not just the smarts. It's that they're sent out through the filter that is the chaos of woman. The chaos of man is a lot less interesting and, in the end, not that chaotic. So a man's smarts can't be expressed as colorfully. A woman like Teal could change moods on a dime and display a rainbow selection of behavioral choices. I called them Smart Moods. It was liberating. And invigorating. Women with Smart Moods fascinated me.

"What are you doing here anyway?" I asked.

"Taking some sun."

"No, but why here?"

She took her time with it. And as she did, my eyes drifted to her feet. She had great feminine feet. They had soft lines, an elegant length to them, and toes that belonged together. Beautiful feet on a woman can be such a lift. If they are proportioned nicely it really makes you feel good about the human race. Because feet can hold the ugliness of the world in them. And when my eyes dragged up her body and took in all that was her nightclub, it was sensory saturation. And beyond.

"Matador Beach had too many people. I wanted to get away. Piedra is more peaceful. Why, you think I followed you?"

Again I remained silent. I didn't want to take that tangent. I just looked out at the blue line in the distance. And switched the subject.

"They say the horizon is thirteen miles. It looks like five."

"And you?"

"I come here a lot."

"I do know. Sydney told me." I nodded and eyed her to see if her comment had any tease to it. It didn't. "Can you put some lotion on my back?"

I hesitated. With my answer. In fact I didn't answer. My voice would have quavered. So I shut up. And dutifully grabbed the bottle. After all, I had to do something.

She peeled off her top and what she uncovered made its presence felt immediately. Fortunately, I had some Oakley ten-dollar knockoffs riding my face so I could take a nice look with impunity. She then turned over on her stomach.

As I massaged her number 4 into her back, my mind drifted from its search of all that is original, and plopped splat on the cliché. All those thoughts invaded my space. And Teal didn't help with comments like:

"Can you do my legs too?"

The specimen before me was for the arts. Her legs were those of a dancer's and the skin felt hot and moist and smooth already. As my hands made their way up from her calves I wondered if I should apply to the wonderful halves bisected by that strand of laughable string. I knew she wasn't going to call the whole thing off if I did. It was there for the taking. I looked over my shoulder for the fiftieth time like the nervous schoolboy trying to study his cheat sheet in the bathroom.

But there was no teacher in sight.

"Didn't you miss a spot?"

"Two in fact."

"And?"

I took my time with it. I was going to hit her where she lived.

"You say I execute. But you just sit around and ponder. So tell me. What are you doing hanging around with Sydney?"

She dug her chin in the sand. Then her head flopped over and she lay on her ear. The one that turned her face away from me. When she spoke her voice was hidden and less audible and it got slightly muffled in the breeze. But I could hear her just the same.

"Is this for your book? Or are you really interested?"

"Does it matter?"

"No, I guess not." Then she raised her head and spiraled it back at me. "Okay, I'll be your science project. But not today," she said. "And maybe not tomorrow. But someday."

I handed her the bottle and stood up straight. "I have to get going. I have a three o'clock meeting."

She took her eyes off me and looked forward again.

"Do you know how many men would love to rub lotion into my ass?"

"Yes I do. I grew up with them. And now we don't speak. But you can catch them at the Coliseum on any Sunday in the fall."

I stood over her waiting for her to say something. She didn't at first. She just smiled.

"Only if it's a home game," she added. I nodded. "Nice seeing you, Heyward. And I liked your script, you know. Let's discuss it sometime."

"Right now, I'm writing a children's book."

"Are you really? What's it called?"

"The Little Soft Penis."

She laughed at that. I was hoping she would.

"What's it about?"

"It's kind of *The Little Engine That Could* meets *Deep Throat.*"

"Vroom, vroom . . . ," she said without exclamation.

And I walked off. Swiftly. Before she could say anything more. She was a Walking Nightclub with Smart Moods. Talk about a land mine.

"Bye-bye, Friday Night Guy," I heard faintly.

She didn't see if I laughed or not. Because I didn't turn around.

The reality is I was days away from any scheduled meeting. But filling up my agenda with imaginary clients was the best course of action. Any dedication I had to maintaining inactive status had been pummeled. Temporarily. Of course I wanted to sleep with her. And make love to her. And fuck her. All three. At once. Yesterday. But I'd never let her know that.

It was the one question of hers I hadn't answered—whether I wanted to have sex with her. Her comment about rubbing lotion into her ass was a test. When you hand a man a sex-laden comment, especially when you have the talent of a Teal, nine times out of ten he'll come right back with a tainted response. Unless he's a novice. I was not a novice. But I didn't bite. I didn't smile. And I certainly didn't massage lotion into her perfect globes. I left, which means I let her wonder. Nothing drives a woman crazier than being forced to wonder.

One question of mine, however, had been answered. Little did Teal know my children's book comment had been a test as well. It was a line of fishing string with a silvery minnow hooked on the end. And Teal had taken the bait. When you hand a woman a sex-laden comment, the responses require more attention. The answers are not as Gym Boy straight as with a man. She can do one of three things. She can ignore it, which means she's shocked, undecided about it, or secretly thinks you're a Mo-ron. She can disavow it, which means she's shocked, undecided about it, or secretly wants to have sex with you. Or she can play along with you, the analysis of which is pretty damn obvious. Teal had played along. Her "Vroom, vroom" was the clincher. At that point I realized she didn't think for one second we were in the same camp.

For those reasons and others, the impromptu meeting on the beach stuck with me for a while. She had called me on a lot. She knew I was coaching Sydney and that I was the Mighty Hippo. But I still couldn't get a fix on her deep character. And she would not let me. What the hell was she doing in L.A.? Was she being the Mighty Hippo too? Had she just appeared at the beach that day? It's hard to forget a woman who shows just enough of herself to convince you there are even more fascinating layers still to be revealed.

I left that day more confused about Teal Harding than I had been prior. Even though I knew a little more.

Teal was right, of course. She was so subtle in her inner mind she knew I was studying her habits. Though I had previously sworn off trying to seize her gold, to find what made her tick, she had hooked me that day on the beach. After that, I was determined to know her secret— to know her private puzzle. It was like placing a filled syringe before a smack addict in midwithdrawal. I had to grab at it.

The Super-cept

A month passed and I did not see her. I wondered what had happened to her. One thing she said stuck with me. The part about Sydney's vengeful character. It was chilling to ponder. It gave me another level of respect for him. Or rekindled the respect I'd had before. I had seen this quality emerge the day we'd made the Pact—when he warned me never to cross him. But when you get close to someone, the walls crumble, life softens, and you begin taking him for granted. But Teal had underscored it with her Smart Moods. It made me firm up. I realized I had to raise my game. I had to get a little bit genius for a while.

One morning in October over coffee and grapefruit sections at the main house, I said it. And when I did, he had no idea it was coming.

"It's time."

Of course I was prepared with the next step. I dressed it down, I played aloof, but I was really two series of downs ahead. And I'd die before I punted.

"Time for what?"

"Whore Weekend."

Surprise climbed all over his face. Before the smile wiped it away. He had no idea what Whore Weekend was about. But he liked the sound of it. Who, if they possessed any kind of politically incorrect penchant, or desired any type of flirtation with their dark side, or merely lived in Hollywood, wouldn't? It was a concept with explosive implications. It was a Super-cept.

It started that Monday with a quick blast of calls, real quick hits, with grabbers, the sexual and dark kind. These hits were administered to only the types we wanted at this party. Women.

I had Armando bring down a burger with fatty stuffings and fattier fries. I was looking pretty pasty and feeling good. A good protein load washed in greasies was in store. It was left on a tray by the pool. By the phone. Sometimes Hell-A wasn't so bad.

I spoke as directly as I dialed. I had rolled my computer out to the patio and tapped into my files. I checked off the desirables of L.A. and the environs, and printed out a list.

In making such dicey calls, let's not forget that I wasn't known for being a dog, or a dick, or a jerk, or a user and abuser of women. I was inactive. I hadn't been piercing their veils and making them cry. If I talked anyone out of their panties I asked them to put them back on soon after because I was only inspecting a stupid tattoo or an appendectomy scar, not their most private privates. Though I still may have enjoyed the view.

So for me to go out on a limb and tell the ladies of L.A. that I was cohosting a party under the flag of prostitution, there was still an element of safety to it. After all, it was being endorsed by me, the Inactive One. And it sounded fun. Having said that, it was early in the week and the phone call I'm sure was like a nerve biter.

In the end, it remained to be seen who would show. I was certain some would try to avoid our party but eventually the dark side would battle and bruise the better angels of their nature. By week's end, their good intentions and safety mechanisms would have taken a beating. They'd not only want to come, they'd be dying to come. For reasons above, I considered my blast of phone calls like a smelling salt, a clarion call to the parcels of darkness out there. And there were many.

Like I said it was a Super-cept. It asked L.A.'s corrupt, jaded princesses of darkness to hold hands and sing. It wasn't a stretch. Dark thoughts, yes. But dark town, definitely. You can check out anytime you like, but . . . you know the rest.

It was an odd fact, however, that on that first day of calls, I received no acceptances. And I got fifteen absolute turndowns for reasons like "I'm going away" or "I'm busy" or of course "My boyfriend wouldn't approve" to which I said repeatedly:

"What a party pooper."

Late in the afternoon, a comely Sydney, wearing a pair of off-white khakis, light blue shirt, and leather braces, put in a visit to make a progress check. I took a break and sucked down a diet cola to keep my mind from drifting away with the afternoon.

"So how's it going?"

"Typical first day."

"How many subscribers?"

"It's still early."

"None?"

"Nope."

He looked at me and thought about it.

"I knew it."

"Knew what?"

"To think that a group of girls are going to come over for a party you call Whore Weekend?"

"I could call it a Hooker Holiday."

"It's not going to work and what's worse is that you'll look bad doing it. As bad as it gets. And so will I. Which is more important. To me. And my business."

He was serious. It was the second time I'd seen him this way.

"You're just going to have to have a little faith. By the time we . . ."

He looked sharply at me. It was a hint to reword my sentence.

". . . I spread the word, at clubs and restaurants, there will be so many candidates we'll have to hire additional security to turn all the girlie-whirlies away."

He cracked a faint grin. "You're a nut."

"That's me. How's Belinda?"

"I'm seeing her tonight."

"And what about Nina?"

"We just had lunch. Then we made out in the car. I'm very close there."

"You have a pretty nice rotation going."

"That's funny. A rotation."

"It's small, but nice."

"I've never had a rotation."

Then he walked back up the lawn. I downed some more diet cola and got back to flooding the circuits with my good cheer. I must say I was surprised no one had signed on yet.

Bad Word

That night, I Sledded over to the Olive and told a few. Then I went to the Monkey Bar and alerted a few more. I was pretty selective. I hit Drai's, Morton's, Chaya Brasserie, and all the haunts dedicated to Woody pussycat fluff.

The stats weren't very pretty. I got a dozen *nos* and *no thank yous*, several *you're joking*s, a couple *you're out of your mind*s, or words to that effect, and one slap in the face. She was drunk, though, and laughed it off afterward. I wasn't worried. Yet.

I decided to extend invites during the day. It would seem less ghoulish and threatening and more good-natured. Appeal to the dark soul in the bright light. Why? The girlie-whirlies may be heated up from the midday sun and open to more risky overtures. After all, daytime is hours away from the danger of night. But the temptation would be placed in mind to cook and simmer all day.

The next day I hit Swinger's for breakfast. I did the King's Road Cafe at high noon. Then I went to Giuseppe's and all the designer boutiques on Rodeo. They threw me out of Azzadine's. No sense of humor. I wondered if I was doing my reputation some injustice. It didn't feel that way. I was approaching the city the way the rest of the con artists approached it. On material terms, on a service basis. I pressed on.

I got some takers but they were types you didn't want to take. We wanted the cream of L.A. Not the 2% low-fat.

I hit Indochine, Matsuhisa and L'Orangerie and Le Colonial and Tommy Tang's that night. I did a full circle around Hell-A. By Wednesday I had covered Hollywood. And secured only a handful.

I was discouraged. I needed to get away from my project. I went to Piedra to watch surfers rip it but the waves sucked. There was one Boogie-boarder chasing a meaningless swirl. I sucked down a beer, though, and that tasted good. Before I knew it, I was doing time in all the girlie spots in Santa Monica and Marina del Rey. On Thursday, I did Venice. I got a few *maybe*s and *call me tomorrow*s, that kind of thing. But the bulk of my responses were in the negative.

On Friday morning, I had a headache and it wasn't a hangover. I had an unfun seminar with myself. Coffee didn't help. It was making me go onstage when I didn't know my lines. All energy and nowhere to go.

I thought I had the perfect idea for the perfect town. I'd felt sure the town with no scruples and no soul would revel in a party to celebrate the prostitutes of the world. Pay-fors from all over America were going to save up a month's salary and fly in for the party. It was going to be that great. This was not to be. I had blown it hugely in big letters. I had lost this battle. Maybe a helluva lot more. The Beethoven-like symphony I had been composing in Bel-Air for Sydney Swinburn had turned totally discordant. It could no longer be considered music. It was bad banging on a drum. My scene had unraveled. I had become bad word.

Panic in L.A.

Of course I wondered if I was just experiencing an insecurity flare-up, the kind only screenwriters and artists suffer. A sort of menstrual cycle for creatives. Only the cause is the massive pressure put on them by a business which will not pay them, consult them, include them, and not let them be a part of—the film they wrote. Or never buy it in the first place, which was the case for most. But I realized that wasn't it.

Sydney called me numerous times. I didn't pick up. I'm sure he was trying me on my mobile but I wasn't using it. I didn't want to report the bad news.

I contemplated moving out that afternoon. And maybe even L.A. Maybe I would return to New York. For good. Or at least until this blew over. That's exactly what I decided to do. I did a quick clean of the guesthouse and Sledded to the airport. Bob the Riot made sure I got there quickly in the HOV track.

When it came down to it, trashing my reputation was my least worry. What was frightening was I had strapped almighty Sydney Swinburn to my back. After all, he was the sponsor. I had taken Sydney down with me. Everything I had worked for had backfired. Instead of helping him, I hurt him. In my rash need for a deal, credits, fame, and recognition, I pushed the envelope too far, too fast. It was all over. I'd never get a script deal. It was over for me in this town.

I figured I'd lay low in Manhattan for a week. Then return with my tail between my legs and move out of the guesthouse. I was going AWOL. I was bad word and I wanted out. I needed out.

I left the Sled in the monthly parking garage. I was sweaty and my pants were sticking to my legs when I entered the terminal.

I thought of the element of surprise I would hit my family with.

They expected me at Thanksgiving, not weeks before. What would I tell them? That I fucked up my career by throwing a whore party that was a bomb? That I couldn't even land a script-polish assignment? That I had miserably failed and I was sliding into the dining room belly-up with both palms open for handouts? What the hell was I going to do?

The more I thought about it, the more I realized if I went back to New York, I would not go home. NFW. I could not stand the embarrassment. Sure, humiliation was only waiting for me in Follywood as well. But Follywood was a place I didn't give a damn about. New York was my town. It was the place I was going to move back to when I had my house in order. By age forty. New York was me.

The ticket lady was staring at me and said "Sir?" for the third time. I didn't register it until another customer stepped in front of me. I mashed his collar and threw him back. After the scuffle, I upbraided myself for being a jerk. Frustration was fueling my aggressiveness. I moseyed out of there to collect my thoughts.

I didn't know why but my left testicle hurt. I think it was due to my blue jeans, which had gotten tighter. I had been eating well thanks to the nutritional spillover from Sydney's main house. And Armando's eggs to order. Some boozing too. Tight jeans for sure.

Reality was dawning. I had to face the music. I had to get a pair of knee pads and crawl up that endless driveway and beg for forgiveness. I had fucked up and I needed help. I had a slight chance since I had gotten him laid. More than once. In this day and age, that counted a lot. I supposed it always had.

Long ago, I had heard someone say a kid may be better off knowing the women of the world early on and having a stable from which to choose than going to Harvard, Yale, or MIT. The road to advancement might be much quicker. I didn't necessarily believe it. But I did believe that, to certain men, women were worth more than gold. I'd hoped Sydney would see it that way.

I was a pretty dejected cat when I pulled out of the garage parking— so dejected I didn't arm-wrestle the attendant for the three bucks I owed for twenty minutes of slottage.

I want to forget the drive back to Bel-Air because it was a total drag.

The car sounded shitty, the tailpipe was dragging and sparking, and my mood sucked. I felt like a low, low, low rider.

Rewrite: Whores & Hustlers

I pressed on the alarm code and the gate opened. I slugged it up the driveway feeling as grandiose as a barroom shorty on a stool with the bartop mashing his gums. I felt devoid of respect, unaccomplished, and towered over by life.

I trudged into the house and Armando met me.

"Mr. Swinburn is in the study," he stressed. "He is eager to see you."

I bet, I thought, but didn't say.

Sydney was seated behind his desk, flipping through a script. He turned the pages three times before looking up.

"Hi, Sydney."

"Look. We have a problem."

"I know, Sydney. I'm here to apologize. I'm so sorry."

He gave me a slightly shaved look. But I didn't want him to speak. I wanted to lay down enough apologetic drizzle so he would be disarmed—if indeed anything would disarm him at all. "Believe it or not, I almost left town. I just got back from the airport."

"What on earth for?" he asked as he stood up.

"I'm ashamed. I don't know how I'm going to make it up to you. I doubt I ever can."

Sydney walked to the front of the desk and squared before me.

"I'm proposing to move my stuff out in the next few days. If you'll give me the weekend . . ."

His face continued with its glaze of confusion. "Move out? What the hell are you talking about?"

"The party. I'm sorry."

"Sorry for what?"

"In case you didn't know, Sydney, we have no guests."

"Are you out of your mind?"

"What do you mean?"

"Every phone line I have, office included, has been flooded with girlie-whirlies begging, I mean begging, to come to this party."

"You're shitting me."

"Your phone has been ringing off the hook."

"I don't get it. No one was confirming."

"They are now. Call it sly, or coy, or playing hard to get, but we're being billed as hosting the party of the year. Girlie-whirlies from all points are flying in for it."

Believing my ears was a problem. I slumped in the cushy chair opposite Sydney's desk, my limbs flopping everywhere. I was a pulseless rag doll. I looked at Sydney and he slapped my knee.

"You did a phenomenal job. It's what we wanted. And beyond."

He was using my language again and it got lost in the more serious implications of one of the world's great turnarounds.

"But you said there's a problem," I reminded him.

"There *is*. Too many women. That's the problem."

"Since when?"

"As of now it's two hundred girls and us. I had to turn down another hundred. We can't handle a scene like that. What do we do, cancel?"

It came to me immediately. "Not cancel. Expand."

"Expand? To what??"

"To: Whores and Hustlers."

"What?"

"Theme change. We'll invite fifty guys—ones we like—and we'll call back the other girlies on the waiting list."

I stood up with renewed enthusiasm. And Sydney met me with an arm wrapping my shoulder.

"It *is* going to be the party of the year," he said finally.

"Not if we don't get that casting under way."

"What casting?"

"For the Tree Girl."

Sure, he was puzzled. Wouldn't you be?

I returned to the guesthouse and rifled off calls to all the lesser talent agencies. The ones with girlies known for more compromising stuff. The Mom-I-Got-the-Parters. And I held an open casting. It took several hours. And looking at all those inspired, beauty-subsidized girls was not a problem. I took it like a man. And when I told a yellow-haired Velveeta stunner from Reno she had the job she said,

"You mean I got the part?"

"Yes, you did."

"Yippee!" Kisses came with it too. She had so much collagen in her lips they were like shorebreak. But I didn't subtract for that. Instead, I showed her to the phone. She couldn't wait to break the news to someone.

"As the Tree Girl!" I heard her pipe excitedly.

The role required her to be tied to the trunk of the big elm in the front yard, wearing a whisper of a bikini. She was to welcome guests and direct them to the front door. She was a mascot of sorts, to get everyone in the right frame of mind. Like the San Diego Chicken. She was the Tree Girl. She was sexy, willing, and totally necessary. For money, we gave her SAG scale.

You bet your ass this party was going to give Star Camp a stamp. Right on the forehead. Never to be forgotten.

Tape the Phones

Instinct is a funny thing. I thought mine had let me down. I thought of all those hours I'd spent getting to know this town. Even though we weren't pals, Hell-A and me, at least I felt I understood her. What happened that Friday made me feel like a real jerk. As a screenwriter, I considered myself a professional student of human behavior. Though I had misjudged individuals, never had I blown it with an entire town.

But in the end I had called it right. I had made an overture to the Darkies of Los Angeles and they responded with interest. A numb observer could attribute fault by citing a paranoiac breakdown as well as a blatant disregard of the basic traits of the city's character. That nothing happens on time. That it is laid-back. It was absurd for me to have jumped the gun and assumed failure.

The Whores and Hustlers' party was going to be our finest hour. It would become the party everyone in Hell-A compared decent bashes to for the next five years. It would set the standard. Why? Forget the fact that it was incredibly well produced. I mean, there was every kind of food, every kind of drink, every kind of place to go off and get sensual or get weird or get wildtime or get lost. This party had it.

The way it started was rather odd. I knew guests were arriving at around seven o'clock, which was sundown. But the thought of wearing a pimp costume was pretty daunting to me. I'm not, and have never been, a costume person. Dressing up seemed so silly, so sassy, so soft to me. I always let the Blips dress up and get the twenty-second laugh or however long it took folks to figure out what the hell they were, then look like a jerk for the rest of the night. I always wore black tie and claimed I was James Bond. It allowed me to avoid party-pooper status and look my best, and it worked nicely with the opposite sex.

But Armando kept phoning me in the guesthouse. I was taking a slow swim. And a slow Jacuzzi, a slow shower, and a slow channel surf on cable. I slowly made it to the fridge, cracked a beer, and sipped it slowly. Because something about that night and that bash seemed too huge. Too great. Too fun. Too everything. A grand stage had been constructed and I was having stage fright. I guess I felt like I'd never be the same person again. That scared me. And to tell you the truth, when it was all over, my fears were realized.

It all began for me with the Bullets ringing in around five o'clock.

"Word . . ."

"Who is it?"

"It's us."

"All of us."

They were on speakerphone, meaning I was on speakerphone.

"Hey there, Bullets."

"You never call us anymore."

"Yeah. You make friends with some studio bigwig and we never hear from you anymore."

"Baby dolls. I've been busy."

"Yeah, right. We heard about Tennessee. And all the dinners with chikitas."

"Yeah, we hear how busy you are."

"Give me a break. I'm a screenwriter. Not a playboy."

"So?"

"So what?" I asked.

"Are you going to invite us to your party?"

"Well, uh, of course. I mean, you know what it's all about, right?"

"It's a whore party," Kelly the Bullet said.

"Sure you guys want to get involved?"

"Well, Suzy does. But being a ho is no big thing."

"As if. You should talk, flopdoll. One shot of tequila and your knees are airborne."

"Oh okay, Ms. Tollgate. The girl who lets every car through."

"Oh okay, Ms. Eiffel Tower. Where everybody's been. And nobody stays."

"My God, such talk? What ever happened to my sweet little Bullets? The kind that cuddle up and think Bambi thoughts."

"Get real."

"Bozo!"

"Fuck Bambi!"

"If it was up Bambi's ass she'd know."

We all had to laugh that one off. My little Bullets had turned into little foulmouthed gremlins. It was kind of fun. I also knew it was the Whores and Hustlers Super-cept that had inspired their naughty chatter. It was an ominous sign. I did not discount it.

With respect to the Bullets, had I been active I might have considered the One-on-Four. Tonight seemed like the night. My guesthouse could easily be the duck blind. Just let the little birdies fly past and pull the trigger.

NFW. No need to complicate matters and waste time on carnal, ego-ridiculous pursuits.

"Do we have to dress up?"

"Only like a whore."

I let them say it and they did. "That's the only kind of clothes we have anyway."

"All girls dress like whores in L.A. or didn't you know?"

"You don't say," I said back flatly. "Party starts at seven."

"As if. We'll be there at ten."

Click! went the phone line. Immediately, I began to second-guess myself. Maybe I shouldn't involve the Bullets in this kind of premeditated debauchery, I thought. But what the hell. They're big girls, I concluded. Little big girls, anyway.

My plaid polyester trousers, bowling alley shirt, and platform shoes looked pretty buggy. So did my scarf and chromy shades. I had a soda-can flip-top necklace and I hung that from my neck instead of gaudier gold alternatives. Besides, any gold I had, I'd pawned long ago. I looked like your average pimpster, the Hollywood and Vine type. "Cheers to you," I said in the mirror.

After three belts of Sauza TQ, I phoned Pacific Bell and tried to get the phone service cut off. Until noon the following day. It was a preventative measure. It was to prohibit me from doing any spastic late-night phoning. Always regrettable.

"I'd like it effective immediately," I commanded.

"Is there a reason why you are dissatisfied with the service?" the woman politely asked.

"I'm not dissatisfied. I'm going out tonight. The phones are just too accessible."

She wouldn't do it without major hassle. So I improvised. I duct-taped all the handsets to their cradles. *Tape up the phones, I'm going out!* was my feeling. I knew this party would be war. And my pimp suit was my only camouflage.

Mom, I Got the Part

After a last belt, I was gliding through freshly cut blades of grass. The music was giving middle earth a good thumping. I think the trees were covering their ears. They were a lot older and wiser and less tolerant. Inside the house, the scene was unfolding like a cross between Halloween meets New Year's with a spin on Hefner's legendary Playboy Midsummer Night's Sex Party. There were girlies everywhere, all dressed like little fuckables with cherries on top.

In fact, I immediately recognized a few of Hefner's vets. Veterans, that is, meaning Playmates. There were some Hawaiian Tropic pageant contestants, some Melrose kittens, as well as a flock of pretty Wams schmoozing away. A few UCLA coeds added an academic flavor. They were tired of playing goody-goodies at their sororities, and they figured they could drink in some of life's taboo lessons without anyone on campus finding out about it. Some Fundies and Frivvies were there too to round out the crowd.

Fundies are the trust fund girls. It's an East Coast term but California boasted them too in the fat-bank communities like Beverly Hills, Malibu, Newport, and La Jolla. You know, the type of girls figure-eighting their towns in Have More cars buying stuffed bunny rabbits and looking for cute guys. In essence, spending Daddy's money.

The Frivvies are another matter. They're gold diggers who specialize in frivolous lawsuits. They're dangerous. They sit at a fat party with eyes the color of bank balances in hopes of landing the fat-cat man of their dreams. If that doesn't pan out, they wait for an ashtray to fall on their knee so they can get all legal and rape the rich, sonofabitch host out of his last dime. Frivvies had to be treated with care. I alerted security.

My next move, as is always when there's such an anthropological onslaught, was to the bar.

"What can I get you, Heyward?"

"Some liquid silver."

"Coming up."

"Hey there, will you be my pimp?"

I looked over and Loni was standing there, looking like she'd just got out of a bath.

"As long as I get first crack," I quipped.

"Still love me?"

"I'll only love you if you do me and dump me, and even then it's in the area of maybe."

"Heyward," she droned.

Loni was an unemployed cheerleader. The poor girl lost her pom-

poms when the Raiders moved back to Oakland. Now she was just another Wam without a franchise.

"How are you, Loni?"

"Can't complain," she said.

"Say, what do clothes look like on you anyway?"

She smiled at that and we touched glasses and my lowballer beat the hell out of her champagne flute. I asked her why she didn't try out for any other teams. She said the Rams moved to St. Louis. I pretended I didn't know. I did that a lot. I feigned ignorance on issues. It wasn't cool to sound like a know-it-all. You're just too informed. Only now it had to do with conservation of energy. I felt the night had a long way to go and I wasn't going to use up my O_2 on Loni Chang's pom-pom employment gap.

Some forgettable mook came up and grabbed her open butt. A "tee-hee" with dimples was her response. This girl was miles away from feminism. I let her be.

I looked around and saw a number of guys, some 8x10s, some Strugs, but certainly not as many as I'd heard were trying to get in. Of course, X-Boy was there. X-Boy was at every Hollywood party. He and his magic tablets were always in demand. He had those black, eight-ball eyes that were now a permanent feature to his skull. He'd been too generous with himself in the young nineties. Though he didn't indulge anymore, he was usually holding. And at a big party, *always* holding. He became Johnny Appleseed for those who wanted their scruples smashed. Already there was a semicircle of girlies surrounding him, pretending to like his goatee.

I decided to sit down and get my bearings. I was not a crasher, or even an invited guest. It was my party. I didn't have to run around and see who was there. I let the party come to me. I found a couch on the side and played voyeur games.

Moments later, a large girl strode past me. It was none other than Pumpkin Butt. Like X-Boy, she was at every Hollywood party. But she was a strange one, and not because she wasn't a nice person—because she was. What made her strange is that she liked her name. In fact, she'd coined it. She was an aspiring rap singer and I think she thought her quirky handle was marketable. I never argued the point with her.

"Hi, Heyward."

"Hey, Pumpster." And that was all we said. We saw enough of each other around town.

The Pumpster was hands down the best party crasher in Los Angeles. Obviously, due to the unspoken requirements of our uber-slim society, it was her rear that was keeping her out of the must-crash parties and she devised ways of getting in. And no one knew how. You'd have to wrap a video camera around her reversed baseball cap, the kind they give to downhill racers, to see how she did it.

But she didn't have to crash this one. I'd invited her.

There were scattered Mom-I-Got-the-Part girls though we hadn't invited many. They always seem to get through security. You know how that goes. Your average Thuggy working the gate doesn't necessarily have the same taste as you. Don't forget, he wants to get his own bang. So he'll make his own deal on the side and take it out in raw trade later. It's called the security skim. What a town, and I live here, was my thought.

As I thought it, coming down the lane was a perfect rendition. She was L.A.-pretty, very tan, with breasts popping out of her No-Not-There dress and curves so sharp they'd make you carsick if you drove them. I wasn't surprised by the Mom-I-Got-the-Part sighting, but I was surprised when she plopped down next to me.

"Hi, I'm Jody. I'm a friend of Sydney's. I live just up over the hill."

"You mean, the Valley?"

"Yup."

"Did you say hi to Sydney?"

"No," she said, and her eyes jiggled nervously. "But he was really busy." She jiggled some more. "This dress makes me burp," she said, and added a giggle.

It wasn't a dress. It wasn't even close. But it was thrusting up her cleavage and I'm sure burping was a problem.

"Let me guess what you do?" I said for grins.

"You don't have to. I'm an actress."

"You don't say."

"I do say. I mean I know lots of girls are actresses and all but I really am."

"I bet you are. I bet you like to play Candyland too."

"You're funny. What do you do?"

"Write," I said.

"No, I asked you what you do."

"I know. I said 'write.'"

"Oh, I thought you were saying 'right' when I was asking you a question."

"Silly you."

"Silly me, I know," and then the giggles followed up. And I wanted to stick an index in her dimple.

"Mom, I Got the Part" was the token response whenever I saw a girl so severely enhanced surgically it screamed out at you as she passed. But they're different than the Wams. The Wams will actually take a waitressing job and work for a living. The Mom-I-Got-the-Parters will do anything. Like the Tree Girl. They're Wams without scruples.

The term derives from a vision I had of those sweet, innocent girls with small-town backgrounds and big-city minds, leaving their quiet, simple nest in the middle of the country and flocking to New York or Los Angeles to become the next Stargal. After leaving their sweet mothers and fathers who are so proud of them for trying to make it as an actress in this big world, the girls feel like they just can't let everyone down.

So I envision that phone call the daughter has been dying to make since she left, exclaiming in utter excitement, "Mom, I got the part!"

And on the other end of the phone, the sweet, unknowing mother erupts in tears and yells to her husband, *"Dear?? Jody got the part!"*

"The *what?*"

"The part! You know, *the movie!*"

Then both proud parents get on the phone and listen to their little girl's story of how she nailed the audition, what the director had said to her, how talented she was, and how much he liked her. Little would the parents know, however, of the horrors involved in what their little girl had done.

The reality of the situation was that she'd gone out and gotten big-time surgery to blimp up her tits and was being asked to expose them, and probably more, to get her "part." Yet, Daddy's Little Girl was telling him how much everybody likes her (her body), how great an actress she was going to be (if she wildtimed the director and still, nine times out of ten, NOT!), and how many friends she has (tits, hair, and body).

Another familiar variation on the theme included, *"Mom, I'm dancing again."*

"Oh, how wonderful," Mom would respond. *"I was hoping you would take up your ballet again."*

Obviously, ballet had nothing to with their daughter's newfound interest in the high-step. What she was masking was the series of ten-dollar table dances she'd been performing nightly at some West Hollywood titty bar. But she would leave the exact type of dancing she was doing sufficiently vague. In case it's unclear, *vague* is the Mom-I-Got-the-Parters' favorite color.

In any case, Sydney's "friend" Jody was a classic Mom-I-Got-the-Parter. It remained to be seen if she had landed any roles, or was just in preparation for that eventuality. And good to go.

She was already looking off into never-never land but I think her mind was even further away than that.

"Are you okay?" I asked.

"I could use a little fun. I've been working so hard."

That was her telling me she wanted me to ask what she was doing. It was threat-free, so I did.

"Doing what?" I asked.

"I've been shooting all week."

She was employing the dental method, trying to pique my interest with each little tidbit, making me pull her teeth. I played along.

"Where? In L.A.?" I asked.

She nodded.

"What kind of shoot?"

And when I saw that naughty sparkle in her eye that fought to be a look of embarrassment but lost, I became a great white in warm and bloody waters. "Come on. You can tell me."

I knew she was aching to ante up. In her own way she was proud she had at least something to say for herself, that someone had employed her, that she was at least part of the Business, no matter how compromising her contribution was.

"I did some nudes," she said.

I stared at her blankly. I think she was expecting some heavy testosterone-laden gaze, that my eyes would light up, my brow would dampen, and my mouth would glisten. When it didn't happen, she assessed my attitude to be more judgmental in nature, and began to qualify her declaration.

"But they were *good* nudes," she asserted.

I looked at her a moment and said it pointedly. "Aren't they *all?*"

I was smiling and she got increasingly defensive.

"No, but it was just like those black-and-white photos Herb Ritts shot of Stephanie and Cindy in *Playboy.*"

"Did Herb Ritts do yours?"

I had to ask it, though I knew the answer already.

"No. But this photographer was really special. He uses all natural light. We did it at Seal Beach where the sunsets are beautiful," she said. "Talk about a challenge," she added.

The challenge part killed me. It really did. Another art photo feminist, I thought.

"Hmm," I said. It was all that was required. And then we exchanged farewells as she sensed I wasn't anyone who could take her where she wanted to go. And that was just fine.

Rich Robot

I must say all the color and all the flesh and all the kinky tresses and undies and spikes and garters had an overwhelming effect on me. And responding to it, I felt so unoriginal, so male. So much the reason I took no notes on the species. For a moment I lost my equilibrium. Like I had popped my ears and was caught in a three-second loss of orientation. There were that many women.

Yet as I gazed across the room, the rest of the party receded into impressionistic relief. One girl stood out. She had high red pumps, red fish-net stockings, and matching red garters, which wasn't a surprise. I will not overlook the red Valentine's Day panties. The bra was the miracle type but it was an impostor compared to her body. That was the mira-cle. Her cleavage would have stood out braless in a maternity blouse blown by the wind in a dark alley. Her hair was that gorgeous strawberry blond and when she turned my way I sensed she had locked on me. I wasn't sure because she was wearing an oval red eye mask and her line of sight was difficult to gauge from thirty paces.

I looked over my shoulder. There was nothing else to see behind me. After all, I was poised in front of a door. When I looked back her way, she was gone.

"Heyward," I heard, and my heart did the triple jump.

I pivoted and it was Sydney wearing a wig with long black tresses and a leopard jacket. He looked great as a pimp. We just stood there and eyed the wall-to-wall exposures.

"I saw your friends."

"Which ones?"

"The Bullets."

"Where?"

"They're at the bar. Chugging punch."

"Of sorts," I said. "I'm going to find them." I started off. But when I did, Sydney placed a pausing hand on my shoulder.

"Let me ask you something."

"Sure."

"What's the word on the Bullet?"

"Which one?"

"Is it Kelly?"

With that I looked at him blankly for a millisecond.

"Boyfriend," I said flatly.

"Oh."

Then he smiled. "They're only one bad mood away."

"That's true. But Kelly is a pretty straight shooter."

"Well, she's here," he said in a suggestive way.

"I know."

A couple palms matted across my eyes. I immediately tried to determine sex and that was accomplished. The firm projectiles pressing into my back gave me a hint. The scent arrived soon after, a sweet perfume that had sugared my pillow many times before.

"Uh, Baby Garbo."

She spun me around and sure enough . . .

"How did you know?"

"Experience, I guess." And Baby Garbo looked mighty fine in her white teddy and stiletto heels.

"You remember Sydney . . ."

"Of course. The rich robot."

His eyes sparkled. If he had minded being dissed by Baby Garbo before, he didn't now. It was one of her best qualities. To dis and be endearing at the same time.

A cluster of Woodies came up, with the energy of your least favorite stalkerazzi, dressed up like hustlers and pimps and jokers, and my thought was that they had overdressed, meaning they didn't need a costume at all. But we were short of guys. Sydney took one look at the group and wanted no part of it. He turned away and Baby Garbo followed suit. Industry gab he wanted none of, especially on this night, and especially not with lesser players.

Then I heard some more yap, yap and noticed Marty, my new agent, had joined the group. Immediately, I was in full discussion with these guys, all of whose names had made me squirm in my seat when their whites rolled. Now they were listening to my agent pitch my brilliance. Why? Because Sydney had given me the symbolic nod by making me his best friend. Amid a throng of four hundred people, who had Sydney's ear? Me. I was the closest conduit to real juice. These guys could get their fingers in the pie of a picture once every three years. Novastar was making twenty a year. You make the call.

It was, if nothing else, a show of force. My newfound force. Standing there in all my pimp splendor and with no credits, I realized I was the Go-To Guy for Sydney Swinburn. In less than five minutes, I had agreed to two meetings and had three business cards pressed in my palm.

At that moment, I felt guilty. I had momentarily forgotten what Sydney had done for me, what he had given me. Total access with a weighty endorsement. So why did I feel bad? No one knew better than me what Kelly the Bullet's romantic status was. And it was nothing. Zero. She had no boyfriend. She had no fuck buddy. She had no make-out dummy. I'd lied to Sydney.

The reality is I didn't want him to hit on her. The Bullet was too fragile. She was a one-man woman. She wanted one set of apartment keys, one TV remote, one phone bill, one shared bed, and one stiffy she could call her own. The Bullet had had that difficult union and she couldn't take another. She had staved off many a midnight muncher to preserve any semblance of a happy smile. She was the type of girl who, if a guy got close, so close he was way inside her rib cage on a daily basis, to a point where tears of joy would flow from her eyes, she would be his. With forever on her mind. She didn't want to play. She was in it for keeps.

Sydney, however, was on a rampage. I didn't see that changing in the near future. Besides, he wasn't the right guy. His life, his way, his demeanor. It would be a classic mismatch.

When I pondered further, I wondered if my reluctance to be straight with Sydney might be attributable to a Greenie flare-up. It's true, I didn't want him to have her. I didn't want anyone to have her. If there was any girl in Hell-A I was covetous of, it was the Bullet. I suppose I feared if anyone got to her, it would drive a wedge in between us and alter our special friendship. And if it was Sydney who was the intruder, all the worse.

Horses and Hawaii

"Hi, baby."

I snapped out of my meditation to find myself surrounded by: the Bullets.

"Heyward!"

"Let's dance."

"Come on."

"How are you guys doing?"

"Great party."

"You're not ready to leave yet?"

"Not yet."

"Why not?"

"Everyone is still trying to get in here."

"Say, we want to check out your pad."

"Yeah, Heyward!"

"Let's go!"

That's exactly what we did. My right arm was still sore from the last time they grabbed me. I extended my left. They yanked on it just as hard. Whoosh! went the team out the door and onto the lawn.

On the dark expanse some of the Bullets ran wild. Then they shot into the guesthouse, flipped on the lights, and tackled the bar. Before I could retrieve some ice, they were slugging Sauza, bypassing the combinants needed for Red. And I slugged right along with them. For some reason I wasn't getting buzzed, however.

Then I watched the Bullets take off their clothes and jump in the Jacuzzi. I wasn't fazed. I had a foot up on the chair, inviting all vices. I was puffing a smoke with tequila on ice in a lowballer. And I was still not fazed. Until an arm wrapped my shoulder. I turned and looked beside me.

"Hey," I said.

It was Sydney. "Nice scene you have going here."

I watched Sydney's eyes fasten on all the enthusiastic breasts of the Bullets popping out of the water.

"Hi, Sydney," said Suzy.

The rest followed with a greeting. I even heard one Bullet mouth how different Sydney looked. It was a compliment for sure. Kelly stood up to swim to the other side of the Jacuzzi. Sydney carved up her wares with an infected glare.

"I was looking for you, Heyward," he began.

"How's it going up there?"

"Crazy. Complaints from the neighbors. Apparently, a couple was caught doing it on their lawn."

I smiled at that. "Good party."

"Tell me. What's the word on Baby Garbo?"

Another blank look took hold of my face. But it was a mask. The lying kind. Because my thoughts were anything but blank. My instantaneous reaction was one of fear. Fear of letting go of an intimate. And that's when the tequila hit me like a ton of bricks. I was disoriented momentarily. I stepped back a second.

"Are you okay?"

I slurred the answer. He asked me about Baby Garbo again. I processed the request as quickly as possible. I felt like a caveman with two rock boulders for brains. Hoping the *clack-clack* of the rocks would yield an idea. It came in short bites. Baby Garbo is going nowhere. With her career. Baby Garbo is a survivor. She's tough. Unless she abuses substances. Sydney makes movies. Sydney can help. *Clack-clack.* After the prehistoric analysis, I green-lighted him.

It came forth from me like more caveman drivel. "Horses and Hawaii."

"What?" He looked at me, making no sense of my drunken, abbreviated talk. So I chopped it up for him.

"Horses. And. Hawaii."

He then assimilated the comment.

"She likes to ride horses."

"*Loves.* Show-jumped as a little girl."

"What about Hawaii?" I could see Sydney's excitement grow.

"Loves Maui. But she's never been to Kauai."

I could have told him a lot about her. That she loved Mexican food, the Gin Blossoms, and anal toys. But what I gave him was more crucial than that. Like information that would penetrate her soul. Because I had gotten close to it. She had let me into her private wonderland.

The word I gave Sydney would yield one hell of a wonder weekend for the best of playboys. But Sydney wasn't the best. He was still among the worst. I was sure this conversation about Baby Garbo represented nothing more than a pipe dream.

"Is Kauai rebuilt?" he asked.

"I don't know, call your travel agent." He laughed at that, grabbed me affectionately around the shoulder. "The north shore of Kauai," I said. "Where it's lush and rain-foresty. There's not much development there. Take her on a Na Pali coast hike. Thirteen miles. And don't forget the secret beaches."

I was spitting out plans to him in my drunken state. Behind me, the twinsies of a Bullet caressed my back and a pair of hands covered my eyes. It was a common L.A. party ploy. Time to guess again.

"Suzy."

"No," and it came with giggles.

"Hurry, Heyward. I'm cold."

"Heidi?"

"No."

"Kelly."

With that answer I got a kiss on the neck. And Kelly strode away, not worried that her sweet body was receding away from me in all its nakedness. And not only me. Sydney as well. If I was less secure I would have thought she was parading for him. The thought had little staying power.

Sydney was still watching her as she slipped inside the guesthouse. He had that look of appreciation. For her. Again.

"One girl at a time," I said to him.

He laughed. "I know, I know." Then his eyes narrowed and he refocused. "We'll stay in Maui. Then we'll take a flight to Kauai later in the week."

I wondered whether or not to bring up the alcohol issue. "She's a Wam. Handle with care," I said.

"You know I will."

"Substances have been a problem."

"You know me."

"She needs encouragement. Reassurance."

He shook my hand. And turned it into a Hollywood. A hug, that is. It was one of love. The conditional kind. But that was okay too.

POST-IT: Conditional love. The town runs on it. Like gas.

It was the only note I made that night.

Gotta Go

Somehow, some way, I left the Bullets in towels laughing it up in the guest cottage. I dragged myself back to the main house. I don't remember the walk it took to get there. Big booze was the excuse.

My midsection was aching and I needed to relieve myself in a major way. The downstairs bathrooms were crammed so I ascended the stairs, stepping gingerly. I didn't want a toesnag or a sudden jerk to break that fragile hold I had on my bladder. At the top of the stairs, I looked down the hall. Sydney was standing there with the girl in the red mask and garters. Of course it was Teal. I eyed her more and my heart pounded more and my pee was all but forgotten. I slapped my chest to shut up my heart. It prompted a squirt right into my pimp pants, which was thematically correct anyway.

The two were quarreling. He was pointing a hard finger at her. I didn't want to be seen and I was already soiled. So I moved off and burst into a bathroom and let it rip in one of the gold sinks. It was either that or piss on the floor. In that bathroom, the toilet was ten yards away. You're such a moron when you're drunk. Maybe always, but it gets worse on fuel.

I wondered briefly what Sydney was doing there with Teal. What they were saying. And that age-old question. After all, she was beautiful. She was more captivating than anyone I had introduced him to. She was better than anyone I had seen. New York included. Except Eleanor. But I had heartstrings attached to her. Physically, Teal was top-shelf. The whole shelf. What were they doing together? It was the most intriguing mystery of Sydney Swinburn and his advantaged life.

It was a brief reverie. When I was done with it a larger worry consumed me. Booze was coming up my throat, doing its best to splatter all over the sink and tiles. I was sure it was the most brutal treatment the sink had ever endured. For me, the moment was just grim. The lowest moment of the party.

I did a quick cleanup, the kind a drunken person who doesn't want to be discovered having made a mess does. That means I ran. I was on the vomit lam and my feet needed to fly.

The party to me now was just people. Like the crowd you see pouring out of portals at the conclusion of a rock concert. You don't give a shit about anyone. The anticipation of the night's event is gone. You just want to get home.

I made it downstairs and wiped my lip. Someone tried to approach me with some boneless overture and I didn't want to hear him and I didn't want him to smell me. The first night of Whores & Hustlers Weekend was over. I think someone politely pretending not to know I was drunk took me to my house. But I'm not sure. When I looked at my bed I saw two of them. I didn't want to punish it with my sordid condition. So I backtracked. I did a slow walk right into my pool and listened to the sounds of the backyard. I floated there peacefully for a while.

The Most Dangerous Scent in the World

When a fraction of my senses came back to me, I pulled myself out of the pool. My shoes did a *squish, squish* all the way to the easy chair with ottoman. It was a two-step process to get to my bed. Get undressed on the ottoman, then slip into bed.

But my eyes made the first move. They closed on me. And then I just tuned out the world and tried to downplay the whirlies that were ruling triumphantly in my head. I took one leg off the ottoman and put it down on the floor. That helped me ground my carcass.

Everything would have been jake, but that deadly *click-clack* resounded off the pavement. It died silently as it hit my carpet. I was too fucked up to open my eyes, so I waited for it, whatever it was, to introduce itself.

"Heyward," it said.

I said nothing in return. Because as soon as the words were released from her lips, the scent, that scent, her scent, came across with it or behind it or in front. It was a sweet, Parisian scent, the perfume name escaping me. And knowing that scent and who it was coming from did nothing to help me open my eyes. In fact they clamped down harder. If

I had a suture kit I would have sewn them shut. Because that scent was the most dangerous scent in the world.

I had a plan. I was going to show this one my best pass-out and nothing more.

I heard her walking around the carpet, stopping, and moving on again. Her breathing was regular but no less hypnotic. It seemed like she was breathing right in my ear. I knew that those beautiful legs and the perfect ass were no more than a few paces away. Then it came right toward me. Right beside me. The light by my chair was considerately snapped off. She had brought the whole nightclub to me.

I'm sure I was quite a sight, sprawled all over that chair looking drunk and wet in my pimp suit. Then I felt a finger lightly touch my nose. I smelled her. It was stronger. It was beckoning me to open my eyes. I wanted to. As much as I wanted to accept a lottery check. But I also wanted her to get the hell out of my house. I couldn't yell at her. I wouldn't yell at her. Part of me wanted her to go. And part of me wanted her to stay and talk and laugh and sip and listen and share her life story with me. Of course another part of me wanted to obliterate my inactive status and shred her all over the carpet. She was that tasty.

I felt her retreat a few steps. Then nothing. There was only the din of a party dying down in the dark beyond.

Then I heard pillow noises, but not a vulgar plop. The sound of a light, elegant, and lithe body settling into a chair. It had to be the love seat, the only chair across the way. I heard a slight exhale, a sensual release. Then nothing.

I heard the pull on elastic. My face broke out in a hot prickly sweat. A few faint clicking sounds followed. There was a wetness to them. It grew louder. And more rapid. So did her breathing. It got heavier. More labored. A wet rhythmic sound was coming across the room at me. I fought hard to hold my sewn eyes shut. I fought hard. Real hard. And lost.

A mosquito's squint did I allow my eyes. They gave me a view I won't forget anytime soon. It was Teal all right, her face made up with a whisper of rouges and reds, faithful to the party theme. Her head was leaning back against the headrest, her wonderful legs parted slightly, and her arm cross-cutting full breasts in lace and extending into her lap. I could see the undulating reflections from the blue pool slash and caress her neck as it craned back. Her fingers danced lightly in her lap.

Sobriety had no business coming back to me. But I had no buzz, no whirlies, and no hangover. Just a pair of wet pimpster pants and a hot throbber held captive by them.

Teal's breathing took on the sound of light, polite moans, polite enough not to wake me up. She was just too considerate. And elegant. And all things unbelievable. A rush of panic struck me. If Sydney ever saw me in this predicament with his Designated Don't Girl, the one never to touch, never to hit on, and certainly never to have her privates out in my living room, it would be all over for me.

It would be worse if I woke up and confronted her as she was doing this. I was frozen in a bath of complete fear. My erection got shy and was replaced by a cold sweat. But she kept moaning and squirming in her seat. I prayed for her little ritual to be over.

Please come, dammit. I'm just a drunken passed-out fool on a chair with no whites, no boldface, no nothing, I thought. *How exciting can that be? Come, dammit, please come!!!*

And she did. She had a hiccoughing orgasm, a burst of climactic release that lasted ten seconds or so. Until the bursts became less and less. And then nothing. All was silent. I prayed for no other noises. Like other footsteps. My shuttered eyes did a quick pan outside and saw nothing and no movement.

What sounds did follow, however, did affect me. It started as a sniffle. Then it grew louder. The sniffles turned to sobs and I saw tears paint silver paths down the sides of her face, taking some mascara-black and cheek rouge with them. It was an awful sight. This was a person I didn't want to be unhappy. She seemed to look at me. I shut down my squint. Vowed not to open my eyes again. Then she let out a sigh of resolution. It contained strong traces of dissatisfaction in it.

I heard her rise out of the chair. The short clacks resumed when she hit the cement outside the glass doors. They moved a few steps beyond, which must have been in the area of poolside. Then I heard her do a peel of the clothes with fasteners being popped and the metal hooks tapping the ground. I wanted to yell "No diving!" but I prayed for the no-diving rule to be adhered to silently. I was dying within. A slight swirl of water came next. And that was a relief. She was swimming in my pool now. The naked bet was a lock.

I opened my eyes. She was standing on the pool steps submerged to her calves, her perfect moon stealing the scene from the real one, and the slight side peek of fully tanned breasts above. I figured everything in her life must be going real well.

I wiped sweat from my brow. Then stepped up to the glass doors and hid by the curtain. I watched her swim. I took her in fully, her face, her nipples, her intimates gliding freely. She was so beautiful in that pool, in that glow, in that place, in that time of my life. She was so much more to me than a Project. I could feel it. I wanted her.

NFW was the response to that. I had come too far. What the hell was I going to do? As it turned out, the decision was made for me by Teal. Lady's Choice, remember? She was out of the pool, looking for a towel and coming back to my house to find one. I reassumed my position again. I gave my best performance of a slump in a chair as possible.

Drying-off sounds gripped me for the next minute or so. When there was a lull I peeked. What I saw surprised me. She was silently inspecting her face. There was a dark band of discoloration beneath her eye, which had been undetectable with the facial cake but now was showing its deep blue life. Then she was done with it. My eyes snapped shut fearing a look my way. Moments later I felt a warm blanket spread over my body and I wondered if a light kiss was coming to my forehead. I wanted it to so badly. When it happened, a slow tear welled and made it out of my eye. It was the nicest gesture I had been subjected to in a long time.

Then I heard the sliding doors shut. And the night was over.

She came, she had orgasm, she cried, she swam, she dried off, she blanketed the sod in the chair. And poof! She was gone. I marveled over what a self-sufficient woman she was. And how self-sufficient all women can be if they decide not to let men mess up their lives. Teal was the best. And I couldn't lay a finger on her. Ever.

The whole episode made me miss Eleanor. And intimacy with a

woman. And all things New York. I was happy to be going home shortly.

I didn't forget the nasty part of that night either. Like, what the hell happened to Teal and how did she get that black eye?

Good News, Bad News

The next morning's awakening was not altogether pleasant. There was a spike in my skull splitting my head apart. As pure as Sauza is, its shrapnel was lodged in my nut. I tried hydrotherapy, meaning a jump in the pool. All that did was make me wet.

The real shocker came when I went up to the main house. I trudged one step at a time with a bathrobe to cover me. I figured I'd see bodies and bottles and beer caps strewn everywhere. And a few all-night X-ers manning inner tubes in the main pool. Still analyzing everything meaningless with that relentless X-wit. But no such thing. The Swinburn mansion was spotless. Amazing little elves must have worked through the night to give the place back its shine. One thing was sure, however. The party was over. And so was Whores & Hustlers Weekend.

I made my way into the kitchen and poured myself some orange juice. The kitchen clock read 3:30 P.M. No one was around. Not even Armando. The house had an eerie feel. So much chaos the night before, and now just the silent sounds of a huge house. I figured Sydney must have gone out for a late lunch or a screening. Then I remembered he was trying to get Baby Garbo to go to Hawaii. I was pretty sure that hadn't happened. The last I saw of him he'd been quarreling with Teal. I figured the ill-will of a no-score evening had gotten the best of him and he had taken it out on the strawberry golden girl.

I searched the office, the screening room, the game room, and the study. I knew eyeing the microdot brushstrokes of Seurat's beachy canvas would make me dizzy, so I didn't look up.

I knocked on Sydney's bedroom door. There was no response. I peeked in and the bed was made and a vacuum cleaner was standing in the middle of the floor like a lonely robot. One of the day maids popped out of the bathroom. She gasped at the unexpected intruder.

"I'm sorry."

"You scare me," her broken border phrasing claimed.

"Where is Mr. Swinburn?"

"He leave this morning."

"Where?"

"I no-no."

"Is there any aspirin?"

"What?"

"Aspirin. You know for headache." She had made me break down my English. I don't know why people do that. Fuck up their own grammar intentionally for someone with language problems, thinking it will be understood better. It didn't work. "Thank you, anyway."

I slipped downstairs. I was already tired and needed to lie down. So I hopped on the gardener's golf cart and hitched a ride back to the guesthouse. I figured I'd lie back poolside and let the world find me.

I gave a few short thoughts to the night before. My recap came back to me in glitches, glossed over with a surreal finish. Very surreal. My recline had all the day-after upsetting meditations. I wondered how I got so ripped. I also wondered if anybody noticed how bad I was. I cringed at some of the incidents. When you're hung over, memories are either good or they're bad. There's no aptitude for anything else. You're too stripped. Your mind is not capable of coming up with anything more refined, descriptive, or defining. Subtleties and nuances are terms for other days. Paranoia strangles them. Things are good or bad. And if you're really plastered like I was, shit is usually bad.

I recalled saying some embarrassing things. That was bad. I remembered talking to a producer about a deal. That was good. Then I remembered Sydney asking the word on Kelly the Bullet. I lied to him and that was bad. But giving it to him would have been worse. Then he asked me the word on Baby Garbo. And I gave it to him. That was fine. Had Sydney gotten her? If he did, he was in for the weekend of his life. I couldn't see that development as anything but good.

Oddly, I could only come up with positives. But I knew that wasn't entirely the case. There was a heaviness to my thoughts that wouldn't go away. There was something bad, bad and dreadful, still lying dormant in my mind like the alien wedged deep in your guts who hasn't deigned to make his gruesome cameo yet. But my synapses were dulled. They were not firing crisply enough to unearth the dark event.

Then I remembered about, oh my God, adrenaline shot through my system. *Teal.* What the hell was that about? I mean she was masturbating in front of me. I shuddered thinking about it. Did anybody see her? Quel wingnut. I was passed out like a possum, sneaky and alive, and she strummed off to me. Let's not go there, was my final thought. Which, of course, was an inevitable invitation for the thought to haunt me for the rest of the day.

Soon after, Armando swung by with a bottle of Tylenol Extra Strength for me. My message had gotten through to the maid after all. Hangovers just give you no patience. You think everyone is as incapable as you.

Armando then explained that the cops had closed down the party around four-thirty. And one officer took the Tree Girl home with him.

"Good for him."

I had to ask him the question and, for some reason, I had a quickening pulse.

"Where's Sydney?"

"I don't know. I thought he was with you."

Armando poured me a glass of water. Every time someone gives me Tylenol Extra Strength, I still fear the bottle might be from the fatal issue that killed people years ago back east. Were some bottles still resting silent and deadly in people's medicine chests ready to snuff you? Could the maid be in on it? Could she be out to get me? It was more hung-over paranoia. I thanked Armando just the same. I ate the tabs and stared stupidly at the red label.

Where the hell was Sydney? When Armando took off, I rang up Baby Garbo. The message on her machine hadn't changed. She hadn't left town. Wams always change their messages. Twice a day.

It's hard to keep up morale when you're a Wam. They want to be contacted anywhere, anytime. That way, when their star call comes in, they'll be readily available. So they leave numbers. Beeper numbers, forwarding numbers, fail-safe numbers, and backup to that, whether it's a friend's house, the Laundromat, or the San Diego Zoo. I decided to beep Baby Garbo. That was a rarity. I never liked waiting for a call to be returned. When I want to talk to someone I want to talk now. Not fifteen minutes from now. In that amount of time, I can lose my enthusiasm for the person. Not in this case.

I felt like shit. I was nailed to my armchair and ottoman. The one Teal had turned into a sex chaise prop for her masturbatory fantasies. What a gal. What a body. What a relief Sydney didn't catch me. And what about her black eye?

Play-by-Play

A few TV channel flicks later, my phone rang. I was right there. I was sure my little Wam Stowaway was lying around Star Camp somewhere, probably the King's Road Cafe, indulging in a little harmless Saturday let's-look-at-the-new-magazines-and-play-with-our-food brunch.

"Heyward?"

"Hey, Garbo. What a night, huh?"

"How do you feel?"

"Scattered."

"You were pretty drunk."

"Yeah, well. Once a year, I let it go," I said. Then I heard some phone fumbling sounds.

"You certainly did." It was a voice, a different voice, a deep voice, and I was talking to a girl no longer. "Hey, buddy."

"Sydney?"

"I'll put you on speaker. We're in the car. There."

"Weeeee!" Baby Garbo shrilled.

I was genuinely surprised. They were together. Way to go, Sydney, was my thought. He was more accomplished than I had given him credit for.

"Where are you guys?"

"We're overlooking a breathtaking cliffside view on the eastern coast of—where, Baby Garbo?"

"Maui!"

"Really."

"We went right to the airport and caught a six A.M. flight."

"Amazing."

"How did your night end up?"

I thought I'd give him the short strokes. It took less energy and was embarrassment-free. "I just went to bed."

"I heard you got sick."

"Did I?" I asked. But realized that was foolish. "Oh yeah, I totally forgot."

"Great party, Heyward."

"You think?"

"It rocked," Baby Garbo yelled.

"Best party I ever had. Thanks to you, man."

"Team effort, Sydney. For sure."

"We're here at the stables."

"We're riding horses on the beach, Heyward!"

"Great."

"Say. Are you okay?"

"Yeah. Why?"

"You sound flat."

"Hung over's the word."

"The word," he laughed. "Thanks for it."

"Not a problem," I said.

Sure I knew what Sydney meant. I also knew Baby Garbo did not. It was a tax-free way of discussing publicly in front of an unknowing partner. I usually love that.

"Have you talked to Eleanor?"

"Not in a while. But we're getting together in New York when I go back for Thanksgiving."

"Call her today. It'll make you feel better."

It wasn't good advice but I didn't say anything. I didn't have the artillery for Eleanor today. The way I was feeling, I couldn't access her the way I would want to. So why send her a negative experience? It could only hurt.

"We're going to go now. But I'll call you later." Then he whispered to me like a five-year-old boy. "And I'll give you the play-by-play."

"Can't wait," I said. "I'm happy for you, Sydney."

"Bye, Heyward," Baby Garbo said.

I said good-bye to both. I really felt awful. I sat there dazed and dunk drunk. Like I'd been playing hoops and twenty guys had slammed on me. I was in a fog.

But I realized some solid career activity had unfolded the night before. I'd set up meetings due to—no question about it—my proximity to Sydney. For that, I had to thank him. No doubt, of course, he would soon see what I had done for him.

Baby Garbo should be happy as well, I thought. By anyone's standards, she'd made out like a bandit. She was a Wam, he was a studio chief. She was taking sun with him in Hawaii. In the end, it could help her career, it could help mine. Anyone would consider that a good L.A. day. Whore Weekend had been a success.

Hurry Up and Wait

Sunday was a great day too. I ran, I lifted, I wrote the rewrite, and I prepped for my meetings. I even browsed through the Internet to read profiles of the honchos I was going to see. I was more excited than I had ever been in Hell-A. I even laid down a moratorium on all L.A. bashing and general dogging of the business for a few hours.

A rewrite I was doing was coming along smoothly and there's nothing like a successful session of work to initiate other creative ideas for your life, your mind-set, and your writing. I had come up with several more script ideas and I was anxious to pitch them.

I was taking Sydney's advice on selection of story. He had taught me to use palatable, commercial genres and weave my own original stories within that framework. That's exactly what I did. I had: a cartoonlike superhuman story; a sexy thriller; and an action-adventure tale, which was my favorite. It had a controversial slant to it, but I felt we were in a period in history, the Age of A, where controversy sold and sold big. Lest we forget Madonna, Stern, Rodman, O.J., and Diana's crash as prime examples.

My slant involved a retired hard-ass, four-star general, a real Starman Squint type whose gay son dies of AIDS, but rather mysteriously. When the father doesn't show up for his son's funeral, his son's gay lover tracks him down and claims, though he was dying of AIDS, he was really murdered. After a show of reluctance, the former general goes on the road with the gay blade and, playing the traditional good-cop, bad-cop roles, with humorous homo/hard-ass content, they resolve the mystery, uncovering a conspiracy which involves a multimillion-dollar AIDS cure scam the gay son had uncovered. The baddies were falsely promoting a drug they knew didn't work. And during the course of the script, the curmudgeon general comes to terms with his son's homosexuality, his death, and gets to know him through this association with his son's lover. In fact, the two become friends. I called it *The Wild Side*, since the general takes a walk on it. I was sure Lou Reed would give us the song too.

I truly wondered if Hollywood was ready for an action-adventure script that involved the AIDS virus. *Philadelphia, Longtime Companion,* and *Kids* showed us they would do an AIDS-related movie but could one be thrust into the action-adventure genre? I wasn't sure. But I hoped they would. They were all on the AIDS committees, Sydney included, but would they do my story?

I had three meetings. With Columbia, New Line, and Paramount. I was meeting with the big guys, the heads of production. That's how much juice I had gotten from my association with Sydney. That was *kewell.*

I had Kelly the Bullet come over and help me with my pitches. She even stayed over. We held hands under the covers. It was nice to spend time with the Bullet again. The next morning we went over my pitch one more time. When I was ready she kissed me and left her lips there a few swollen seconds.

I gassed up the Sled on the corner. I even paid for full-serve because I didn't want to get any gas on my shoes. I didn't want to smell like a grease monkey. No longer was I coming out of left field. I had some stature. I had a great pal in Sydney Swinburn. And I had a great agent. Hopefully, I had the goods.

The meetings went "well," which means nothing other than the hurry-up-and-wait game. What I did not get were rejections. I sensed they were skeptical about the action-adventure piece. You're talking fifty million for that picture and if the public reacts negatively to the subject matter, you've got a weighty bomb on your hands. No studio executive wants to shoulder that type of burden for the rest of his career.

I felt my best shot was with the sexy thriller. They all told me they'd give me their decisions after the Thanksgiving break, meaning next week. That was okay too. I was leaving for New York that evening.

But here I am talking about the business and I promised I wouldn't. Overall I was happy with my day.

Before I left for the airport I got a call from Sydney. He and Baby Garbo were still in Hawaii and were planning to island-hop to Kauai for the holiday. He gave me the word on their activity. It involved some nice dinners, some nice chatter about their points of commonality, and some good screwing on the beach with fellatio support. I was happy for them. After all, spending that much time with a supermogul was likely to yield Garbo some form of career boost. And for him, she was a dream.

I packed lightly and sent the last script I'd written ahead. I never registered it with the Guild and mailing it to yourself is a way of doing it. Besides, you never know whom you might run into in New York. Like Starman. Or Stargal. Who might magically want to star in your pic *if you only had a copy for them to read.*

You're right. I *didn't* count on it. But it only cost three bucks.

Queen of the Could-Bes

On the flight to Kennedy my mind wasn't really on the family reunion. I was more focused on seeing Eleanor. In fact, I couldn't wait to see her.

She was quite a girl—stylish, cosmopolitan, educated, beautiful, smart, the whole refined deal. She was Queen of the Could-Bes, meaning in this era, rightly and wrongly, everyone was comparing the world's beauties to models. Clearly, Eleanor could be a model if she wanted, but she didn't care to. The Could-Bes were a notch above the models. They were more empowered. They had style and breeding. The Could-Bes were the thoroughbreds of the nineties.

In the end, a Could-Be would never want to be. She would never stoop to it. She didn't have to. She was usually educated enough to make it on her own and very successfully. Or she was wealthy in her own right and didn't need the money. Style and beauty is quite a package after all. It was the models who were crashing the Could-Be parties and not the reverse. After they had their stint with fame, they yearned for social stature. And Eleanor and the Could-Bes were already there—way ahead. And, like I said, Eleanor was the Queen. Every guy in New York wanted to date her.

Not only was she well-bred and dynamite-looking, she was cool. She was not a show-off or stuck on herself, and she had a good sense of humor. At the same time, everything she did testified to her cultured up-bringing. She could discuss business, art, literature, and most topics of the day. I also liked that about her.

In addition, Eleanor respected me. And that didn't hurt. She knew the struggle I'd been going through. I sensed she'd be proud of me. That I was associating with a power guy would demonstrate I was making the proper inroads and turning things around.

She had a slender but curvy figure that clothes hung from elegantly. Her body was well-appointed and it was all hers naturally, due to nothing and no one. She was the envy of her peers. Also important, she could, and would, eat junk food with the best of them. Let's not forget she loved Drive-Thru. Another bonus.

Hot shit. I was coming home. At last.

Park Avenue Blast

It had been over a year since I'd been to New York. I was staying with my parents on Park Avenue, which was cool. It would be nice to see those digs again. I hadn't lived there in so long, maybe ten years, and I was ready to embrace all the nostalgia that would come my way by the sights, the sounds, the scents, the decor, and everything else that conjured up mems of an era gone by.

I didn't talk to my parents often. My real father had died when I was ten. He was a Wall Streeter, the relaxed type, and he came from money. Big money. And yes, all that early privilege had ruined his ambition. His great-grandfather was one of the country's foremost industrialist heavies and had founded a textile empire. But my dad's father took a big hit in the Crash of '29 and the Depression afterward. Old Max's heart eventually popped from the strain. Any money that was left was split between my dad and the gal Friday my grandfather knocked up before his death.

Harlan was my real dad's name. I think I was named Heyward because it was close to Harlan, but not so much that I'd drown in his identity. I was happy for that.

My father just never did get it right when it came to business. The lives of leisure his ancestors led had taken their toll on him. He was conditioned to having it easy, and when it got hard, he had a great name, a great face, and some great suits, but he couldn't compete with the city's aggressive breed of have-nots. Nor would he ever lower himself to. The fortune just dwindled. When my father died unexpectedly of a heart attack in 1975, my mother was left with very little except an apartment on Park Avenue. The Hoons had really dropped the ball financially.

Donald Loach is a drunk for the most part. He had met my mother on a bender and married her soon after. She'd needed a security blanket. He needed companionship. They liked each other, but neither of them married for love. Donald had some money from a trust fund, but not much. They lived comfortably but measuredly in her apartment on Park. That means they had limits. They were still attending those social-climbing affairs with all those **boldfaced names** in the society columns but they were really **pretenders.** They didn't have the money to keep up. But they tried.

My sister, Courtney, was a sharpie. She was living in Boston doing paralegal stuff and was preparing to attend law school in the fall. In college Courtney wasn't much of a student. She'd gone to Wellesley and she excelled when she applied herself, but who doesn't? She had a boyfriend, a black guy named Thelonius Thomas, whom everyone called TNT. He was a deejay at a Boston nightspot called M-80, which I thought was appropriate.

Courtney was always kind of a slut. Like me. Which doesn't mean she was loose. She just exhibited traditional male behavior. Like most female sharpies in the nineties. She wasn't going to swallow all those archaic mores designed to hem women in. She indulged whenever it suited her. If you're careful, why not? Passion is about the only thing to look forward to sometimes. Besides, I think her generation got a raw deal. With war, terrorism, AIDS, robotic techno music, eighties glam revivals, condoms-or-else, baggy mugger clothing, the O.J. trial, and Pamela Anderson, they'd taken a lot on the chin. So get it where and when you can, was my feeling.

I was looking forward to seeing her, actually. She was the one spot of my own blood that mattered the most. Don't get me wrong. I loved my mother. And not because I felt guilty for not loving her more than I did. I really did. She was my mother after all. My brain and sensitivities and warmth and my love of the arts came from her. What annoyed me was how full of it she was. Mom was a Climber. All this Park Avenue bunk really mattered to her. She was always on that fearful grate, fearful of saying the wrong thing, looking the wrong way, buying the wrong stationery, fearful of anything that might be looked down upon. She was so wrapped up in what people thought. It was maddening, it really was.

The Loach was a Climber too. Though I'm sure his heavy intake slowed his climb. It was said he was a partner in a law firm. I didn't really believe it. In fact, he never did much of anything except drink and play backgammon at the University Club. How did he even get into clubs? you might wonder. Like most of the unworthy members did. He was smooth enough to suck up to the important boozing blue bloods on the membership boards. And after enough hangovers together, enough steam rooms full of their own fatness, and enough cocktail parties, the power elite would put aside their previous prejudices and see him as one of their own. He looked right, and that was enough. It usually is in the end.

Loach married my mother because she looked right. She still had a damn good figure, and she'd schooled herself to know and say the right things—to the point where she was overbred, even more so than the authentic social mavens. She married him because—I hate to say it—she needed backing to keep up her social status. My dad hadn't left Mom well off, however, and that's never fun for a woman, especially one from that era. How many options do they have? Remarrying was the only cure.

Anyhow, Mom and the Loach lived there on Park Avenue boldfacing around and upholding the tenets of sophisticated society as best they could. I'm sure you can imagine the load of crap I had to deal with when I went home. The phony rules and laws of propriety and class and elitism, for starters. And I rejected it. After all, I was no inheritance boy. And I knew it. Big money had been advertised by all the Fundies I grew up with, but no fund was coming my way. I'd been living in a reverse ghetto. I'd been falsely conditioned into behaving like a rich kid. It was taking me and getting me nowhere. Just like a ghetto. I was aware of it early on. It was why I moved to Hell-A.

What did my family think of me? The usual. You know, the rebel goes west to join all those tacky, classless movie people. The usual Park Avenue, WASPy, boldfacer blast. I'd heard it all before. Twice. I mean stuff like "Why did you go to an Ivy League school to be in the movies? You could have done that after high school" was one argument. Or, "You could have studied movies on a VCR." Then there was "It's so plastic out there, how can you do it?" Or the usual anti-Semite stuff. Or just the Hollywood Big Three.

Has there ever been a conversation you've overheard that made you forever change your sentiments toward that person? It happened to me. I heard this discussion between my mother and the Loach. It let me know where he really stood, how he really felt, beyond all the faux niceties and Christmas presents with *Love, Donald* notations.

He told her I couldn't make it in New York in business. That I had moved to Los Angeles so no one could keep tabs on me. That comment didn't bring the Loach and me any closer. One time I threw a drink in his face. His drink. That was when he called my mother a bitch. I can call her a bitch but I'll be damned if I'll let some bloated, mouthpiece drunk do it, was my feeling.

But enough about family, I thought. There were more important things to think about. Like, where I was going to go that first night in town. I didn't know what was hot, hopping, or happening anymore. First, though, I'd have dinner with Eleanor. I couldn't wait to see her.

Mother Issues

Paddy the doorman greeted me with a smile and a dumb Irish joke. Doormen really are strange. How could they sign up for that job if they weren't? They all looked like they'd just finished digging a shallow grave series in the park. With metal air ducts. But I liked Paddy and it was nice to see him.

Our apartment was the only spread on the twelfth floor. I stepped inside and plopped my bag down. I stood in the foyer and smelled those old familiar smells, the ones that reminded me of Life cereal, bloody noses, and my Creepy Crawlers set. I looked into the corner hall mirror and saw my mother sitting in the living room, fighting off a crossword puzzle. My mother was a real sharpie and she could dust off a *New York Times* checkerboard in minutes.

"Heyward?"

"Yes. Hi."

I moved into the living room. She rose, approached me, her powdered cheek leading the way. I kissed it dutifully. She looked older. Her lips were riddled with little miserly WASP lines. The kind of lips that would not tip any city waiter more than 15 percent and that was calculated before the tax. Beyond all the pretensions, Mom was a nice person though and meant well.

"Ooh. Look at your hair."

"I didn't have a comb on the plane."

"I mean the color."

"I haven't been outside much. No sun."

"But it's so dark."

"Dark hair's big out there," I said. "You look well," I added to head off any further commentaries at the pass.

"I look awful," she snapped back. "I thought you'd be more tan."

"I would be if I wasn't in L.A."

That meant I wouldn't take a tan from L.A. I wouldn't take anything that tried to break me down and dull my Blade. But Mom didn't know what I meant. She didn't know a lot of what I meant. In fairness to her, I didn't ever really let her know what I meant either. That was my own quirk.

I think Mom was generally disappointed with me. I think she thought all I needed was a little straightening out and I would be that good little blond boy in the Prince Charles haircut she had tried to package all those years before. She was very appearance conscious. My tan, my hair, lint, etc. I hate to say it, but if a person was physically unattractive I really think she had less time for them. Kind of like the rest of the world, I guess.

It's funny. I got along great with her brother, my Uncle Bobby, and Aunt Sammy, her sister. They were good people and though they enjoyed visiting us, I sensed they frowned upon their sister's assumed status, though it had never been discussed with me.

"However you get your drive, use it" was my credo. I was determined to do it my way. And show them. All of them. To have ego just because you belong to the Brook Club, the Racquet Club, or Maidstone was pathetic to me. I can take arrogance when it's warranted. But I hate it when there's no support. In my mother's circle there was little or no support. Just accident of birth stuff. Inherited money, fancy French ties, tassels, Gucci loafers, and anything else that helped these Climbers feel special and elitist.

"Your room is ready. Lulu came." That made me smile. Lulu had been our maid for thirty-five years and she was like a second mother to me.

"How is Lulu?"

"Well her arthritis is giving her some trouble."

Mom was great at talking illnesses. Of course that's what happens when people get older. Mom would give you full inventory on what malady everyone she knew was afflicted with. In addition to the competitive illness talk, the gossip also included inheritances, scandals, romance, some fund-raiser politics, social muscle wars, who was getting good boldface, who was nouveau, and who was pretending to be a WASP when they really were a Jew.

She rattled off some other maladies of people I had long since forgotten and finished it up with, "How long are you staying?"

It was a typical question in a WASP household. My kind of WASP household. The real meaning here is "When will my program be back to normal again?"

Death by Mothballs

Sometimes I wished I could shake Mom in a cocktail shaker. I wished I could peel away all the layers of WASPery, all the worries of how everyone perceived her, all that social armature that allowed her to soak in an elitist bath without reflection. But she had worked hard at getting to this place. And her socially backward son who crept into town once a year at best was not going to make a dent in her armor.

But I didn't blame her. I knew how difficult the world was out there. And with respect to me, is it any better to have screen whites and bolster your ego from that, than it is to be listed in Manhattan's Social Register and the New York social magazines and to attend all the right parties? Of course there is product involved in the former case. But just like I wanted to separate myself from the other Wannabeasts and Blips, and therefore the rest of the world, she wanted to separate herself from the other orders.

"I want to talk to you," she said, suddenly serious.

"Oh?"

"Yes." She followed it up with a strong glare and held on it. I knew whatever she had to discuss with me was in the realm of reprobation.

"Now?"

"Uh, no. The Duponts are coming over, I have to prepare for that. You can join us if you like."

"Uh, no. In fact, I'm going out with a friend."

Though she'd invited me, deep down I knew she didn't want me there. I was capable of saying anything at any time which to me were just my views on life. But "anything" to her was potentially embarrassing.

"So why don't we wait until Wednesday. How about Wednesday lunch?"

"How about Thanksgiving? You're having a dinner, aren't you?"

"I want our talk to be more private. The Scanlons are coming over for Thanksgiving."

It went on like this for a while. Until we settled on Wednesday tea. Our relationship consisted of talk of plans instead of normal pleas-antries. And the more she tried to plan, the more I tried to dodge.

"What else are you going to do while you're in town?"

"I don't know yet."

"What time are you going out?"

"What do you mean by that?"

"I mean tonight? Do you want dinner or are you going out for din-ner?"

It irritated me to be the project person that had to be sat down, and fed, and talked to, and put into someone's box, someone's appointment book. My only weapon against it was vagueness. I offered witty stuff like *Could be, How do you mean?, I'm not sure, Dunno, buh!* from my days in Florence, *Peut-être* from my days in France, *You don't say?*, and:

"*Maybe . . .*"

"Well, if you want certain foods like cereals or lunch meats, make a list and put it in the kitchen."

"Okay."

"How's Los Angeles?"

"Same."

My mother never asked me about my work or what I was writing. She claimed she didn't understand it.

"Your sister's in tomorrow." Then she looked at me and sighed. "Okay, I have some errands to run. You know where the fridge is."

"Thanks."

And that was it.

To my mother, "errands" meant a lunch at Mortimer's, a visit to

Louis Vuitton to see if her key chain had been fixed, a drop-in at Hermès to check on the latest scarves, or a stop-by to do a wave-wave at the Colony Club. The Big Yawn for sure. But that was Mary Dexter Hoon Loach. My mother.

She knew early on what to copy and exactly how to do it. She was razor-sharp that way. And what she had copied and modeled herself after was now part of her. She'd acquired a thorough understanding of what it took to be a kick-ass social warhorse. She knew her What-Tos. What to say, what to buy, what to wear, what to about everything. And she incorporated it into her character seamlessly. You'd have thought she'd had centuries of elitist breeding behind her. She knew more about it than my father, who was the real thing.

Anyway, she was off on her errands and that was okay. The motherly aspects that might lure me into having her hang around were long since gone anyway. I wasn't going to beg for them or give her a guilt trip or try and dig them out. She was contaminated. Maybe I was too.

I plopped down my bag in my old room and I almost died of moth-ball asphyxiation. If the smell of mothballs doesn't make you feel like you really don't belong somewhere anymore, the green lily pad wallpaper print will. I felt like I was in some tragic Palm Beach cocktail party. My room used to have solid gray walls covered by my sixties propaganda posters. I had plastic peace signs, beer signs, STP flower stickers, Easy Rider posters, and a Stoned Again poster showing a guy having a brain meltdown in six frames.

Now the scheme was a lily pad nightmare with pillows that said cutesy blurbs like "Don't mistake endurance for hospitality." They belonged in those cars in L.A. with the fluffy license plates. I tossed the pillows in the corner and put my bag on the bed.

What I did next was watch a little New York cable TV. I liked seeing my old New York news anchor heroes again. I had caught a lot of bad news from those cats. Like John Lennon's death. And Son of Sam. They were like family. Bill Beutel, Chuck Scarborough, and Michelle Marsh. They also looked a lot older.

When I got bored of the box, I took a quick shower, wrapped a towel around me, and sunk into my favorite chair. It was the chair in which I'd done all my scratchwork in high school. I didn't like desks. I liked the cushiony feel. It made me feel less confined.

As I sat there motionlessly, I immediately felt sad for my old pal. Sure, it still had the same down-filled cushions. But Mom had turned the chair into a gay blade. She had given it a makeover. It was bright green now and part of the lily pad set. It was like a dog with its fur shaved off. But I told it not to worry. That it didn't have to impress me. I knew it had balls. After all, it put up with me and anything my ass had to offer for all those years.

Rebel Trips

There was one thing I didn't give much thought to at all. Hell-A. It would take days before I would give life there any thought. I wasn't even thinking about Sydney. It seemed so far away. The blood in my veins felt like shouting. I was so happy to be back on my own soil. So happy.

I wore a pressed white shirt and the black cashmere blazer Eleanor had given me at Christmas the year before. I retrieved my camel-haired coat from the closet that had the sniffs of mothballs and you know why.

My cabby was a jerk who didn't know the city, but pretended he did, and I loved it. He took the FDR Drive right into a jam due to construction. When I woke up out of my "I can't believe I'm back in New York" reverie, I had to scold him and get him back on track. New York has a way of getting your Blade back immediately. It's the energy of the place. You're not going to be fucked with, you're not going to come in second, you're not going to let someone outdo you. And you're not going to let a cabbie take a bad route if you know a better one. It was a healthy environment for a Wannabeast. The music was that of a knife sharpening.

My mother was critical of everything and everyone. But she considered Eleanor a dream. In Mom's eyes, she could do no wrong. She knew all about her family lines, which helped. She knew more about Eleanor's genealogy than Eleanor. Of course I didn't confide in my mother my feelings for Eleanor. Or that I was seeing her that night. After all, this was the one girl who, on my twenty-fifth birthday, my mother told me I could never get.

"What makes you say that?" I asked.

"Well, first of all, you don't have a job."

Fair enough. At the time I said, "Writing is my job."

"I mean a real job. One she would consider a job."

Then my saturated stepfather chimed in with his own invective. "Look. She could have anyone she wants. Why would she go for you?"

There are certain things that are painful in life. But there's nothing more painful or debilitating than your mother telling you you're unable to accomplish something. You might expect it from your father. That's how dysfuncionado father-son relationships usually work. But when your mother is a dream dasher it's the worst. It really is. Mother is supposed to be your patron saint, your dedicated supporter even when she may have genuine fears about supporting you. When Mother is not there for you it's a little more than crushing. It crushes your spirit. It crushes *you.* Until you get rid of it. The only way I was going to get rid of it was prove her wrong.

It's true I had a huge crush on Eleanor. And I knew I had to make good to get her. I felt I was one step closer. I was on my way. I had made serious inroads in L.A. and I was on the brink of a breakthrough. I was so excited to share it with Eleanor. But I would never let my mother know any of this.

In my younger days, I used to go out with the greatest selection of sexy lowlifes, it repulsed her. And I was all too overjoyed to do it. There was an immense satisfaction quotient there. The less class, the better. If she was randy and raunchy, I was the man. I'd drag the Betty home to 780 Park and introduce her to everyone, the doorman, the night custodian, I'd even give them a little peek of her garters or undies and say something witty in front of them like "Send up the justice of the peace, Paddy, we're swapping rings tonight, right, slapshot?" Then I'd French-everything her.

Or I could be more creative. "Baby, let's go upstairs and dry-hump." I was a moron for sure. But I swear I could think of no finer moment than to have maMa walk into my bedroom and drink in the sight of a nice Afro-American gal tucked sweetly on my chest. Along the lines of "Look, Ma, no hands!," I would say "Morning, Ma, meet Shanaynay!"

She always gave me the same response. Bulging eyes, a huff, and a slammed door.

Of course the other reason I didn't tell my mother I was secretly courting Eleanor was that if I failed, I sure as hell didn't want to prove her right. If you combine my need to make it in the film industry, and my need to score the coveted New York darling, you come up with some heavy pressure weighing on my heart and soul. Not to mention stiff probability statistics stacked against me. But those were my goals and I was determined to achieve them. In the smallest of nutshells, that was why I was such the indefatigable Wannabeast.

Reunion with Eleanor

I considered Indochine an odd choice of restaurant for Eleanor. She didn't usually like to frequent popular eateries. She had been seen enough during the day and on the street and in the magazines that by the time dinner came around she'd be happy with a bowl of soup in solitary confinement. But this had been her choice.

I was so excited to see Eleanor I had to quiet myself down. I gave myself a quick pep talk that featured things like *Don't name-drop, Don't come out with all the new news at once,* and *Don't blow your wad too early. Let the atmosphere and the table talk breathe, wait for her, stay cool and calm.*

She was such an old friend, I felt the pep talk was silly, but just the same, it seemed like this meeting was different. Not because she had changed at all. Not because the scenery had either. Or the price of the bus fare, or the color of the taxis, or the New York accent. It was me. I had had a modicum of success. I was on my way. Even if I wasn't, I felt like I was, which can make all the difference anyway.

A better indicator of how I felt about myself was this. Finally, on this night I was going to tell her how I thought, truly thought, about her.

Upon arrival, I was happy to see we had won the booth wars. Eleanor was already seated prominently on the right bank when I got there. It was a weighty slot, proof that Eleanor had standing. Sure, she looked great. For her, that was the easy part. For me it was easy too, to be excited about having dinner with her. The joint was swollen and loud.

"Hello there," she said in her elitist Exeter drawl. But it was a soft version and not offensive.

She stood up and we kissed hello and she performed hers lightly and to the side so as not to lose all the grease on her lips. I suffered a mild correction but the disappointment didn't last.

"Look at you," she offered.

"Hey there, El," I said with a breaking grin.

As she sat back down, I gave her the glance-over. She had a silk print scarf so fashionably draped around her neck, it fell with regal accuracy. So chic. I could never get a scarf to mind me. It always ended up in a wrinkled roll as if a dog had been tugging on it.

"So how are you?"

"Overjoyed. To be out of Hell-A."

"Really?" And she did sound surprised. "Why?"

"Are you being serious?"

"I hear you've been having quite a time of it."

And she sipped on the drink she had already ordered. It was white wine. She had a sly smile, the one someone cracks when they think they have something on you. So my spine stiffened ready to mount a defensive.

"Me?"

"That's the buzz. Flying here, flying there."

"Where?"

"With some sort of studio bigwig?"

"Oh, Sydney. We took a trip, yeah."

"You're being modest."

"How so?"

"I hear . . ."

"You hear what?"

She reached over and matted her hand on mine. Finally some touch, I thought. It's always great to get that. The earlier the better. "Not that it matters to me. I think it's great."

I didn't like hearing that. I never like it when a person you're crazy about doesn't give a shit what kind of madness you've been up to. It's a way of telling you you're not in their emotional sights.

But I wanted confirmation.

"You mean with ladies?"

It came out sarcastic from her. "No, *men*."

"I look but I don't touch."

"I hear you've had . . ." And then she swallowed it.

"What?"

"Well, that you're out a lot. And you had a theme party. What was it called, Sextasy or something?"

Gossip is never correct, was the best thought that shot through my mind. My face prickled as blood overloaded it, and sweat seeped into pores that had been taut, clean, and dry. Damn straight, I was uneasy. My only defense was to laugh. She didn't share in it.

"Don't believe everything you hear."

At that point, a waiter whom I would have paid handsomely to show up came of his own accord and I ordered up.

"You seem rather gossipy. Don't tell me all the infotainment shows have body-snatched you too."

"I'm a bit hyper. I just worked out with my trainer."

"You look great." And she did. She had a black turtleneck sweater on that I knew was cashmere, but I felt it anyway. Touch, remember? "Wait a second. *Trainer?*"

"Can you believe?"

"The new you."

"The new and improved me. I figured I might as well try this fitness thing before I die."

"You've never needed it."

It was true. I'd seen her in a bathing suit often. Many New York women and men can deceive you. They have so much clothing on, you often can't tell what's beneath. But she had an amazing shape. And she wore clothes that didn't show it. But hinted at it in a tasteful way.

"And how are you?" I asked her, and showed a face charged with enthusiasm so she couldn't possibly revive any of the previous subjects.

"Great, really."

"Work?"

"Very busy," she said, and let the topic die. It was almost as if she wanted to hear my news first. "So tell me. What's been happening?"

"I did a polish and a rewrite. And just pitched a story before I left. I'm waiting to hear on that."

"Sounds exciting. Congratulations."

"I just want to get enough projects so I can live wherever I want."

"New York, I suppose."

"And other places. Maybe Paris. Or Tuscany."

"I just got back."

I nodded and thanked her for the postcard.

"Then I'll fly out there for meetings and retreat back to my house and do the work."

"Sounds like a good plan."

"Are you going to stay in New York?"

I knew the answer. Eleanor could never leave the city.

"Funny you should ask. I was toying with the idea of moving to Los Angeles. I was talking about it today with my mother."

"Los Angeles?" I was shocked. Truly. "Why?"

"I don't know. I've been doing the New York thing most of my life. A change might be good."

"What would you do?"

"The magazine is opening a West Coast office." She finished her wine and continued. "Besides, there's something I've been dying to tell you. I'm taking acting classes. Two nights a week."

"Acting? Really?"

Oh, no, I thought. It had hit her.

"I know you don't approve. But I'm really enjoying it. It's amazing how it enhances communication skills. Your ability to listen and hear people . . ."

"I can't believe what I'm hearing."

"What?"

"You becoming an actress."

"It's nothing yet. It's secondary to my magazine work. The reality is the magazines are so bent on star culture and gossip now. We need an office there, to get the better scoops, the better interviews. They want me to do it."

"My God. The town is a mess."

"You don't like it, I know. Perhaps I will. You've been there a few years and you miss New York. I've been here the entire time. I'm a little tired of the same people, the cold winters, the flock out to the Hamptons every summer. There's more to L.A. than L.A. too. There's the mountains, Northern California, San Francisco, Oregon, Hawaii."

"You don't like the mountains."

"True. But, well, I can always come back to New York."

"You want to give up being the kick-ass Manhattan editrix? The most sought-after, plum job for any woman? The real thing? And become an actress?"

"I'm just saying I feel like expanding my horizons. I feel stifled. Besides, I've always thought that going to Los Angeles is a sort of rite of passage for anyone growing up in America."

I didn't want to say it and I held back for as long as I could, then I said it anyway. "Are you out of your mind?"

"What?"

"You're going to hate it. And acting? It's the most demeaning and degrading profession known to man and womankind."

I didn't really believe this but the Mighty Hippo in me took over. Naturally . . . Needs, remember?

"Why are you saying this?"

"'Cause I've been there. I know you won't like it."

"Heyward. You have that 'You're a puzzle, and I've figured you out' tone. I hate that. I'm not one of your computer profiles."

"I do know you, Eleanor."

"Not that way you don't. You've chosen to know what you want to know."

I remained silent. And stunned.

The rest of the dinner, you could call my mood shell-shocked. Which means it was more of a state. I couldn't believe what I'd been hearing. Eleanor, Ms. Young World Sophisticated Lady of New York, was heading west to all that pollution and contamination and freeways and collagen and burrito stands and chili dog people and no bookstores and smogs and shakes and everything I loathed. It irked me with arsenic, meaning it killed me. It was mind sodomy. If that wasn't enough, it sucked the wind right out of my sails. The dinner and reunion I had been waiting so long for was becoming a festival of a thousand horrors.

Boat Ride to Nowhere

I started to drink. It started politely with a Kamikaze. I guess the idea had been planted earlier when I was thinking about shaking up my mother.

And the spirits got progressively more hard and rude. My only mixer was ice. Which was something I usually didn't do. But I wanted it pure and clean with a line of credit directly to my cortex.

I kept reannouncing it in my head. Eleanor was going to Star Camp. I had been scratching and clawing and playing it down and sacrificing and starving and biting the bullet a million times over, and, in general, dying daily of the lack of what I would consider any kind of positive humane nourishment, all in an effort to fight my way back to New York, only to find the girl of my dreams within dreams was seriously considering setting up shop in L.A. and embarking on a life of Wamhood. The Rangers losing the Stanley Cup in game 7 would have been better news. I ordered more bourbon. And drank it.

And then the dizzying procession of heroes of café society descended on us. It featured beauty junkies, voyeurs, suitors, tuggers, grabbers, Fossil Men, Remora Men, and Of-the-Moment Men who passed by the table and gave their salutations to Eleanor while I chugged away stupidly and silently on my brown booze. What made me seethe even more was the fact that her face lit up each time a new person came by as if it was such a relief to be drawn away from me and our morose and ugly little dinner. Grimmer than grim.

She engaged the onlookers splash-happily, the same types who would normally annoy her at a nightclub and whom I would threaten with a throat transplant. But it was better than talking to me. When there was a pause in the procession, she did the logical thing. She went to the bathroom.

And I called myself Stew.

It gave me time to think things over. And drink some more. I needed to think things through and I only had six minutes to do it. I'm talking about eastern standard latrine time, the average time allotted for a woman's pee and powder-up session. Any less and she's probably making a phone call, any more and she's probably doing drugs.

I called time-out. I realized I had put too much hope and expectation into this one little blippy dinner. For our long-standing relationship it was, and would be, a blip on the radar screen. I was pressuring it. I had invested all my hopes and dreams in her. The weight of my Great Sacrifice was levied upon her shoulders. I wanted too much. Too fast. I was hurling myself at her emotionally. I'm sure it was surging forth from me. And she didn't like it. It repelled her. It made her tell me I didn't know her at all, which, in case the significance is hazy, is an act of repulsion.

The thing is I had done without for so long in L.A. Like a girlfriend. Like a relationship. Like a little love from a place I wanted it to come from. So now that it was in front of me, I was grabbing at it. Everything I had taught Sydney Swinburn to do, and not to do, had been lost on me. Isn't that always the way? You can properly analyze behavior and strategies for everyone else's romances. But when it comes to your own, your emotions sneak up on you like a sniper and hit you with a peck of lead in the skull. It turns you into a needy, emotional Frankenstein monster and you chase with big shoes and big green arms extended.

I decided to take my foot off the gas pedal and just calm the fuck down. I was going to take her by the hand, help her step on the deck of my little outboard, have her sit in the bow, look at the seas ahead, motor out to a deserted island, and drop her off on the seashell beach. And just take off. Distance, distance, distance, was my thought.

I figured as soon as my boat was comfortably across the ocean from her, only then would normal life return to our table. Not pressured life. Not life that would make her run away. I would end up with a pretty girl across from me who was more interesting and interested in me and what I had to say.

A new drink came my way and I didn't give it much of a chance. It didn't even tickle my throat going down. I only remember asking for another before the waiter passed out of earshot.

I saw a figure, a gorgeous figure in black and tan, coming toward me, a figure that had treasure at every outpost. She was so stylish, so hip, so together, so with it, so on top of it, and beautiful. Holy shit, was my pixilated thought.

And she smiled at me and I stood up and let her slide into the booth and then a couple more guys came up to the table, said hi-how-are-you? and took off.

"Those are nice guys," I said in a measured way, with an even, non-threatened tone.

"Do you know John?"

"No, but he seems nice," and the he's-a-dick thought came to me immediately. But a *be cool and distant* reminder overrode it.

Of course my positive endorsement allowed her the room to tell the truth about him. Life is funny. "Well, he's just another New York party boy, but he's perfectly nice." No doubt, had I said he was a dick she would have said he was an incredibly good person with exceptional character.

"Why don't you go out with him?"

I said it to further distance myself from her to make her feel a little abandoned by me and all the pressure I had been giving her.

"What makes you say that?"

Great, I thought. My pep talk was working. "I don't know. He seems like your type."

"My type?" She didn't like hearing it. I loved saying it.

"Maybe."

With that she extended a hand across the table and placed it atop mine, no doubt not enjoying being abandoned by me and my affections. It's amazing how it's so easy to get someone interested in you when you're not interested in them. And pretending you're not interested is almost as effective. Unfortunately, that was all she had to do. With that one gesture, of her placing her hand on mine, that iron constitution, my iron constitution, that was so firmly in place and unshakable, went out the window. All the laws I'd told myself not to violate were forgotten. A wedge of sentimentality surged through my brain, my pickled brain, in a way that can only happen when you're drunk. Things happen in waves. But that was a tsunami. It made me crack. I couldn't believe what trailed out of my mouth.

"So what about us?"

"Us?"

"Yeah."

"What do you mean?"

Shit, I thought. I was out there all alone and standing nakedly holding up a sign. With a huge heart on it. And no matching sign from her reciprocating my sentiments. My one-sided crush was platformed. Brutal.

And, of course, I had to stay assertive. I was too drunk and stupid and ego-driven to let it die. So she could punish me further with cruel definites.

"Come on. You know what I mean."

"No, I don't," she said absolutely.

"For years, you and I have had a thing."

"A thing?"

She was making me join the fourth-grade spelling bee contest and drag it out letter by letter. And I was forced to use cliché language I hated.

"A connection. Admit it."

"Well, yes, I guess. But only as friends, Heyward."

"Really? Only as friends? Doesn't the thought ever cross your mind?"

"What thought?"

"To get it on. Make love."

"Heyward, you're drunk."

"Come on. You're telling me you don't want to have—or never have wanted to have—a relationship with me?"

"That's exactly what I'm telling you."

"Never?"

"*Never.*"

The Courtesy Kiss

I felt like I'd been run over by a Humvee. But the only thing keeping me alive was the booze looping through my veins.

The rest of the dinner became a huge haze I don't remember well. Except dropping her off in a cab. She gave me a kiss on the forehead. A forehead kiss. It was like the bronze medal. Worse. She did it out of pity too, I am sure. Like the merciful tennis ace who's got you down 5–0 in the set and he gives you a courtesy game. She gave me a courtesy kiss. And it's unbelievable I could reach through all the disappointment and still crack-wise.

"You better watch out, Eleanor. Or I'll go model on you."

She smiled. She knew that a guy going model on his girlfriend in the nineties was still a legitimate threat. And the fact that I had no chance at her amused her enough to shovel the following:

"It's not entirely true what I said, Heyward. I have thought about it. Obviously. Or you wouldn't have felt it. But I don't think it's right. I like you. No. I love you. But not that way. Maybe that will change. But right now I'm doing my thing."

The scarf that she flicked around her neck served as punctuation for her departure. And my dusting. I hated the way it fell perfectly again on her shoulders.

I remember screaming so loud in the cab that the cabbie kicked me out and made me get another one. So I did.

I don't remember slipping inside my building, taking the 'vator ride up, and getting into bed. But I do remember needing to keep one leg down on the floor.

At seven in the morning I found myself in my clothes still. I had the worst hangover known to man. And Eleanor was doing her thing. The thought of the evening sent huge chills up my spine. My dream girl notion was over. My coveted New York darling was going to be coveted all right. By some other Hero of Café Society. Not me.

Life sucks, was another thought.

Holiday Health Drill

It was Thanksgiving Day and nobody gave a damn. Including me. I was so bitter I was thinking crude thoughts. One involved a particularly raunchy quote I remembered. *If the Pilgrims had shot a cat on that famous day instead of a turkey, we'd all be eating pussy.* A Darkie ensued as I pondered what would happen if I shared that little spot of wit at the table. Nothing good, I figured.

I smelled the scent of holiday cooking and the closest I got to enjoying it was making my way to the bathroom. And it took character. I threw down four aspirins, one for each appendage. Or two for my headache and two for that disappointing chat with Eleanor. The beats of the conversation replayed in my mind and made me feel about as big as a midget in high-tops.

I did a twist on the shower handle and let it rain down on me. Had I not been hung over and depressed I might have thought nice nostalgic thoughts. This was the shower in which I'd contemplated all my morning thoughts when growing up. It was the shower I was forced to dunk in every Sunday in my youth, the shower in which my cousin Cheryl Janes bathed while I spied on her to see her naked, the shower I learned to crack off in, the shower my girlfriends hid in after a secret sleep-over, and certainly, the shower I employed for its hydrotherapy after a few thousand shimmering nights of boozing. Like last night. And hydrotherapy was all I could get out of it.

A knock on the bathroom door was followed by my mother letting me know everyone was sitting down for the afternoon dinner.

"Is Courtney here?"

"Yes."

That was a comforting thought. My sister could help take the heat off me, meaning I wouldn't have to stand alone and explain off my life the entire time.

The previous night's clothes smelled like a bonfire log so I went with an orphaned turtleneck sweater I had abandoned years before. Of course, it smelled like mothballs. But it was better than wearing a smoky cloud and the mems it would stir up of that disastrous dinner.

I walked unsteadily into the dining room having contributed not even a can of jellied cranberries to the affair. But I didn't have any guilts about that either. This was family after all. It served them right for putting the whole thing together.

"Hi, Donald."

"Heyward."

A handshake followed and that was the only real warmth we shared for the rest of the day. It's one great thing about being a grown-up. You don't have to pretend anymore. And I didn't. Not that he didn't have any warmth in him. But I don't think my mother having kids from a previous marriage ever sat well with him. Especially since we were offspring of a superior man, my father. The Loach and I were cordial and that's all.

"Can I get you anything?" He was standing at the bar already, giving himself a refuel of hi-test. At the bar, at any bar, Donald Loach was like a baseball manager in a dugout. Totally in his element.

"I think I'll stick to water. For now anyway."

When you're hung over and you have to speak, don't you sometimes feel like your face is as big as a lampshade?

"You go out last night?"

"I'm still out," I said. "Do you see anyone here?"

He didn't bother to think through my sense of humor. He just stood there and did what he did best. Sip. The guy was such a Donald. There was no better name for him. He had all the characteristics. Uncoordinated, pudgy, humorless, boring. I must say, I was glad he was named Donald. I felt that name on anyone was an insult. So all I had to do was call him by his name and I'd be speaking my mind.

"Donald."

"Yes?"

"Never mind."

I got a wraparound from behind and I knew who it was. The only one in my family capable of that type of spirit and affection was my sister, Courtney. I spun around and *did not* give her a Hollywood—a Hollywood Hug, that is. It's the thick one saturated with good feeling that the big-budget producer gives you when he knows he's already hired on another writer. None of that. I gave her a real hug, an expression of real warmth, from me to her.

"When did you get in?" she asked.

"A little while ago."

"How are you?"

"You're already asking too many questions, if that's an answer."

"Love the hair," she added. And she meant it.

We hugged again.

"How's TNT?"

"Fine."

Courtney had visited me in L.A. once and we actually had a good time. Not that we didn't usually, because Courtney and I got along great. Even the most contentious of siblings can find some harmony when they've been through the weird-parents mill, but our sensibilities were more spot on than that. It was just that you never knew what a town like L.A. would do to a visitor. It had great weather while she was there anyway, and that gave her a nice Boston thaw.

"I hear you're getting work."

"It's looking up. I guess."

"It's about time that town utilized your mind."

"Now, if only New York doesn't destroy it."

I told her what I had done to myself the previous evening. I told her about Eleanor too. She knew about my feelings for her. But she was less of a fan than me. She thought Eleanor was less virtuous and more of an operator. She was probably right. But no woman was good enough for me, according to my sister. Sisters rule.

The fact is, everyone was a little envious of Eleanor, however. She just had too much going. She could get any guy she wanted. Anytime. And keep him. That wasn't the case with my sister. Though Courtney was pretty and smart, she couldn't pick and choose like that. She could get Starguy for a night, a week, a month maybe. Like most girls can. Guys are so easy, remember? But to keep him? No sir. So I wasn't sure if my sister had taken that position because she was right, or protecting me, or because she had a case of the Greenies, the hissing feline strain.

At that moment, Donald came up to me and said to me what he always said to me upon my return from L.A.

"Looking pretty pale."

I returned my response, which was also the same every year.

"Well, you know me, Donald. I hate the sun."

It was our token little ritual of communication. It was like a quick, wooden exchange out of an Ionesco theater of the absurd play. We repeated it like robots. Looping every year. But you couldn't blame Donald entirely. After all the breakdowns due to heavy booze intake which includes memory loss, synapse short-circuits, and the originality coma, you could expect him to loop it up. Besides, he sensed I didn't like him much. Why should he make the effort when he could spend the time getting a refill?

The Loach's one saving grace, from my perspective, was that years before, when he was going through a blistering midlife cracker, a crisis I'm talking, he took off for a week to Bermuda with a girlie undergrad from NYU. He and Mom patched it up soon after, as all later-in-lifers do. At that age, sex with others hurts less—it's the pride thing that is bothersome. *Just do it quietly* is the credo. So no one is socially compromised or embarrassed publicly.

Which is not to say I was a rabid supporter of the event, but I must confess, it made me find Donald a wee bit more interesting.

I settled into a puffed-up chair and I saw Donald look curiously at me a moment, as if something was different. It was probably my hair. But I'm sure he was easily scared off of his perception, because he had misfired so many times by now, he didn't know if his recollections were figments or inaccuracies his pickled brain had once again dreamed up.

The Scanlons were a no-show, which invited no objection from me. Like I said, I was feeling rather shy. So the four of us were ushered out of the living room and into the dining room, where a very festive meal was spread out with wisps of hot vapor rising from each dish. There we were, with all that history, all those hours logged together, and very little to say. So we made out like most dysfunctional families in search of holiday harmony do. We faked it.

It all started with some good old competitive illness talk. And my mother led the charge. I'm sure you know the drill: who has what, who has it worse, who's had it longer, and what it will take to get rid of it. It was pleasant reunion fare. Of course Mom started with me.

"Have you been feeling well, Heyward?"

"Great."

"Have you been taking your vitamins?"

"No."

"You should."

"I eat when I need to eat."

"Caveman," Courtney interjected. And I smiled at that.

"Yes, but you don't eat the right things."

I wanted to groan but I sat on it. It was partly because my mother was doing her best to dish out holiday parcels of maternal goodwill, the kind that made her feel she still had some connection to motherhood. But she did it with such pale conviction that it was difficult to respond seriously to.

Partly also, it was because my nerves were burned. When you send that much booze through your body you can feel psychologically stripped of any kind of protectionary exoskeleton. You're opened up like a raw wound, constantly being stung by whatever hits it—water, air, touch, words. At that moment I looked at my hand and saw a stamp on it. It indicated I had been somewhere else that previous night. And I didn't remember where. It must have been an after-hours club. New chills made my head vibrate.

While the group caught up on Courtney's life, I took a few spoonfuls of yams and mashed potatoes to decorate my plate. The orange and white thing attracted me. The food didn't. I certainly wasn't hungry. The only food group I would be eating from that day was the ibuprofen family. In fact, a slight tug of nausea forced me to excuse myself, get up, and down a few more tablets in the bathroom. I heard Courtney telling them I'd had a rough night. It was more than rough. More like ruinous.

When I returned to the dining room, the illness confessional relay had only reached Donald. He cited a vicious low-level pneumonia that had hit him in October, completely debilitating him. I thought of how arduous his trips to the University Club bar must have been after being hit by that viral punch. It went on like this and every time he mentioned *office*, I substituted with *bar*.

"I was having trouble sleeping, I woke up in pools of sweat, and I had no energy. I'd be in the office and suddenly I'd feel exhausted and weak in the knees. And I had to return home."

"Didn't you see a doctor?" Courtney asked thoughtfully.

"Yes. But he thought it was just a cold. He gave me some antibiotics for it and told me to stay out of the office."

"You only took them for five days," Mom chimed in. "You're supposed to take them for ten." And she shook her head.

Donald just sipped on his vodka-with-a-splash. And I would have dared anyone to try and find the splash. Right then, I decided to lighten up. Sure the holiday was a sad and bitter ritual, and these people were vulnerable to criticism, but they weren't responsible for my foul mood. *She* was.

I thought about my "What about us?" line and I cringed. With more chills for frills. How could I have said it? Especially after the calming dialogue I'd had with myself and the perfect strategy I'd devised to give it all a rest? The ironies of life were socking it to me again. I had cracked like a farm egg.

With the great ladies, there's a fine line between losing her and winning her over. You can be so close it's in your palm but those last gestures are crucial ones. You don't grab. You don't offend. You don't get aggressive. It is more prudent to continue to wait. Let it go another night. Because in the end, it has nothing to do with you. It's all her. She'll let you know when it's time. It's Lady's Choice. I knew it. I coached it.

Forcing the issue will make you crack. And in most cases, she'll be gone forever. I decided to leave that thought alone. In fact, I decided to leave my mind alone altogether. It was just too stripped. Call it fragmented weirdness, but I was one shuddering, hung-over bastard.

"When it didn't go away, the next thought was that it was meningitis," Donald said.

"Mononucleosis," Mom corrected him.

"Yes, that was it. Or maybe even hepatitis."

"Yes, I hear different strains of hepatitis are reaching epidemic proportions. There's hepatitis C now. And it can be fatal."

"Finally, they called it the Subway Flu. It was a low-level form of
pneumonia. Everybody in the office got it. And I took the proper med-
ication. And, well"—he coughed—"I'm feeling much better."

He washed his cough down with you know what. What an advertisement, I thought. For what? Well, whaddaya got?

Then it was Courtney's turn and she offered up some tale of a sniffle she'd had but that was it. She obviously knew we were in the grips of
the holiday health drill but she was better at dealing with it than me.

Wrong Spelling

At that moment, my mother slid an envelope over to me. She didn't look
at me either when she did it. That made me leery.

"It came here. I don't know why."

"What is it?"

"It's from some film company, I guess," Donald said with arms
crossed and eyeing me steadily.

"No," I said. "It's from the Writers Guild."

"Are you a member?" Donald asked not without a legitimate curiosity that seemed too significant.

"Yes I am." And he looked directly over at Mom as if his suspicions
were being met. "I changed my membership from the East Coast Guild
to the West Coast," I qualified.

I opened the letter and read. "It's a letter of confirmation."

"And they know you?"

"Yes. I am a member, I told you."

Mom just sighed. "For an accredited agency they still don't seem to
be able to spell your name correctly."

I looked sharply over at her.

I didn't want to get into this. I didn't ever want to get in to this. I
never thought they'd find out. But they did. Maybe not. I played along
the only way anyone smart ever plays along. Dumb.

"How is it spelled?" Courtney asked.

To avoid any incriminating spew, I just made like the contents of the letter were lengthy and I was still reading. It was a three-liner if the truth be known.

"H-o-o-n-s-t-e-i-n," Donald offered.

"Hoonstein? It's probably a misprint," Courtney remarked.

"Is it, Heyward?" Mom asked. I looked over at her. "Are you spelling it that way?"

"No."

They looked at each other.

"That's not what we've heard."

"What have you heard?"

"It's intentional," she said.

"Who are your sources?"

"Informed sources," she responded. I said nothing. "Would you consider the title page to one of your scripts as proof of an informed opinion?" she asked.

I did a quick flash through my memory banks wondering if I'd left any wallpaper behind. But I was too rattled. And hung over. My face was now on fire. It was possible they saw a script page. Then I thought, No way. I was about to lie my ass off and tell them a typist got my name wrong. But I saw a copy of one of my scripts suddenly appear on the table. Then I remembered how it got there. I had sent that script ahead. I had written my mother's name and address on it. And she'd opened it. I was the People's Choice Award–winning moron.

"Yeah. I spelled it that way."

Courtney held her napkin to her mouth and muffled a burst of laughter. It made me chuckle too but my face worked to keep its seriousness.

"Excuse me," she said, and ran off, consumed by uncontrollable heaves.

"Where are you going?" I asked with the implication of "Don't leave me now!" They were both looking at me. "What's the big deal?" I asked.

"You've made your name . . . ," Mom began with.

"What?" I asked. Of course I knew where she was going with this. So

I wanted her to spell out her anti-Semitic remark to make her feel fool-ish even though she wouldn't.

"Jewish," Donald finished off with. I looked at Donald and his eyes were locked on mine.

"And it's why you've colored and curled your hair, isn't it?"

"I didn't curl my hair!" I burst out with. And more laughter reverber-ated from the hall. Courtney was the culprit, of course.

"Why?" Donald asked.

Sure, I made him work for it. "Why what?"

"Why all this?"

"That's my business, Donald."

"It's ours too," he said.

"It's none of your business." It was a typical stepson defense: claim-ing no bond to the stepparent. It gave me more time.

"Well, it is mine," Mom snapped. "Do you know at Mortimer's yes-terday someone asked me if your father was Jewish? And me too?"

"No, I didn't."

"And I know it's because you're out there playing a Jew for your own reasons, or gain, or whatever."

"It's happened more than once," Donald added.

I let everyone get a little more acquainted with each other. That means I kept my mouth shut.

"Sometimes I don't know about you, Heyward," Mom added.

"What does that mean?"

"I think you're . . ."

"What?"

"Overpressured."

"Overpressured?"

"Too pressured. Overly so."

I played around with my food for a bit. I mixed the orange with the white.

"Look, it came out pumpkin," I said of my food mix. "How turkey day of me."

"What?" my mother said, hurdling over my nonsense. So I answered her.

"Is that a way of saying you'd like me to see someone?"

No one responded. Which was their answer. Clearly they wanted me to see the Gods of Park, Mad, & Fifth. It's a firm. The psychiatric kind. Those are the only residences where people can afford to hear their bunk. And in this neighborhood seeing the Gods was the only solution for parents who had kids who were disappointing them—either by getting shitty grades, smoking pot, or just carving a different path. Growing up is another way of putting it. That wasn't to say some kids couldn't use therapy, including me, but I considered it an overused crutch. It was usually called upon in cases where the parents hadn't spent enough time with their kids to guide them properly because they've been too busy flying to the islands, connecting the dots socially, or boozing silently and tragically on their own.

"Why?" I continued.

"I think you'll stop at nothing," Mom said.

"Well, maybe that's partially true."

"That is true," Donald added emphatically.

"Maybe that's what it takes. In some families that drive may be considered admirable. But in this house ambition is like a dirty word."

"Heyward. Calling yourself a Jew?" Mom griped. "I think that's a little beyond ambition."

Courtney came back into the room and sat down.

"I don't call myself a Jew."

"Oh, no? What do you say?"

"I may have said I'm 'half' on occasion."

Courtney belched out again. "I'm sorry," she repeated again. She enjoyed my sense of humor. The more bitter and weird I got, the more she loved it.

"What on earth for?" Mom asked.

"Look. I don't say anything usually. Just because there's a 'stein' on the end doesn't mean you're Jewish. I leave it up for them to decide. I just think it flows better."

"Flows better?"

"Yes, on a script. They're used to names like that."

"What are you saying?"

"Clack-clack. Hello? Because there's a serious Jewish lobby out there. In case you hadn't noticed, the Jews are a major force in entertainment. Just read the credits of any movie or TV show or magazine masthead. I'm tired of getting lost in the shuffle. It may not be because I'm a WASP but I don't want anything to hold me back. That's all."

"John Huston wasn't a Jew," the Loach interjected. "Neither was John Ford. And those Italians. Francis Coppola. Or Martin Scorsese."

"Should I now list all of them who are?" I asked.

"Come on, Heyward. They're all whores out there," he continued.

"What's that saying?"

"If you have the product, they'll buy it. They don't care who you are. It's a business."

"I think Donald's right. If you've got something they think they can make money on, then it doesn't matter what your background is."

"Well, maybe I don't have the product," I trailed off with.

"I don't know. I don't know what you write."

"Well, how would you?" I looked at her and immediately I wished I could take that one back. I didn't want to go there. "Look, let's just drop this."

"Yeah, it's Thanksgiving," Courtney added.

Donald was still looking pointedly at me. And accusingly. So was Mom.

"Who is Sydney Swinburn, Heyward?" she asked.

I didn't know this was coming. I really didn't. "He runs a movie studio. You've heard of him, haven't you?"

"Yes, I have. But who is he to you?"

"He's a friend."

"Has he helped you out? In the business?"

"In fact, he has."

"How so?"

"He's introduced me to Hollywood for starters."

"And what have you done for him?" Donald asked.

"How do you mean?"

"I mean, what does he get out of this friendship?"

"He gets my companionship. In whatever we do."

"And what kinds of things do you do?"

"We attend screenings, go out to dinner, we took a trip to Memphis."

"What for?"

"There was a festival there." I didn't think I should get into the girlie thing with them.

"A film festival in Memphis?"

"What is this, the Inquisition?"

Donald got up, drifted to the bar and poured himself another one. His back was turned to me.

"We've heard some things," my mother added.

"I'm sure you have. You're always hearing things at these luncheons and dinners full of interesting and significant people."

She shook her head.

"Like what?" Courtney asked. She was trying to help, but the effect was to condone the interrogation by demanding follow-up.

"The . . . well . . . word that we got was you're a procurer."

"A procurer?" Courtney asked.

Donald blew it out flatly. As flat as a Nebraska back road. "He's been pimping girls for that Swinburn character."

I sat silent for a moment. My nerves were too raw to deal with this. But I had to.

"It's not true," I said eventually.

"What's not true?" the Loach asked.

"Look. We're both single. We go out together," I said offhandedly. "Sure, I've introduced him to people I know. He's introduced me to people he knows."

"People or women?" Mom asked.

"Both. So what?"

"*So what?*" Donald shot back. "So what?? Smearing your family name? Embarrassing your mother and me and your sister for the umpteenth time? Is that all just *so what?* to you?"

"Donald . . . ," Mom said.

He stood there looking at me, his face twitching he was so irked. Then he sipped. He followed up with a slow walk back to the table. And for the first time ever he was showing a little moxie. I couldn't believe it.

"You think you're so smart," he said. "You know what people think of you?"

"Donald, let's stop it!" Mom snapped.

"No! He needs to hear it! He needed it years ago. You went out there to hide. Because you couldn't make it in this town. And now you're a goddam pimp for some kike mogul! Way to make it, Heyward! That's really making it!"

His face was beet-red now. And he followed up with a vicious coughing attack. I waited for it to end. It took a minute or so. Mom fed him a glass of water. After he finished sipping it, I angled a look at my mother. Her eyes were filled with water.

Then I stood up.

"I'm sorry, Mom. I never meant to embarrass you." Her chin trembled. "And I didn't mean to upset your household. That includes you, Donald."

I moved out of there and didn't look back. Bags are easy to pack when you don't care how you pack them. It's just one big stuff. Courtney came in and gave me a sisterly hug. A damn good one. But it didn't help my condition. I wanted out. Of there. Fast.

"Where are you going?"

"The Gateway."

"What's that?"

"It's my favorite motel. The roadside kind. Only it's right in Manhattan. On Fiftieth and Tenth. It's cheap and comfy." I added a twisted smile.

"I'll visit you there later."

"That's okay."

She had tears in her eyes now. Family. What a bonus.

"Hey, don't worry about me. I do fine."

"I know you do. I'm proud of you, Heyward." More hugging came.

"Just refer my calls there, okay?"

"Want me to get you anything?"

"Like what?"

"There's tons of food."

"Yeah, grab me some pumpkin pie."

Before I could tell her I was kidding, she was gone. And back immediately with a foil pouch of a holiday dinner without the family, which I considered a better value.

I emerged from the bedroom I had grown up in, preparing to leave once again, as I had done a few thousand times before. But this time was different. I was not coming back. When you have a disturbed childhood you make odd alliances with odd objects. Like my made-over chair. My eyes gave the room's furnishings one last drink for the memories. Then I was out.

Mother was standing near the door. The Loach didn't have the nerve to.

"I'm sorry, Heyward."

"Sorry for the bad word at the club."

That hit her right in the eyes. They watered again. "Please stay."

"It's not your fault. I know you mean well."

"I just wish you could do something else. Like write for a magazine. You're so talented. If you could just change your business."

"I have. I left the approval business a long, long time ago."

"I know," she conceded. It was actually a nice thing to hear. With that one line it told me she was aware of how full of it she was with all the society climbing. "People do what they can," she added.

I nodded. I almost uttered a "Happy Holidays" but it sounded like overused irony for bad TV. She gave me a good-luck peck on the forehead. Less than soon, I was giving my back to the building I had grown up in. Soon after that, a cabbie took me away from it all. Forever.

T-Day at the Gateway

The Gateway was at its holiday best when I arrived. A big cardboard gobbler was pasted in the window and a few random gourds were riding the check-in counter. I quietly signed in and paid my dues.

"William Shakespeare, huh?" asked the concierge, who was definitely taking on too much status with that title. He had a puffed stomach, a tired face, and a Camel filterless sticking from it with a look like he didn't care if I checked in or not.

"Do you care if I check in or not?"

"Nope."

"That's the holiday spirit."

"You objectin'?"

"Nope. S'why I came."

Then he coughed and it sounded like thunder. When the thunder stopped he said, "I been waiting for ya just the same."

"Sir?"

"You got a message."

"For me?"

"No. Last night's ref," he quipped sarcastically. No one gives off better wiseass than New Yorkers. It's crucial language. Love that.

He handed me a slip of pink preprinted message paper. I figured it was Courtney trying to get me to come back and help satisfy everyone's holiday dreams. But it wasn't. It was from my old pal Sydney Swinburn. He had obviously tried to get me at Park and my sister gave him the number.

Of course one mystery needed to be resolved.

"How did you know I was me?"

"Guy said you'd use some fancy name to register with."

That made me smile. It was a first for that day. I thanked him, gobbled, then took a ride five floors up and manned my holiday suite. It had a big bed and a tube. So I turned it on and let the blue haze flicker in my face. By now I was starved, of course. So there I was, in my rented rack, on the West Side, on Thanksgiving Day, munching away on white meat and pumpkin pie wrapped in foil, like any other holiday schmuck.

Then I remembered that old *Playboy* magazine cartoon fossilized in my mems where the guy with the grim, beady eyes has just finished fucking the stuffing hole of the turkey. And his lecherous face cracks out of the side of his mouth: "Happy Thanksgiving."

I was just disturbed enough that the memory kept my smile alive. Then I got a nice dose of food coma and passed out for the hell of it. And some rest.

Soft Boys and Dinosaurs

I awoke around midnight. I decided to go for a short walk. It turned into a long one. I walked all the way to SoHo. And back. I slipped into some night haunts that had sprung up while I was out wide left. I stopped by Spy. And Wax.

The highlight of the evening was getting through the door thugs at the Bowery Bar. When I did a demographic check of the four door bozos I devised a strategy, and bullshitting had nothing to do with it. Of the fab four one of them was fay and it was very clear. He had been a door stopper in the eighties when gay guys were a viable choice for brassing. In this era of smashmouth anabolic bouncers this guy was going against the grain. But he had the keen eye for cool people. He had a shaved head now and a few earrings.

I took the door penetration trick right out of my eighties bag. If you were solo, the trick was just to offer up a little flutter of the eyelashes to the Soft Boy bouncer and you'd get an instant edge on all the pushing and shoving hard-asses. If you were with another guy what you did was look weakly and adoringly into your partner's eyes so the Soft Boy knew he was ramming you enough every night to give you that dreamy docile look.

So when Soft Boy looked my way, sure enough I softened my gaze, gave a rosy, weak smile, and made my face melt a little. Let's not forget I let my head go loose and bobby. Before I knew it I was being asked how many were in my party. And I delivered it equally soft, almost in song.

"Just me, me, me."

I was ushered through a crowd that now hated my guts and wondered how a gay guy got priority over all their macho slop. I was thrust into the glass doors and got a masculine grip on myself again. I literally added a Sicilian grab of my crotch to help it along.

But that was all the fun I had. I saw some people I knew but I felt strange. They felt strange to me. I didn't drink a drop that night and I left the bar early.

That night I found it difficult to sleep. My mind was churning and there was a tempest swirling in my rib cage. I thought about that holiday dinner. And how I had resisted. And what it took to do so. Sure, I could have gone off on the Loach. I could have asked him if he had ever done anything with his life. I could have asked him if he ever had a goal. And achieved it. And I could have called Mom on questioning my character. And I could have questioned hers. Like why she ever married Donald Loach. It seemed that the union with him was against nature and all its laws.

I could have told them both I was no inheritance boy. That no one was giving me any money. That no one was going to make my life a series of trips to the Colony Club or the U Club to play backgammon. That neither of them knew what it took to make it. That they were a dead breed. That no one gave a shit who belonged to what club. That no one cared whose family came over on the *Mayflower*. That the have-nots would screw you over faster if they found out yours did. That all that matters is what goddam boat you have now and where it's docked. That the have-nots have crumbled their walls, tossed their Social Register, and moved their kind out. That my mother and Donald Loach were dinosaurs. Because of their own stupidity. That it was a meritocracy now and their breed had become nearly extinct.

I could have told them that was precisely the reason the Hoon fortune was all gone too. That Harlan Hoon hadn't adapted. That he'd wasted it all. And I could have told them I was actually happy he had fucked it all up. Why? Because it gave me a chance.

I could have told my mother I saw nothing wrong in introducing a guy to girls. That the guy was too busy to meet people on his own and that he could help me professionally in return. That it could get me to a point where I could live and exist and buy a house and have a wife and a life. That I was determined not to spend my life at the edge of somebody else's table.

And that I deserved it too. That I had the goods, I just needed a break. He could give it to me.

And I could have told her if she was disappointed with me and objected to who I was, what I was doing, and what I had become, then we were obviously at a stalemate.

But I sat on it. I sat on the thirty years of bitterness welled up in my chest. And stepped away from the table. And I was happy I did. I think

I had shown maturity in doing so. In fact, I was proud. I don't know how I did it but I did.

Changing Islands

Early the next morning I awoke feeling sad. It had nothing to do with my disastrous dinner with Eleanor. Or my Park Avenue mother, or the Thanksgiving dinner call-down, or the fact that I was a hybrid blue blood, or wishing my father wasn't dead, or making better decisions when he was alive. It was what had happened between me and my town.

The town that had nurtured me for so long, the town I looked up to, and respected, and idolized was no longer there for me. I was no longer its son. It was a foreign land with too many new faces. What had been my little crib no longer felt warm and homey to me. I was an alien. I even started to see the people as rude and abrasive and stuck-up.

Maybe I'd been away for too long. Maybe I hadn't nurtured our relationship. Maybe it had changed on me. Or maybe I was the one who had done all the changing. Maybe I had gotten soft out there and lost my ability to communicate with it in the way I was used to. Maybe I was just too L.A. now. In any case, the New York I once knew, my New York, was no longer mine. It was someone else's. Or maybe no one else's. But certainly not mine.

The phone rang.

"Word," I barked with a Homeboy snap. It was one of those theatrical telephone responses an odd mood can bring on.

"Happy day after Thanksgiving," he said.

"Easy for you to say."

"What? Where'd you go last night?"

"Some trendy hole. You still in Hawaii?"

"Change in plans. I'm going to St. Bart's."

"Great island."

"Have you been?"

"No, but that's the word."

"So how did it go with Eleanor?"

Of course I wouldn't tell him what happened. Maybe because he had landed so much gaga recently and I hadn't and I didn't want to seem inadequate. Basically, I wanted to show strengths, not weaknesses, especially with the girl I told him was my treasured one.

Bet your ass I was insecure about my proficiency at this point. Many men aren't configured this way, meaning overly sensitive to the statistics of how well they are doing with women. Most get over it in grade school and, if not that early, in high school or college. And then they move on to marriage and constructing a future around a family. But if you've been a holdout all your life, whether it involved swashbuckling, unabashed drageurism, an inability to settle down, or just being not ready, things like not feeling attractive to the opposite sex matter. I was configured that way. So I lied.

"Oh great."

"That's great, Heyward. I'm really happy for you." And it sounded genuine. And it forced me to think of the Walking Nightclub. In visual terms, the reverie was like focusing on a red patch for a while and then looking off and away only to be blinded by its primary opposite, green. Sydney's questioning regarding Eleanor made me wonder about *his* Designated Don't Gal.

"Have you talked to Teal?"

"Always," he said, and nothing more. And he coughed a bit. "Listen, I heard you did a nice job on that short."

"Really? You heard that?"

"It was well-received. I don't know the specifics."

And that perked up my mood.

"So when are you taking off for St. Bart's?"

"Whenever I want. I'm taking the studio jet."

"You taking Baby Garbo?"

He stuttered at first. "No. She's home in San Francisco."

"And?"

"She's very excited. She got a role in a series."

"Really? How great . . . Did you help her?"

"Maybe . . ."

"Nice," I said. And if you're wondering, the answer is *Of course.* I had an envy flare-up, the *Why her and not me?* kind. It was inevitable. But I shook it off. "So you obviously had a good time."

"I'll tell you all about it. I just want to get this island trip together."

"Who's going with you?"

"It's what I'm calling you about. Who's around? Do you know?"

"What about Rhonda?"

"She went home for the holidays. As did most of L.A."

"What about Giselle?"

"She went skiing."

"Hmm. It's sort of last-minute."

"I know. You want to go?"

My happy nerves jumped and I thought about it. It took all of a second and a half to accept.

"Can you get away from the family stuff?"

"I'll do my best," and I had a laugh with myself.

Then he got down to business. "I can't have the jet stop in New York. But call my travel agent. You have the number, right?" I said I did. "So who else? I hate to have this whole jet and not fill it. What about the Bullet girls?"

"That's a great idea," I said. "Kelly I know is down in Laguna. Heidi's in the Palisades. And the others I think are around too. Hold on."

I quickly rummaged through my bag and pulled out my electronic organizer. Then I rattled off a dozen names with numbers. I got an immediate rush of enthusiasm and blood returned to my face and I was sitting up now on the edge of the bed.

I thought about calling Kelly the Bullet but I knew how much the bill would be if I started rifling off calls from the hotel.

"You want to give her a call, Sydney?"

"Sure."

I gave him the number and I didn't need my organizer to do it.

"You going to leave tonight?"

"Or tomorrow morning."

"Call me here at the hotel and let me know. Or leave a message. If I have any other ideas, I'll let you know."

"Thatta boy. Just call my travel agent and she'll take care of it. And don't worry. You're going first-class."

"See you, man."

'Til Death Do Us Part

I had a sudden rush of good feeling for Sydney Swinburn. I was feeling so low and here was this guy who was making it easy for me. Of course I knew why. But still. It made me feel better. In one phone call he'd done more for my morale than my hometown city had done in two days. What had started as a bad family reunion with friction, resentment, and gloom turned into a sunny vacation on a jewel of an island in the Caribbean. Life was looking up. Way up. And seeing the Bullets would make it even better. Hot damn, was my feeling.

My fragile quality and hangover stress were miles away now. I felt refreshed and happy. I took an immediate shower to prove it. I knew I had avoided a lengthy seminar that would have featured wallowing and feeling sorry for myself. Conceivably, I could have lain in that hotel bedroom for some real debilitating days of darkness, wrestling sheets, watching offbeat channels, and phone-ordering abdominal exercise machines I'd never use. But not now. Now I was thinking about buying the loudest bathing suit in the loudest colors with the most vocal print pattern imaginable. My whole soul wanted to scream.

When I got dressed I made my calls. I was going to get the quickest flight to the islands known to man. I couldn't wait to soar upward in the plane, cut through some thick clouds that were holding the East Coast hostage with a cold grip, find the sun, look down, and give New York my tallest finger.

Because that's the way I felt.

I made my arrangements with Sydney's travel agent and scored a flight in minutes. Then I did a shove-all pack that took milliseconds. I still had three hours before my flight, but I wanted to spend them at the airport. That meant a lot to me. That meant I was getting out.

And that's precisely what I did. I hung out in the airport bar and read a newspaper. Then I munched on two Pizza Hut pizzas. Love that. The fact that franchises are in the airports now and you don't have to eat those shitty hot dogs and nachos with that awful cheese goo on top. My trip east was starting to feel like a holiday for a change. I even bought some coconut sunscreen and smeared it on my face just for the smell.

All's I can tell you about the next twenty-four hours is that the sleet storm that had kicked up the previous evening forced Kennedy Airport to shut down. I had the option of returning to the city but I opted against it for reasons noted.

It was during that day at the airport that I came to a few more realizations. L.A. was now my town and I better make the best of it. I'd dug in there and I had to respect it a little more. I even felt myself missing a few aspects. Like the Sled. And my Duke. And Bob the Riot. My whole dysfunctional family unit was out there. And I missed them.

The real reason I wanted out of New York so fast was clear. I was embarrassed. I didn't have enough juice yet. I didn't have enough accomplishment merits to go back and rub it in their faces. Though I knew I had gained a boost in stature, it wasn't visible or tangible or identifiable to anyone else. Especially back east. I made a pact with myself. I was not coming back to New York until I had the goods. I wasn't going to take or eat any more shit from anyone. Ever. Not in that town, anyway.

If the New York trip showed me anything, it showed me I had made my choice and now I was committed to it. There was no going back. I had chosen fully my lot in life. It had the tensile strength of "'Til death do us part." No shit. I had to stick to my guns. Career was all-important. All roads led to it. And all roads went from it. Without career commitment, I was just another Blip riding on a planet, three away from the sun in the thousandth galaxy of a billion, frighteningly close to nowhere.

I also realized I could never land a girl of Eleanor's stature with just glamorous irons in the fire. I needed some real glam, I needed some real results, I needed for her to want me, for her to look up to me. That was the only way. Sure, I was a pro at grabbing all those fun, spontaneous, pretty girlies from modest backgrounds. I looked pretty good, I had a gift for gab, parents liked me, I went to all the right schools, and had a personality that didn't suck. But to get someone like Eleanor, I needed more. I needed that X factor.

Except it wasn't an X. It was not a variable. It was specific. Very specific. It wasn't money per se. It was stature. In my field. I would not accept anything less. For me to fall short of that was a life not worth leading.

Hollow Day Stowaway

My flight to St. Bart's was among my best ever. As we rode high near the sun, my whole body was bathed in good feeling. I started feeling better about my life. I dashed off the disappointment of my sojourn in New York by thinking about the exciting new avenue I'd paved for myself in L.A.

I had a few thoughts too. I wondered whom Sydney had enlisted for the trip. Though it was a holiday, I figured he'd get some girlie-whirlies to change their plans. After all, he had a jet, a name, and beaucoup bucks—those qualify as lubricants. I'd given him enough numbers to try, that was for sure.

I never phoned in a good-bye to Eleanor. But she didn't phone me either. For a split second, I wondered if I should have invited her. I decided against it because she probably had some other obligations. Besides, I figured I needed to let that dog lie. To put some distance between us, so that the bad night we had would recede in memory to nothingness. Her memory.

I was excited to see the Bullets. I hoped Kelly had signed on to the trip, especially. It would be great to see her. On the island. In a bikini. Swimming. Laughing. And no bullshit—with me. The inactive one. It made me reminisce. I thought about how we met, how we became close, and that crazy, crazy night.

It was January. It was an eerie day. And eeriness can make even an L.A. uni-day memorable. It was one of those days that felt hollow. Right from the beginning of breakfast. Breakfast was hollow. My afternoon run was hollow. I found myself in an equally strange mood. The feeling of the entire day was that of a calm before the storm.

The Bullet came over in the early evening. She was feeling pretty low. Kelly often came to my place when she was down. We could just lie around, listen to music, do the Blockbuster thing, and she could laugh at all my bitterness. She'd lose her pain in my angst and think life wasn't so bad after all. A morale boost.

That night I made my special garbage spaghetti. It consisted of frozen vegetables, garlic, and onions, all sauteed with turkey meat and red sauce, which was half Newman's Own and half salsa. It was the hot sauce that gave it the extra bite. The Bullet loved the dish and after putting down a girlie plateful, she lay back defeatedly on my futon, stuffed and displaying a swollen Buddha belly.

After dinner we contemplated a movie. I had a VCR but only one cassette. It was *The Umbrellas of Cherbourg*, the French musical that had catapulted Catherine Deneuve to stardom. I'd seen it a hundred times already but I never tired of the opening credit sequence. The aerial-angled camera frames a rain-slicked cobblestone courtyard and a parade of multicolored umbrellas passes beneath in and out of frame in a beautifully choreographed ballet. It's my favorite four minutes in cinema. And I turned it on to many a guest. Best of all was the fact that I didn't know anyone involved in the whites so it didn't ulcerate me the way most credit sequences do. After all, the "Le Scénariste" billing had gone to a foreigner, and he was probably dead by now anyway. *Tant mieux.*

Kelly had never seen it and the medicine ball in her stomach quashed any desire to head home. But as the love story progressed she became increasingly emotional. In French film tradition the ending is not a happy Woody one. And it was just depressing enough to push Kelly over the edge. There was something on her mind she had never told me about.

"What's the matter?"

"It reminds me of Lawrence."

"Your ex?"

She nodded.

She had told me about him before and I liked nothing about the profile. It was her You Don't Know Him Guy. Every girl has one. Eventually. The type that is inwardly and outwardly one hundred percent prick with not an ounce of goodness, and it's as clear to you as summer rainwater. But she's blinded. And, of course, *you don't know him.*

The Bullet's You Don't Know Him Guy was an agent on the Star Camp rise. I hadn't been surprised at all when they broke up. A You Don't Know Him Guy always makes a mess. But the way in which her relationship ended was more painful than I'd imagined.

"What happened?"

"You don't want to hear it."

"Of course I do."

She then told me in between sobs that she and her man had been very much in love. And she got pregnant. She wanted to have the baby. And he told her at first that they should. But a week later, he changed his mind.

"What did he say?"

"He said he didn't love me anymore."

"Just like that?"

And they never saw each other again. The Bullet was crushed. And then she'd gotten an abortion. Alone.

"Why didn't you have the kid?"

"Because I didn't want to have to deal with the child's father for the rest of my life. He's a cold, heartless bastard. And the last thing I wanted to do was have a child that came from him."

Good answer, I thought. But that's why he gets the big bucks, was really my feeling. He was an agent after all. It had happened two years ago.

"You get involved with these guys and all you are is the next girl in line. You're just a moment. I don't want to be a moment, Heyward."

And the Bullet poured some more. It was heart-wrenching for sure. I held her close. I didn't say wow. But I felt it. Here she was, another relationship casualty. The walking wounded. A quarter-slice was missing from her melon, and it would take time for the missing wedge to fill in. But it would. I knew the formula. She just needed some time to herself, some good work to boost her self-esteem, and some new wildtime with a new man.

"In five years, it won't make a difference," I said. "In two years, even. Maybe a year. It's important to work on the self now."

"What self?"

"Your self. Ever done that before?"

"I've had boyfriends since I was fifteen."

"Precisely. You needed this. Imagine if you'd stayed with that guy, had the baby, and then cracked three years from now because you never worked on the self, never got to know who you were and what you were about, and woke up one day hating the way he laced his shoes in the morning? Relationships are tough enough when the two of you are soul-mates, let alone when you're still unaware who you are and you force a mismatch."

I paused a bit and looked down at the Bullet's head cradled in my arms.

"I like you, Heyward."

"Same ting."

"Same ting?"

"Yeah, it's the way Akeem Olajuwon says 'same thing.'"

She laughed through the tears. "You're so weird." And I laughed too.

My reminiscence made me more excited than ever to see her.

La Femme Blonde

Sydney had booked us a couple of suites at the Hotel Carl Gustav that overlooked Gustavia, the island's little port town. I couldn't get hold of him but I was sure he had heard I was delayed. The mini-Mok buggy brought me to the hotel and I loved the warm air surging through my face on the roofless go-cart.

The Gustav was a gorgeous hotel inset on the hill with the rooms and suites terracing down the slope. I gave my bags to someone who mattered, told him my name, and then followed him down the stairs to my suite. It was a beautiful suite with a bedroom, a porch, a view of the harbor, and a dipping pool. Little birdies were overdoing it in the shrubbery that surrounded the porch. It gave the suite the privacy aspect. Cool. I gave him dollars and some kindergarten French.

"*Uh, est-que Monsieur Swinburn est là?*"

"*Oui. La chambre 212.*"

"*Est-qu'il y à des autres femmes avec lui?*"

"*Oui. Une femme blonde.*"

"*Et des autres?*"

"*Je ne crois pas. Une seulement.*"

He only brought one girl, was the news. I found that odd. "*Kelly?*"

"*Oui, c'est ça.*"

"Elle est dans quelle chambre?"

"Deux-douze."

"Aussi?"

"Oui."

My heart bounced around hard. It was a moment I was not prepared for. The Bullet had stayed with Sydney the previous night. The night I couldn't make it. Because I was delayed. Holy shit, I thought. Sydney had snagged the Bullet. I was shaken. I was stupefied.

I guessed Sydney must have run interference with her. He must have given her some information to cause a rift between her and me. To break down our bond of intimacy. She wouldn't have done it otherwise. And I knew damn well what it was.

I threw my bags down and told my heart to shut up. I slipped out of my suite, gave no respect to the blazing sun, and looked for room 212. I didn't know what my approach was going to be. If they were still in bed together what was I going to do?

The grace of God staged it such that a maid was leaving the room as I was stepping down the tiled walk. The door was retracting with a spring delay and I silently crept up and halted it with my shoe tip. At first look, the suite was much bigger than mine. My breathing was labored and anxiety was a part of it too.

I peered into a glass doorway and saw the Bullet lying pretty stark with blond tresses cascading everywhere. The hair was haphazardly strewn like seaweed on the beach. The duvet was riding low and she was sunny-side up. Her skin was sunburned, and she had no tan lines framing her breasts.

I thought of the day the two of them had spent together. How she'd been lying nearly naked for him all day. Sydney had asked about her frequently. Add to that, her being alone with him on a Caribbean beach and what do you get? A no-brainer. Griffey going yard over the right field wall, at worst.

Like a twitchy rodent, I nervously searched for any kind of detail that would indicate consummation. Like condom wrappers, soiled sheets, or a diaphragm container. I didn't see any. I scanned the room. I saw only cutesy feminine clothes, like little shorts, little tops, and little shoes. The

Bullet was so cute. I didn't see any additional luggage. There was no evidence of cohabitation.

Maybe Sydney hadn't taken her down. Then I thought the answer must be in the bathroom. That's where all sexual and gender identifying articles would be. But I couldn't slip in there. What if she caught me?

The mystery was killing me.

"Hello there," I heard in a whisper. I jerked for sure but not violently. A brotherly hand matted itself on my shoulder. Had the greeting been more aggressive, I would have jumped out of my skin.

I spun. Sydney was standing there. I tried to drain away the debate consuming my mind, to not show any concern.

We exchanged pleasantries.

"Join me for breakfast," he said flatly.

Power Breakfast

I followed him up the stairs to the hotel's four-star restaurant which overlooked a wide pool and that breathtaking panorama of the harbor. To fully appreciate the setting, I needed a counterpart, the female kind. With thoughts like that, I knew I was getting ready to hop off that inactive roster. My head was starting to house the limitless recordings of the undersexed male mind.

We went through an inventory of our time spent apart. Sydney told me about Baby Garbo and Hawaii, and an interesting liaison he had subsequently in L.A. He was very confident. He had come to understand the finer points of aggressive womanizing. It's amazing what a series of sexual conquests can do for a guy's self-esteem. I was generally happy for him.

After our holiday recaps, he gave me a string of ideas, all his, and none of them forgettable.

"Heyward."

"Yeah?"

"I really like her."

And my mood sunk like the *Lusitania*. Here it came. His word on the

Bullet. I was hoping nothing had happened. Sure I was possessive of her. Partially because I knew I couldn't have her. But also because I knew that Sydney, for the first time in his life, was experiencing what it was like to be what he had always dreamed of being. A playboy. He was shuffling through women, making up for lost time. If the Bullet was going to get involved, it was for a long time, maybe forever. Not a weekend. I didn't want her to be a night notch for him.

"You do?" I asked hollowly.

"And I think she likes me."

I processed this as the renewed ego of recent conquests speaking out. I'd seen it before. Ever since grade school. Then he told me how they had experienced a "connection" on the plane. "A real connection. You know what I mean."

Meanwhile, I remember telling the Bullet Sydney wasn't such a bad guy, to give him a chance. Because she didn't like him or guys like him. The Hollywoodies. Her bad experience, remember?

"We both like the same books," he added. "She loved *The Gods of Gunfire.* It was her favorite movie. We had some wine. It was pretty cozy. Just the two of us on the plane. And you know how that's a lubricant."

I couldn't believe how my words were being sent back, haunting me. And why was it just the two of them? I wondered. What about all the other phone numbers I'd given him? He never mentioned even calling anyone else.

"Sure," I said with manufactured enthusiasm.

"Then we had a beautiful candlelit dinner last night. She was drinking. Telling me personal stuff."

"About what?"

"Ex-boyfriends. What she likes in a guy. Didn't you tell me she had a boyfriend?"

"Uh, yes." I was hoping I wouldn't get busted on this.

"She never mentioned him. Even though I figured they obviously weren't that tight or she wouldn't have come with me."

Of course he left out the part that he used me as the bait to get her to come in the first place. But with his new, swollen disposition, all of that was now translating to him as his own irresistibility.

Then he leaned in and spoke softly. "You know, Heyward, all the while we were talking, I swear I was falling in love with her."

"You fall in love with every girl."

"No, this is different."

"It always is different."

"I'm telling you. We clicked."

It was like those interminable seconds before the doctor gives you the needle in the keister. You fear it's going to hurt. You know it's going to hurt. But I had to hear it. So I asked him and made my facial muscles alter my grimace.

"Then we went back to the room. And took a swim in the dipping pool."

Though my pulse was thumping, I delivered this in the tone of a frat brother, rather than a jealous maniac. "Naked?"

"She wore her bathing suit."

"She did?" I asked, masking the relief.

"Her bottoms." And Sydney smiled.

"And we drank some more wine."

"Then?"

"Then we went to bed."

"Together?"

I needed to dial 911 because he was taking a sip of orange juice when I asked and I thought if he didn't answer me soon, I was going to have a thunderous coronary.

"No. She went to her bedroom. Mine is just on the opposite side. Didn't you see it?"

"No," I said. And I wished I had, dammit. It would have saved me the six months on my life I just lost listening to this tale with all the Greenies, Darkies, mind-racing, and senseless paranoia.

"But I kissed her good night."

"Long?"

"Not really. It was a peck. But I tell you. I felt like the Super Bowl MVP when I went to bed."

"That's great," I said with more hollow enthusiasm. And he used one of my similes too, I thought. Grim.

"And today we just hung out at Governor's Beach."

I looked at him again. "Topless," he confirmed.

What a breakfast, I thought. I would have rather had an Egg McPolyp in a Jersey mall and risked a faulty stool than hear this.

"She got pretty burned, actually." Then there was some silence. "Heyward. I'm asking you. Help me with this one."

"What?" I said with a pointed look.

"I know you've helped me with every one. But this one I really want." He paused again. Then added this. "I'll never forget it."

I said it guardedly. "She's a good friend."

"I know," he said. "And I know she's going to ask you."

I went silent. He knew this girl was important to me. And losing her was worth something. "It'll be worth it for you in the long run," he added.

We locked gazes after that. Until I nodded contemplatively.

"I'll see what I can do," I said.

He offered a weak smile. "Good."

Forget It

At that moment, I looked over and the Bullet was standing there looking at me. So cute. So sunburned. So sexy. So much of everything I loved about women. She ran to me like a little schoolgirl and she didn't need a little Black Watch plaid skirt to do it. We hugged and pretzeled and kissed and had the warmest of embraces. It gave me a nice sense of power. Of my power. Of my strength. It was a real turn of the cards.

The Bullet sat down and ordered some juice.

"Is it fresh-squeezed?"

"Yes, Bullet," I said.

She smiled at me. But her eyes betrayed a mind digging into something.

"I hear you're in love."

I said "What?" with a quizzical expression, but I really wanted to say

"I knew it." But not to her, to Sydney, because I did know it. It's what I had surmised had happened when I'd falsely considered them linked.

"You have a girlfriend," the Bullet offered.

"Where?"

"Don't *where?* me." And she looked to Sydney for support. He kind of shrunk there in his chair. He had purposely, meaning strategically, let her know I was linked up elsewhere. He knew it would weaken our bond. Smart.

"Your friend Eleanor," she added.

"Oh," I said. "Eleanor's just a good friend."

With that, the Bullet looked over at Sydney and he eyed her for a flash then quickly turned his head away. It seemed as if the Bullet was smiling. But her mouth didn't move.

Eventually, we got off the subject or it fizzled out. I really can't remember. Because I didn't give a shit what else was said. From that moment on, I was altered inside. Sydney had used one of my axiomatic ruses, but not against the male competition. Against me.

Of course his maneuver had an element of risk. It could backfire. Claiming someone is taken can further fuel an attraction. What you can't have and all. For all he knew, it could drive the Bullet right away. Closer to me. But he was smart. He hedged and hinged. He hedged it by sweet-talking in my ear. He hinged it upon some implied career advancement talk. I'm sure he hadn't forgotten the profile I'd given him of her. That she was a principled, old-fashioned girl. This would mean another guy with a girlfriend was off limits. He knew that. His knowledge of her psychological makeup reduced the risk that telling her about my relationship with Eleanor would drive her toward me, rather than away.

So, in the equation, he figured he'd get the Bullet to either stiffen toward me or be more drawn to me than ever, which was less likely; and, at the same time, he would neutralize that by making sure I repelled her, repudiated her, refused her. So she'd be left standing there alone. And vulnerable. And maybe, just maybe, she'd want to seek out a little revenge. On me. And give him further consideration. And, given the assumption that she would be opened up in good old island ways, meaning naked and near naked all the time, heating up, burning her flesh, sweating, oiling down, moisturizing up, cooling down, taking swims, doing the frog kick, dunking in hot tubs, with warm bubbles rushing between her legs, all those erotic things that happen in tropical places and all that would put the burner on her, all erogenous zones included, *eventually,* she may want to roll over from her stomach and let her legs drift apart and yield that fine source of womanhood the Gods of Good Genes had given her. Add a little booze and it could accelerate the whole deal. It was a pretty good bet. Like pre-bite Tyson in three rounds or less. And if I was off limits, there would only be one guy there for her with the necessary equipment.

That's all *if* I corroborated Sydney's claim about my romantic status and repudiated her. If.

I pondered the issue the rest of the day. While we took a swim. While we drove the island. While we lunched at another hotel. While we hit tennis balls. While we did all the things three people not romantic with each other do.

I wondered what Sydney would do if I announced a crush on the Bullet. And used all the weapons in my arsenal to seal her affections. Because I had to give her hope for something. I couldn't just take her away from a situation and not offer up anything in return. If I was going to run interference on him, which I truly felt was for her own good, I'd have to offer myself as the reward. I still had that much romantic influence over her, I thought.

I wondered what Sydney would do. Would he cancel the trip? Would he never talk to me again? Would he blackball me? I didn't think so. After all, he really hadn't done that much for me yet. Not anything concrete that had turned into dollars. And Lord knows, I'd been instrumental in dishing him a pretty fine assortment of pretty fine ladies, from First Ball In on.

How could he complain at this point? He'd had Graceland Tammy. He loved that. Then he'd had Baby Garbo. He never thought he could score her. Horses and Hawaii. I fed him that with a spoon. Not to mention all the other teeny-weenies, layups, and random girlie-whirlies I fed him with less character. Rachel, Chantal, Martine, Binky, Lola, Travels with Men, Inga, Captain Mustache, Daphne, Fux Young Boys, Wendy,

Christy, Two Credits Short, Check the Passport, Priscilla, Toni, two Brunei Babies, and a Dubai Darling to name a few. And there were others. Could he really turn on me?

The Dismantling

I made my decision. I was going to dismantle the foundation and groundwork Sydney had laid. I was going to run interference on him. The steps were easy ones. Out of my high school pages. For me, it was like mailing a letter.

First, I would tell the Bullet that Sydney had a crush on her. She would tell me she knew already. I would then tell her that it was more than that. That he was pumping me to give her good word on him, to boost him up in her eyes. That would flatter her slightly. And turn her off too. That he was so easy. So there. But more significantly, so plotting. Then I would tell her that what I had going in New York was nothing. That Sydney had confided that to her to break the bond we had. She would then see him as even more conniving. So the person she thought was so nice and considerate was actually plotting, deceitful, and desperate. And the Bullet didn't need to hear much negativity when it came to Hollywoodies.

Let's also take into account Sydney's most likely *inflated* assessment of how much the Bullet liked him in the first place. That would mean it wouldn't take much at all for her to be turned off by him. If this was true, my ruse would almost be overkill. It would go that much easier.

After that, I would just open my palm and let my personality fly, something I held back on in front of girlies Sydney had been pursuing. I would just have fun, tell Sydney to have fun, that it was the only way to win over the Bullet. Then we'd all have fun & stuff. Swimming, bathing, scuba diving, eating, riding bikes, exploring the island, whatever.

Would I then tell Sydney that she wasn't interested in him? No. I would tell him everything was okay. That in time, I believed it could work between them. I would tell him that she just got over a relationship, that she was confused and a little lost and it was a vulnerable time for her. But not to worry. Maybe in the future.

Then I wouldn't say another word.

Waves at Play

I remember sitting at the Hotel Gustav bar when she came out. She had a sheer orange St. Tropez strapless dress on and her burned and tanned body stood out voluptuously against it. The Bullet had an undeniable shape and her breasts were peering through, daring everyone to have a stare contest.

We hugged not once but three times. I could taste her burned flesh just looking at it. And I did when I kissed her protectively on the shoulder. Then we kissed lightly but we held our lips there. The Bullet and I were back together, thick as thieves.

Sydney was in his room returning calls, so we ordered up. The Bullet had a rum punch. I stuck with mineral water. I wasn't in the mood for drinking. When I raised my head Sydney was standing there looking at me somewhat awkwardly. Somewhat, for lack of a better phrase, miffed. His eyes were afire.

"Whoa, you scared me," I said. It was a surprise.

"Is everything okay?" the Bullet asked him.

"I had to fire an actor."

"Off the set?"

He nodded and looked decidedly stern as he ordered himself a ginger ale. Then he looked at the Bullet and smiled weakly.

"Tough business," he said.

All I can say is the dinner was one of the oddest I can remember. Sydney was very serious, almost grim throughout. He said very little. I'd seen him endure more than just an actor being fired. I asked if there was anything else wrong.

"No," he said evenly. And he forced a smile. Meanwhile, the Bullet continued to slam down rum punches. And they were punching her in the frontal lobes.

After dinner, Sydney decided to retire. He gave the Bullet a good-night kiss and he seemed to try and make it more than that. It was a strange move. If he actually was going for her, which he was, I considered him beyond that level of nighttime proficiency. Then he glared at her awkwardly. The Bullet just giggled it off.

"Let's go to the beach," the Bullet said.

So we did. I drove the mini-Mok and had a pretty good idea what was going to happen. She'd go skinny-dipping, would try to get me to go, would try to kiss me, and I'd have to tell her not to, that she was drunk. But I couldn't flat out reject her. I would play along somewhat.

Holding hands, we went down to the beach and the Bullet stopped and planted the biggest, wettest kiss on me in recent memory. It was totally unexpected. I had no time to protest. Then her dress came off at her behest and that beautiful body danced and pranced in the moonlight. And I watched it and its happy feet rush excitedly into the water. She beckoned me. I didn't comply. Until she rushed up and started lifting off my shirt.

"Come on," she said.

"No." Then I told her I had caught a cold in New York and didn't want to get wet.

Moments later, I was in the drink with her. She was splashing around laughing it up. I looked up at the glowing, silver orb. I loved those late-night ocean nights. I would have loved to have been there with someone I was in love with. Oddly, Eleanor didn't come to mind. Someone else did. I wondered where she was. And what she was doing.

I swam underwater a moment. The one thought that struck me was how easy the dismantling was going. It wasn't even a challenge. All the better, I figured. I was saving the Bullet from a potentially bad situation. When I resurfaced, she was already on the beach, drying herself with her dress.

I walked up the beach and joined her. I put my pants on. And we sat there looking out at the night ocean, so vast, so deep, so far away and so near.

"I want to fall in love, Heyward."

I looked at her. She was resting back, looking skyward, her arms propping her from behind.

"You will."

"But it's hard to find."

"What is?"

"My type."

"Maybe you shouldn't think in terms of types."

"What do you mean?"

"If types were so great you'd still be with someone you think is your type. Type is high school. Think in terms of other things. Like character."

She pondered it. "What's she like?" she asked eventually.

"Who?" I asked anyway. Of course I knew who she meant but my immediate reaction was to show ignorance.

"Eleanor."

"She's a bright girl. You'd like her. I'm not in love though."

She looked over at me sharply. Then smiled. "You're not in love with Eleanor?" she asked in a drifting skeptical tone.

And it irked me. Sydney must have laid it on thick, I thought, with respect to the degree of my involvement with Eleanor. "No. Why are you smiling?"

"Nothing."

I decided it was time to initiate a chord or two of the dismantling.

"Sydney likes you," I said airily.

"I know," she said as I had anticipated. "He likes you too," she added.

I pondered that though I faux-smiled just the same. I wasn't really prepared for it. "He told me to say nice things about him to you," I added.

"Did he?" And she looked at me somewhat powerfully. It was not a vulnerable gaze at all. My statement was intended to make her ponder the implications, to make Sydney seem conniving. But there was no fear, no apprehension, no confusion in her expression. She didn't bat an eye.

"Yeah. To give you good word on him."

She nodded. But she had a question prepared already, as if what I'd said didn't matter. "He told me you said I had a boyfriend," she said instead. "Why did you tell him that?"

"I was protecting you."

"How so?"

"Well, I didn't think you were necessarily ready. And he was asking about you. I said that to keep him away. For your own good."

"Heyward, how many times have you told me I am not in control of my life?"

"I've said it to you before, yes."

"That I'm holding on to immature ways of thinking? That it's time for me to move on to different pastures? Haven't you said that to me?"

"Yes."

"You even said the other Bullets hold me back, didn't you?"

"Not exactly. I said hanging together can do two things. It can be helpful and secure to have a clique of friends. In a town as dangerous as L.A., support systems are needed. But they can also be stifling."

"Well . . . ," she said, and paused to reconsider.

I knew where this was going. And I was torn here. First I didn't want to knock Sydney. And tell her the real reason I was blocking him from her, that he wasn't right for her. But I couldn't really be honest with her without doing so. Obviously, I was thoroughly disappointed how tragically off track our beach chat had gone already.

"Didn't you tell me I was caught in a freeze from that other relationship?" she resumed. "That I was stuck. You said, 'You're in a place where you don't want to be any longer.' That it was okay for a while to 're-group, revitalize, and recharge.' But 'it's time for you to shed that skin and evolve.' And I said, 'Evolve into what?' And you said, 'A modern woman. To be alive again. To live again. It's time to break fucking out, Bullet. Take a chance.' Remember?"

I was amazed at the precision of her recall. "Of course."

"Well, I remember. I wrote it down. And memorized it. And I've been waiting to apply it to my life."

"Why are you telling me this?"

"Well, I have."

"You have what?"

"I've taken a chance."

"You have?" And my words just hung there, in need of an answer. A quick answer.

"Yes."

"With who?"

"Heyward, I slept with Sydney last night."

I just let the sound of the waves play. I was so stunned I forgot the mother tongue. And my own version of it. I might have said "Really . . ." but I don't remember very well. The porno flick of the two of them in the rack was already on the screen and I was eating popcorn to it with all the other paying-customer schmucks.

But I still couldn't believe it. So I gave her a chance to reveal the lie of it all. "He told me you just kissed."

"I told him to. To not say anything. I wanted to tell you myself."

"And Sydney?"

"He agreed it was the right thing to do."

And then I flashed on Sydney's behavior earlier. His willingness to let us spend an evening together. And that bizarre kiss good night he gave her that she'd laughed off. He knew full well I was no longer a threat. He had taken her down already. No wonder he'd been so confident at breakfast that morning. His assessment of how much she liked him hadn't been inflated. The connection he spoke of was legitimate. They had done more than kissed and she had been less than topless. And they probably had plans for tonight as well. It hurt.

"And that's why you came out with me tonight?"

"I wanted to tell you, yes. And honestly, Heyward, honest to God, I didn't know how you'd feel about it. I agonized over it. I asked myself, 'What would Heyward want me to do?' And my mind brought back all the advice you had given me. You're upset, aren't you? I didn't know you would . . ."

"It's okay, Bullet," I said, employing the tone of the losing pitcher. And I handed the manager the ball, heard the boos, left the mound, and walked into the dugout. "I want you to be happy. You know that."

"I know," she said. "But even though you have a girlfriend you love, I still felt I owed it to you to explain. And you know what?"

"Tell me."

"I feel guilty."

"Don't. My advice still stands." And releasing those words was like bench-pressing.

"Do you still love me?"

"Of course I do."

At that moment, we went silent to each other for a while. And I processed the full blast with a flash reenactment of the events. And when I was done, I had one question to ask.

"Tell me, Bullet. Why did you smile when I said I wasn't in love with Eleanor?"

She looked at me. "Sydney told me you would say that," she said evenly.

"Did he?"

"He also told me you'd say other things you said. He knows you very well. And he really loves you."

I bet he does, I said to myself. And he should too. It was like loving the state after winning the lottery.

"There's something else you said to me," the Bullet continued. "'Take your time. A relationship will find you.' But I did take my time and I don't know if this thing with Sydney is anything or not but there's only one way to find out. Right?"

I didn't say anything. I was drowned in my own thoughts. They weren't about the two of them in bed, or about whether their union had a chance, or that my friendship with the Bullet might be forever changed. What was of prime, stupefying significance was the fact that Sydney had outmaneuvered me. He had dismantled my efforts before I could dismantle his. Basically, I had taught him so well, he had used my own teachings against me and snagged my little Bullet. That's what was leaving me noiseless.

The maneuvering had been there at the outset. I had let Sydney choose the girls for the trip. I'd let him do the phoning. And he chose only one girl. Purposely. Knowing full well he was going to hedge and hinge. And fearing I would still rebuff him, he backed it up with some counteractivity to quash any of my attempts to run interference.

There's no question it was all my fault. I had given him an entire cross-country flight to work on her. To tell her how much I loved Eleanor, how much I wanted to marry her, how much my family wanted me to marry her. And he would tell her how I had run interference on him by lying to him. By claiming she'd had a boyfriend when she didn't. It would make it seem like I was the grand conniver. So that he could break our bond. And he did.

No one knew better than me how I'd fucked it up. I let him take her on his plane, the Law of Taking Her Away from Herself, and gave him the coveted Uninterrupted Seminar, some real quality time, with a member of the opposite sex. He hadn't enlisted any more girlies. Another girlie would have been a distraction. He knew the girlies might get lost in each other. He just wanted the three of us. I was the bait to get Kelly there in the first place.

But that wasn't really where the miscalculation lay. The error here was in my assessment of Sydney himself. I had underestimated him. I never deemed him capable of such an act. His level of proficiency in aggressive womanizing had far exceeded my estimates. He had fooled me. And made me the fool.

Nowhere was it more evident how much a fool I was than on our ride home that night. It was a symbolic trip for the Bullet and me. The two of us in that little car were numb to each other. We didn't talk at all. She was quiet. And I was speechless. Anything more would have been overkill. There really wasn't anything to say. We were just two headlights bobbing in the night.

Chest Fight

We arrived at the hotel, swapped a good-night peck, and parted ways. I went to my suite. And she went to his. I took a couple Tylenol PMs. I didn't want to think about the late-night gift Sydney had just received. I didn't want to think about anything. I wanted sleep.

The next morning, my room phone rang and I picked up. Sydney asked me to join him and the Bullet for breakfast. I said I would as soon as I could find my clothes.

They were both seated at the breakfast table between their adjoining suites, and the table was full of jellies and jams and honey, coffee and pastries. It was so cheery I felt like kicking it on its side. The Bullet had a skimpy top on and the rim of her nipple showed. But I quickly averted my gaze. She was a different person to me now. She was of a different sex. She was one of the guys. Not even. She was neither sex. Of course it was my ego at play but how else do you survive without employing such defenses?

"Hey there," Sydney said as I stepped in.

The Bullet looked up at me and flashed a weak smile. And she couldn't hold on me any longer. I understood. I sat down and Sydney poured me some coffee.

"How do you feel?"

"Like a pothole," I said. And I sneezed too. The cold I had dreamed up on the beach had become a reality.

The Bullet excused herself and got up and went into her room. As soon as she disappeared, Sydney cracked a radiant smile and patted me on the shoulder. He whispered it.

"Everything cool?"

"Sure."

"She told you, right?"

"Yup," I said nonchalantly.

"I've got to thank you. I mean the first night was great but last night, wow. I think it relaxed her to have your endorsement."

Sure, I remember the Endorsement of a Close Friend axiom he was speaking of. He raised his glass of orange juice with a smile. I touched it with mine. I had to.

At that moment, she returned to the table and Sydney quickly put a seal on it and destroyed the silence immediately with:

"Anybody interested in going scuba diving?"

And I looked at him. He really was good. His mind was active, thinking ahead, all the angles, processing, and spewing out words laden with strategy. I tried to give myself a pat on the back for that, but somehow the self-praise didn't raise my spirits.

"Love to," I faked. The Bullet shrugged, her nipple rim jiggling as a result, though I shouldn't have been looking. Some neutralized entity she was, I thought.

Later, after breakfast, when she went to take a shower, Sydney tried to finish off the story with all the juicy horror. But I interrupted him with silly questions like "What's the time difference here?" and "Who's the president of St. Bart's?" I just couldn't bear to hear the play-by-play. It was high-percentage, high-velocity torture. Every shot was a hit.

"She has an incredible body," he felt compelled to add anyway.

It was like saying Michael Johnson is fast. "That's great." And I gave him my best "yes, *love* the taste of cod-liver oil" smile.

"What did you say to her?" he said with a glow, as if I'd worked another magic assist for him. Which in essence is what I'd done, only unwittingly, and months ago.

"I told her to take a chance."

"Brilliant."

It was brilliant, all right. Brilliant enough to ruin the rest of the vacation for me. I had driven the Bullet right into his arms. With some cornball, self-help doctrine I'd heard a million times and laughed off its cliché tenets half as many. Not really. I tried to drain the bitterness out of my thoughts but it was difficult. This one hurt. More than you can imagine.

That day we did go scuba diving, which was something I had no interest in doing. Submerging with big tanks, making my ears pop, having my nose bleed, breathing irregularly, and getting all paranoid in the head was not my idea of an easy day. I figured diving's requisite toothy barracuda would make his cameo appearance, sense my wounded rhythms, and want to play meat kabob games with my limbs.

But Sydney put on the gear, and the diving instructor coaxed the Bullet into suiting up too. And they had a lot of fun. I sat on the dock like a chump. And then we had a quick lunch at a roadside hamburger place, and then they went to the beach and had a good time. I went back to my room and reracked for no fewer than five hours.

When I pulled it together and showered, I met them at the hotel restaurant and they were waiting for me. The Bullet looked exquisite in white and Sydney had a white dinner jacket on. We ate, and not to my surprise, I was about as much fun as a case of poison sumac. They had spent a great day together, they were sunburned and healthy, recounting the fun they'd had underwater, and I sat there like Mr. Blip. My personality was in the shitter and I kept it there.

After dinner, they insisted we dance and they forced me to watch. Eventually, we went home and separated. I went to my bedroom. They went to theirs.

All I can say is the chest fight I had for the next five or six hours led me to believe that Sydney had the time of his life that night. Of course I had my own anxiety from the night before, but if you piled on top of that all the positions I pictured them in, you'd get a better sense of the pain I was fighting off. After all, it was night three of their union and the sex always gets better. I had to swallow it. I had to swallow it all. I had to lie there defenseless and contemplate their passionate moves.

Of course I was jealous. I hadn't had sex in I didn't know how long. And Sydney got the Bullet. If you think it was an awful night for me you're forgetting the devastating part.

Dear X

I took a shower around 4 A.M. and let the hot water try to clear out my head and calm my anxiety. And wash me off too. I felt like I needed a good cleaning. The thought came to me while I was squat in the tub letting it rain down on me.

Part of me died in those days in St. Bart's. I didn't know if it was an amputation, a jettison, or a new phase in a metamorphosis. But some outer carcass of mine was left there in that hotel suite on that foofy French island.

The next couple of days I kicked back and took in the sun and made myself have a good time. It wasn't that difficult. While they were doing their thing, what I did on that island was to start writing. Not script pages or anything. But postcards. I scratched off a few and sent them off to ex-girlfriends who had dumped me horrifically in the past and now had live-in boyfriends. What I would do was write loving and adoring notes in the dirty Hallmark card idiom, fraught with sexual longings, all in remembrance of our fun and frolic, lovemaking included, just so it would plant a seedling of doubt in Mr. Right Now's mind of his woman's allegiance to him. At worst, it would cause a discussion at home. Maybe even a fight, which is the result I was going for. Of course she'd say I was crazy but the seed would be planted. Of course, also, I only did this when I was feeling extremely low and wanted to get back at someone. That was the case in St. Bart's. I sent seven cards.

Shame and Eggs

On the last afternoon, I had a beer at the hotel bar. There were several other couples there. At the end of the bar was a guy clocking me. He was handsome, neatly dressed in white linen pants, blue blazer, and sparkling links. He was neatly slicked and neatly coiffed. Nothing was out of place. Clearly, he was a Soft Boy. Since it was a very heterosexual place, honeymoon couples and the like, I assessed his game. My best guess was he was hoping for a gay-curious hetero to get a little drunk and sloppy. So he could maybe guide him back to his room and show him how the other half lived. That was his dream. And if he was lucky he'd get the ultimate prize, a virgin hetero who had given it up only to wake up the following morning to confront the only breakfast he could swallow. Shame and eggs.

The sighting was no surprise. I'd seen this kind of character at the Olive and the Monkey Bar. Always poised at the end of the bar. Waiting like a cat in the reeds. Ready to pounce. But what did surprise me was this guy approached me.

"You're Heyward Hoonstein, right?"

"Yes."

"I'm Ludwig," he stated sternly in a crisp German accent.

I said hello to him.

"We met at your whores and hustlers party. Well," he laughed, "you may not remember but I escorted you back to your cottage. You weren't feeling that well."

I was pretty shocked. I did in fact vaguely remember someone bringing me back.

"Better than I did the next day," I quipped.

"Of that I am sure," he said with a pointed laugh. "You're with Sydney Swinburn, aren't you?"

"He's here, yes."

"I see he has a new girlfriend."

"I wouldn't say that."

"And you?"

Ludwig stared directly into my eyes. My analysis had been correct. The look I returned to him told him I wasn't gay and I wasn't gay-curious. "Thanks for the help," I said, and extended my hand. We shook.

"Maybe we will see each other back in L.A. Here's my card."

I took it. He smiled and drifted off. And I lay the card on the bar.

I considered the interlude a new station for my morale. A lower one. Sydney was with the Bullet and I was getting chatted up by an international homosexual dilettante in rippling summery linen. But I didn't want to give it much thought. I'm just grateful I didn't pass out that night of the party.

But let's not forget Ludwig did rub it in. I had no recourse but to think about the Bullet. I saw her differently now. Clearly, she was no longer the Bullet, my Bullet. She was a different person. I didn't treat her differently, but deep down I felt it. I guess seeing her differently was a coping mechanism. I decided to give her a new name. From now on, she was Neuter Bullet.

Sensitivity Override

On the flight back to L.A., my moods vacillated. One minute, I was quiet, reflective, and regretful, and the next, I was delighting in my raised standard of living. Though I couldn't take credit for it, it was great to be relieved of the daily pressures most people must contend with. Sure, I had bills to pay, but it was at a tremendous discount.

I was with Sydney Swinburn, yes. But I had my own identity too. And I had stature. I had a name. A new name. And a damn good address. And when it got right down to it, leaving ego behind was the most important thing. Every time I got depressed about something I'd lost, I'd find strength in all the advantages I'd secured for myself.

Like I decided back in New York, the life I led in L.A. with all its trappings was my life. And Sydney Swinburn and company were now my family. Disrupting that would be foolish. I would have to start again— not from the bottom, but close to it. The thing is, in Hell-A, power is the perception of power. I was perceived as someone who had the goods. By association. Without Sydney, I would lose the foundation upon which my newfound stature rested.

For these reasons I couldn't get too worked up about losing Neuter Bullet. And if I did, I made sure I didn't. I'd lecture myself right out of my bad feeling. It was a tool for survival. The best way of putting it was sensitivity override.

I awoke from my mile-high meditations and glanced to see Neuter Bullet sleeping soundly. *No doubt from all the pounding her body has taken, I thought.* When I looked over at Sydney he was looking over at me.

"Are you okay?" he asked.

"Yeah, why?"

She walked around naked in front of him every day.

"You haven't seemed like yourself these last few days."

"I'm me. Don't worry."

"Is it her?"

"What?"

"Are you upset I got involved with her?"

"No way. I think it's great."

He had his mouth on her breasts.

"Really?"

"Really."

He looked at me like he didn't believe me. So I decided I'd cover myself. My gloom was too damn obvious. So I threw it elsewhere.

He shoveled his hands under her twin globes while he was fucking her.

"No, it's true. I haven't been feeling that great."

"Why not?"

"Well, a lot of things. You know my family reunion wasn't much fun."

"What about Eleanor?"

"What about her?" I asked sharply.

"I thought it went great with her."

"No, actually. It didn't."

And I don't know why I said it. But I did. My only reason was: why not? Which always sucks as a reason. You usually pay for *why-not?*s.

"Really?"

"We just had a bad night. I hadn't seen her in a while. She was preoccupied. Rushed."

"Did you talk to her about it?"

He knows how she tastes.

"Not really."

So I told him exactly what we said. Minus the crucial stuff. Like "I don't want you, Heyward, you're a loser." It made it sound like everything really was still okay. It was defensive for sure. It was a partial opening. I'd never go full. It would be suicide. Because one of the last axioms is Never Divulge the Whole Truth—either to friends or to lovers. It can only be used against you. And will. In this case, I was sure of it.

"Sounds like everything's okay."

He did her from behind.

"I guess."

Then his face lit up and he looked over to me.

"You know what you do?"

At this, I was incredulous. Here Sydney Swinburn was coaching *me*. I couldn't believe my ears.

"Well, you know already."

"No, please tell me."

He shaved her. Maybe not.

"You know, romantic chess. Don't call her for a while. Then send her some flowers. Then call her. You'll be back on track. Flowers always do it. It sounds corny. But it's true."

"Thanks, Sydney. I'll keep that in mind."

I just sat there, simmering away. All the way to LAX. I couldn't believe it—romantic chess tips from Sydney Swinburn. It was a new low.
She took him whole. Beaucoup.

Fam Reunion

I must say, it was the first time I could remember looking forward to landing in Los Angeles. It's no wonder. New York was awful. And St. Bart's sucked. Los Angeles was now looking like Paris.

The limousine dropped me off at the house. I pecked Neuter Bullet good-bye on the cheek. And the kiss she returned might as well have come from an Iraqi leper. The two of them went for lunch.

I, however, took a nice stroll in the backyard, stepped into my not-so-humble abode, looked around at all I had to be thankful for, the real Thanksgiving for me, and took a dip in my pool. It let myself know unerringly that I was back home. And happy to be there.

"Chirp, chirp," went some birds, and I noticed it. Maybe I should get more into nature, was a thought.

I figured I'd stay away from Sydney for a few days. We needed that kind of break. At least I did. I needed to regroup. I decided to pay a visit to some friends.

I lifted the garage door and saw my old pal staring at me, headlights and all. I coughed the Sled up for a start and promised her a new milk shake. Then I wiped Bob the Riot's face. He had a light film of vacation dust. Bob was talking to me again. In case the point is muddled, *absence makes the heart grow fonder* works for HOV dummies too. I tossed some moldy lemons and I motored out the gate. It was nice to be back with the dysfunctional fam again.

As the car climbed up PCH against the sun, I saw a red lip-smack in the middle of the windshield. I wasn't sure who was responsible. It had probably happened during the whores and hustlers party. The shade of stick was dark. Maybe mulberry. I figured it had come from a sister, or a white-faced vamp tramp.

First I stopped by my favorite tree and filled up the console. The Sled had that musty, unused smell and all the new citrus gave Bob and me a nice break.

La Piedra, my favorite beach, was just about as nice as I had ever seen it. The sun was out but it was not that hot. Surfers with full suits dotted the break. One rider took off on a nothing wave and made something out of it. Obviously, Shred was working off all that holiday food.

I moseyed around the shore awhile and it was peaceful.

I didn't do much that night but calm down. I was tired. I was seeing my agent in the morning. I was excited to hear the results of my studio pitches. I figured just one shot in the arm like that and I would be on my way. I wouldn't have to deal with any more of this. In New York. Or in L.A.

Just one break . . .

Word on Me

I was feeling pretty confident when I went into my agent's office. I looked tan and healthy and I felt good about the material I had delivered to the heads of production I met with, and my chances for getting a deal.

Unfortunately, that was not the case. One studio after another had rejected my pitches. I heard things like "The emotional throughline is not strong enough," "Good characters, weak story," and "We have something like that in development already." Marty also said that the pitch market was weak. The studios weren't buying pitches from A-listers, let alone no-credit forgettables like me.

During the course of the meeting—and I won't give you details because I promised I wouldn't, because agent talk and Star Camp talk in general are intolerable—Marty praised my efforts. He also said I only had one recourse. To write a spec. A spec is a four-letter word to a screenwriter. It means busting your ass without a contract. It means work but no pay and hope it sells. It was a dismal prospect. I was fed up with writing for nothing.

I asked Marty if I could get another rewrite job. He said the town was closing down for the holidays. They were all waiting until after the first of January when all the Star Campers came back from vacation. It would be futile to send me out now. And unfair. The executives were thinking about Hanukkah. And Christmas. And Sun Valley. And Aspen. And Gstaad. And that hellhole, St. Bart's. Not about offering a rewrite job to Heyward Hoonstein, faux Jew of the Year.

As I watched the lips of my superagent move, I felt superdejected. But I couldn't really complain. I sensed Marty was looking out for me. Whether it was because he was acting genuinely or because of my relationship with Sydney, I couldn't be sure. Ego told me no. My gut told me maybe. And I always go with my ego to a fault. It's easier on the psyche. But the last bit out of Marty's mouth did perturb me.

"So how's Sydney? Big Sydney," he said with a laugh.

"What's so funny?"

"Oh, nothing. I hear he's pretty wild."

"Really? How so?"

"Well, I mean, they say—"

"Who says?" I cut him off.

"A girlfriend of mine who knows a girl he's been going out with."

"What did she say?"

"She said he's quite the ladies' man."

"She did?"

"Well, isn't he? You ought to know. You live there."

"What else does she say?"

"What do you mean?"

"What does she say about me?"

"About you? Nothing really."

"Come on, Marty."

"Well, nothing. Just that you're around. And you know a lot of people."

"Girls?"

"Yeah. She said that. And that, well, you . . ."

"I what?"

"Well . . ."

"What?"

"Take it easy, Heyward."

"I *am* easy," I barked, and I could have bitten lead pipe. "Tell me."

"Hey look. I don't care. I'm your agent. And I'm going to help you make it in this business, okay?"

"What did she say?"

"Forget it, man. It's petty."

"Don't give me that shit. Did she say I hook him up?"

"Did she? Well, she said that you know the women and, yes, you introduce them to Sydney Swinburn."

"Uh-huh. Well, you can tell your friend to mind her own business."

"Hey, lemme tell you something, Heyward. It's a small town. Real small. As small as it gets."

"What do you mean?"

"I mean, she isn't the only one."

"Oh no?"

"What do you do? Live in a vacuum? You think all this carousing with one of the town's giants at glamorous parties doesn't get noticed? In L.A.? How about with a microscope? Hello? Now maybe no one tells you this, because they don't want to piss you off or they want to stay on your good side 'cause you got an ear to one of the top guys in the business. But that doesn't stop them from talking behind your back. On E-mail even. Come on, man. Kick it out of the Dark Ages."

I was silent.

"Look. I tell you this as your friend. Okay? Just be aware."

"Okay."

"And, as your agent, I tell you to get back to work. Got it?" I marched over to the door. "And don't tell him what I said."

I nodded and split.

Bowwow Art

Agent Marty was right. Deep down I knew what people had been saying about me. But I had put a deaf ear to it. I wanted to believe the brotherhood I was getting from Sydney was because I was a talented artist. And the attention I was getting from Hollywood was because I was a Word-Star-Waiting-to-Happen. Of course, I knew what they were really saying out in Star Camp, that I was a middleman of flesh.

I laid low for a while. I wasn't feeling very well. I tried to come up with a new story but nothing really seized my imagination. Armando told me Sydney went out of town for a week, which was fine.

Days later, for whatever reason, I received a flurry of phone calls. The first call was from Sydney. I screened it and didn't pick up. He was inviting me to go to Sun Valley with him for Christmas. Ten minutes later the phone rang. It was my sister telling me how nice it was to see me at Thanksgiving. I screened that one too. She also said the Loach had gone into the hospital. She didn't say why but I had my suspicions.

Five minutes later the Jolly Jumping Lying and Cheating Bastard called in. Again I did not pick up. He was alerting me about a performance art exposition in Venice in which a naked man lives in a big cage pretending he's a dog. It's called Bowwow Art. I guess the Jolly Jumper felt we had outlived each other's usefulness and he had to offer up something to reclaim my attention. But Bowwow Art?

Then Sydney's secretary rang and left the details of the Sun Valley trip. She also said Sydney would be gone several more days than anticipated.

I decided to drive around. I took Benedict Canyon Drive with a purpose. It was a long straightaway. I didn't want to think about turns. I just rode aimlessly. To be honest, I felt kind of lost. I didn't know what to feel about where I was and what I was doing. The mood held some bitterness. I ended up on Mulholland. And I thought about Loach and how the hospital must be giving him fits by now. That the intravenous unit's liquid was clear but not his kind of clear. Then I thought of my mother and what her likely reaction to the latest illness would be. I was sure she was happy. She had a new project on her hands and new exciting things to say on the Wrapped Weenie circuit. She could use all the new hospital buzzwords and really juice up the party.

I must say I did feel bad for not having picked up on Courtney. So I pulled into the Glen Center on Beverly Glen and called her with a phone card. But she wasn't in.

Hard to believe but true, I next found the Sled drifting south through Brentwood, Santa Monica, Marina del Rey, and into Venice. It was that kind of uni-day. But I was determined to give it some definition. To accomplish something. Anything.

The gallery was pretty easy to find. I went in with few expectations. I was asked to sign in and I said no.

"I saw him do the aardvark in Moscow," I added, and the gallery attendant didn't argue.

As soon as I entered the room, he barked at me. He was in a thirty-by-twenty-foot gray cage. He was poised on his haunches, spiked collar around his throat and wearing nothing else. He wasn't the most evolved *Homo sapiens* I had ever seen. He had a simian look and a hairy ass. And his dingus was dragging along the cement floor. I hoped for his sake it was callused over already. I perused the pamphlet and learned his name was Gunther and this was his third stop on his world Bowwow Tour. That was solace. He was used to the inconveniences by now. Further reading indicated he had bitten a man in Zurich. I was sure it was a publicity thing and I hoped the victim was a film producer. Gunther had a doggy bowl and a cushion the size of a baby mattress. Man, I felt for him. The things we artists do, was a thought.

I took the forearm guard off the wall and held it up to the bars. I let the padded jumpsuit alone. I didn't want to get in the cage with him. He hopped over on all fours and did a jump. I let his teeth snare the arm guard. I had trouble looking into his eyes even though I was letting him go through his performance. I guess I was embarrassed at the extent of his humiliation. I hoped he was the kind of person who got off on humiliation. Then I wondered if indeed I was humiliating myself more, the way my life had been going lately. Was there really a difference between Bowwow Art and my foolish Follywood follies? I couldn't really decide.

He continued to bark at me. And not happily so. I wondered if he had an interior vision of me and sensed I was like him. And he didn't like seeing me. He had his own pain and didn't want any of mine. If the truth be known, I hated seeing him. More chills riddled my spine and arms. And it was a hot day. A last glance at his résumé stated he was also an actor, a poet, and a screenwriter. That said it all.

Before taking off I quoted General Joe Stilwell for him. "Don't let the bastards grind you down," I said, and I credited the General too. Because everyone used that phrase and no one ever credited him. It hit my writer's conscience. After all, I was still a paid member of the Writers' Resistance Movement. When he continued to bark I got annoyed. I pivoted around, aimed my uneven halves at him, and asked him if he wanted to sniff my butt.

He barked louder and I was out of there. I had had enough culture for one day.

Bowwow Art. I'm so sure.

On the drive home, somehow I felt okay. Though the exposition was disturbing, I felt mildly invigorated. I felt like I wanted to fight. Or at least not take any shit. And maybe that was the point of Bowwow Art. I immediately felt better about Gunther as an artist. Of course I wondered if seeing him perform such a degrading act had made me feel better about myself—had reminded me that no matter how much you feel you're bending, there's always some fool bending a little more. In any case, I felt good. At worst, I had accomplished something. I had defined the uni-day. I had gone somewhere. And seen something.

You Bet

For the next two weeks, I worked on my spec, outlining and reoutlining. Sydney called in from time to time. He was visiting the various sets of his productions. It was nice to spend some time apart. I was a little burned-out from our routine.

One afternoon I was limbering up for a run and he was standing there in the driveway. We swapped updates. Then he asked me to join him for dinner. He had invited a few girlie-whirlies and he needed me to round out the table. Somehow I didn't mind.

"Who's coming?" I asked.

"Well, there's Julia, who's coming as my date." I looked at him with an askew glance. He was toying with this one as of late. "I mean I had to. Right?"

I said nothing.

"And there's Wendy, her best friend. But then there's Angel who I really want."

"More than Julia?"

"Yeah, Julia and I have, you know, done it fifty times now. Thanks to you, by the way."

"Don't mention it."

"I mean I did the work," he was quick to say. "But you introduced me. Pretty good team, aren't we?"

Again, I didn't say anything.

"Angel and I met at a benefit in Toronto a couple of weeks ago. You remember. You set me up with George, who set me up with her."

Of course I remembered. George was the social Go-To Guy in Toronto. All towns have them. And I knew my fair share of them.

"Anyway, she's in town for a little while."

"Why don't you go out with her?"

"Because I want to use Julia. To impress Angel. It never hurts, right? To show her I'm a wanted man, right?"

"That's right." It was another axiom I'd taught him early on.

"So. Would you mind coming along? To talk to Julia while I make time with Angel. You know, keep her happy."

I found this amusing. He wanted me to be his Storage Man. I didn't say anything. I had other things on my mind.

"Let me ask you something, Sydney."

"Anything . . ."

"Do you think you might have a rewrite job for me at the studio? Or a polish?"

"I think we're all covered for now."

"You *think*?"

"No, I know. I mean, I know. I'm it." And it made him crack a smile.

"Well, if something comes up, let me know."

"You bet. You know Sun Valley's a great place to write. I know so many scriptwriters who live there. They just fly in for meetings. Not a bad life, huh?"

"Not a bad life," I said. And I swallowed it like I was swallowing a Japanese beetle. It tasted bad and the thought of it was worse.

"That reminds me. Who do you want to bring to Sun Valley? I mean let's just fill the house. Girlie-whirlies galore, you know? And maybe I'll even save a couple for you."

Sure, he laughed out loud. It was that kind of remark. An obnoxious one. The fact is, I hadn't accepted his invitation to go to Sun Valley. But I hadn't rejected it either. But he was used to people who said nothing to his generous overtures. To him silence always meant yes. And rightly so.

Before leaving, I took a long run to clear out my head. The drive over to Le Colonial restaurant was grueling. Sydney went over all his conquests, recent and old, and told me how much in love every gal was with him. It was largely unbearable. I thought I'd pry him off himself and his braggadocio stream and put him on the spot, though he wouldn't know I was aware he was on the spot.

"Have you spoken to Baby Garbo?"

"No. Why?"

"Just wondering," I followed up airily.

"She's been shooting a small picture in Europe."

"That's good. What about Neuter Bullet?"

"Who?"

"Uh, Kelly. The Bullet."

His spine seemed to straighten as he drove.

"No, well, the Bullet and I, well . . . She wanted something more permanent. And I told her I just got over a divorce. After a long marriage."

"Really . . . "

"But I understood where she was coming from. You know. Well, why not, right?"

"Why not what?"

"Why wouldn't she want to link up? With something more permanent. I mean, wouldn't you?" He was indicating all that comes with being Lady Swinburn. Then he added this. "Although that's what you've got."

And he laughed coarsely. It was a put-down. I let it go. It was the first of its kind. Little did I know, he was just warming up.

Shy Guy

Dinner was predictable as were the girls and their personalities. I went to the bathroom immediately to let others settle into seats and give me the chance to choose my own. I didn't want to sit next to Julia and force tactical diversionary chatter with her. I would not sit next to Angel either. I wanted to leave no room for doubt. It would show Sydney I was not interested and, once again, inactive. Which I felt I was.

I always put myself off in Siberia. Siberia in this case meant next to Wendy, Julia's friend, a young lady who was passionate and interesting. But she would not have satisfied a beauty junkie. Or even an indiscriminate night-notcher for that matter.

The table covered the same old yawn, yawn Star Camp subjects. The actresses, the actors, their performances, and Novastar's lineup of movies to come. Another bimbo, another night, was my feeling.

A waiter moved in on us and took a drink order.

"Do you make frozen margaritas?" Angel asked.

"No. Only on ice."

"Oh, no-sy." She did say it, I swear. It killed me.

"Well, I'll have that anyway. Maybe crush the ice if you can." The waiter gave me one of those polite on the outside, fuck you and the pickup you rode in on, on the inside looks.

"I'll have the same."

That remark was no surprise. To me anyway. It came from Sydney and I never saw him drink tequila. But I taught him to exploit opportunities, to show points of commonality, even if it takes ordering what the Target Girl orders. That he was employing these strategies in front of me was making my arm hair stand. My hair had been standing a lot lately. Ever since St. Bart's.

"So what are you girls doing for the holidays?" he asked.

Two piped up they were going home. And Angel said she was going to St. Bart's.

"I was just there," Sydney shot back.

I figured he wouldn't say I was there with him. And he didn't. I didn't care. He just wanted to one-on-one Angel and give the conversation a chance to right itself elsewhere. To take it out of the communal and put it in the personal. Meaning him. There's a way to do it. Sydney knew how. From you know who.

They did chat for a while. I sat there silently. Sydney I'm sure wanted me to talk to Julia, who'd been left idle, but I didn't want to. I didn't want to talk to anyone. I was the resistant poodle, unwilling to jump through the flaming hoop. I would bark like Gunther, but I would not talk.

Then Wendy smiled amiably at me. I smiled back. Oddly enough, it occurred during a break in Sydney's line of chatter with Angel. He'd taken the pregnant moment to clink glasses with her, another gesture to keep the one-on-one alive and thriving. He then took a long draw on his drink.

"You have to pull teeth to get anything out of him," Sydney shot over at Wendy, referring to me. It was definitely out of the blue—our blue, not his, however.

"What?" Wendy asked.

"Heyward. He's kind of shy." And then Sydney laughed too.

"That's me. Shy guy." I didn't smile and I didn't frown. But my mind immediately raced to "just one contract *shy* of saying up yours to all my detractors."

"Is he really shy?" she asked as if not convinced.

"Tell her, Heyward."

I didn't say anything, so she asked me directly. "Are you shy?"

"Shy of my goals, yes."

Then came this:

"Actually, his girlfriend dumped him back in New York and he's inconsolable." He laughed harder. I couldn't believe my ears.

"And you know why?" I asked them all. " 'Cause she heard I was hustling women for this romantic black hole out here in L.A. and that, well, was the end of *that* union."

I belched out in laughter too. It's a good thing I did too because my remark made Sydney go white in the face. But he was forced to laugh, or else it would have looked true. And bad for him. I could tell his poise was hanging on for dear life. When it's not in your genes to be a social whirlwind, well that's the way it goes. People who aren't naturally affable can be knocked off stride so easily. It's like knocking off clay pigeons with a .22.

Suddenly, I had made up my mind about something. There was no way in hell I was going to Sun Valley. Not with this guy, not the way he'd become. A monster.

The Big Ha-Ha

After I let my fires die, I had a pleasant talk with Wendy. She wasn't very attractive, she wasn't a Wam, and she didn't live in Hollywood. That was refreshing. She was a nurse at the UCLA Medical Center. Of course it forced me to consider my Wannabeast drive, and all our Wannabeast drives, and how useless we were, and how we really contributed nothing to society but a few diversionary laughs. And how, for the most part, it was all for our own ego support. And how this nurse was really out there helping people less fortunate, giving her own time to make someone else, not herself, feel better.

I felt ashamed. Here I was bent out of shape because I didn't have screen whites. And because my buddy and his ego were grating on me. I felt stupid, and silly, and petty, and ugly. I wanted to wash with six bars of soap. I felt all alone, so not a part of what was going down. I felt like a moron. I hate my life, was another thought.

I was so engrossed, I didn't even notice Wendy get up and go to the bathroom.

"Why are you so talkative?"

I looked over and saw Sydney having a mild altercation with Julia. Typical relationship-breakdown stuff. The kind that has nothing to do with one party. And has everything to do with the other who is sweet on someone else. And they have no recourse but to blame the innocent. I glanced right and saw Angel giving me her best eyelash flaps and a smile that wasn't painful to look at.

Then what she said registered. "Me?"

She nodded.

"I'm a part of the Big Ha-Ha. And I feel rather alone."

"The Big what?"

"The Big Ha-Ha."

"What's the Big Ha-Ha?" she said, and laughed too, though I knew she wasn't laughing at me.

"It's empty. It's me. It's you. It's the menu. It's us flying through space and time and spinning around on an imaginary axis. The Big Ha-Ha."

She sipped on her spirit, whatever it was, tequila I guess, and smiled, somewhat intrigued.

"So what does it mean?"

"Absolutely zero. Nothing. The joke's on you."

"I can't hear you . . ."

With that, she got up and her wonderful body settled next to me in the chair vacated by Wendy. I noticed Sydney registering it all, but I also noticed him trying to not care.

"But come on. It must mean something."

It's all you have to do to get the attention of a woman. Or anyone for that matter. It's called dropping bizarre. But dropping bizarre doesn't work as effectively in L.A. You get that weird or weirdo labeling usually. L.A. is obvious. L.A. is blunt. L.A. is not witty. L.A. is knocking someone over the head. Dropping bizarre works in New York. There it's the stuff of legend and stars. New York is crawling with junkies for the bizarre. As soon as they sense something is weird they get all tingly inside. They are attracted to it like magnets. Once again, configuration rules.

POST-IT: For Title File—Configuration Rules.

I sensed Angel was either one of two things. She was a little off and out there, meaning receptive to dropping bizarre. It genuinely accessed her. Either that, or she was bored. They can fool you. A bored person can click into bizarre but only until something else, something completely conventional, relieves their boredom. Because they're really not turned on by bizarre droppings, or comfortable with them. They're pretending to be accessed. And the fact that all this went through my mind tells you how bored I was at this table.

Having said all this, I really wasn't trying to be bizarre. I was saying what I was feeling. Which is also how to get someone's attention. To not try. It's even more effective than dropping bizarre.

"Why's the joke on me?"

"Well, not you. *Everyone.*"

"You too?"

"The laugh is louder for me."

"You sound so pretentious."

Of course she was right. Though I didn't care and wasn't trying to be pretentious, that's how it sounded. It made me like her a little. Instead of not at all.

"Good word. I usually only hear that one back east. Did you bring it out here?"

"No."

"Watch out. They'll fine you."

"For what?"

"The syllable count."

"You've got an attitude."

"I hope so."

"So tell me. What's the Big Ha-Ha?"

"Don't you feel you're being laughed at?"

"By who?"

"By life, by God, by whatever you believe in."

"No. I love God."

"I'm sure you do. Did you know God's a Leo?"

"He is not. He's a Capricorn."

"Just testing . . ." And I was. I was waiting for the "Really?" which I often get. With Follywood fluff. No shit, I was in an ornery mood. But so what? Look at my life. And the people I hung with. The only cool thing I had going for me was my license plate.

"Tell me, Angel, do you know when a relationship between a man and a woman is consummated?"

She looked at me warily as if it was a trick question. I told her it was not.

She nodded yes. "Uh-huh."

"When?"

"When they start fucking." And I was happy she used profanity. It would add poetry to my follow-up.

"Wrong. When they start *farting*."

And that got her. Go figure. You never know when you're going to crack a girlie-whirlie wide open. She was holding her guts in. So I didn't leave her alone.

"Anyone can fuck. And they do. Look around this room. Look at all these people here with no regard for who they let climb on top of them and get all sweaty and piggy with."

She was roaring and I don't know why but I kept it coming.

"But can they fart comfortably in each other's presence?" And I held up a professorial finger. "That's the true test!"

She wiped the tears from her face and I sipped on my margie.

"I bet you write good dialogue."

I laughed at that.

"Nope. Bathroom graffiti's my thing."

"What are you writing now?"

"I'm finishing a sexy thriller."

"What's it called?"

"*Deep Snout.*"

She laughed but didn't know why. Yet. She was waiting for the encapsulation.

"It's doggy porn, actually."

The laughs kept coming.

Out of nowhere, I got a vicious tap which was more of a slap, on my shoulder. I turned around. It was Sydney looking down at me, his face taut, and very specific.

"Friends don't do that to friends," he whispered tensely in my ear.

He was miffed and then some.

"What?"

"You know what I mean."

"Well, I meant nothing. I'm just sitting here."

Sydney looked at me with that harsh glare and it cracked somewhat. His face softened an inch. Then he waited for Angel to turn away. Wendy, however, was spot on with us, sensing the tension. It reminded me in flash form of the pettiness of it all.

"Okay. Sorry. I just thought . . ."

"Never, Sydney. We've been through too much for that."

Having said that to him and shaking hands, and watching him take his place back next to Julia, there was nothing more in the world I would have enjoyed more than grabbing Angel by the hand, have her go down on all fours, peel up her mini from the back, and give her the Big Hurt in front of everyone. It was a dream. But that's what dreams are made of. My dreams anyway on that night.

Friends don't do that to friends? Well, if they don't do that, what do they do? Help them with their careers? Not a chance.

The Politics of Farewell

Before the dinner was over, I did the right thing. I apologized to him. I told him I was out of line. With that, he apologized for having made the remark that prompted it. Using material that was very sensitive to me against me. Ostensibly all was cool again.

When it came time to leave and everybody was considerably happied up, I sent quick eyes to the girls to see what their next move was. The answer was in their faces. You either see resolute faces, indicating they know what they're doing, meaning going home, or fuzzy, lost expressions, indicating they're looking to be led. Not that I cared, but it was always a way of finding out if there was life after the party. The whispers Angel exchanged with Wendy indicated they would politely back out of any further frolic.

"Let's go for a drink," Sydney said to me. "I think the girls are game."

Then he saw them moving in on him. "What do you all say about a drink? Maybe the Bel-Air Hotel?"

"No thanks, Sydney," Angel said. "We're tired. I have an early morning tomorrow."

"So do I," Wendy added.

"Okay, well . . ."

Then I watched the politics of farewell take place. The way it unfolds can be exciting. It's so telling. If you consider human beings like charged little particles, ions, for example, which are propelled by other ions, or repelled by them, the politics of farewell can easily be understood.

Out of any group or gathering, any two people who are most drawn to each other will save their farewell for last. They'll kiss and say good-bye to everyone else, but they will save their object of attraction for the end. Of course the attraction may not be reciprocated, but the person who has the crush or interest beyond casual will always make it known by virtue of his or her farewell.

I was interested in seeing how this one would play out.

Angel, who was pretty enough to spur interest in saying good-bye to her, bid all of them farewell first, the maître d' included. Then she moved right in on Sydney.

"Thank you, Sydney."

"You're welcome. Let's do it again."

"I'd love to."

At the same time, Wendy approached to say good-bye. I kissed her warmly on the cheek. She was a good person and I knew it. So together, so into what she was doing, so not giving a shit about who had movie credits and who didn't. Cool woman, for sure. I was so happy to be around a woman who wasn't involved in the fray, in the scam, in the rigmarole of the sex raffle. She was just a good person. I sensed I was starved for the breed.

At this point, Wendy said good-bye to Sydney and Angel squared before me. Our noses weren't far apart. It made me nervous.

"Good-bye, Mr. Ha-Ha," Angel said. And then she grazed her nose tip past mine and gave me one on the lips. Then she started off, but swiveled back around with her back to Sydney.

"Call me sometime," she said.

I just looked at her as she was waiting for me to ask for her number. I didn't. I just nodded that I would.

"Do you know my number?"

I shook.

"I'm listed," she announced.

At that moment, Sydney came back over, and momentarily after that, Julia returned from getting her coat from the checker.

"Oh, there you are," Sydney said to her. And we both looked at her and smiled.

The ballet of human interaction never ceased to interest me. It holds so much truth. Especially the politics of farewell. Table seatings can be equally revealing for romantic leanings. But they're usually ruined by chance. And late arrivals. Body language is, of course, a great indicator too.

And the body language between Sydney and me indicated we weren't going to go out for a drink together. It was silently understood.

Cheek, Not Lips

The drive home was somewhat quiet. Until we got back to subject ground zero. Which, of course, was a real puzzler.

"I think she likes me."

Here it goes, I thought. But I had to ask whom he was talking about. Even though I knew.

"Who?"

"*Angel,*" he said emphatically as if I wasn't thinking straight.

"Think so?"

"Do I think so? I mean we had eye contact throughout dinner. We like the same music. She's cool, don't you think?"

"Sure," I said.

"And what a body." I let that go. "Did she say anything to you?"

"About what?"

"About me . . . " And he looked over again as if I was out to lunch or something. "Are you okay?"

I flatly said I was.

I really wanted to let him have it. I was sick of the runaway ego and preoccupation with self and talk of his crushes, imaginary and otherwise. I was fed up. I had been feeling somewhat low recently. After all, Romance was the area in which I excelled and I hadn't received any ego satisfaction recently. For my ego to stay afloat, I was waiting for other things like some triple-jump career strides. But that wasn't happening. I had done nothing to service my ego in a long time.

Allying myself with Sydney Swinburn helped, knowing I had New York and all that solid educational background helped, and getting a new agent and a name in Follywood also was ego supportive. But I still had an ego debt and it needed to be filled. I was fragile. I hadn't had any good female warmth in a while and I was due. Or at least coming due.

There's no doubt Sydney and his constant chick chatter exacerbated the whole thing. Making fun of me didn't help. I mean the more he got laid and bragged about it, and the more I didn't and watched, even though I wasn't trying, the more it made me resent him. It also worked on me in such a way that I was starting to get insecure, insecure in an area that I had always been a master. I had a personality that didn't suck, remember? And shit as stupid and ridiculous as the Big Ha-Ha was always floating through my brains which could impress a bored tablemate in no time.

Which is why the conversation in the car took the following turn.

"Well, Julia was there. That didn't help."

"You thought it would," I said.

"I did. But you never know in these things," he confessed like the Master of All Women he had recently believed himself to be.

"I don't think she's interested in anyone."

"No?"

And I was on the edge of my seat because I knew where this was going. So I chose my words carefully. Like,

"Nope."

"Why not?"

"Because she just got over another relationship."

"She told you that?"

"No. Wendy did."

"Huh . . . ," he said. "Well, she wants to go out again. She said she really wanted to."

That was when I took the chat to another level. It was more of an Irascible Me for sure. But as much as I wanted to hold my tongue, I couldn't.

"Yeah, well, I wouldn't get your hopes up there."

"Oh no?"

"No."

"Why?"

"Because she's spraying it everywhere."

"What do you mean?"

"She was working the room."

And it was as easy as chewing gum for him. "Well, who else was in the room?"

No shit, this guy was out of control . . .

"Not just the room. The table."

Then he looked sharply at me.

"You?"

"She told me to call her, yeah . . ."

"Well, she knows you're my friend. Did she give you her number?"

"In essence."

"In essence?" he asked challengingly.

"She told me where I could get it."

"From me, right?" And the way he said it, he was convinced she was not trying to hide anything from him.

"No, actually. From the phone book."

There was a long pause. It was his move. I wasn't going on the offensive, that's for sure. But I knew he wasn't done. He wanted to have no argument on the issue of being the Master and he was going to keep it rolling until I agreed with him or the discussion turned up the anger enough to call it quits. Which was not the best path for a friendship. A crack usually results.

"We had a connection. You know it when you feel it. If I had asked her to come home with me she would have. I guarantee you."

"How about she's nice to you because she knows you're in a power position? That doesn't mean she wants to go to bed with you. She'd be a fool to be a bitch to you."

He looked at me with a face slashed with fury.

"Look, I'm just trying to help you make the proper reads," I qualified.

"What makes you so sure you're making the right reads? I mean who have you fucked lately?"

I laughed that one off. But it did irk me. Later.

"Sydney, I could say the same thing. That we had a connection. I mean she kissed me good-bye on the lips, the whole deal."

"Me too."

"No she didn't. She kissed you on the cheek."

"What are you talking about? Right on the lips."

"Cheek. Not lips. I saw it."

Then we argued about that for a while. He protested vociferously. Right then and there I wanted the Feminist Fairy to fly by and say, "Men are so funny." Or "so stupid." Or "so predictable." Or "so childish." Because we deserved it. We are absurd beasts. But that's just it. We are beasts. Every last one.

"Look," I said. "The girl turns her back to you, asks me to call her up and go out. What do you want me to say?"

"Oh, so she was after *you*?"

"I don't know."

After all, I couldn't say yes. I wanted to. But it would have sounded so stupid and needy. So I let the thought hang there. And slowly murder him.

But it didn't. He wouldn't let it. Denial came fast.

"Bullshit. She knows you're my friend. She'd never go behind my back. She's an aspiring actress, remember? How about she was being nice to you because she knows you're close to me?"

It was a substantial point. Hell-A makes every point like that substantial. It was better to capitulate. After all, who knew who was right. Maybe he was. I was feeling low enough to think he could be.

"I don't know what to tell you. She's a sly one."

We pulled into the driveway. I decided to come off my stance that she was interested in me. Just to preserve the peace. Of course I hated to do it. I had swallowed so much of this kind of shit for so many months, I needed my stomach pumped.

"Look, all I'm saying is she's not dependable. I wouldn't take her clapping eyelashes as a sign of anything other than she's just keeping her options open."

He had an eerie response to that. He didn't say anything. We went in the front door, bid each other good night, and I went out the back.

Ear to the King

I sat on a chaise lounge for a while and listened to the hum of my pool heater. With the water glowing blue and me staring at it, I came to the realization that I had been treading water like a swimmer hoping to see the faraway island. Finally, I'd spotted the island and I was going to swim ashore. It was all suddenly clear.

Sydney Swinburn was never going to give me the career boost I really needed. By helping me win my professional freedom, he would lose control of me. I would fly and fly free on my own merits. I was potentially a shooting star that he didn't want to see shoot across the sky. Because he would lose his power over me. And his ability to use me. That was it about these power figures. It all comes down to that. Power. They know how to use it. And they know how to keep it. At all costs.

He would fund anything—a trip to Manitoba, a trip to Mars—if it helped him score pussy. But that was it. He was after his own, and it had been that way ever since he saw me emerge from a bathroom with four girlie-whirlies in tow. The man put me in his sights, sucked me in with a nice place to live and with sky-high promises, and did not deliver.

And I was in no position to blame him. In my Wannabeastly way, I'd exhibited no better conduct than he. Of course I had delivered for him. Sure, I'd been given a kick-ass residence, but I didn't care about living well. I never would have gotten involved with him if the sole prize had been a higher standard of living. I'd rather live like a pauper and have a career with credits than live like a prince without.

Sydney was smart. That was for sure. But since I knew what his M.O. was, and since he hadn't yet deciphered mine, I felt like I had an advantage, however slight. Not that he wasn't aware that I was in search of career advancement. He didn't know I knew he would never give it to me.

Should I continue to be his close friend? *Damn right,* I should. Why? To promote myself and remain in that position of having an ear to the king. To force the town's players to respect me and eventually entrust me, befriend me, get in good with me, and employ me. That, I was sure, was the path to getting my contract. And then I would be off to the races. If there had been any doubt before, there was none now. Our relationship would be uncut, uncensored mutual manipulation at its best.

I made like Gunther and barked. Poolside. With no one around. "Ruff! Ruff! Ruff!"

In seeing my predicament this way, I felt a tremendous sense of relief. The weight of all those misguided hopes was off my shoulders. I felt like a flyweight boxer. Light, quick, and with an endless reserve of energy.

That night I spent the bulk of the time burning and churning in my bed. I had to keep taking the covers off or exposing a leg. I was sweating. I was like a human steam engine rolling around, conjuring images of meetings, exchanges, and interludes with power people and taking charge of all situations. I was ready to take charge. I was ready for success. I was a rabid dog with a bone. And I was going to foam at the mouth all over town until I got what I wanted.

Let's not forget also that during all that churning I came up with the idea for my new spec script.

I started writing that night and by six in the morning had twelve pages. I couldn't sleep. And I couldn't wait to get back to work. There was a wild animal within me and I had to let it out. I hadn't had the feeling in years. And knowing it was back got me thoroughly excited.

The Crack

POST-IT: The Crack
There is nothing more exciting than a new friendship. It's full of promise and excitement. It's like having a crush. You want to be with them and tell them everything. And fear no reprisal. But after a while, the relationship cracks. And you feel it with all your nerves. Suddenly your friend annoys you, preys upon you, makes you bitter and irritable, after only a whisper of provocation. And you want to lash out though they may not be feeling the same upset. You really want to strangle them and all their little habits that one time you found appealing. I'm not sure what triggers the crack. Maybe it is that familiarity breeds contempt, that human beings can stand their brethren only for so long. The Greenies accelerate the Crack. But once the Crack appears, it is difficult to mend. Like a crack in cement. You can patch it but eventually the Crack reappears, recracking all the adhesives and patches you've spackled. A solid bond of friendship finds no equal in strength until it cracks. Then it's like a knee injury. It's never the same again.

The next couple weeks I treaded lightly on the property. Sydney asked me to go out a few times but I declined. I told him I was working on My Newest and I didn't want to play until it was done. The reality is a crack had appeared in our relationship. As soon as we were in the same space, you could feel the tension. I could no longer stomach his unrelenting blasts about who loved him and how much. If I spent any time with him I would immediately feel myself slipping into contrarian mode, meaning I could not resist resisting him. I could no longer give him ego strokes. I could no longer coach him. He didn't want to listen anyway.

So what did I do? I got serious with My Newest. It was coming at a furious pace.

With my downtime, I had a new spot of interest. And intrigue. And it all started in an all-American way. At 7-Eleven. I was in there one afternoon in search of a way to pick myself up. For the late-afternoon idea push. I was bored of the usual caffeine offerings. I wanted something new. I ended up just getting some normal coffee and doctoring it with some punishingly sweet amaretto creamer.

Two Dots

Just as I was backing out of the slot and seeping into that delicious parking scramble 7-Elevens are famous for, I saw her. She slid into the spot next to mine in Sydney's Jag, but I swear she did not see me. She popped out and hurt everyone with the way she looked. For girls and guys alike it was *no way*. *No way* to look like her and *no way* to have her. You just had to be content that you were human and she was on your team. Or that eventually she would die. Or get old or something that made her succumb to gravity's pull. But that still didn't work. Because it was the Now and she was there in her little black skirt and tank top. Hurting everyone. Ouch.

She settled on a diet soda and a pack of cigarettes and I watched the clerk try to make small talk with her. She gave him a mild smile and it was enough to make him break like he'd just had a baby boy.

You see, my subconscious had been working on me with respect to this one. Teal was the most interesting subject I'd come across. Don't forget my penchant for finding the little riddle in everyone. Though I had copious sound bites in the Teal file, exact transcripts of all our conversations included, none of them added up to anything resembling deep character. She'd remained a raging mystery to me. This was above and beyond her physical merits. They worked on me another way. They had been massively suppressed as a result of the Pact. And of course the danger added to the allure. And mystery. Not only was I largely ignorant of her background but I still hadn't gotten to the bottom of her relationship with Sydney.

It had been nine months already and still I had no gold on her. Before I hadn't wanted any. It was hers to keep, remember? But no longer. I wasn't scared anymore of the Sydney retaliation factor. That was final proof the Crack had appeared. I wasn't going to break the Pact or anything. But Teal's gold was something I was attracted to and wanted to have.

I tailed her, staying one car behind and one lane over. I followed her into Beverly Hills keeping my distance. She parked in a lot on Rodeo and I slid past and found an empty space. In my rearview I watched her step into the La Perla shop. That raised my blood temperature a notch. She was exactly what the lingerie designers had in mind when their horny little elves were sewing all those cups and crotches together in Laceland.

She came out carrying a petite, elegant shopping bag. She then went across the street and emerged from a sunglass shop with a new pair of Jackie O specials. Curiously, she walked in my direction, but my car was shielded by a big-ass sapphire Rolls. No doubt it found the Sled cute and cuddly and was trying to sniff its rear bumpers.

Teal stopped and yanked on a pay phone and dialed. Of course I wondered whom she was calling. I didn't know whom she knew, if indeed she knew anyone. She was one ultracurvaceous question mark. With two dots instead of one.

I decided it was time to get back to my keys. I had some more ideas, some more Post-its, and a few new bursts of dialogue. I let Teal be. To beat the hell out of the rest of L.A. I was already bruised and it took under a half hour. And she'd gone lingerie shopping too. But for whom? Sydney? And if not, what other lucky sonofabitch?

When I returned home, I booted up my computer. Then played my answering machine. Sydney had called to remind me about the roster of potential candidates for Sun Valley. I still hadn't accepted the invitation, though Christmas was only a week away. Marty called to ask how the script was coming along. And then there was this:

"Heyward. Stop studying me. I'm not for your files and I'm not a science project. Don't follow me around. If you would like to get together as friends, let's do it the right way. I'll be at Le Petit Four at five if you want to join me for tea."

I was stunned. It was me she had telephoned while I was tagging her. I checked my watch. It was already a quarter after. I figured it was too late. That means I drove fast. Sunset Boulevard saw a whish and nothing more.

The Sled dove into the back parking lot and I slotted it unevenly. I ran up the back stairs of Le Petit Four and into the dining room. She was not there. Then I checked the porch. There was your normal Sunset showing. Only with a few more European and Arab types. There wasn't a pale face or a flat chest in the group. But there was enough lip gloss to lacquer a parquet floor.

In the corner, all alone and sipping silently on a teacup, was Teal. She spotted me and gave a half-wave. She wasn't smiling. I marched over and stood before her, not sure what to expect.

"Hello," she said.

"Hi, Teal." And I sat down. "I thought you told me you were giving yourself up to science."

"Whose science?"

"Mine."

She took a draw on her cup. "I said *someday*."

"That day hasn't arrived yet?"

She said nothing. I felt uncomfortable. There was something on her mind and it wasn't thoroughly pleasant. I ordered a double espresso.

"You seem disturbed," I said.

Again she just tilted the teacup rim and took another tug. With the cup in front of her face and her buggy frames there wasn't much to look at. It left her ravishing instead of drop-dead.

"I am, I guess."

"How come? Or rather, I take that back. I won't ask."

"It's okay. My brother upsets me."

"The fireman?"

"Not anymore. He quit his job."

"What's he going to do?"

"He wants to visit me," she said in a tone that sunk into some form of discomfort.

"What's wrong with that?"

"I don't want him to come down here."

"Why?"

"It's not him."

"Him, or you?"

"Both. I don't particularly want him to see me this way."

"What way?"

"Living the way I do."

"How do you live?"

"Shut up, Heyward," she snapped.

I looked at her, hoping for some form of explanation. It didn't come.

"What's the matter?"

"What's the matter? You're so full of shit," she shot back.

I was not prepared for this. Not this way. Not from her. "Why?"

"How do *you* live?"

"What's that supposed to mean?"

"It's the same question, only I guarantee you have a lot more to answer for."

"Do I?"

"Yes you do."

"How so?"

"Come on."

"Come on what?"

"You don't want to go there."

And she was right. I didn't. Or at least I wasn't sure. So I hedged.

"Could it be that I have more to answer for because I confess to my shortcomings? While you take the easy route?"

"Which is?"

"Hiding."

She stayed silent.

"Forget I said that. We can take up your case another time. Let's just deal with me. So let me have it."

My words even surprised me. To the point where I didn't think it was me talking. Something deep down was guiding me to take this line. Telling me I needed to. Call it a need for abuse, self-inflicted punishment, or psychomasochism.

"No. You really don't want to, Heyward."

"Sure I do."

"I don't want to make a project out of you."

"You already have. And you know it."

She knew I was right. But my comment had more to it. The dare aspect. My heart started to pound. I'd never swum in adverse waters with her. I sensed it could hurt our rapport. Maybe destroy us and our little connection. 'Cause no matter how much you want to know the truth sometimes, when you get it, it can prove to be the stuff of lifetime resentment.

But I had to know what she thought of me. Sure, I was scared as hell. She still said nothing. So I ran one past her.

"If you don't tell me, then we're going to delve into you. And the implications of your being Sydney's Stowaway."

Teal flared a fiery look at me. And then pondered a beat. Then she sat up in her chair and leaned in, elbows on the table.

"Well, where should I begin?" She said it in a wavering voice, like it was something she didn't want to say. "The categorizing, the hypocrisy, or the introductions to women?"

I felt emotion rise in my chest. Some water seeped into my eyes. They were filled by the time I spoke.

"Take your pick," I said in a voice that cracked like a sugar wafer.

"You like hurting people?" she asked.

"Have I hurt anyone?"

She held on me a beat longer. Then her face crumpled. She couldn't hold back the upset any longer. "I'm sorry" came out in between heaves.

"No, you're right. I've been dealing with these issues for some time now. It hasn't been easy." I looked at her directly. "But you're wrong about one thing. I wasn't following you to study you. I just like it when you're . . . around. Whether you know you're being *around* or not."

She topped my hand with hers and looked at me fondly. "I always come unglued before holidays," she said, and added a wet laugh.

Immediately, I flashed on the thought of what her family history was and what would make holiday time a difficult time for her. Then I told my analytical mind to shut the fuck up. Then I realized it was okay. Because it wasn't that I wanted to make a project out of her. I really cared. And when you care about someone, you want to understand the reasons behind their emotions. Especially if they involve tears and sadness.

She wiped her face with a napkin. And tried to smile. When she did, I did too.

"You forgot to tell me something," she said.

"What about?"

"You never told me about Wednesday Night Guy."

And she let out a big laugh that was a relief from the upset. It made me laugh too, through the tears. And what was just as funny is she really wanted to know.

"It's actually an uphill battle for Wednesday Night Guy."

"Why?"

"Because Wednesday Night Guy gets caught in no-man's-land. He's smack in the middle of the week. He's too late for being someone's Monday Night Guy and he's too early for the weekend. He gets caught in between. Wednesday Night Guy never gets laid."

She was laughing pretty hard. I was happy for that.

"And he's usually a big drinker. And watches ESPN's *SportsCenter* even as it loops. Those male barflies all lined up in a row at your favorite watering hole? Wednesday Night Guys. All of them. And the more they drink, the more they can't figure out why they're not getting laid."

When she stopped laughing she clasped my hand even more gently than before. "You inspire me, Heyward."

"Do I?"

"Yes, you do."

"Why?"

She didn't answer. Until the next subject hit her. "Tell me about your new script." And we both laughed little awkward laughs.

And after I went to the bathroom and freshened up, I did. And she listened. I could tell the story was engaging to her. When we got to the part I was having difficulty with, she offered a suggestion. A damn good one. I was further impressed by her. She seemed so wise. So knowledge-able. So beyond her years.

"Why are you looking at me that way?" she asked.

"What way?" I asked guiltily and wiped the glaze from my face.

She leaned in. Her lips slowly moved toward mine. And at that mo-ment, I saw everything. Everything great the world had to offer. Includ-ing that mulberry shade of lip paint smacked on my windshield. It wasn't a sister or a weird-for-weird's-sake vamp who had put it there. It was Teal's stamp. And it was coming right to me, homing in on my lips. They touched. Lightly. Then it was over.

"Heyward," Teal said in a cool, even tone. "I have to tell you some-thing."

And she was about to. Until, not only the moment, but the rest of the afternoon was shattered.

"Hello, there."

It was coming from behind me. I looked at Teal. Her face showed startle. I swiveled. Sure. It was Sydney. All of him. There was so much of him, we couldn't see the sky. He was blocking it like nature's goalie. His face was as tight as Saran Wrap on a bowl of beans.

"Hi, Sydney," I said.

He looked at me. Then at her. Neither of us was a favorite.

"Join us," Teal said. "We're having tea."

"I noticed."

He sat down and went silent. Then he drew out a cigar. And leaned back. And lit up, slowly turning the stick in his fingers.

"Have you decided what you're doing for the holidays, Teal?" he asked eventually.

"I'm going home, I guess."

He nodded slightly. Then he looked at me.

"Excited about Sun Valley?"

"Sure," I said, and mustered up as much enthusiasm as I could. It was not a time to look guilty or think guilty thoughts. Even though that's how I felt. Even though I shouldn't have. After all, it wasn't I who had initiated the kiss. I had put myself in that compromising position, how-ever.

That was my mind trail. And I immediately got off it. Because it was probably making my face register guilty again. Thoughts are like crayons and they sketch a new picture each time. And your face is the canvas. Unless you're a really good actor or just crazy and then the countenance gets all scrambled up anyway.

Sydney stood up. He was like a coffee stirrer for all the silence. He looked at Teal. "Well, I'll call you later." Then he rested two-ton eyes on me. "See you back at the house."

Then he took off. Teal and I didn't have much to say. A sobering canopy had been laid down over us. What could we say?

She rose.

"Don't worry, Heyward." I just looked at her. "It was my fault. He knows it too."

"What makes you think it was your fault?"

And we just looked at each other. She squeezed my hand one last time then spun and walked up the street. I didn't follow. I didn't want to. I sat back down. And tried to piece together what had happened.

Interestingly, I discovered that what had happened is what I'd wanted to happen. I had put myself in that position for a reason. My thoughts of ignoring Sydney's retaliation capabilities were proof. I wanted to get caught, to cause some form of rift.

There was too much pressure built up. And I needed to release it. I later realized it was why I had my temporary block in the second act of My Newest. The Crack with Sydney was in my way. And the only way to get rid of it was to release the pressure. And crack it wide open.

Bridget Unplugged

I didn't want to go home. Somehow I didn't have that homey feeling. I buzzed around awhile giving thought to what Teal had said. Tea is usually a warm, pleasant time. Friendly chats and all, with sugar cookies and ladyfingers. Not that day. That tea was grim. I couldn't blame her for what she'd said. I wasn't happy about the hookups either. I wasn't sure if I'd been hurting people. I tried to keep it clean. It worried me. But those were things I knew already. What I didn't know was how she really felt about them. She seemed more understanding that day at Piedra. Apparently not. It worried me more.

I drove into my old neighborhood. I sauntered into the Olive, the Monkey Bar, and came upon a Nogul who needed one eye tightened. Noguls make me impatient but when a Nogul is shoveling it at you with screwy eyes, it's that much more irritating. Because the bullshit is coming from all directions. It's like Marty Feldman saying sincerely, "I'd like to go to bed with you." I mean, what do you say to that?

Then I dropped into the bar at the Peninsula Hotel. I guess I was looking for something. Or someone. I felt like the little boy who's been bad. And gets caught. And now he's going to be really bad. Real swell stuff.

Two feminine hands attached themselves to my rib cage. From behind. I wasn't sure who it was. The scent was unrecognizable. I spun finally. It was a surprise. It was the Last American Virgin.

"Wayward Heyward," she giggled.

"Hello, Bridget."

And she leaned forward and planted both uppers and lowers on mine. It was the most enthusiastic kiss she had ever given me. So nice, I could tell she was drinking a dry white wine.

"What are you doing here?" she asked.

"Futzing around. You?"

"I was having a drink," she said, and covered her mouth to burp. "With a friend," she added.

"Where's the friend?"

"He took off."

I nodded. She just stood there smiling at me. She was tipsy for sure. So we yapped for a while. She kept pushing me to have a drink. I stuck to ginger ale.

I must say Bridget looked beautiful that night. She was dressed for the murder of all things male. She had a tight-tight black strapless on, stockings, ruby lipstick, and her hair pulled back in a ponytail. Her face was tight and bright like she'd been getting her sleep. There were better bodies out there. But not many. Everything she had was tight, together, well-proportioned, and sexy as hell.

This girl was not seen very often on the Hell-A circuit. She chose her evenings. Let's not forget her mind was unfettered with thoughts of some insincere jerk who was alternately doing her and doing some bungalow sins with another Wam or Mom-I-Got-the-Parter. She didn't give it up, remember? She was all together, enhanced artificially, of course, but all together. No one had bragging rights on her. But what got me were her long slender fingers. And the fact that they never left my knees and thighs. It was a direct appeal to my inactive status.

Not before long we were very cozy. She landed two more kisses on my mouth. The next time I kissed her back. This all turned into making out at the bar. The thought of having a crack at Bridget Unplugged gave me midwaist sensations. There was a tightness in my pants. It had been so long.

Glass or Gun

I asked the concierge for the cheapest room they had. As I was about to pay for it, Bridget muscled in and gave him her credit card. I protested. She wouldn't be denied. I denied her anyway.

She giggled in the elevator. And down the sixth-floor corridor. Her dark stockings made that sexy thigh music beneath her dress as she walked. A champagne basket arrived shortly thereafter. And she giggled at the room service jockey who brought it.

I was seated in a padded chair. She was kneeling before me, with both arms resting on my knees. She was telling me about growing up in Arizona. She had been a cheerleader at ASU. I had always heard Arizona State had the best-looking college girls in the country. She was a damn good representative.

I don't know what spurred her on that night. Which probably means I do. One Bad Mood. It works for virgins too. But the reasons behind that. The why me? stuff. She'd never treated me specially before. And I hadn't treated her specially either. Maybe it was just that dumb. But I never had the sense she had a crush on me. So I asked her.

"I don't. It's your car," and she laughed out loud. So did I.

"My car?"

"I love your car."

"That's all?"

"That's it." More giggles. When they stopped she had a moment of bobbing candor. "No. I've always watched you. The way you cruise around town. You're always with women. But you're always a gentleman. And you never seem to be involved with any."

"You like that too?"

"Love that. I'm so sick of all these guys running around trying to fuck me. Like I don't know what they want. Hello?"

She looked at me. I sent the look back. She perched on her knees, slid hands up my outer thighs, found a speedbump on one side, and it didn't scare her. She hooked her hands around my waist. Our heads met. We kissed. And kissed some more. I was so excited. I really was. It had been so long.

We rolled around the bed for a while like a couple of seals on Prozac. Her leg was embedded in between mine. I kissed her with less restraint. The metal of my belt buckle clanked with the silver of hers. I took a breast in one hand and it was large enough to make the hand feel child-like. I didn't move it around a lot. I didn't want it to get lost.

She grabbed my crotch and found what had been poking at her legs. It was wonderful. Really wonderful. So wonderful I made her stop. And I sat up.

"What's wrong?"

I told her I didn't know. And that was a lie. She sat up and poured herself another wine. She was pretty drunk at this point. I was dead sober.

"Are you seeing someone?"

"No."

"You're scared. Aren't you?"

"Of what?"

"Me."

I looked at her. And what was behind her comment registered. I didn't say anything.

"I understand, you know," she said softly.

"You do?"

She sipped a sip, came back over to me. She knelt before me again. And stroked me. Where it hurt. I turned my head significantly away. It made her stop.

"Make love to me, Heyward."

It was a pretty bold comment, I thought. I shook my head anyway. Then I looked into her eyes. They weren't registering any disappointment. Rather, there was still a notch of determination in them. She wasn't done with me yet.

"I understand your apprehension about being the first guy. You don't want that responsibility. But I'm going to tell you something, Heyward. You're not."

"What?"

"My first guy." I looked sharply at her. "I'm not a virgin."

I wasn't shocked. But I was surprised. She was telling me because she thought it would free me up. So I wouldn't be worried about being her First Guy. I think any guy would have grabbed a glass at that point to join her. Or a gun. To shoot me.

I didn't do anything. That's when her face finally surrendered a little.

"You surprised?"

I said I was. And then I asked her questions I already knew the answers to.

"Protection" was her answer.

And it was a damn good reason.

"It's a rough town," she added.

I said she was right about that. I looked at her. She looked great. So sexy. So honest. And so tipsy. In a small but nicely appointed hotel room. I kissed her once more. Hard. And then I got up to leave.

She didn't lose respect for me. The hug we shared in the doorway told me that much. I just told her I hadn't been myself lately. More accurate words were never spoken.

It was true. Bridget was no more a virgin than I was. It was her calling card. To help her bust out of the periphery. Another ploy by a Wam Beast to separate herself from the pack. That was her con. In a con man's town. And why the hell not?

There's no question I was turned on by her. The reality is I was in love with someone else. And her sensual offering at the bar hit me at a vulnerable time. I had just been with Teal and my hormones were raging. But I knew any extensive activity with Bridget would be absurd. Either that or a blast. I wasn't sure. I wasn't sure of much anymore. But I didn't want to turn Bridget into the substitute teacher. I was one good mood away. But my mood was not good.

Ugly Word

It happened on the stretch of the freshly watered grass between the big house and my smaller one when I got home. It sounded like this:

"What the hell do you think you're doing!"

"What?"

"Fucking with me that way!"

"What are you talking about?"

"Teal! That's what." And he was busting a hose in his forehead.

"She asked me to join her for tea."

"Why?"

"Because she wanted to."

"She did, or you manipulated her?"

"You want to hear the message?"

"I saw the makeout session."

"Sydney, she was upset. She bent over and kissed me. Did you see it? Because if you did you'd know I didn't make any move toward her."

I had more to say but since he wasn't yelling again yet, I felt encouraged to pause. In fact, I didn't know what he was doing. It was eerie. I knew he was steaming though. We were in the middle of the grass expanse and the tall lofty pines were our judges. After a while, his silence made me secure enough to offer up some explanation.

"Sydney, I think I've been pretty generous with respect to the girls we've been interacting with. I think I've acquiesced, let's say, every time."

"Every time what?"

"Every time I get a bat of the eyelashes from women you're pursuing."

"That was no woman. That was Teal."

"And nothing happened."

"You let it happen. Why?"

"The kiss?"

"Yeah, the kiss."

"I don't know. Maybe I wasn't feeling that great. And when she moved toward me, I just froze."

"You weren't feeling that great? Not feeling too chipper? Oh, poor little Heyward Hoonstein. Well, you can shove your feelings right up your ass. Do you know who you're fucking with?"

I stayed silent.

For a moment. And then I had to do it. Call it fate. Call it wiseass. Call it stupid. Call it balls. Call it a tragic flaw. Or my inability to resist resisting him. Or call it the release I needed.

"Lady's Choice, Sydney." I couldn't believe it rolled out.

"Oh? Is that it?"

I stayed silent.

"You want to play games? You want to get competitive?"

"Not really. It doesn't matter that much to me."

"You're so full of shit. You just haven't gotten any pussy at all. That's why you did it. You've been watching me pull all the girlies and it pissed you off. So you were going to give it to me. You're as competitive as it gets. You're just pissed I've been getting all the chicks."

And it started coming up my chest. I was secretly fuming.

"Sydney, are you out of your fucking mind? I've laid girls in your lap, told them to talk to you, boosted you up. You barely knew how to kiss when I met you."

"Is that what you think?"

"Yeah. That's what I think."

"You think I need you to score chicks?"

"No. I guess you've gotten them all by your own brand of charm."

"You're pressing it."

"Well, pull your head out." Then I listed off the roster of girls I'd set him up with. It took a minute or so. "Tell me I haven't done anything for you . . ."

"And what about the Bullet?

"What about her?"

"Come on, Heyward. Play dumb with dumb people. Not me. You ran serious interference on me. Telling me she had a boyfriend."

"I was protecting her."

"For what reasons? For your own selfish use."

"Bullshit!"

"And you know what I say? Fine. Let the games begin. And they did. And who ended up with her? Huh? I sent you and all your little girlie tricks to the back of the class. I played opossum games, knowing what you wanted but not letting you know I knew. I outsmarted you. And that's why I was the one fucking her."

The amount of energy that came from his voice and that was released from his face as he said these words indicated how much and for how long he had wanted to say something like this to someone like me.

"You need help," I said.

"You need the truth!" he snapped. Then looked at me. Silence fell. He lowered his tone. "The reality is, Heyward, look what I did *for you* . . ."

And it came out of me like a clogged motor gets rid of some spontaneous combustion. With a firecracker blast.

"Yeah! Tell me! I'd love to hear this!"

"How about I've given you a life! A name! Before you met me you were a nobody!"

"I still am a nobody!"

"That's right. And it's not my fault!"

"Telling people my work is subpar."

"I never said that."

"You never say anything. That's saying everything. It's called a negative endorsement. It's all about pussy for you. That's all you give a shit about. You don't care if I ever get a deal. In fact, you don't want me to."

"It doesn't matter what I want. It's Darwinian out there. Only the fittest. You either have the product or you don't! You haven't proven to anybody you have it."

"I don't have the product?"

"Not that I can see."

"You ever looked?"

"In the beginning, yes. Look, Heyward, one of these days you're going to have to face up to some realities."

"Like what?"

"Like maybe you don't have it."

"I have it. You don't want me to get it."

"Don't blame your lack of success on me."

"You're just a selfish fuck."

"And you're a selfish hack."

"Conversation over," I said. And I started to charge back down the lawn.

"Is it, Heyward? Where are you going? To your room? The room I gave you?"

I stopped short. "You're going to hit me with that?"

"Reality, you mean? Bet your ass. You're a goddam country club rebel spoiled brat who hates the fact that he can't cut it out here. Now you got two choices. You either comply with the rules of this house or you go back to your Boys Town bungalow."

"And what are the rules, Sydney? Finding you more pussy?"

"You're damn right!"

"That's the kind of friendship this is, right?"

"Don't talk friendship to me, you dumb fuck! To insult me with that shit? You know the deal. You're here for one reason and one reason only. To find me girls. That's why I brought you aboard. Not because you went to an Ivy League school, not because you look nice or speak hip, or throw a good spiral. I got you because you know pussy. And if you get a career out of it, great. I'm happy for you. But frankly I don't give a shit either way. I brought you along and gave you a life and a name for one reason. Pussy! To find it, meet it, be nice to it, and introduce it to me so I can *fuck it!* And you'll do it. And you'll like it. And I don't want to hear another fucking word about it. You got it?"

"You're a prick, Sydney."

"And what are you? A *nice person*? You've been using me as much as I've been using you. That's how it works out here. And you know it. Only lady luck isn't on your side."

"Yet," I said.

"Yeah, well, until she shows her face, your best move is to shut your goddam mouth, go to your room, and think of a nice crew you can put together for Sun Valley. Make the proper calls. I want heat. I want flow, I want overflow. I want a stable, Heyward. So we're the buzz of the goddam mountain. Got it?"

And I couldn't believe it. He was cracking a smile too. Then he finished it off, which was finishing me off, with this:

"If you're smart, and I know you are, you'll make the calls."

Then he advanced on me and patted me on the shoulder like a first grader on the first day of school. The goddam awful fucking truth of it is, I was.

Cinq Soft Boys

It should be no surprise I didn't sleep that night. I lay on my bed totally drained. I replayed the conversation over in my mind. What he said, what I said. I said as much as I could without us coming to blows. After all the pondering, I noticed my hand was twitching on the bed. My ankle found rhythm to an old Pink Floyd song too. A wave of relief entered my frame from head to toe. I had wanted to tell him those things for so long. I felt freed up. Hugely so.

I got my ass out of bed and wallowed no longer. I began to peck away on my portable and I didn't stop until I felt it necessary to make my personal calls midday.

For the next few days, no one bothered me, which indicated the household knew something was afoot. And that was okay. I didn't care anymore how I was being perceived. I didn't care if people knew I was Sydney's best friend or worst or if we were on the outs or not.

And here's the proof.

I moved out of Sydney's guesthouse the following week. But not before I dutifully set up a group of unforgettables to join Sydney on his hired jet to Idaho. I told him I needed to stay behind and work on My Newest. But you can bet I would have paid handsomely to have seen his reaction to the guests.

Soft Ludwig was a neat and nice guy from Hamburg. I'd met him unknowingly at our party and then became reacquainted with him in St. Bart's. You know who he is. I ran into him again at the Olive during a twilight tour. Of course he kept wanting to initiate hetero crossover flesh talk with me. I only spoke to him for a few minutes while waiting on a middleweight producer. And before I left, he gave me his card. Again.

When it came to Sydney's trip to Sun Valley, I called on Ludwig to help me corral the talent. Sydney said he wanted a stableful, and he wanted to be eyed by the entire town. I was going to do my damnedest. And from what I heard later, I succeeded.

You see, when he arrived with his entourage at LAX, he saw five gaping, dripping smiles broken in his direction, all waiting for directions to the private jet. You see, not only was Soft Ludwig soft, so were all his buddies. There was Soft Serge, Soft Gil (pronounced with a soft *g*), Soft Sven, and Soft Maurice, all wondrous globe-trotting homosexual dilettantes. Soft Ludwig extended his hand to Sydney, and told him he was a friend of mine, then he introduced the four other Boys one by one. Sydney had more than a slight jump in blood pressure. And I was surprised to hear that he didn't walk out. He graciously sat down with them and explained there was a mix-up. He offered to pay for their trip to Idaho but claimed he'd already invited other guests. And the Soft Boys took the plane tickets. And had a great time.

Me, on the other hand, I moved out. There was nothing left for me at Sydney's place. Our friendship I considered to be at best in hiatus. We didn't speak for another few weeks.

The Three Kisses

Besides, I needed to finish off my spec and I had a rush of new ideas, rewrite and the like, that freed the piece back up and out of its second-act lock. I was cooking again. I was up all night, caffing up hugely, and working like a mo-fo. Everything was coming to me like flying comets and it was all I could do to keep my fingers moving fast enough. My mind was trapping and catching little pieces of dialogue, words, and ideas. I was very ripe, in that flow, the one you pray and wait for. And when it comes you just don't stop. You take what you can from a brain that is unusually highly sensitized, because it may not happen again for weeks. And usually in one of these bursts you figure the entire puzzle of your project out. With alternative choices. And backup for that.

It was the first time I'd been happy, truly happy, in a long time. I felt loose, unbounded, versatile, open, honest, and together. Besides, I thought my work really had a chance. How did I know that? I felt there was no way the piece could not sell. From any angle I looked. If it didn't sell, I was going to throw in the towel. I'd made up my mind.

More significantly, a strange feeling had set in which was more telling. I didn't care if the script sold or not. Which was not entirely true, but part of me really didn't give a flying fuck anymore. That also seemed to be an indicator I was onto something. After all, I'd never felt that way before.

I wrote a few more hours before I slept. Then I took a nap which consisted of nothing more than me turning over and over in bed, too excited, too wired, too dazzled by all the thoughts of the new characters and their words going off in my head.

I awoke in the afternoon, poured a hot pot, and made the last corrections. I printed out, along with a title page, three-hole-punched the paper, bound the script with light blues, and inserted brads. I was done with My Newest. It was a damn good feeling. I wasn't going to turn the script in to Marty yet. I wanted the overnight to let the draft settle in my mind. The morning after I'd finished a script there was always a trail of little refinements I liked to make. I figured I'd get the final, final draft to him the following afternoon.

For the next few hours I packed up my shit. I used the same boxes I'd used in the move from West Hollywood and had stored in the garage. Armando came down at one point and I explained to him I was moving out. I think he knew already. Maybe he was going to tell me to anyway. In any case he helped me lug bags to the car.

It didn't take long to pack up. I had only moved recently and I even remembered packing tips to help me from the previous move. It took two trips to get all my stuff.

On the second trip, I thanked Armando for all he had done for me. And just then as we'd finished shaking hands, I got another visitor.

"Heyward . . ."

I did the surprised thing and jumped. I didn't need a butler to tell me who it was.

"Hello, Teal."

"I hear you're leaving."

"Yeah . . ."

"How come?"

"It's time to move on."

"Why?"

"The Big Gray Monster is dead."

"What about all your science projects?"

The question stymied me. It made me really take her in, and I wished I hadn't. She looked too goddam wonderful. Her hair was up and pulled back tight and a plaid skirt was wrapping her lower half and I considered it lucky. I'd always been jealous of the bedrooms, clothes, and pets of beautiful women. They always get the best views. Unobstructed and the subject is never shy.

"You look nice, Teal."

"Thank you. I was at an audition."

I was standing opposite her now, holding a box between us. Even though Armando was sifting some floaters out of the guesthouse pool, I didn't feel nervous. The thought of Sydney and the Pact was a distant one now. A silly one now.

"I think you're making the right decision."

"Do you?"

"Yes." And her voice softened to a whisper. "It's what I was going to tell you that day. When we were interrupted."

"What were you going to say?"

"That it was never going to work out. He would never help you." And she gave a careful glance in Armando's direction.

I nodded. I knew that already.

"And that's why I was hard on you. Not because I think badly of you. In fact, it's just the opposite. I wanted to embarrass you into really looking into your situation, and it got out of hand. For that, I am sorry."

And it became clear to me.

"You knew he was watching. That's the reason you kissed me."

"That was one of the reasons," she sent right back. It was a nice missive.

We just stood there gazing at each other. Like the first time we had that interior vision of each other. I smiled eventually. Then so did she. She moved forward and pecked me on the lips. But somehow, it was more than a kiss. Though the stamp did not last long, with that one gesture, she gave her entire self to me. It held all the intimacy of more serious involvements. Only it came through her lips. I was disoriented for minutes. It was definitely time to go.

"Good-bye, Teal."

"Good-bye, Heyward. Good luck."

"Never too much of that."

And I walked off toward the driveway.

"Heyward?"

I stopped and turned.

"You know if you ever want to say hi, I'm up there on Soledad. Number 22319."

I smiled faintly. I was still dazed. Then I walked back up the yard, got in the Sled, and motored off. I didn't worry about phone messages because I left a forwarding number on the guesthouse machine.

I calculated I'd been living at Sydney Swinburn's for eight months now and I had gotten no deal. Nothing. But I lived well, that was for sure. And there were those three kisses. One on my windshield and two on me.

My chapter in the life of Sydney Swinburn was over.

Bye-Bye, Bullets

I moved into a dive hotel on Wilshire Boulevard in Santa Monica called the St. Regis. It was $30 a night with a Denny's right across the street. So for $32.99, I got a bed, shower, and a mother-lode breakfast. Which was cool. The hotel manager at the St. Regis gave me room number 6. I could park the Sled right outside it and I liked that feature. Unfortunately, there was no bellhop to go with it. Once I moved all my belongings inside, I lay down for a while. I actually dozed off. I hadn't had much sleep lately.

Though I still had a sleep debt, I awoke happy and recharged. I decided to make a drive-by and see who was around. I brought the script with me. I let Bob the Riot sit on it and guard it. While I drove, I looked over at it, all bound and new and full of promise. At stoplights I thumbed through pages and reread lines I'd reread tons of times already. I even read out loud to Bob. He approved silently. He even liked the title though he'd heard it before.

I stopped in at the Olive and issued a few greetings. A bunch of Noguls were there. How did I know they were Noguls? There were some telltale signs. First, it was a Festival of I's. Everyone had an "I" story and their "I"s were like swords that cut each other off. Because everyone had a better story to top the previous and in a better place with a better group of people and a better girl. Noguls always sounded like they were doing coke. *Hey, what you're doing is great, but what I'm doing is better.*

"One night we went over to the Stone Man's place."

"How is Oliver?"

"You know Olly."

While I sipped on a clear soft drink, I listened to them name-drop names of people they saw from afar and didn't know and hadn't met. Of course none of their Nogul buddies were ever present to corroborate or contradict the story. Exciting shit always happens to Noguls when they are alone.

"Michael was there too."

"Eisner?"

"No, Douglas."

"How was he?"

"He looked good. He's so funny. He always calls me Bub."

"Really? He calls me that too. Funny."

"Guy's a great guy."

"Great guy."

"Great . . ."

Oddly, their presence didn't irk me. I felt relieved. I then stopped by Bar Marmont. It had just opened up and I'd heard it had quite a good swell. I was not disappointed. At first, anyway.

It all started like this.

Suzy and Mindy, two of the Bullets, spotted me. I was actually pleased to see them. There's nothing better than seeing friends you were close with, but grew distant from. Obviously, this separation had been mostly my fault. I just hoped they'd accept me back. Some people never do, after all.

When I approached them they gave me subdued looks. I asked them how they were and they gave me the innocuous "fine." And nothing more.

I figured they were giving me the brush because I dropped out of their lives. So I decided to give it a rest. I chose the pay phone. I dialed my number but the phone just rang and rang. Either someone was on it, or the machine had been turned off.

I started to the bar and then ran into Mindy again.

"Hey there, friendly," I said.

"What?"

"Are you mad at me?"

"Whatever, Heyward."

"What does that mean?"

"Let's not get into it."

"Into what?"

"As if you don't know."

"Know what?"

"Listen, we're off."

"Let me get you some Red."

"I don't drink Red anymore. No one does. See ya."

Their dismissive behavior had me baffled. "Say, have you seen Kelly?"

Mindy's clock on me was ice cold. Then came the SoCal sarcasm. It was high-schooly, the kind with the ninth-grade-equivalency rating. *"How nice of you to ask,"* she snapped.

I clutched her arm.

"What the hell is going on?"

"I don't want to get into it."

And I clamped her wrist. *"Get into it."*

"You don't know . . . ," she said flatly. And suspiciously.

"No . . . "

"You mean you haven't seen her?"

"No."

"She's not living up there?"

"Up where?"

"Up at that guy's house?

"Sydney's?" She nodded. "What are you talking about?"

"Look, Heyward. I gotta go."

"Listen. I moved out. I have no idea what's going on. I haven't seen the Bullet in weeks."

"She's doing drugs."

"Drugs?"

"Every night with your guy. Swinburn."

"With Sydney? He doesn't do drugs."

"Well, he's got her doing it."

"But he's in Sun Valley."

"I don't know. She calls in sometimes. All crazy and stuff. Tells me she's there. With him. Gives me a mobile number. I call. She never picks up. I don't know what's true. But she's all messed up, Heyward. And you got her into it."

I couldn't refute what she was telling me. But I had introduced her to Sydney Swinburn. That was for sure.

"I gotta go."

"Look, I want to talk more about this. What's your number?"

She just shook her head.

"Good-bye, Heyward."

Flash!

I was shocked. I didn't know what to do. I went to the pay phone and called the Bullet. I got her machine. I stood there catatonic for a while. All enthusiasm for socializing was drained out of me. I got out of there.

I drove the Sled west back toward Santa Monica but found myself heading up to Sydney's. But when I arrived there, the alarm codes weren't working. They had been changed. And Sydney's cars were not there. I still wanted in.

I thought about it. I knew how to get in there. Behind the security house there was a wall bordering the neighbor's property. I scaled it and found myself doing a dew dance down the back lawn and into the guest-house.

My answering machine was not on. The plug had been separated from the wall. I reactivated it and played it. Sure enough, my agent Marty had called.

"Heyward. Where's the script? Didn't you finish it?"

Then there was a message from Courtney. She was in New York. The Loach had been hospitalized again. She was "comforting" my mother. *Comforting.* I wondered what that meant. It didn't sound good.

I walked back up to the main gate to greet the security guy so as not to alarm him. I would tell them I was getting a last few things. But there was no one there.

As I advanced on the alley at the side of the house, I saw a quick flash light up the immediate area. It prompted me to slow my pace. Then another flash splashed in my eyes and I could tell it came from a lone car, Sydney's dark stretch limousine parked in the driveway. The windows were tinted black so I couldn't see inside. Another flash barely showed two figures in the backseat. My pulse quickened. It looked like she was in his lap.

I went around the side of the car. One of the windows was down slightly and I peered in. And it was a vision. It was a man and a woman in a compromising position. But the man wasn't Sydney. It was Monkey Man, Sydney's prick driver, sitting back in the seat with no pants on, and he was aiming a Polaroid camera down at some girl. Her rear was bare, she had a tiny midriff top on, no panties, and high white boots. She was a blonde and her ass was facing me, while her head was bobbing up and down in his lap. She was blowing him.

He tapped her skull in a Stone Age way and her head withdrew itself from him. When it did I was forced to see his erection glistening in the little disco lights of the limo's interior. Then I saw him raise a baggy of white powder, extend his hand into it, take out a pinch of it in his thumb and forefinger and flick the contents on the head of his cock. Then she pressed an index against one nostril and sniffed up the whiteness off the tip of his member.

At that moment FLASH!

Monkey Man had taken another photo, the sick midnight chronicler he'd become. And then she resumed sucking again. I was beyond stunned. He did this repeatedly. He'd give her a pinch, lay it down on his member, she'd snort it and finish it off each time with a suck, until he felt like giving her another pinch. It was strongly depraved and my senses melted in an extreme and perverse way.

I remained there for one reason. And one reason only. To find out who the girl was.

Clack went the camera as it ejected the newest snapshot, and, without even looking at it, he Frisbeed it still dark and undeveloped into the middle of the limo floor where it met with dozens of others piled there, already alive and in color, starring faces and body parts, mostly hers. The photos showed the two of them in all sorts of positions and acts, but I was too far away to make out any one in particular.

Then I saw it all. Monkey Man maneuvered the girl aggressively around. He steered her by her hair. She was a slave to his touch. This guy ruled her. *Whatever he wants, he gets* was her expression. She about-faced on her hands and knees which left her ass now facing him. That was when she looked my way. And my eyes were stymied by the sight. It was the Bullet. An ulcer, the bleeding kind, was a close cousin to the feeling in my gut.

She had fried platinum hair now and her face looked robbed of anything good. She was a fortnight away from nourishment. She was all of twenty-three and looked fifty. Her eyes were bobbing around in her head. So messed up, like Mindy had said. There she was, on her hands and knees, looking straight ahead, with her ass spread wide, at the face of an ugly and despicable man.

Monkey Man did another pinch of powder and sprinkled it on her ass. Then I watched him lick her up and down until all the white was gone and then he zeroed back in on the center of her crack and ate out her rim. It was the most sick and heinous thing I'd ever witnessed. My heart just thumped away wildly, like I'd been running for miles and stopped suddenly.

As he worked away from behind her, her eyes tried to roll around and show she was enjoying it, but they didn't make it all the way around. Her nerves were too frazzled. She had lost all feeling.

Then what happened was what always happens after bad things happen in Hell-A. They get worse.

Monkey Man got on his knees, leaned forward, grabbed her by the hair, yanked her head back with one hand, and with the other, guided his dick into her ass. He pounded away, tearing away her midriff and groping the two breasts that fell out with his freed-up mitt.

For the next three minutes, I found myself on my knees around the side of the house, puking up a variety of intestinal fluids. It was the worst night of my life.

The Vet

Outside the hospital, I sat in the ambulance. I looked at my knuckles and saw the dried blood on them. I was still trembling. You see, I hadn't exactly taken off after viewing that grotesque display. After shooting up my guts in the shrubs, I returned to the car, spread the door wide, and beat the living fuck out of Monkey Man. We were never friends and that wouldn't have helped him anyway. I really wanted to separate his face but I let him off easy. I just gave him six slams in the area of the nose. When I left him his condition was out. And breathing. He'd come to in about five hours. And it wouldn't be fun. Before leaving, I took a couple of his sleazy snaps in case he wanted to get legal with me.

During the melee, a horrified Bullet just coiled in the corner as small as she could. And sobbed. The tragedy of it all is she didn't even know what she was sobbing about. I grabbed her by the hand, but she wouldn't move. Then she lunged at me and pounded me in the chest, yelling "Why? Why? Why?"

Sure I cried. And told her I was sorry.

I called an ambulance with the limo phone. Not for him. For her. Then I ushered her out to the street and we waited. We didn't speak and we didn't discuss it. There was no point. She was weeks away from coherence anyway. Her nerves were like swizzle sticks. They had to have been to let a toad like that invade her personal spaces.

The ambulance came shortly thereafter. I demanded to join the medics on the trip to Cedar Sinai. I held the Bullet's hand all the way.

I stayed at the hospital until nine the next morning. Kelly had been given sedatives and was sleeping soundly when I left. A driver eventually joined me in the ambulance and fractionally revived me from my recap meditations. He gave me a lift back to my car.

I was a basket case. The emergency was over and the reality had seeped in. So I just pulled over. And stopped the car. Right on Sunset Boulevard. I had to. I couldn't drive. I just sat there in the car like an idiot robot. I felt like a Vietnam War vet who had just seen too much. But it wasn't the haunting vision that had the devastating effect on me. It was that it was all my fault. I felt like I had gotten my war buddy shot and killed.

It was clear there was a chasm of activity I had not been aware of. If the Bullet had been relegated to performing grim acts with the Monkey Man, it was all too obvious the degree of dementia Sydney had enjoyed

with her. He had made a pass-around pack out of her. My friend, the
Bullet. She was nothing more than a hand-me-down to him. I felt like a
total fool. More than a fool. A moron. I was a moron. These scumbags
had been tipped off to her fragile character and they exploited it to the
end. Of course I tried to keep Sydney away from her. But so what? I
knew how the town operated. I never should have put her in the same
space. I hadn't protected her.

Welcome to Hell-A. Again.

Eventually, with thoughts still dividing my head, I found the
willpower to start up the Sled and drive unevenly back to the St. Regis.
A few cars honked at my unsure vehicle along the way.

I didn't sleep that night.

It was the first week in January in Los Angeles and Heyward
Hoonstein had a new script and nobody gave a damn. Including Heyward Hoon.

Thursday Night Guy

Sydney had played me. He had played me good. All word on him had
been wrong. He was a cordial and respectable man on the surface, a fear-
some businessman beneath that, with a charming innocence in his inter-
personal relations, but truly a dark lord beneath that. He ran with four
levels of deception. He was a Hell-A all-purpose player. He had pulver-
ized every gal I had put before him except that prima donna model with
the great life story. If her story hadn't been great before, it was now. She
was the smartest of us all. She insulted him, showed him no respect, and
went on her way. She gave him everything he deserved. And I thought
she was retarded. The reality is she ruled.

I truly detested Sydney Swinburn. But I didn't know what to do
about it.

I went to my room, showered the filth off, and lay down. I spent the
day holed up there going over the horrific details of a life that had run
amok. My only break was an early evening stroll down Wilshire. I
walked up to a franchise drive-thru and ordered some real trash. They

told me to go inside because I had no car. I told them to cram it. I didn't want food anyway.

I retrieved my jacket from the hotel and barked an order to the Sled. I said a few more curse words to Bob the Riot and motored back up to Sydney's. I wanted to rip him a new rim. But he still hadn't returned.

I drove deep and high into Bel-Air. I knew the street I wanted. I'd been there with the Bullets at another party. I parked outside a number I had memorized.

I trudged up to the door and tried it. It was locked and I wasn't shocked. No one in the hills ever forgot the Manson murders. I scanned the front yard of a manicured lawn with flowers. I was looking for a large object. Like a log or something. To break down the door. I opted for the bell.

I rang for a good minute or so. I heard some noise upstairs.

"Who is it?" was asked of me from inside.

"It's Friday Night Guy."

She opened the door. And looked me up and down. Her face was pressed on one side with pillow lines and she still looked sleepy. Her lips were dry and just-awoken. There she was. The Walking Nightclub. I still wasn't sure if she wanted me there or not. Until she said, "Dressed in Monday Night Clothing." She delivered it in a parched voice, and an almost smile came with it.

"On a Thursday Night," I said. I grabbed her and gave her a fierce one. Her lips tasted as I'd imagined, as I'd felt, only better. She was wearing a sheer mini-nightgown and probably a robe too but that I didn't notice. My hands couldn't help but hold her tight. Her skin felt like it did that day I gave her a massage at Piedra. Only better. She was so soft, so curvaceous, so beyond, so drop-dead. This gal would ruin men for other women.

"I've been waiting for that for a long time."

"Me too," she said.

She took my hand and led me inside.

"I'm going to make some tea."

She asked me if I wanted any. I declined. I followed her into the kitchen. That was no surprise. Before I knew it, I had taken her down to the floor. We made out until the kettle whistled. Teal didn't hold it against me.

We hauled ourselves up and she made all those clanking noises of tea preparation. I just stood there. Then we settled on the shaggy carpet in her living room. There was a fireplace and some logs smoldering in it.

I told her about the Bullet. If she was surprised, she didn't show it. After all, she knew Sydney better than me. She tried to tell me how much better. I wouldn't let her. I didn't want to know. Even though I did. But I couldn't handle any more L.A. darkness and its bag of secrets, lies, and deceptions. So we sat there and covered other topics. I kept it pretty light as I didn't want my morose cynicism to come out.

"What were you like in high school, Heyward?"

I tried to smile even though my emotions hadn't rebounded sufficiently yet.

"Were you the one always raising your hand to give the right answer?"

"I was more narcissistic. I only answered a question if the rest of the class couldn't get it."

"So you had it back then?"

"Had what?"

"The need."

That was true, though I had never retrieved that memory before and assimilated that way.

She looked at me with a curious expression. Like she was flipping through her own back data files. "Someone once said, 'I'm sick of not having the courage to be an absolute nobody.'"

And I did recall it. It was from somewhere. "Who said it?"

"Zooey."

"Salinger's Zooey?" I asked.

"Is there any other?"

I thought about that. "I love Salinger. But he's scary."

"Scary?"

"And dangerous."

"How so?"

"He's a rallying cry."

"For who?"

"Freaks."

"You think?"

"The world is full of Holden Caulfields. But some of them never get rehabilitated. They're one hot day away from being in tomorrow's papers. They come to that point of chaotic hopelessness and can't turn back. They go off the edge. And before you know it they're burying peaceful neighbors in sand traps on golf courses. Travis Bickle and the like. Assassins and mass murderers adopt Salinger as their own. And *Catcher* as their Bible. Like it's all the proof they need."

"Who did you say?"

"Travis Bickle was Schrader's taxi driver."

"You mean Scorsese's taxi driver."

Normally, I would have objected. But somehow giving the director the credit instead of the writer didn't bother me. I really didn't care anymore.

Then she smiled at me. "Yeah, well, it's either that or they end up in Hollywood."

It made me smile a real smile. It was a first in a while.

When we dried up on books, we talked about family. Mine. And my life growing up in New York. And as I spoke I could tell she had a question ready for me.

"I don't really get it."

"Get what?"

"Here's this kid with fair hair, who's cute, smart, from a decent family, whatever *decent* means. Why the hell are you so bitter?"

Damn right it was a good question. *So* good I didn't want to answer it. So I suggested she answer it herself.

"Me?"

"You've studied me. Maybe as much as I've studied you. Why am I so bitter?"

"I'll give it a stab," she said. And it didn't take her long. "The *fear*."

It was a damn good answer too. If she was saying what I thought she was saying.

"Of?"

"That you have the capacity to not make it. Just like your father."

The answer felt right. She was on it. That primal fear had made me go my Wannabeastly way. I knew I could blow the whole deal. It was in my family. It was in my bloodline. It was in my genetic map. Like Zooey, I didn't have the courage to be a nobody. And maybe I didn't have the wherewithal and fortitude to be a somebody. I feared I would die the slow death of an Unknown in the murky middle. The legacy of Harlan Hoon truly scared the hell out of me.

You see, I've always thought everything comes down to genes. That your physical and mental characteristics are genetically linked. Even ambition. And I was scared I didn't have it. Or enough of it. My father's statistics had showed me that much. And in this way, I underestimated what my mother had brought to the table. She came from a long line of unimportant people. And I didn't give her enough credit. I had been running scared. It's what made me the Wannabeast I was.

I thought about my mother for a second. And flashed on the various run-ins and disagreements we'd had over the years. I realized that our relationship didn't need to suffer anymore.

Teal was looking at me. "Are you okay?"

I stood up. And paced an aimless circle. Not more than six steps. And I had my reply to it all.

"I came to say good-bye," I said. No, I hadn't thought about it previously. It just came out of my mouth. But I loved the sound of it. It seemed so right, so perfect, so much what I wanted. A heaviness was lifted immediately. My frame felt lighter.

Teal's face was now etched with concern.

"You mean you're leaving town?"

"Yes."

"Where are you going?"

"Home."

"Home? You mean New York?"

"That's the only home I know."

"I didn't know."

"Neither did I," I affirmed. "But before I go, I'd like you to tell me, what else was it you wanted to say to me that day at the pool?"

She thought about it. "That you should get away from him. Before he destroyed you. I knew it would only get worse for you. You're not friends with him anymore, are you?"

"Not entirely," I said, and found a pinch of amusement with my wording.

"He'll never help you, Heyward. Which is to say he'll never buy a script or an idea of yours or pay for a project you're involved with. He'll never pay to help you. But he'll spare no cost, untold millions, to hurt you if you cross him. That's the way he is. I've seen it. I'm warning you. Always remember that. That's what I wanted to tell you."

I didn't say I had come to that realization on my own. The *he would never help me* clause. But the underwriting of my destruction I hadn't thought of. Who would? Some time passed as I sipped on that Darkie for a while.

Then Teal turned to me and smiled faintly. She said she admired me again.

"You must be really stuck."

"Stuck?"

"For a role model."

And then she sat beside me. "I'm going to tell you about myself."

"That's okay."

"No, I don't care if I'm your science project."

"You're not." And it came out all at once. What I'd been feeling for months now, but was burying deep every time it tried to come up for air. "I love you, Teal."

She looked at me. And her face just stayed there. Her right eye spilled a single drop. It moved sweetly down the edge of her nose. My eyes were now framed with water. I had let it live. Finally.

"I love you too," she whispered. And the whisper made it all the more potent. We embraced. "That's why I want to tell you about me."

"That's why I don't want to hear."

"But . . ."

"Ssssh. It's all yours. To keep."

Then her face crumbled slightly. And she wept. I moved in close again and held her hand.

"He takes care of me, Heyward."

"Ssssh."

"He hit me. After I spent the day on the beach with you."

"Quiet . . ."

"I don't date. I'm not an aspiring actress. And I don't go on auditions."

"Hush."

"I'm twenty-five. I want to have a family."

"Shut the fuck up, Teal. I love you. And I don't want to know. I don't want to know anything."

More tears streamed down her face. And I hugged her. Our cheeks were pressed together. My lips trailed back until the corners of our mouths met. And then we kissed. And kissed. Like we hadn't kissed before.

Our heads revolved slowly back and forth. I think the kiss lasted ten minutes or so. The kind that you had when you played spin the bottle and you finally got the girl you wanted and both of you ended up just leaving the game and making out. Only better.

I unpeeled her robe. I climbed at her sideways and kissed her everywhere. Her neck, her lips, her forehead, I sucked on her breasts, her belly button—even the mound on top of her privates. I wouldn't go further with that unless she gave me an indication to. But I didn't think she was stressed about it. I continued down her thighs, her calves, and then I sucked on every one of her toes, slowly, adoringly.

I can't remember wanting a girl so badly.

She responded to the touch. Arching her back, shuddering, chills were rippling up her legs and arms. Something told me she hadn't had sex in a while. It was not only in her response physically, but the look in her eyes. If that was true, what a waste, I thought.

But I didn't ask her. I didn't want to know anything about her. Just her being there in that space with me was enough.

Strawberries

We kissed more. And we chatted. She tried to talk again about herself but I wouldn't let her. At about five in the morning, we lay down in bed. There was no pressure at all. No pressure to stay, to leave, to make love, to not. It was just the two of us enjoying each other's company.

The phone rang at about six-thirty. Our lips were almost kissed out. The top layer of skin on mine was barely hanging on. She ignored the ring. So did I.

She bent forward and gave me another wet press. If I was going to do anything in life, I was going to make her feel good. Because at that moment, it was all very clear to me. Her deep-seated, inner pain was as significant as mine. And it was all the more reason to let her keep her secrets. They might well be the only thing keeping her together.

I undid the tiny silk ties to her nightie and let it fall off her shoulders. I did notice the nightie had a La Perla label. And she saw me notice it. I looked at her and her mouth curved warmly. It was a smile of confirmation. That day I tailed her in Beverly Hills, she'd been lingerie shopping for somebody all right. Me.

Though we had been touching each other all night, this had a different feel to it. I went down on my knees as she stood before me. She braced my head between her thighs with her hands, her nails gripping my scalp.

I stood up and turned her around. My head was buried in her neck. I was sucking away at her, giving her a mark that would last. She was doing nothing but hearing the sounds of her backyard through the bathroom window. I was sucking her so hard I tasted her blood. I was drinking her. I wanted to.

As I sucked her neck, I drifted a gentle hand below. I watched her raise up on the balls of her feet, her arches extended, her legs trembling all the while. In the mirror, I saw her eyes, hidden behind her cascading mane, roll back in her head.

I then turned her back around. I took her hand and clasped mine around it. And I led her back into the bedroom. She seemed as if she was in a trance, a dream dance of sorts. I couldn't get enough of her. I eased her onto the bed and let her lie back. I alternated from kissing her and licking her lips to sucking her. I could taste more blood I was drawing so hard on it.

Her head drifted into my lap and I grabbed her by the strawberry strands. She went free on me.

The only problem with letting her go free on me is I was watching her the whole time. It made me want to be the consumer rather than the consumed. I lodged a finger beneath her chin and raised up her head. I saw her lip bleeding where I had bitten it. I kissed it and got rid of the red.

I recoiled for a second and observed from afar. The long legs were joining in such a perfect convergence, with things waiting there. Waiting, waiting . . .

Then she spun around and sucked me again, all the while I cupped her breasts.

And I didn't say a word . . .

She looked at me at one point and asked me with her eyes, "Will you do it now?" And I just shook my head slightly and motioned for her to look straight ahead. Sure, there was toe-sucking and kissing and hickey-stamping, and we both had numerous red, blue, and purple marks all over. But that was the hard part. Staying away from the act was difficult.

And she didn't say a word . . .

Then it was time.

I drew her out of my lap. She looked at me. I looked at her. She looked wistful, almost sad, almost of another world. The sensations were just all too electric. But we both had more in us.

And we weren't going to use a condom.

NFW.

Not after all this. We were going to defy our life and times and all the warnings and all the negativity of a generation that had been shortchanged. We were going to laugh in the face of the age, the Age of Astonishment. It was the Big Ha-Ha. The joke was on them. It was my feeling.

It was going to be raw. It was going to be perfect. The way I'd enjoyed it in my teens. The way it used to be. In the old days. Doesn't everyone yearn for the good old days? We were no different.

I gently positioned her legs apart. Then I sat back and looked at her. And then her face. We locked eyes. And then I drove right through her. I saw her eyes roll. So did mine. Teal was genius.

In and out of her was a great feeling, her legs wrapping me from behind was another, her hands resting on my cheeks was still another, and sucking her left breast was a fourth. Let's not forget the psychological deliciousness of it all.

It went from me on the top, to me on the side, to me from behind, to me sitting straight up. I was doing it all. And it wasn't all about me. It went to her on top, front ways and back, her lying on me, her straddling me. We did it all. And invented more. It was remarkable. It was indescribable. It was like . . . *word.*

It was twelve-thirty when we broke. I was famished. We had some tomato and mozzarella sandwiches which I devoured. But just looking at her made me want her again. With half a sandwich left, she was bent at the waist over the cutting-board island in the kitchen. We did it there. We did it again upstairs. We did it everywhere two people could fit in a space.

It continued into the late afternoon. Until she said just this.

"Are you really leaving?"

"Yes."

"When?"

"When I leave here."

A nap found its way into our life. When I awoke several hours later, she was gone. But only downstairs. And then we went at it into the evening with no inhibitions, no protection, and every formation. We did high-impact stuff and we did low-impact stuff. There was one thing that was no longer uncertain anymore. My romantic status. I was active. I was proactive. And I was reactive. More like radioactive. And it all had to do with the woman I loved.

We awoke in the early morning and went at it again. We had blood tats all over. My neck had a new sprawling birthmark. The last four times we did it I asked her the same question.

"Are you sore?"

She said yes each time. But we weren't going to stop.

I remember waking up while atop her around noon the next day, my shriveled contribution still inside her. The movement of me climbing off her woke her up. Her face looked pretty puffy from all the crying and love-making. In the end, she made love a hell of a lot more than she'd cried.

"I missed you," she said.

It was the most beautiful thing I'd ever heard. Has anyone ever said that to you? That you're so precious to someone you're being missed during the unconscious hours. Even though you're in the same bed. If no one has ever said that to you, I recommend it highly. It's a good time. For the insides.

I slipped downstairs and looked for some sugar. I saw my favorite form. Cookies. There was a box of Pepperidge Farm giant Sausalitos with three left. It was an unheard-of notion for me. Leftover cookies. There was never such a thing as leftover cookies in my kitchen. They were always downed in one sitting. I mean, how could you let those last cookies get away?

I took a shower. Teal had a cup of coffee for me. She was fully dressed. We had all those sweet, loving gestures for each other, the kind you have with someone you've just made love to for the first time.

"I think you're gonna need a turtleneck," I said to her.

"You too."

"Are you hungry?"

"Maybe some fruit."

"There're oranges. And an apple."

"Maybe I'll have the apple."

And we both smiled at that. And I ate it.

And then I got dressed. She pecked me on the forehead. But still she seemed distracted. That's when she told me there was a car outside.

"What do you mean?"

"A car . . . ," she repeated.

"Whose?"

"One of Sydney's guys."

"So he knows."

"Probably. He always has somebody watching me. I like it actually. I get scared."

I headed toward the door. I didn't forget to tell her something.

The Mole Game

"By the way, you ought to have that looked at."

"What?" she wondered.

"That thing."

"What thing?"

"That mole."

"What mole?"

"On your," I began but needed the right word. ". . . leg."

"I have a mole?"

"On your leg. But closer, uh, to, your . . . ," and I trailed off in a leading way.

"Really? You're kidding me."

"No."

"What does it look like?" And she poked around her front through the blue jeans.

"It's brown."

"Is it big?"

"Pretty big."

"How weird."

With that, the pants came down.

Which is what I had been waiting for. Then she slipped her G-string to the side and searched. I watched her intently roll her leg flesh back and forth until she looked up at me.

"I don't see anything."

At that point, I just plunged myself inside her. We reeled back, falling to the ground, and did it one more time.

On the way to my car I waved to the thug who was watching over Teal's household. Sydney knew. Well, it served Sydney right. Though he hadn't broken the Pact per se, he had committed some very severe violations. I didn't even think we were even. But making love to Teal made it close. Real close. The fact is I didn't give a shit anyway. About Sydney, or the Pact, or the revenge aspects. I had made love to the woman I loved. And that was it.

Sky Word

I flew back to New York that night. On the red-eye. I was looking forward to seeing my family members. Each one of them. Even Loach. For the first time I was aware of my own behavior and how it might have affected my relationships. I was aware of my faults. And the breakdowns they had caused. And I wanted to tell them.

I wasn't really worried about what I was going to do with my life. I figured it would come to me in time. I felt like I was starting over again. Somewhere on those streets in Los Angeles the Wannabeast in me had died. And all the related pressures and tensions had seeped out of my frame. Though the death was sudden, it had been a long time coming. I felt tremendously light. And free. It was the greatest feeling I had had in a long time. I was a prisoner no longer. I was me, reacting to things my way. Not through some Machiavellian filter. Just me.

Prior to departing L.A., there were a few things I did and a few things I did not do. I called the hospital and discovered the Bullet had checked out. The nurse I'd met when we admitted her told me she had returned to Newport Beach. To rest. I considered that good news.

The Sled I left at Teal's house. I knew I wasn't coming back. I told her she could give it away or sell it to a friend if she wanted. As long as the friend would take care of her.

As for my computer, I sent that ahead. But only after I deleted all my Gold files. I didn't feel any sense of loss. They represented a lot of entries, a lot of interviews, and a lot of toil. They also represented a brashness and an insensitivity I wanted to leave behind. They represented another me.

I was done with categories. And little riddles. And weakness and all the other guides to Deep Character. I had spent so much time categorizing, reducing, encapsulating, and coining moronic buzzwords, it made me sick. I had probed too many people's puzzles. I had invaded too many interiors. I had ripped the guts out of too many people and whittled them down to my own little brand of nothingness. And it wasn't right.

I didn't want to label. I didn't want to classify. Gone were the terms

Blips, Wams, Strugs, Noguls, Mom-I-Got-the-Parters, and all the rest. I cringed at the thought of them. Because in the end, I realized I'd become nothing more than Buzzword Guy. I'd rationalized it all by calling myself the Mighty Hippo. I'd been embracing the notion that hypocrisy was an essential part of the human condition in Los Angeles. That there was no way around it. It was the biggest lie of all. It didn't make me the Mighty Hippo. It made me a hypocrite. Plain and simple.

I didn't want to reduce, to boil down and close down anymore. I threw my Blade out the window. I wasn't paranoid, or worried, or wary of people. I'd let them have theirs. I wanted to open up. I wanted to start fresh.

Of course, I gave thought to Teal. I was still glowing from our time spent together. But I knew there was a lot of pain she was sitting on. And she had to deal with it her way. Without some love interest playing the enabler, selfishly yessing her to death and making her postpone a long-overdue date with herself. She had to come to terms with it all and I would only be in the way. The truth is we had to work on ourselves before we could have any hope of working together. I had called myself on my bluff. Teal had to too. I hoped she was ready to do that.

I considered our union a point of departure for both of us. Her gold was hers to keep. Until she came to terms with it. Then I would listen. With open ears. And arms. If she wanted me to. And letting her keep it was my expression of love for her. I believed that. Before I left we made plans to get together in a few months.

There's no question it was going to be difficult being apart from her. I knew I would be thinking of her constantly. And of course I feared losing her. Sure, it was a sad good-bye, but I felt this was the only way.

Dealing with the self is a difficult thing. It takes courage. I prayed for her not to run away. From me. And herself.

At the airport I wrote her a letter to further explain my feelings. And mailed it.

That flight was a wonderful burst through the skies. Life seemed like such a privilege. I was truly enjoying myself minute to minute. And of course I took Bob the Riot with me. He rode in the empty seat beside me on the plane. And that was it. I was leaving Los Angeles, but not in a bitter way. Finally, I knew what it was like to be Shred, my surfer pal. The pressure was off. The Beast was dead. And I was relieved. *Free,* is another way of putting it.

I was coming home. For good.

Coming Clean

Well, it wasn't meningitis. And it wasn't mononucleosis. And it wasn't the Subway Flu. The Thanksgiving holiday health drill had misdiagnosed this one. It was plain old liver failure. That's what Lenox Hill Hospital admitted the Loach for. And they were keeping him for a while. I considered it pretty good news actually. The Loach would be scared enough to curb his heavy intake ways.

My mother, however, was a cause for more concern. She was in a deep depression. Like the rest of the country, she was taking happy-hap pills to stabilize her moods, but she still was in pretty bad shape. It was quite a scene to come home to. Especially after my recent upheavals in Los Angeles and my subsequent departure.

When Mom first saw me she burst into tears in an overly saturated and mushy way. Courtney had warned me about dropping any bad news on her. Or not even bad. Just news. She couldn't handle it. I tried not to. I didn't think leaving the Sled in Los Angeles would affect her. But, well, you get the picture. Dr. Sherman, our family doctor for forty years, told me it would take time. She would pull out of it eventually.

She obviously had been on much shakier ground than I'd thought previously. Clearly, the Loach's getting sick and being hospitalized pushed her over the edge. But I hadn't known she was on the edge. I really hadn't. I sensed there had to be some fallout eventually for all her empty boldfacing, but I never thought it would be this bad.

We did share one afternoon that was special. It was the day I apologized to her. I didn't leave much out. I told her I was sorry for all those embarrassing things I'd done when I was young. Like free-cursing at her parties, bringing all the ethnic types home for show, buying her Timberland boots for Christmas and calling them her Social Climbers, proclaiming that lots of Afro-American people had my name now, and just general jerkish kid behavior.

I told her I was aware of all the sacrifices she'd made while we were growing up. That I'd been selfish and inconsiderate. That for all the areas where we'd disagreed, she had always possessed a good heart. That I never gave her enough credit. I was too busy looking for it myself. That I finally realized that life is about the journey, not about the destination. And in the end, it wasn't about her. It was about me. It was my problem.

But what was foremost in my mind was the realization of what I had been doing with my close relationships. And how I had maneuvered and manipulated them. The discussion that night with Teal when she picked off my primal fear of failure was the catalyst. That's what really made me leave Los Angeles.

There had always been a fundamental decency in my mother. And in others. But I pretended there wasn't. I ignored the goodness. I needed enemies. I needed people to fight against, to feel unfairly conspired against, in order to create an I'll Show Them atmosphere. I had invented. I'd invented a world stacking up against me which included faux-piling adversities with the people closest to me. My family.

Why? To give me drive. Something my father never had. I was playing catch-up, remember? So I invented obstacles and tension and the Underdog and the Victim and the Opposition and the Uncaring Mother and the Wicked, Drunken Stepfather and all those things that turned myself into an angst-ridden, bitter, Machiavellian Beast. And it wasn't fair. And it wasn't right. Not even close.

I felt ashamed.

If the truth be known, I wasn't sure if I should bring up all this stuff with Mom. I didn't know if she could handle it. But I really thought— I really did—that if she knew the way I was feeling, even though some tears would fall, she would emerge from the conversation with more positive thoughts about me and my life, and her and her life, and the subjects would no longer be depressing to her.

But she didn't cry. Not yet.

At the conclusion of my apologetic blast, after all that venting and confessing, she killed me. She looked at me steadily and said with sincerity, "Get ahold of yourself, Heyward." And she added a smile. That made me laugh. Hard. To a point where she began to doubt the humor of it.

"What's so funny?" she asked.

"You are."

"I am?"

"Yes."

"You've never laughed at anything I ever said."

"I know."

"Everyone always told me how funny I was. But you always made me feel like I was the most unfunny person around."

"I guess I didn't want anyone else funny around. I needed all the praise myself."

"So I stopped being funny around you . . ."

"I'm sorry."

And she looked at me. And caressed my face. And at that moment, more than any moment in my life, I felt like I had a mother. One that felt, watched, and listened. We had both been through big battles and were scarred enough to be able to put down the arms and get back to being human again.

Yet what did send tears to her eyes had nothing to do with us. It was when I apologized to her for my treatment of the Loach. I told her I had been pretty hard on him. That I, in need of someone to affix blame to for my shortcomings, had found him a suitable punching bag. I had exploited him. And for that I was sorry.

That was when she reached over and gave me a nice squeeze.

"He really is a good man," she said.

I didn't respond and not because I disagreed. I was going to say, "There's no question he's always been there for you." But it would have sounded like a backhanded insult. So I just let it be.

After that afternoon, a lightness came back to our relationship. Mom and I took walks together. Watched TV together. I escorted her to Bergdorf's, though she didn't want to buy anything. So I bought her a nice cashmere scarf. Black, of course. One thing we did not do was discuss the future. But that was okay. Me and Mom getting along in the present was fine.

"I'm frightened," she said one day in the kitchen as I was preparing tea for her.

"Don't be," I said immediately. "Courtney and I are with you."

"How bad is it, Heyward?"

"What?"

"Me . . ."

"You're fine."

"I know I'm not fine. I don't feel fine."

"You just," and I sent a flash prayer to the Gods of Good Words for the follow-up, ". . . lost your way momentarily." And I looked straight at her. "And so did I."

And her face crumpled. She bowed her head apologetically. There was a long silence but I sensed pressure building in her chest. She heaved one big heave and looked at me. Her face pressed out some water.

And she reached over and clutched me close. "I love you, Heyward."

And I must say it sounded nice to hear it. "I love you, Mom."

"I'm so proud of you," she said into my ear.

We embraced a long time.

Obviously, I'd lied before. I did return to my Park Avenue home, though I swore I never would. But that's one good thing about homes you grew up in. You can always say you're never coming back. Even though you still can.

Don

The truth is, there was no lying involved. The old Heyward, Heyward the Beast, never did return to that house. It was a new era. And a new me.

When I arrived he was on the phone. He didn't look too bad either. His face was pale but it had always been pale. On his bed was an opened box that had been gift-wrapped. There was a brand-new backgammon board in it. And there was a gorgeous flower arrangement.

His eyes steadied on me as he wrapped up the phone call.

"That's right, Parkinson. Tell the boys I will see them next week. And thanks for the new board. I'm having my way with the nursing staff. It's the only group I consistently win against."

And then the Loach hung up. "Hello, Heyward."

"How are you feeling?"

"It could be worse, I suppose."

He looked at me as if studying my face. I could tell he was about to comment on how I didn't look tan. You know, our little holiday conversational loop. His mouth separated, but somehow nothing came out. He must have remembered I had been back for a month already and wouldn't be tan. That was good. His memory was on the mend.

"So you're back for good."

"For now anyway. We'll see."

And we both shared weak smiles. I watched him look at me in the room, not knowing what to do. So he just started talking.

"I play backgammon with Parkinson. We play at the U Club. And I don't have the foggiest what it is. He's not a better player. I'm much more experienced. But he always beats me. He beats Fowler and Bancroft too. But he doesn't play Rohn. No one plays Rohn . . ."

I cut him off. "Donald?"

"Yes."

"Can I call you *Don*?"

He was frozen for a second. "Cripes. It's what," and then he stuttered. Then turned it into a cough. It was a false move. I wondered what was behind it. "It's what my father called me," he finished it off with. "What on earth for?"

"I like it more."

He looked at me a beat. I had no idea what he was going to say. If he was going to tell me to shut up. Or just change the subject. Or ask the nurse to have me removed.

"Be my guest," he said finally.

I advanced on the bed and extended my hand. We shook.

"Okay, Don."

I saw what looked like some form of bad lunch on a tray beside the bed. I was going to ask him how the food was, but I decided not to.

There was no need to get chitchatty now. We had had our first conversation and that was enough.

Wild Vibe

Don came home a few days later and it was rather funny. There we were. The four of us. Roaming around in each other's space. Something we hadn't done in a dozen years or so. We had coffee together, shared newspapers, and sat down to established meals at established times. It was nice for everyone. Courtney eventually returned to Boston but it was like this for a couple weeks. And no one seemed more pleased than Mom. She started to laugh again. She felt much better. And the name Don caught on. It was a keeper.

One day, Don asked me to join him at the University Club. He couldn't drink, of course, but he wanted to visit his backgammon cronies. And cronies they were. I met Deacon, Bancroft, and Parkinson. And Parkinson, well, he was the kind of guy you loved to hate. Arrogant, bloated, elitist, spoke with a condescending drawl, was a braggart in all games competitive, had a Princeton gut, a Yale brow, a Dartmouth capacity for drink, and the blood-drained face of a Harvard man. And he went to Tufts. I guess you could say he felt he still had something to prove.

As we entered the high-ceilinged game room, they were all assembled. And they gave Don a warm welcome. He was a little nervous, I could tell. And he was aching to play. Parkinson chided him, of course.

"Donald, I haven't been able to pay for my new screening room since you dropped out. I was counting on you."

Ha, ha, ha, I thought.

"Should we have a go?" he challenged.

"Not today, Parkinson," Don said.

"Come now."

"I'm not up for it really." Then he looked over at me. "What about Heyward?"

And Parkinson looked at me and I could tell he wasn't sure. I still had

Coerte V. W. Felske

the air of a rebel, though I knew some, if not all, of my demons had been quieted. But to these guys, I was not reformed enough yet. If at all. I still gave off that wild vibe. He smiled anyway. "Sure," he said with artificial confidence.

I sent a look of protest to Don but he ushered me forward.

"Are we really playing?" I asked.

"Yes," Don said.

Then I spoke in whisper. "I don't have any cash on me."

"I'm backing you."

"I haven't played in five years."

"That's okay. You have great dice."

"I do?"

"Hey, what's all this coaching stuff?" Parkinson protested. "No holding hands."

And that one irked me. That's when I put on my prick face. It came easy. One look at Parkinson was all it took.

All I can say is sometimes in life Someone is really looking out for you. I took three out of four games and two hundred dollars from Parkinson. That included one backgammon and one double game. He paid up immediately with a check off a Greenwich bank.

"I don't accept out-of-state checks," I said for the fun of it.

I must say Don was ecstatic. He walked all the way up Park Avenue laughing it off. Nailing Old Parkinson was his finest moment in a long time. And from what I learned later, it had broken the spell. Don proceeded to clean up on him the rest of the winter until Parkinson stopped going to the club. It killed him. It really did.

The News

Don and I became friends during those cold days in February. Who could have predicted that? Certainly not me. We took walks in the Park together, him in his long overcoat and me in my Lands' End hunting jacket. Quitting drinking made him much more accessible and interesting. I could tell his brain was responding positively too. His memory improved and his personality was much more lively. After all, I had been convinced previously he had none.

One afternoon we were sitting on a park bench near the Hans Christian Andersen statue. I looked at him. And I had to ask.

"So. What was she like?"

He looked sharply over at me. My face showed an expression of mild interest. But not the spying kind. He processed my comment. When he assimilated it to the point where he was sure I could be asking none other than That Question, he paused another second and said, "She's a great girl."

"How did you meet?"

"We met at the Bathing Corporation in Southampton. Her parents were friends of my brother's family in Connecticut."

"How did it start?"

"I asked her to join me for dinner in town. But she wanted to go skating. I hadn't been skating since I was a kid. But we ended up having a terrific time."

And of course I thought of the old rules on that one.

"And Bermuda?"

He just looked straight ahead and smiled. That was an answer. Anything more would have been too much. Then his face turned more serious.

"She liked me very much."

"I heard."

He looked at me. He was about to divulge something a little more private. I could feel it. But he held off. And I was glad. I think I knew what he was going to say anyway.

"We're moving," he said instead.

"Really?"

"Yes."

"Where?"

"We bought a place in Cos Cob." It was where he was from. "We're going to live there. It'll be better for your mother. Less hectic. New York doesn't have the same appeal to her. We'll come in for essential evenings. But the place is yours."

"When are you leaving?"

"Next week."

"Next week?"

He nodded. I just looked at him. It was surprising news for sure. I wondered why they hadn't told me. But I didn't ask. It was their business anyway.

His mind then drifted off. He took on a curious expression. It lasted a while. I could tell he was enjoying reliving it. So I let him. "I never had a chance to discuss it with her."

"Who?"

"Caitlin. Your mother and I got back together and that was that. I always felt bad about that."

"Where is she now?"

"She lives in an apartment in Greenwich Village."

"So?" I asked suggestively. He looked at me. "You have her number?"

"Yes. She sent me flowers in the hospital."

And I remembered the colorful arrangement. At that moment, I walked him up to the pay phone.

"Go ahead," I said. And I slotted a quarter in. He took the phone and shuffled a bit, and even brushed his hair back. He was nervous.

"Hello? Caitlin. It's Don."

He looked at me with a smile. It was the reason he stuttered in the hospital that day. *She* was the one who called him Don. Not his father.

"I wanted to call you for the longest time. Thank you so much for the flowers. I'm feeling pretty well, actually. I just wanted to say—I know we never spoke—and for that I am sorry . . . you're a wonderful girl . . . Take care, Caitlin. Good-bye."

He hung up and didn't move for a few seconds. He then spun around and looked at me.

"Thanks, Heyward."

And we didn't say another word the entire walk back to the apartment. But the whole scene made me miss someone. Teal.

Dethroned

I ran into Eleanor once. I had accompanied Mom and Don to a ball at the Met. I was surprised to see her mainly because I hadn't thought of her in a long time. She was on the arm of a guy named Bradley. He seemed nice enough. Eleanor looked great actually. And as she was telling me she was moving to Los Angeles to work for a movie magazine, the whole package which was her person came surging forth. I saw her mouth moving, her hands gesticulating, and little baby hairs in her hairline blowing in the draft of the ballroom.

Looking at her I realized she was no more than another marionette in the Heroes of Café Society play. The artificiality of her existence was plain as day. I was smiling inside while I listened. And was relieved I hadn't fallen for it. It was obvious I hadn't been courting her for me. I had been courting her for others. Like my mother. And Don. To prove to them I could win over the coveted eastern establishment wondergirl. To explain, I'll resort to my discarded sardonic shorthand. Eleanor wasn't Queen of the Could-Bes. She wasn't Queen of the Maybes. She wasn't a queen at all. She was no more than a Trust Fund Gal bored of her notoriety on the East Coast and now needed praise from the left. How did I know? Well, just as a former alcoholic or drug addict can spot the telltale behavior in others, I, a reformed fame hound, saw all the unmistakable signs. Money, fame, beauty, and power—they're all drugs. If you are configured in a certain way. Don't let anyone tell you differently.

Eleanor approached me three more times that evening. It was proof I was giving off a different series of pulsations. I felt my life was heading in a nice direction. So I thanked her for showing me that, however unknowingly. And for defining herself as well. Then I walked away from her for the last time.

But the best part of our reunion occurred when I rejoined Mom and Don. That's when Mom said of Eleanor, "She's very fake." It meant more to me than she knew. That was when I knew everything in my family was going to be all right.

A Chair for Bob

It was nice living in the home I grew up in. It was also strange. I had never had the place to myself before. It was what you dreamed of in high school. And college. No 'rents nowhere. But I was thirty. And in a thoroughly confused state as to what I wanted to do with my life. I wasn't going to go out to socialize or anything. I didn't know how to approach the city yet. I felt I had time. After all, the pressure was off. I wanted to collect my thoughts. I found ways to occupy myself. I sat in the library and read dead books.

One night I answered the ringing phone. It was around nine P.M. It was a surprise call for sure.

"Heyward!" The voice was male and it held a lot of excitement in it.

"Yes?"

"I have some really good news."

I knew the voice but I couldn't place it yet.

"I hope you won't be angry with me. But I did something without your authorization. I tried to find you but . . ."

And now I successfully processed the voice. It was Marty my agent. Former agent. "What did you do?"

"I put your script up for sale."

"*Age of Astonishment?*"

"Yes. It sold for four-point-two-five million dollars."

I was silent. It took time to translate words to number form in my head. The decimal point mixed me up. But the millions part clarified it. "Really?" I asked in a way that was as much shock as it was enthusiasm. The truth is, I hadn't even thought about the script since I'd left it somewhere. And I didn't know where.

"*Really?* Is that all you have to say?"

"I'm speechless."

"It was quite an auction. At first we were worried. That we weren't getting enough heat on the script. But word got out, get this, your old pal Sydney Swinburn was after it in a big way. His company was buzzing about it. The bids just kept rolling in."

That was one for the ages. Sydney had bid on my work. I couldn't believe it. Especially since I was sure he knew what had happened between Teal and me.

"Where have you been?" Marty asked. "I've tried everyone to get your number."

"Uh, here. In New York." And I explained there had been an illness in the family.

"What did you do, just pack up and leave?"

His question was less interesting to me than the thought I had that overrode it. "Four million dollars?" I heard myself ask.

"The biggest spec sale in ten years. Great, huh?"

"Tell me, Marty, how did you get hold of the script?"

I had an idea how but I wanted to ask anyway.

"In the mail. Why?"

"No one dropped it off?"

"I, no, I don't think so. But I'll check with my secretary. Why?"

"No reason."

"You did a great job, buddy. When can you come out?"

"Come out?" I was put on the spot. I started to conjure up a flaky response. But I then realized I wasn't on the spot at all. He was. It was my life. A life that was no longer dependent on what he had, and what Los Angeles in general had, to offer.

"They want to get rewrites going right away."

I told Marty I wasn't interested in writing the next draft. And they should go ahead and hire another writer.

"Are you kidding me? This is what you've been working for your whole life."

"I have nothing to say about it, Marty, other than I just am not interested anymore in a movie-writing career."

He threw a few incentives my way. After all, he saw me as a real moneymaker now and it was in his interest to do so. I didn't blame him one bit. It's what agents wait for. The day they can cash in on clients they've been bringing along. He mentioned a sequel to my script, adaptation work, high-paying rewrites, and a directorial gig down the road.

I told him I'd think it over. And not because I wanted to play games. Because I really didn't care.

"Thanks for all the help," I said. Then I told him where to send the check. I knew he was stunned. He didn't seem to want to get off the phone. But we did. I made sure of it.

I pondered my good fortune. I thought about everyone who had made it all possible. The Sled, my landlady, even Sydney to some degree. But most important, I credited Teal. She had proved to be the catalyst. She'd kept me going. She had gotten me away from Sydney. And she was the one who ultimately had taken the script out of the Sled's backseat, where I'd left it, and mailed it in to be put up for sale.

I tried to call her but she wasn't in. It was my second attempt at trying to reach her.

Then I thought about the sleeping bag in the back of the Sled. It had been placed there for this very day. You see, I had made a promise to myself long ago.

The first thing agents, friends, family, and fellow colleagues in the celluloid fight tell you is that when you hit it big, whatever you do, do not go out and blow your money. On a car, a new house, a boat, or something extravagant. As a creative, you don't know when the next check is coming. *So don't blow it* is the thinking. I had my sleeping bag in the trunk of the Sled ready for this occasion.

What I intended to do was sleep out all night long in the Sled, in the parking lot of the Porsche dealership in North Hollywood, and, as soon as the doors opened in the morning, I was going to buy the baddest-ass, newest version of a Porsche I could find. And tell everyone to fuck off.

The thought made me smile. And tense up. It conjured up memories of an inner angst, a burning drive, a Wannabeastliness, a Buzzword Guy syndrome, not yet long gone. Now it was just a nice memory that held some irony.

I was happy the script sold, however. Don't misinterpret the significance. It meant I wouldn't have to rush into my next career venture. And I would find my own new ways to spend it. Like maybe buy my mother a nice car for Connecticut. And definitely reupholster that lily-pad green chair that had been compromised by her. After all, it was going to be Bob the Riot's permanent perch. When his talents weren't being called upon on trips to East Hampton on the Long Island Expressway.

I found the implications amusing. All I cared to do for myself with this windfall was to get my HOV dummy a nice seat in the house. Then again, Bob deserved a good chair.

But I do not discount the self-esteem aspects of the sale. I'd done it. I'd pulled it off. I hadn't been wrong about my career choice, after all. I was capable of succeeding in that Tough Business, Man. That sat well with me. It was a nice jolt. No one could say now that my work didn't sell. Not anymore.

The word on my work now was commercial. Over four million dollars' worth.

There was only one way to describe it. *Word* . . .

The Jack of Tarts

Over the next few days, I saw myself written up in every entertainment publication. Marty apprised me of the rainbow of offers from the studios. I also received an outpouring of phone calls from old as well as new friends.

I went for one of my afternoon walks in Central Park. It was something I looked forward to every day. It had all started that day with Don. Watching the dogs frolic, and mothers roll their little ones, and joggers pass by full of life and red cheeks, was invigorating.

The day was cool and crisp but full of midwinter sunshine and a memorable deep blue sky. I heard it from behind.

"Heyward," the voice said.

I spun around. I was definitely surprised but oddly my pulse didn't quicken. Which was a good sign. I was silently glad this guy didn't affect me much anymore.

"Hello, Sydney."

He looked pretty tan and healthy and looked out of place in the wintry surroundings, as most visitors from sunshine states do. He met me with a firm handshake. He was wearing a heavy leather knee-length jacket and black jeans, part of the wardrobe I'd fitted him over with. The thought of the makeover made me cringe a little, I must say, and all the reminders that came with it.

"Congratulations."

"Thanks."

"Quite a sale."

I nodded.

"Now you're on your way."

"I suppose . . ."

"Has it changed your life yet?"

"No."

We just looked at each other a moment. The exchange was strained. And that was as good as it was going to get. The flashes splashed my eyes at that point. The Polaroid flashes, that is. I tried but had difficulty getting beyond that imagery, but I let it go to stay in the moment with him.

We talked about the terms of the deal and he was surprised when I informed him I was not sure if I was continuing on with the project. That led to some silence and I was set to extend my hand to say good-bye but he kept talking. I slipped my disappointed hand back in my pocket.

"We liked the project," he said.

"I heard."

"I think you, if I could be so bold as to say, heeded my advice. It was gritty, funny, irreverent, but accessible as well. Commercial, in fact, is what I am saying. You finally did something commercial, Heyward."

"That's what they say . . ."

He stared at me with those slate-gray eyes and they looked as hard as the rock they were colored after.

"In fact, we made a bid on it."

"Really . . ." It was a flat "really" that hid my knowledge of the issue.

"More than one, actually. But when it got up there, well, we've never bought a script for that much. But we were in there for a while."

I didn't know how to respond to that. So I didn't. But I felt a knot tightening in my stomach.

"But that's your career, and I wish you well with it."

I considered the remark odd and eerie. It was a transitional comment with something else implied behind it. So I decided to take my own initiative and not let him rail me down some path of his own choice.

"It is no longer," I affirmed.

"At least you have the freedom to make that choice."

I nodded. That was true. And right then I realized I didn't want to shake his hand. So I started to step away.

"But there's some other business that I think we should go over. And it's more unpleasant."

I halted my retreat.

"Shoot . . . ," I said powerfully, as if I was in a hurry.

"You know what I know."

"I think so."

"Well, if you don't, let me explain. I know what happened with Teal and you. Nothing goes on in that house I don't know about. And I know why it happened. I even understand it in a way. But I cannot overlook the violation."

"Violation?"

"Of our agreement."

It made me smile. One of those smiles that has nothing to do with joy, or glee, or any form of pleasantry. It is all theater and an artificial way of saying *Screw you, you prick* to someone.

"And how do you think you treated your end of this pact?"

"I respected it."

"You respected it? Is that because you haven't met Eleanor yet?"

He just fastened on me with a weighted glare. I watched him draw a cigar out of his coat as well as a small cigar blade. He carefully chopped off the cigar end and walked over to a nearby trash basket and tossed the nub in it. He then lit up and twirled the cigar in his hand to get a healthy burn. Then he puffed it a few times and returned his gaze to me.

"I'm going to tell you a little," and he pretended to choose his words, ". . . anecdote, shall we say. It takes place in Paris. You've been to Paris, right?"

I gave him a bit of a nod.

"There's a little boy who walks into a church in Paris, the Sacré-Coeur to be specific. Do you know the church?"

"Yes, I do."

"Of course, you studied there," he remembered. "And this little boy is not overtly religious but he has shall we say strong moral fiber. He sees people lighting candles and tossing money into the coin box. A little further up, there are a few more candle stands. He advances on them and stops before two stands in particular. He places his five-franc piece in the box and lights his candle from the flame of another. Now, of the two candle stands he is standing before, one has only one candle there placed by another church member. And the other has none at all. Normally, they have a hundred candles illuminated. But of these two stands, one has one candle lit, and the other none. It's empty. My question to you, Heyward, is where does the boy place his lit candle? On the stand with one candle? Or the stand with none?"

"On the stand with one candle."

"Why?"

"Because he doesn't want the other candle to be all alone."

"That's right, Heyward. Do you see where I'm going with all this?"

I didn't say I did, but I did. I didn't say anything.

"The man who places the candles together is the sensitive man. A compassionate man. A man known for teamwork, understanding, and a love of one's brother."

He puffed out a stinky cloud before continuing and it mixed with the cool air and became even more white and thick. And disgusting.

"Your error, Heyward, is you put your candle on the empty stand. It's a move that indicates me, me, me, all alone, on a pedestal, by yourself, all fueled on the self without any regard for others. With respect to us, you and me, you placed your candle above all others, including mine."

"Or did I place it on your pedestal?"

"You fucked with the wrong guy, Heyward." Then his voice just crackled. And it speared right through me. "And I warned you."

"I love your analogy, Sydney. Funny that it takes place in a church." I turned slightly and drifted back a step. "I'm going to leave you now. I'm sure God is waiting for you back at your hotel. And though you may not care, I don't want to keep Him waiting."

"Stay right there!" he said, and it came out like the sound of a gavel smacking a desktop.

I just stood there. He punished the stogie on the ground. And the last stinkies drifted by.

"You're going to listen to me. And mark my words. You're never going to forget what I'm about to tell you." He moved toward me a couple steps. His face wasn't that far from mine. "I gave you one instruction in this life. And you violated it. I won't even get into the extent of the violation. But nevertheless. I told you not to lay a finger on her."

"And what about you!" I snapped. "Look what you did to my friend."

He remained silent. Then a portable phone beeped from deep inside his clothing somewhere. He unearthed it and answered.

"Yes? Okay." Then he mouthed to me not to say a word. "Put her through." He waited. "Hi there. Sleep well? You're still in bed?" And Sydney laughed slyly and looked at me. "Did you have a nice time last night?"

And oddly, his portable cell had a speaker function. And he brought her in. Live. For my benefit, of course. And it was a bed voice, one that indicated sex, that she was still rolling around in the sheets. And the next burst confirmed it.

"Of course. But it's like an ice chamber in here. The thermostat says *fifty-five degrees!* Mind if I turn the heat up?"

And Sydney smiled at me with that sick smile.

"Course not."

"Never a dull moment," she said in her characteristic way.

"Never," he returned.

"When are you coming back?" she asked in the tone of the sexually vanquished. It was a voice I was familiar with. It belonged to Vanessa Lewis. She had caved in, after all.

"I'm in a meeting. But soon, baby, soon."

"Make it sooner than soon."

I was almost numb to this kind of thing. But not yet. I felt a surge of self-loathing for having contributed to this guy's pathology.

Sydney hung up and looked straight at me.

"I don't know how I did it without you, Heyward." And he laughed a laugh that was heard around the park.

"You're full of shit, Sydney. You fucked my friend. Then passed her on to your help. She's just the one I know about. You're the sickest, most disgusting, and depraved motherfucker I have ever met. You sucked me in, used me for my introductions, fucked a rosterful, and did nothing for me in return. And you have the nerve to tell me you expect obedience to some stupid pact?"

"And how did you play it? You came on as some kind of friend of mine. Who wanted to help. Your ambition was oozing out of you. It was so obvious it had color. You were here to use me, to suck me and my connections dry, to advance your own agenda. And you know what I say to that? *Fine.* Welcome to Hollywood. That's the town. I expect it."

And he moved in a few inches closer.

"Yeah, I raided your pussy bin. I lied to you when I had to. But it wasn't a stretch for you. You're a whore, Heyward. Just like everyone out there. You would have sold your soul for a contract. And you did."

I didn't know what he meant by that but he wasn't done.

"You claim ties to a pristine heritage but you were as bad as any huckster working the Sunset Strip. Until you hit it with that script, you were just a pimp with a pen. The Jack of Tarts, to use your speak. And I saw you coming a million miles away."

I looked at him and I didn't show any surprise. Even though I was.

"You bet your ass I targeted you. I'd seen you dancing around the bars for a year. I was waiting for you to come. To my party, to my table, to my house, wherever. And I knew you would. You were looking for a way in. I was just waiting. I knew everything about you before you crashed. I am that on top of it, jerk-off! And you thought you could bring your Ivy League bullshit here and outsmart and outmaneuver me? You dumb fuck! This is the big leagues, boy! It doesn't get any bigger. And no one plays it like I do. And now you're fucked. In the worst way. Not the Hollywood way. That would be too easy. My fuckin' way!"

Sydney was red in the face. He stepped back and let his fury subside. When he started up again, and he did very soon, he had a tone of voice

I disliked. He talked not like an enemy or an adversary or a stranger or an acquaintance. He spoke to me evenly, in an even tone, like he was my friend. It was his most demonic display to date.

"Heyward, there's always purpose behind my actions. You saw the mystery and the tension of my relationship with Teal. There's a reason I take care of her. She is a special case. She's not well. She's sick. If she wasn't sick, I would have married her long ago. You see, she has the Badge, Heyward."

I froze there.

"And now you have it too. Unless you're some medical miracle, one of that tiny percentage of people who are immune to HIV."

A chill went up my body.

He scanned my face for a reaction. I had one. But I didn't give it to him. I would have died first.

"I put her out there for you, Heyward. On a platter. For you not to touch. And you touched. The poor girl did not want to fuck you, my friend. She fucked you because I made her fuck you. Everything she did, her hands on you, her lips on your cock, her pussy around your dick, all was signed, sealed, and delivered by me. She told me she'd never exchanged so many fluids in her life. She said you sucked the blood right out of her neck. And I told her to let you."

As I looked at him I wondered when he was going to stop. But good old Sydney. He had more for me. Destruction was his game, remember? And if nothing else depicts his degree of depravity, this might help.

"Heyward, you wrote a great script. And the bidding price was five hundred thousand and I put in a bid for seven-fifty. When it went to a million, I went to a million and a quarter. When it went to a million-five, I went to a million nine-fifty. And when it went to two and a half mil I went to three. On three and a half, I went to four. I went to four for you, Heyward. And then I let it go. But make no mistake about it, I helped make your script sale stand alone. And it does. I knew the other studios wanted it badly. More than me. I just kept upping the bids. What I'm telling you is, I never intended on buying it.

"And again, I have my reasons. Yes, Heyward, I gave you advice on your work, I gave you stature around town, and I made you more money than you deserve. I made you a millionaire four times over, which in turn has now given you your coveted fame. Heyward Hoonstein is a household industry name now. The pseudo-Jew name that it is."

He dragged a look over my face to see if I would acknowledge the fact that he was onto my name change from the beginning. But I didn't give him anything. After all this, my false claims of being Jewish seemed pretty insignificant. And I wasn't going to give him anything anyway. Not even a frown.

"You're front-page news in all the trades, the magazines will all want to do a spot on you, and the infotainment shows too. You're famous, Heyward. You're a celebrity writer. Which, no matter how you slice it, is still a celebrity. No longer are you the guy at the edge of somebody else's table. It's your table now. You can order what you want, invite whoever you want, yuck it up however you want, and you have the honor and privilege of paying the check. Which is a privilege, let me tell you. Because the best blessing is to be able to pay for it. Which you can. Now. You stand alone, on your own, with no supports. What an accomplishment.

"The unfortunate setback to all this is, you may never get laid again. And you know why. When the word hits the street, the word that you are sick, the word that you are HIV positive, the word that you have to swig a cocktail of protease inhibitors on a daily basis, you won't be able to buy a blow job on Forty-second Street. And you can bet your ass you'll never find that socially prominent wonderwoman you're so desperately searching for. You're fucked. You can't get laid. And you can't go out in New York and confront the infamy. The two places you love most, you are banned from. Your hometown. And the interior of a woman.

"None of this would have mattered to me if you hadn't become famous. Because then you could just put blinders on and go around and lie to people and still get your bang. I wanted you to be a celebrity. I needed you to be famous. It was the only way to handle the violation of our pact. Now you're just another celebrity case of HIV positive. You're a pinup boy. A lecture circuit kid. The word is out. And you know what the word is? You're fucked. Place the ribbon on your lapel and weep, Heyward Hoonstein. You fucked with the wrong person."

I stood there a moment and took it in. All of it. And he just stared at me, waiting for a response. I said nothing for a good half minute. Sure, I thought of all the horror. And a future altered. And all the other gruesome details of my new predicament. So I felt compelled to give him this:

"I love the park at this hour, don't you?"

His face twisted up a bit. It wasn't the reaction he wanted. So he overrode that with the cliché smug smile.

"If you'll excuse me now, Heyward. I have a four-thirty flight. I have to get back for a meeting. And you were right. It is with God. I'm taking Him to a screening of my new movie. The word on it is it's pretty strong." He stepped back and turned away and said it behind him. "Good-bye, Heyward."

I didn't say anything. And we didn't shake hands.

Bud

There I was. In the park. The park that had seen me through a few eras. From the bowl cut in my single digits, to the Prince Charles cut I had in my doubles, when my mother ruled my hair, to the long hair with part in the middle in my teens, to the spikes in the Hair Wars era of the eighties, to the shaved head, to the crew cut, to the generic, capitulated thirty-something short hair. In these later years, of course, whatever my mother didn't like became my style. I was a pretty obvious kid, actually. I thought people were silently awarding me genius status, for my strange cuts. But now I was certain they weren't. It was pretty standard rebellious stuff.

And there I was. In the park. The place where Don and I became friends. There I was. With some severe news about my future. Oddly, the thought that really incensed me was that the motherfucker referred to the unfortunate condition as the Badge. It seemed as bad as the bad behavior it took to get me there. The Badge. Here he was on all sorts of left coast entertainment AIDS charity committees wearing the red ribbons, making contributions and all. And on a free moment in New York City, with the industry not listening in and all guards down, he was calling me the equivalent of a nigger with AIDS.

Another fleeting thought—I was bombarded with them for the next hour or so—was how he had gotten almost boringly biblical with me. He had introduced me to Teal, set her up as the Forbidden Fruit, and then just behaved horrifically with no fear whatsoever of the consequences. Because the place where I could hurt him most, meaning the worst, meaning the best, was a trap that would result in those *grave consequences gravely felt* he'd spoken of. I would be kicked out of the Garden and sent to some form of hell.

And what did I do? I made like Adam and took a whopping bite of the apple. I mauled it in fact. And left the core. Maybe more. Maybe less. Of course I remember actually eating that apple at Teal's house. At the time, we both flashed on the significance and found amusement in it. Little did I know. But it was another identifiable little spot of cheeky irony for the log and I had to conjure it up and let it roam. I wanted my mind to access all areas and directions, paths and channels with this one. I'm talking memories.

I decided not to go home. I wanted to walk some more. And ruminate on the new blood looping through my veins. And the implications therein. I thought about Los Angeles. And how desperately I wanted to be. I had been a Wannabeast. I wanted to be. And now I was *it*.

I thought of myself as the indefatigable Wannabeast and the price I had to pay to have the table in my own name. And, yes, it gave me an odd sensation to think of the buzzwords again.

And of course I thought of Teal too. After all, she was the star of this little gem. It was her little secret. Her little riddle. Her chunk of gold that I'd told her was hers to keep. All along she had been riding poolside with a hidden life and secret status as a hired assassin to a supermogul. It was so absurd it sounded cinematic.

I sat on a park bench and tried not to cry. Each jogger that passed by was a welcomed reprieve. I forced myself to think about each one of them and their athletic form and their pace and their apparel, anything

I could. Anything to divert my mind from the brutality at hand. It was difficult.

It was late afternoon by now and I found myself at the swing set near the children's zoo. I rested my weakened carcass in one of the hanging loops. I stared down at the sand and my feet made senseless patterns in it. Shoes are just not the right shape for sand sculpture, I thought.

Then suddenly I felt some pressure on me. It was coming from my left. When I looked over there was a little boy with blond hair and a big coat with a hood that he was peering out of. He was looking directly at me and if I hadn't known any better I would have guessed he was sizing me up. He remained that way an extended moment. Then he looked back over at the sidewalk. Then back to me.

"Can you push me?"

I guess his flash appraisal of me indicated I'd do for the job.

"What's your name?"

"Sammy."

"Hi, Sammy." And I said it with a smile. I wasn't so sure he cared, though.

"Can you push me now?" It was clear. He wanted to be pushed.

"Of course."

And as I moved behind him, I wondered where Sammy's next of kin was. He obviously had not adhered to all the don't-talk-to-strangers propaganda that I'm sure had been drummed into his head all these years. He had his own program with a ruling body of one. He reminded me of someone I knew well. And for all his toughness, he couldn't have been more than six years old.

And I shoved him nicely. After a few thrusts he was all over me.

"Higher!" was the only word he seemed to know.

Then I heard some commotion behind me. A woman was conferring with a passerby. Then they both looked our way.

"There he is!" And she came running toward me.

"Sammy! I was looking all over for you."

"Look how high I am, Mom!"

"We have to go." Then she turned to me. "Hello."

"Hi. He needed a push."

"That's not all he needs." And the weary look in his mother's eyes indicated Sammy and his fiercely independent streak was taking its toll on her.

"Higher!"

"It's time to go," she announced.

The requisite plead came. "Just five more minutes."

I looked at the mother. She sighed. I stepped back. "Time to go, Sammy," I said. And the mother gave me a thankful look like it was the first break of its kind she'd received all day.

And without the permission to kick and pump further, Sammy's swing eventually died right under his little behind. He hopped off. And his mother grabbed his hand.

"Say thank you to the man, Sammy."

"Thanks, bud."

Bud. That's all I was to him. Some schmuck with willing arms and the ability to push through time and space. I couldn't believe it. At that moment I was convinced. I was a believer. The kid was going to take over the world. He knew what he wanted and he was going to get it. The Buds of the world were going to have to take it on the chin with this one.

24 Dark

It had been some twenty hours. Dinner the night before had been highlighted with the news I'd made four million dollars. And tea the following day revealed that I'd been infected with a deadly virus.

I sauntered back to the apartment, took a lonely ride up the elevator, and slipped inside my bedroom. I lay down on my bed and looked at Bob.

"I'm fucked, Bob."

He let me continue. But I didn't want to. The thought of talking out loud to my HOV dummy at this dark hour was even more depressing.

I thought about Teal. I didn't hate her. She wasn't hateable. But what she did, well. I knew she'd been isolated. She did try to confess something to me numerous times. It must have been about her condition. I called her again, but again, no answer and no machine.

In the end, I should have known. I had prided myself on making the proper reads. I had certainly seen enough flaws, and weaknesses, some evidence that something was amiss. For certain, I'd seen her sadness. I saw it the night we shared that first interior vision of each other. I had realized her gold was something special and hidden. But this? I was baffled. I turned my phone off and just felt the blood move through my body.

The dark and horrifying aspects didn't hit me until about four in the morning when I leaped up in panic, chest heaving, anxiety having its way with me. I took a hot-hot shower to calm down. When I returned to the bedroom, I saw my sheets were twisted everywhere.

I made coffee. I made eggs. But I didn't consume either. It was good just to do something. I was sixteen hours into my new life and it was about time. I stared at my palms and examined the veins. And I gave in to the Darkie about the tainted fluids swirling beneath the skin. How could I not?

The buzzer rang around nine. I was lying on the couch in the living room. I picked up the house phone.

"A Ms. Harding is here to see you."

My heart either jumped or I skipped a breath. It was somewhere in there. And still negligible.

"Send her up."

The elevator spread and she flew at me, wrapping her arms around me, kissing me, in between hugs.

I led her into the apartment.

"Was Sydney here?"

"No. But I saw him in the park."

"Oh, Heyward, I'm so sorry." And her face started to stream. "What did he tell you?"

"Just the bad news. That I was infected."

She lunged at me and held me close. "It's not true."

"No?" My eyes were flooded.

"No. Of course not. I would never do that to anyone. Especially you."

"Why didn't you warn me?"

"I tried. I called you all yesterday. You changed your number."

I nodded.

"Once I heard Sydney had gone to New York I knew he'd drop this on you. When I couldn't reach you I took the first flight."

"So you're not HIV positive?"

"No."

"Why did you tell him that?"

"So I wouldn't have to sleep with him."

That was her con. In a con man's town. It was even better than Bridget's.

"I tried to tell you."

She had. But I couldn't speak. I just looked at her.

"I love you, Heyward."

We embraced some more. And shed some more tears. It was nice. Real nice. We stayed there holding each other for a while.

Just as I was feeling a bit comfortable it dawned on me. It started as a slow seep, of a subconscious analysis born of the simplest forms of common sense, and then it broke through all cerebral blockades and flooded my circuits.

"That's why you put the script up for sale."

She smiled a faint smile with a face full of water. I hugged her and kept on hugging her. This girl had beat them all at their own game. She was tops. She was all that and a mile more. We made love until the evening news. The sports segment. It's the last one.

Pure Gold

She'd said it that night. At her place. In the Hollywood Hills. She said it and I should have heard it. It was so loud neighbors should have complained. She explained how Sydney would never invest in any project that would help me in my credit and acclaim wars. But he would pay any and all exorbitant sums to set me back if I crossed him.

After I left town she read My Newest and sensed I had something to sell. With an understanding of the subtlest points of the human condition, which includes a profound working knowledge of the functioning of the darkest minds in the darkest towns, she'd concocted a ruse that would set the standard for all others to be judged.

How do you get your life provided for, take four million dollars out of Hollywood's vast kitty, and, at the same time, never give away a piece of yourself? She had an answer to that riddle. And that was her gold, the secret of all secrets.

The woman had chosen Los Angeles in order to drift a little, so as not to confront the larger issues of a life that had beaten her up, haunted her, and paralyzed her from making something of herself. There was a sadness I saw in her the first night we'd met. It was that interior vision I'd had of her. She had recognized pain in me as well—pain—the kind exacerbated by Mighty Hippo rationales and defensive propaganda. This was a girl who had a rare mind and tremendous abilities. But she didn't know what she wanted out of life. Fortunately, she had the strength to hold off from making any rash decisions. She needed time to figure it out.

So she set herself up with a man who had deep pockets and strong L.A. roots. I'm sure that took her away from her pain and allowed her to exist worry-free. He was a comfort. A human Linus blanket. Then she did what anyone with powers of keen analysis does. She made a science project out of him. If for no other reason than boredom. When you're that smart you find ways to occupy your mind.

Soon after, and I'm sure it was a fairly short soon, Teal uncovered Sydney's Achilles' heel, that neon weakness he had for gifted women. A weakness that had been slowly murdering him. For this man lacked the wherewithal to charm them his way. Throughout his life, he had been stifled, shunned, and rejected from that circle of princesses. And this beautiful creature was the only advantage he ever wanted out of his advantaged life. And he opened his heart and his home to her. And for good reason. In return, she gave herself to him, most fully, in every way. Except in matters carnal.

Teal had lied. She had lied so she wouldn't have to extend herself, the way the rest of the town's flock of women had. The ones in search of fame, or security, or a part, or some demented fun, the normal ones and dysfunctional types alike. She claimed she was infected. That was her con. In a con man's town.

It was a tale spun from her past as a nurse in Africa, that she had contracted it there nonsexually. The confession preyed on the sympathy of the mogul and took her out of the pool of sought-after talent. It became their cherished secret, the secret Sydney held on to, and it provided him the intimacy with the type of woman he had always challenged himself to attain. He had her and held on to her even though physically he could never experience her. She was a million-dollar armpiece. What she offered him was an intelligent voice and ear, as well as a loyalty rarely found in that town which was infested with low-level schemers and oozing con men. He could depend on her at any hour. His reward was a gilded friendship of soulmate proportions.

And since she could not provide for him in that special way, he had to look elsewhere. So he befriended a desperate, identity-starved New Yorker with a fame complex and a deep sense of inadequacy, but one who also possessed a certain wit and social savvy and access to a bevy of lovelies. The screenwriter manqué had everything the supermogul needed. And desired. And for her, this find was perfect. A godsend. He could fill that void in Sydney she couldn't, and this arrangement gave her more of what she wanted most. Time. To think things through.

But along the way, something happened to her she hadn't counted on. Her emotions gave way. Maybe it was the coincidence of meeting me and the synergy we shared that swirled up her wonderful womanly chaos. Maybe it was simply that she saw someone in me who was so close in deep character, including the shared pain, that maybe it made her feel vital and human and not alone. Maybe it had *nothing* to do with me but, rather, was something that had been lying dormant within her and was time-released. Whichever, her emotional being did release—for reasons that are still her own, and she most likely has not yet come to terms with.

Teal knew how Sydney would react to her giving herself to me. She knew he was apprised of all of her moves. And mine. And so she executed her plan.

Of course she was not sick as Sydney had been led to believe. But her protection was that he thought she was. There would be no fallout between them. Just another secret piled atop the rest they already shared. After the consummation, she knew he'd consider me a carrier, and that it would be only a small leap for his deviant mind, one she already knew thrived on acts of brilliant vengeance, to conceive the angle of making me page-one famous and turning me into a headline poster boy for the virus, which would serve as my destruction. All he had to do was raise a few bids. To give me my credits and fame and, at the same time, alter my life. Forever.

It was genius. Teal was genius.

The full unraveling came to me as Bob and I watched her sleep in the bedroom of my Park Avenue apartment. And the extent to how much she cared for me was not lost on me. And in turn, in seeing her design as clearly as I did, it was hard to love her less. My sentiments have not changed.

My life experience had taken me to a point where I could no longer stomach jotting down the little notes on people's souls. I had violated too many private parts. That's why, back in L.A., in those last days, I'd balked at her attempts to come clean. But having now processed what had occurred, at least partially, I can say with full conviction, it is the greatest stunt I've ever heard of, let alone witnessed.

The reasons behind that deep-seated inner drive which drew her to Los Angeles and, in turn, to Sydney Swinburn remain a mystery. I'm sure I will learn of them in time. Or maybe I won't. The reality is I don't give a damn.

What I can surmise is her spirit had been trodden and was barely alive or near dead. And perhaps that is why she repeatedly told me she admired me. My passion, as misguided as it was, held her respect.

Teal needed to feel. She needed to love. She needed her own passions to be ignited. She needed to believe in something. And act upon it. And that was why she did what she did for me. But I'm convinced that is only a fraction of what her needs truly were. And are. And I am convinced that is what she is still trying to work out.

Of course, there remains the issue of the unforeseen bomb being dropped on me in Central Park and its ferociously cruel aspects. How could Teal not prepare me?

The truth is she had no idea Sydney would reveal the news to me. She assumed, as would I, he would take a far crueler path and not want to prepare me for the misery. That he'd let me run free to boast about my fresh new career and make the proper aggressive maneuvers to keep it thriving. That he'd let me make my fame a twenty-four-hour job and turn myself into a better star and fortify and cement it all in. So the dark news would hold that much more drama.

I certainly didn't hold it against her.

Teal awoke briefly and looked at me through clapping eyes that were fending off the brights of the bedside lamp. She smiled and whispered sweetly, "Your blond roots are growing in."

"I know."

"I missed you."

Those twenty-four hours, which had such a wonderful start and a chilling middle, culminated in a triumphant end. That night, as Teal fell back asleep, I went out for an evening paper. And after I purchased it, I strode back up the sidewalk like any man worth four million-plus, with a kick-ass pad on Park Avenue and a gem of a girlfriend, would.

Calmly.

Word

One thing I did not do was forget the West Coast people I had spent time with and cared about. I kept in touch. Kelly enrolled in a general studies program at the University of California at Irvine, which, in effect, disbanded her clique, allowing the other girls to get on with their lives. For the better. Louise, however, formerly known as Baby Garbo, had a consumption setback and lost her sitcom series. She just couldn't kick her booze habit. It was what I had always feared. Some people, I guess, just can't ever seem to get it right. Maybe this would prove to be the kick that would turn her around. I hoped it would be.

But there was one bright surprise. A month after I returned to New

York, I received a small package. It was postmarked from Kauai, Hawaii. The guy to whom Teal had given the Sled had sent me a letter. He had broken up with his actress girlfriend and shipped the Sled to Hanalei, a small surf town where he was now living. Of course the letter was from Shred. I was happy for him. And I was happy the Sled had made it to a place with authentic tropical climes. A remote Hawaiian island seemed a nice place for her to retire.

The package also included something I cherished at one point in time. The twin license plates were wrapped together. *NFW*, they announced to me, reminding me of the life I'd led in Los Angeles at the height of the Age of Astonishment.

The attitude hasn't left me. Just the bitterness. I write feature articles now for urban periodicals of the day. They all seem to have a decidedly NFW stamp to them. I try to out the ironies, injustices, and incongruities wherever I can. I hope to eventually start my own magazine in this idiom. I have a title for it.

I did see Sydney Swinburn one more time. It was eighteen months later at my movie's premiere. I was sure he didn't think I'd show. How could I, after all? In his mind, it would only be public embarrassment for me. Sure, there were rumors. But Teal and I didn't mind. They'd been propagated by people I didn't care to appeal to anyway.

If the truth be known, it was nice to see Sydney. And it was nice for him to see me. With Teal. On my arm. And I must say, both of us looked pretty damned healthy. It really was quite a night. And difficult to describe. Words don't really do it justice. Only one word could. And we both know what it is. We really do.

In the end, you can't care so much. It enables you to free up, let loose, and let a better life in. And that's when things start to happen. And you realize what you were striving for wasn't important anyway. So when results do occur, it doesn't matter as much. If at all. And it shouldn't. What does matter is the new, bright life you've availed yourself of. Life is the journey, after all. That's what I learned anyway. So I say stop caring so much. Which is really caring more than ever.